"A rip-roaring thriller that both entertains and [...]
of post-traumatic stress disorder (PTSD) is ter[...]
do more to educate the lay public about this serious disorder than a thousand public service announcements on late night television. He weaves the pain of the PTSD sufferer with psychiatric and military history in a seamless manner. He now joins David Baldacci, Lee Child, John Katzenbach and Stephen Hunter as one of the novelists who keeps the reader up late, too engrossed to turn out the lights."

— Charles B. Nemeroff, M.D., Ph.D.
Leonard M. Miller, Professor and Chairman Department of Psychiatry and Behavioral Sciences Director, Center on Aging Chief of Psychiatry, Jackson Memorial Hospital Chief of Psychiatry, University of Miami Hospital

"Spanning a hundred years, the engrossing narrative blends fact and fiction and shows how little we have changed in our attitudes to mental illness, most particularly PTSD. This book is, in turns, a newspaper expose and a crime thriller. Just how much of it is true? For once the reader is left desperately hoping that what he is reading is pure fiction."

— Professor David Taylor
Director of Pharmacy and Pathology; Head of Pharmaceutical Sciences Clinical Academic Group, King's Health Partners South London and Maudsley NHS Foundation Trust Pharmacy Department | Maudsley Hospital | London

"This thesis novel barrels a long faster than a speeding bullet fuelled by Stahl's customary brio and with his hyperthymic 'voice' in evidence ... and with Stahl's mission to ensure that the lay reader does not equate PTSD with cowardice and that many current military psychiatric practices are addressed. As ever Stahl, and his protagonist Conrad, seek not merely to educate but to change practice."

— Professor Gordon Parker
University of New South Wales, Australia

"*Shell Shock* is rooted in the past and the indisputable truths continue to resonate—for which it becomes nearly impossible to tell where the fiction stops and the story continues—in a fast-paced read that is reminiscent of Dan Brown."

— Chad B. Clement
U.S. Navy SEAL (Ret.)

"For as long as humans could write, hard-to-swallow truths have been delivered in the form of entertaining stories, and *Shell Shock*, is no exception. Gripping and thrilling to the very end, Dr. Stahl's story entertains while highlighting the mental health consequences of warfare and the historic denial of same. The modern era is no exception, making Shell Shock not only enjoyable to read, but also timely and inspiring."

— **Lieutenant Commander Dr. William M. Sauve**
former U.S. Navy psychiatrist embedded with the U.S. Marine Corps in Iraq during Operation Iraqi Freedom

"*Shell Shock* is not only a page-turner but a *tour de force* first novel by renowned psychiatrist Stephen Stahl. It is sure to be a major motion picture."

— **Louann Brizendine, M.D.**
New York Times Best Selling Author of *The Female Brain* and *The Male Brain*

"When you finish the incredibly timely story of the last 100 years of PTSD, you only realize that this gripping tale of Stahl's mixture of civilian and military approaches to trauma have highlighted society's failure to confront important human problems. The similarities of the consequences to warfare for individual fighters regardless of the conflict are striking. ... I cannot wait for the sequel."

— **Dr. David Kupfer**
Chair of the Task Force for the Diagnostic and Statistical Manual (DSM) of the APA, and former Professor and Chair, Department of Psychiatry, University of Pittsburgh

"*Shell Shock* is a novel that should have appeared decades ago, and examines battles and how they affect soldiers' mental illness. ... [It is] an unusual blend of military history, thriller, and psychological suspense story. ... [It is] well-done and involving on many levels."

— **D. Donovan**
Senior Reviewer, *California Book Watch*

"A thrilling detective story that movingly captures the experiences of war's psychological casualties. *Shell Shock*'s fast-paced narrative takes you on an eye-opening journey from the battlefields of World War I through the conflicts of today. Breathtaking and enlightening!"

— **Dr. Paul Lerner**
Associate Professor of History, USC, and author of *Hysterical Men: War, Psychiatry, and the Politics of Trauma in Germany, 1890-1930*

SHELL SHOCK

SHELL SHOCK

A GUS CONRAD THRILLER

STEVE STAHL

HARLEY HOUSE
PRESS

First Harley House Trade Paperback Edition: July 2015

Published by Harley House Press
Carlsbad, CA 92008

www.harleyhousepress.com

100% acid-free paper

Printed in the United States

Library of Congress Control Number: 2014959456

ISBN: 978-0-9863237-0-6 (hardcover)
ISBN: 978-0-9863237-1-3 (paperback)
ISBN: 978-0-9863237-2-0 (eBook)

987654321

Dedication:
For Meredith, Staff Sergeant,
US Army Infantry,
World War II, and my hero.
For wounded warriors of all times.

Letter to the Reader

Although a work of fiction, *Shell Shock* is based on real events dating from World War I to the present. Part thriller and part historical fiction, *Shell Shock* traces the true story of Private Harry Farr, a real character who served in the British Army during World War I and was executed after being treated for *shell shock*. Subsequently, his daughter uncovered the treatment of her father by the British Army once records from World War I were made public, seventy-five years following the end of the war. She tirelessly lobbied for his pardon well into her nineties and ultimately achieved this for him and 305 others executed for cowardice but who had *shell shock*. A memorial has been erected in Great Britain in their honor.

D Block, Netley Hospital was an actual treatment center for lower rank soldiers and the doctors who treated Private Jennings in this story are based on known characters who were experts in hypnosis and faradization (a type of electrocution). Lieutenant Warburton is entirely fictional, but the hospital where he was treated, Craiglockhart, was real, and the characters Siegfried Sassoon and Wilfred Owen were true life poets who were hospitalized there, and Dr. W.H.R. Rivers, another true life psychiatrist, treated them. Many of the World War I characters are based on actual newspaper accounts and these are quoted here.

The Maudsley Hospital in London is an authentic place and thrives today in South London. The author was an Honorary Consultant there in the 1980s. The Bethlem Royal Hospital is the present-day version of "Bedlam" and has a psychiatric museum there. The Imperial War Museum occupies the site where the Bedlam hospital once stood. Dr. Augustus "Gus" Conrad is entirely fictional, as are all current characters. However, like Dr. Conrad, the author has trained at Stanford University, was on the faculty in psychiatry there, lived in Los Altos, drives an Aston Martin, and is a best-selling textbook author as well as an Honorary Fellow at Cambridge. The author lived in Harley House in England and Little Hadham, a small village in rural Hertfordshire. Like Conrad, the author has also trained military mental health professionals at Fort Hood and many other facilities and has visited the real vice chief of the army at the Pentagon, as well as having treated many patients with PTSD.

Contemporary events and characters in *Shell Shock* are entirely fictional, although based on actual experiences of the author. The scenes in the Pentagon, Stanford University, the University of Cambridge, Madingley Hall Cambridge and Harley House are all based on actual places.

The story of psychological reactions to war described in this novel is based upon a disturbing pattern of lack of recognition and treatment of these conditions by the military throughout history, and continuing today in ways that are at best inadequate and at worst shocking, particularly by the U.S. Army. Unfortunately, this continues today unabated, despite the heroic efforts of countless mental health professionals on active duty and civilian contractors dedicated to the care of military members and veterans. It is an issue of military culture and leadership. This part of the story is real. This novel is an attempt to enlighten the reader about these problems, how they came to be over the past 100 years, and to provoke the reader to think about them, with the hope that changes can be made in time to help future warriors who sacrifice not only their lives, but increasingly, survive but lose their well-being, for us. We owe them the very best treatment, rather than make them into cowards.

Steve Stahl
Carlsbad, CA
March, 2015

"Of every 100 men, 10 shouldn't even be there, 80 are nothing but targets, 9 are real fighters. ... We are lucky to have them, they make the battle. ... AH, but ONE, one of them is a Warrior. ... He will bring the others back."

      – Attributed by some to Heraclitus, c. 500 B.C.

Prologue

FRANCE, AUTUMN OF 1915:

Jennings had been sitting in a deathtrap for months now. Living in trenches made him think joining the army was a disaster. One of the worst things was the war was separating him from his precious bride back home. His Sarah would be bringing a newborn into their lives later this year, but Jennings wondered if he could stay sane or survive to see his cherub child. The young Yorkshireman had come to realize the worst thing about the Great War was not the separation from his beloved Sarah, as bad as that was. He hoped the war would soon be over and they'd be reunited. The worst thing wasn't even the filth, the smell or the squalor. Nor the fighting, as pointless as that was. The Great War was proving to be lethal to a degree never before experienced in history. It would prove to be the "war to end all wars" before it was over.

No. The worst thing wasn't even those rats—including the brown ones that gorged on putrefied bodies, eating the eyes and livers and leaving behind gruesome remains of a soldier's duty—or the dead horses or the torturous moaning of wounded men lying on stretchers in the open air. Jennings agonized even in his sleep by the sounds of such suffering. The worst thing wasn't even the chill from being waist deep in mud, as penetrating an annoyance as that was.

It's the shell fire that shocks you, Jennings mused.

The five-nines with their black smoke—Jennings and the others called them Jack Johnsons after that black boxer from America. The whizz bangs and the four twos and the minnies—they each had their own distinct sound. Jennings felt like an animal sitting in a burrow waiting for one of them to blow him straight to hell.

He decided once and for all: *It's the shells. Yes, they're the worst thing.*

SUNDAY

Chapter 1

NEAR PALO ALTO, CALIFORNIA, A CENTURY LATER:

Kneeling to touch the names Emily and Patricia on the grave markers, Dr. Augustus (Gus) Conrad suddenly heard the screech of tires. He recoiled as his nostrils were scorched by the smell of noxious gas. He could see flames ignited by fuel from the punctured tank of the car. Exploding glass windows and a horrible grating sound of crunching metal assaulted his ears. He trembled as terror seared his guts. *Here we go again,* Conrad thought as the flashback gripped him and began to tear apart the fabric of his body. A deafening silence now descended upon him as he visualized himself in his driver's seat right after the crash on his way home from Stanford University Hospital. Neither his wife nor his newborn daughter had any chance of surviving the accelerating pickup truck as it T-boned their side of their car. Seated in the driver's seat, Conrad had only suffered shoulder and back injuries. His family was killed instantly upon impact.

The cemetery, illuminated by the brightness of the mid-morning sun, belied the darkness it held beneath two grave markers that bore the surname "Conrad." Looking at the two names near his feet, Conrad found himself alone and bombarded with painfully familiar emotions. Usually he avoided this place. It made him face the burning torment of unresolved feelings about his loss. *What sort of demon causes a soldier to plow into a car on purpose to murder a young mother and her newborn child on their way home from the hospital?* he asked himself.

The contrast between the highest and lowest points in his life made him wish he could burst out of his skin and scream to the high heavens. But as always, his tears abruptly shifted to anger as he heard over and again "not guilty ... not guilty ... not guilty"—twelve times from jurors polled following their verdict in the manslaughter trial of the crazed driver.

Willing himself back to the present, Conrad felt the irony of being a psychiatrist accountable for helping soldiers with post-traumatic stress disorder—PTSD—when he'd been so painfully victimized by one himself. He wondered if he could ever be effective when he was so conflicted about PTSD. Conrad knew this particular visit would put his emotions through a ringer that would last for days. But, he also knew he couldn't face the soldiers in the Wounded Warrior Brigade without first reappearing at the burial site of his wife Emily and newborn daughter, Tricia. He owed that much to their memory, and to the family he might have had but now never would.

Thinking back to that day months after the deaths of Emily and Tricia, Conrad recalled seeing the defense lawyer talking to reporters on the steps outside a California courtroom after the verdict. "On behalf of my client, Corporal Stephens, we wish to express our deepest regrets to Dr. Conrad and his family for their loss and thank the jury for understanding this was a horrible accident and not manslaughter. Given the horror Corporal Stephens witnessed in Iraq, his PTSD continues to prevent him from a successful reentry into society. Sadly, but through no fault of his own, he experienced a beastly flashback as he drove home that night, thinking he was accelerating his Humvee away from hostile fire to save his platoon. Corporal Stephens lives with the guilt and shame of two deaths he feels responsible for, but we thank the jury for finding him not guilty. We hope Corporal Stephens can find a way forward with his life as this tragedy, in many ways, is as much his as it is Dr. Conrad's."

Seething with anger, Conrad took a deep breath, avoided looking at the graves again as he walked away, and resolved to put his loss behind him. Striding purposefully towards his car, he vowed to help every last soldier in his power try to cope with the *shell shock* of modern warfare, now better known as PTSD.

MONDAY

Chapter 2

EN ROUTE TO THE PENTAGON, WASHINGTON, D.C.:

The syncopated rhythm of helicopter blades beat upon the ears of Dr. Augustus Conrad, Professor of Psychiatry at Stanford University in Palo Alto, California. He was whisked away at a moment's notice this morning, with orders to board military transport bound for the Pentagon. Apparently the Vice Chief of the Army wanted to talk to him. And the Vice Chief didn't like to wait. Conrad was trying his best to remain composed and enjoy the ride.

"Look over there," his companion Libby Warburton shouted in his ear above the roar of the helicopter as she pointed out the window. "The Washington Monument."

Turning towards her to respond with his lips next to her ear, Gus Conrad noticed Libby's kind eyes lighting up. "You're right," he responded, wishing he could share her enthusiasm.

"And there's the White House," she continued. "Amazing." Their chopper flew right through restricted air space, past the Washington Monument, and then made an end-run around the White House. In a moment, Libby pointed again. "Whoa, that must be the Pentagon below."

"Now that's a stunning view," Conrad shouted.

"Brilliant. Looks like an entire city."

"Biggest building on earth. From up here you realize how truly massive it is." Their helicopter circled for a beat over the headquarters of the world's most powerful military, and then, with a go-ahead signal from the ground crew below, the pilot descended with a certain level of élan directly in front of the gargantuan, five-sided edifice.

"Quite the royal treatment, don't you think?" Libby asked as they descended.

"A royal pain if you asked me. I'd rather be working with the soldiers at Fort Hood."

"Evidently, that's not your call this morning."

The chopper slowly finalized its descent. Gus Conrad looked over at Libby, refusing to acknowledge he was a bit smitten with the single mother of a young army sergeant. He'd been immediately attracted to her tender spirit when he saw it in action at Fort Hood. She ministered with great kindness to young soldiers with PTSD assigned to the Wounded Warrior Brigade where she worked as a civilian nurse practitioner. Conrad also thought she was beautiful in an uncontrived, natural way.

As the chopper settled firmly on the ground, Conrad shifted uncomfortably in his seat, wincing as the helicopter lurched, causing him to fleetingly recall—but just as quickly dismiss—the car accident that was the reason for his chronic back pain. "It's great you're coming with me on this little junket to the Pentagon, Libby," Conrad finally said aloud, leaning over to touch her shoulder as he spoke directly into her ear so she could hear above the continuing roar of the helicopter engine, still idling after landing. Conrad knew Libby could see through his self-righteousness to his big heart. He hoped maybe she could help him soften his approach for the upcoming meeting with army brass. He had to guard against his tendency under fire to become overly certain and talk down to those who disagreed with him. That certainly wouldn't work today.

"Glad to come along. I'll certainly try to help you from becoming your own worst enemy by alienating important people," Libby replied as she positioned her lips close to his ear. "Do you think you can behave yourself during your discussion with the Vice Chief and his underlings?" she shouted, attempting to communicate with Conrad above the continuing roar of the helicopter blades as the pilot finalized his landing papers and flipped switches on the console in front of him.

Conrad admired her relaxed beauty as she spoke. Her flaxen-colored, shoulder length hair fell naturally about her soft face, punctuated with light-blue eyes that always seemed to show interest in what he had to say. *Not that she's my girlfriend or anything like that,* he thought. *But not a bad figure,* he admitted to himself. Libby always dressed in a modest, simple manner. *No plunging neckline necessary,* Conrad thought as he sneaked a quick look at her ample breasts.

Conrad thought for a moment, then began writhing in discomfort, this time from what was coming from his memory and not from his back. "I'll try, but I suspect the army's gonna lambaste me because of my criticisms of mental health treatment for their soldiers."

"It wouldn't hurt if you were more obvious in showing your commitment to helping the soldiers with PTSD rather than to banging heads with the leaders of army psychiatry."

"Guilty as charged. I'm also pretty sure they're not happy with my testimony for the defense of Sergeant Bales." Conrad had recently served as an expert witness for the defense of Sergeant Robert Bales, the U.S. soldier who killed sixteen Afghanis—nine of them children and some as young as two years old.

"You mean that soldier who killed all those innocent villagers?"

"Yep." Conrad noted some sort of welcoming party in army fatigues was beginning to assemble at a safe distance on the lawn outside the Pentagon, presumably to escort them inside.

"When I read about it in the papers, I was ashamed I had become an American. How could you possibly have testified on his behalf?"

"Everybody deserves a vigorous defense, even a murderer. And there's another side to the story."

"Really? What could that possibly be?"

The long spin-down of the helicopter blades still in progress, Conrad and Libby waited in their seats, then Conrad continued, "I uncovered several facts about Sergeant Bales and his rampage. It was fueled by drugs Army Special Forces gave him. Of course, the army didn't want to admit this, but they gave him anabolic steroids—plus illegal alcohol and various tranquilizers. Bales was actually taking more than a half-dozen different drugs that night, including a dozen Benadryl pills plus all sorts of caffeine supplements equivalent to over 200 cups of coffee. All that plus 'roid rage."

"Amazing. That wasn't in any of the news stories about the case I read. Didn't Sergeant Bales still get a life sentence without the possibility of parole? That should've satisfied the army."

"True enough." Now speaking in a normal tone of voice as the turbulence from above had almost completely faded, Conrad continued. "I wonder if the army's also upset about the statements I made in the press about the various Fort Hood shootings. You know, I linked the last one to the army's denial of psychiatric care for the shooter, who killed three soldiers and wounded sixteen others before committing suicide that day."

"Yes, I know. From what I've seen at Fort Hood, while the army doesn't provide sufficient mental health resources, they're still really sensitive about appearing in the press as unresponsive to all the PTSD and suicides of their soldiers. Everybody's giving the army a hard time for doing the minimum for soldiers with mental health issues, and then dumping them as soon as possible into the VA."

Both Libby and Conrad now unbuckled their seatbelts and Conrad asked, "You mean the same Veterans Affairs Department that has inadequate capacity, and lets veterans die while they sit on a waiting list?"

"Yeah, Gus," Libby sighed, "the very same VA." Just then the copilot jumped out and opened the door for Libby to help her exit from her side of the helicopter. She gathered her purse while getting ready to hop out.

"Pardon me if I think that soldiers are only supposed to die on the battlefield and not on a VA waiting list," he shouted after her.

Conrad's door was then opened by an enlisted soldier and he stepped to the ground and began to approach the welcoming party. Libby joined back with Conrad in front of the helicopter and responded, "Suppose they could be bringing you here to thank you for being a great advocate for soldiers with mental health issues?" She then turned to look at him with an impish grin.

"Yeah, sure, I bet they've got some sort of a medal for me when I get in there. More likely, smart aleck, they want to kick my ass for that preliminary report I sent to them about the horrible situation with mental health care we've both seen at Fort Hood since we began working there."

Just as they continued approaching their small platoon of escorting soldiers in army fatigues, Libby responded under her breath, "I guess we're about to find out which one it'll be, and I don't like your chances that it's gonna be the medal."

Chapter 3

THE PENTAGON, WASHINGTON, D.C.:

"This is a fucking disaster in the making," railed Brigadier General Andreas Rossi. Rossi was senior aide to the Vice Chief of the U.S. Army and head of its intelligence unit. The army was General Rossi's entire life. He knew his dedication bordered on paranoia when he thought his army was under fire, whether by mortar shells or political opportunists. Rising from the table to his full six-foot stature, General Rossi preferred to stand, assuming a more comfortable and familiar erect military posture. He liked to stretch upright into his full confrontational frame from which he could pace and work off the nervous tension he always felt whenever his army was being threatened or criticized by outsiders. He realized this motion could be simultaneously intimidating to others, which he often used to good purpose to get what he wanted.

"Don't go off the reservation on us, General Rossi. It's all under control," Dr. Ellen Richards said as she winked at Rossi and refused to be bullied. Dr. Richards was a Lieutenant Colonel in the U.S. Army, and chief of army psychiatry. Rossi just glared back at her. Despite scowling at her, he couldn't help but notice she was pleasant looking, almost attractive. Mid-40s, a bit short, with bleach-blonde hair tied up in back army style, and an ample figure, Colonel Richards looked powerful to him in a sexy sort of way in her dress military uniform.

The Vice Chief, Four-Star General Peter Morelli, shook his head, continuing to stare down at the conference table where he and Colonel Richards were still sitting. Having served for over thirty years, General Morelli was officially second in command for the entire U.S. Army. Everyone knew, however, General Morelli was really the man who ran the army. The so-called Chief of the Army, his boss General Casey, was mostly a hand-shaker who dealt with the chiefs of the other military branches, as well as the president and Congress. Rossi admired General Morelli as a leader who had earned the loyalty of the soldiers he commanded, leading warriors rather than pandering to government bureaucrats. "How're we gonna handle this next meeting at the top of the hour with the doctor who's working for us at Fort Hood?" General Morelli asked, almost to himself.

"The civilian is Dr. Augustus Conrad, professor of psychiatry at Stanford. A big shot in his field," offered Colonel Richards. She looked at Rossi as she spoke, returning his glare with a smile as she delicately swept a mischievous strand of blonde hair behind her ear. "Dr. Conrad has been working with army psychiatry programs at Fort Hood as a consultant. He's part of our plan to associate army mental health programs with leading figures in psychiatry as a positive public relations move."

"Fucking left-wing bleeding-heart academic," Rossi boomed back. "He's a public relations disaster if you ask me. I had army intelligence put him on 'watch' status ever since he testified for the defense in the Bales court-martial. The asshole tried to make our Special Forces look bad. One more unfair criticism of army psychiatry by that bastard in the press and we'll move against him. Turns out we have intelligence contacts in Germany and Argentina who've also had Conrad under surveillance for years. We've agreed to cooperate with them in case they decide to move on him."

"What do you mean by that, General Rossi?" Richards asked. "Gonna eliminate Conrad for felony 'disagreement with the army?' Haven't you ever heard the cliché about catching more flies with honey than with vinegar?" Richards continued, batting her eyes. "By the way, what about the Germans and Argentinians?"

"Never you mind, Colonel Richards," Rossi retorted as he blew Richards off. "Army generals all over the world have their own ways of dealing with their enemies and threats to national security."

"Tone it down, children," General Morelli sighed. "We've got better things to do than bickering over difficult professors who work with us."

"Conrad should have served as eye-candy for the press," Richards continued. "But he just doesn't cooperate."

"Well, he'd better start cooperating after he meets with us today," Rossi said as he paced up and down next to the oversized conference table.

General Morelli looked up at Rossi. "You're both missing the point. We need more than good publicity. We have a real problem with post-traumatic stress in our soldiers returning from deployment. Keeps me up at night, I tell ya. Don't mind admitting I gotta use trazodone for my own insomnia ever since coming back from commanding the ground troops in Iraq. Rossi, hand me that stack of cards over there on the table. The ones by my Bible."

"These?"

"Yes," General Morelli said as he pulled off the rubber band holding together a bunch of laminated cards looking like a bundle of driver's licenses.

"What're those?" asked Colonel Richards.

General Morelli handed them to her. "They're the pictures and personal details of every soldier who died under my command while I was leading the troops in Iraq before I took this job. I keep them by my side to remind me who I'm serving."

Rossi's eyes bulged out of his head as he gulped in amazement. *The old man really gives a fuck about his troops,* he said to himself.

"Problem is—" General Morelli paused mid-sentence to clear his throat as his voice broke from emotions obviously welling up from inside. "Problem is, I don't have a stack of cards for all those who're still having trouble with post-traumatic stress due to serving in combat under my watch. I fear that'd be a very tall stack. We owe it to our soldiers to do something about these problems. So don't you guys make this seem like simply politics. There're countless soldiers who're really hurting."

After a long pause, Colonel Richards delicately broke the silence. "Yes sir, General Morelli. Agreed. And to do the right thing by those soldiers, I take very seriously we have to get our behavioral health programs in order. The contract with Dr. Conrad was an attempt to boost our psychiatric programs at Fort Hood. The morale there still remains quite low in the aftermath of the shooting incidents over recent years, and the way the press linked them to problems with army mental health programs."

"No thanks to you, Colonel Richards," Rossi said with a snide grin, beginning to pace directly behind her. "I seem to recall when I reviewed your service record to approve your promotion to lieutenant colonel, you'd been the supervisor of the psychiatrist Major Hasan who turned out to be the first Fort Hood shooter. A psychiatrist! Son-of-a-bitch killed thirteen and shot another thirty innocent souls. Mostly other mental health workers, if you can believe it. You failed to recognize his dangerousness and actually promoted him instead of drumming him out of the army."

"Of course I'm well aware of that and need to tell you how honored I am you promoted me to head up army psychiatry anyway. I'm fully committed to turning it around."

"Well, at least we're gonna fry Hasan's ass now that he's gotten the death penalty," Rossi responded. "I'll make sure of it."

"Yes, certainly not the poster boy we want for an army psychiatrist," Colonel Richards replied, blushing and obviously having a hard time finding words. "And now we have to deal with the aftermath of the second mass shooting that occurred at Fort Hood just as the psychiatry programs there were beginning to get back on their feet. Remember Private Ivan Lopez, the second Fort Hood shooter? He was a psychiatric patient there at the time. He killed four, including himself, and injured an additional sixteen. He was complaining of poor treatment for his PTSD and depression. He also was outraged at bureaucratic delays about getting permission to take leave to attend his mother's funeral."

"This isn't simply about circling the wagons and protecting army psychiatry from external criticism, like that from Dr. Conrad," General Morelli stated with an exasperated look. "It's about fixing the problem. Listen to what Conrad writes about his observations at Fort Hood:

> '…Cadre thinks PTSD is not a mental illness but weakness.'
> 'Nurses have inadequate access to psychiatric records.'
> 'Nurses say that soldiers in the Warrior Transition Brigade get too many medications.'
> 'Nurses say that soldiers in the Warrior Transition Brigade get too many opiates.'
> 'All the serious incident reports involve prescription opiates from army medical personnel plus alcohol.'"

"If this report's true, we'd go from toasted to roasted in the press," General Morelli said. "I don't want another Walter Reed medical scandal on my watch. I want this corrected."

"Fucking *Washington Post* journalists," Rossi fumed. "That same bitch from the paper who wrote the story making Walter Reed into a medical scandal several years ago has another story in today's paper about problems with the psychiatry programs at Fort Hood. She's the same fire-eater who won a fucking Pulitzer Prize several years ago for her series claiming the British executed their own soldiers who had *shell shock* in World War I. She'll do anything to discredit the way the military deals with mental health issues," Rossi spouted as he paced back and forth behind the conference table where Richards and Morelli remained seated.

"Yes. That'd be Jennifer Roberts of *The Washington Post*," Colonel Richards interjected. "A real enemy of the army and of army psychiatry."

"Some muckraking reporter who never spent a minute in combat has no right to exonerate cowards by making them mental," Rossi ranted. "Cowards are shit. I'm sorry, but a good night's sleep helps more than any session of touchy-feely psychotherapy. I appreciate that some of the weaker among us can get battle exhaustion, but come on, they get over it. Instead, we had to make baby-sitting services for the so-called 'psychologically wounded' and form Warrior Transition Units that waste a lot of good manpower and money taking care of these zeros."

"Andy, knock it off," General Morelli retorted sharply to Rossi. "You'll never get that second star unless you can understand how sensitive this issue is. It's not simply about cowardice. There's such a thing as a *psychological war wound,* whether *you* want to admit it or not. The army is really behind the curve on identifying soldiers with this problem, and treating them. We've been passing our soldiers with post-traumatic stress along to the Veterans Affairs hospitals for too long, and avoided dealing with the problem ourselves. Colonel Richards, I want you to make this right. And General Rossi, grow up."

"Yes, you wouldn't want to derail your fast track status to a two-star major general," Richards said, batting her eyes ever so slightly at Rossi, all the time attempting to tame that rambunctious strand of blonde hair behind her ear.

"Call it what you want," Rossi responded. "With all due respect, I think PTSD is just another name for slackers and drama queens. And those who commit suicide just want the easy way out."

"That's not going to work with a world-renowned psychiatrist in our next meeting, General Rossi," Richards pleaded. "Conrad's also the best-selling author of numerous psychiatric textbooks and hundreds of scientific articles. We need a better plan than insulting him in order to neutralize his influence. We need to get him to quash his report to buy us time so we can fix things before another army psychiatric scandal explodes in the press."

Looking at Rossi, General Morelli spoke, shaking his head in disapproval, "Rossi, you're hopeless. Don't let Conrad hear you talking like that. That's why we have Richards here. You'd better stuff it when Conrad comes in, and let Colonel Richards try to work her feminine charms on him and handle the meeting," he said flatly.

"I guess that's my job, to show the army has a heart," Colonel Richards said, gracefully placing her hands together over a voluptuous left breast. Morelli continued to stare at the conference table dotted with half-spent water bottles as Rossi swallowed hard, looking at what Richards was covering with her hands. "At least we should make a show of appearing as if the army has a heart when we interact with *The Washington Post* and high-powered academics like Conrad," Richards continued. "For our upcoming meeting, I think we should simply point out to Conrad the army takes mental illness seriously and spends vast resources inoculating soldiers against suicide and PTSD with *resilience training*."

Rossi added, "PTSD is really due to poor recruitment, poor training and ill disciplined soldiers, not due to some psychiatric disorder caused by combat. When we have the gifted, the intelligent, and the strong as members of our army, they create a spirit of purpose and authority, and there is no PTSD. In fact, in well-commanded units today, we see no PTSD at all."

"General Rossi, I'm afraid that's an old-fashioned point of view," Richards chimed in. "And even if there's some truth to it, that attitude will get us nothing but grief from the likes of Conrad and that reporter Jennifer Roberts."

"It makes me wonder whatever happened to the idea that warriors who go to war come back all the stronger for the experience, standing tall and proud for having served their country well with only a few weaklings who fall by the wayside," Rossi asked, now feeling deflated.

"I agree with you in part, General Rossi, but that kind of talk is no longer politically correct," General Morelli shot back. "We need to use psychiatry more than ever as an acceptable tool to show the civilian world we care about psychological wounds, especially when they occur in our brave soldiers."

"Brave soldiers don't get psychological wounds," Rossi countered, taking a seat and feeling dejected, but having to make his point.

"Maybe so," General Morelli responded, "but that's irrelevant, unfortunately. The White House and Joint Chiefs put the military in an impossible situation fighting these wars. Even with all our active duty soldiers, reserves and National Guard, we never had enough manpower to really implement the 'surge.' With the demand on the army to place huge numbers of troops into combat, we've been forced to make our soldiers serve long deployments with little dwell time between consecutive deployments. I know that wasn't right, but it was the only choice I had."

"Yes, I agree the Iraq and Afghanistan conflicts have taken a huge toll on our warriors," Rossi agreed. "Armed conflicts have never lasted so long. I really feel bad for what we've asked of our troops."

"And don't forget, the long duration of deployments is not the only reason for our soldiers' burdens. Because combat deaths have actually been so low, soldiers have survived to serve many repeated deployments," General Morelli said with a long face and downcast eyes.

"Troops only served a year in Vietnam, as you well know," Rossi agreed. "Most of our current troops have pulled multiple deployments for over a decade now."

The general seemed to recoil as he noted aloud, "No soldier has ever been asked by his leaders to fight in combat for such an extended period time as this before. I'm gonna have to live with my own role in sending too many soldiers into combat for too long a time."

Richards shot Rossi a sly look out of the corner of her eye, and then gave him a long seductive glance. Rossi thought to himself, *I gotta nail that bitch tonight.*

Richards then chimed in with a winning smile. "That's why we have to balance the needs of the individual with the needs of the army. Unfortunately, in time of war, the interests of the army come first and that's partly why we're seeing all this PTSD. You've already emphasized, General Rossi, we have powerful enemies out there in the liberal media and academia, so we have to address these things in a more sensitive and enlightened manner. Otherwise, we'll get even more pushback from them, and that risks alienating our support in Congress and ultimately, our budget."

"I still say mental hygiene is the 'rectum of the army' and psychiatry in the army exists to eliminate our unwanted wastes," Rossi said as a smirk grew across his face.

"Lovely way of putting it, Andy," Richards said rolling her eyes. "I can't wait to see how you and Dr. Conrad are gonna get along."

Chapter 4

PENTAGON, WASHINGTON, D.C.:

As Libby and Conrad walked away from their helicopter toward the welcoming party outside the Pentagon, Libby asked, "What's that? With such an impressive building, I'd have thought they would've at least cleaned the walls," she said pointing to an ugly black blemish on the exterior of the Pentagon.

"That's a piece of burnt wreckage from the 9/11 attack, built back into the wall on purpose during reconstruction in defiance to the attackers and as a reminder," Conrad replied.

"Amazing statement. Seems like I can still smell pungent fumes of jet fuel coming from that black scar."

Within a few steps they were met by a small troop of soldiers headed by a beaming young female sergeant. She was slight and professional-looking in crisp army fatigues with three chevrons on the front of her uniform subtly betraying her rank. "Sergeant Williams, sir." The soldier shook Conrad's hand and smiled at Libby. "Right this way."

Conrad and Libby were ushered through an airport-style metal detector into a large waiting area. Sergeant Williams stated to the clerk at the reception desk, "This man has been pre-cleared to see General Morelli, E-Ring."

The clerk, another army sergeant, replied, "Here's his pass."

"What about her?" Sergeant Williams asked.

"She's not cleared and'll have to wait here," the clerk answered.

"Wait a minute," Conrad said, feeling Libby was being slighted. "I want her to come along as well. She's my training partner and obviously made the trip with me."

"Sorry," the clerk replied. "Orders."

Libby immediately responded, "That's okay." Pointing to her shoulder bag, she continued, "I've got lots to read," and sat down and pulled out the latest issue of *Real Simple*.

Feeling a bit unsettled, Conrad excused himself from Libby and followed Sergeant Williams through a maze of incredible complexity for what seemed to be an eternity. "Don't you ever get lost in here? The hallways seem to roll on forever."

"Rumor is, some people are still wandering around this building years after entering," Sergeant Williams joked. "After all, this is the largest building in the world. We're now well on our way. See, we're just now entering the E-Ring, where all the brass have their offices ... Secretary of Defense ... Secretary of the Army ... Secretary of the Navy, etc. And of course Chief and Vice Chief of the Army, which is where you're going. They call it E-Ring because it's the outer ring, starting with 'A' in the center, then 'B' and so on with the fifth, the largest and highest profile, the 'E-Ring.' It forms the outer perimeter all the way around the building. Ah, there it is. Second office on the left is where we're going.

Conrad then entered a huge office suite with a central reception area and two enormous inner offices, one to the right and one to the left. Standing just to the right of the reception desk was an older man in battle fatigues and combat boots.

Combat boots, Conrad thought to himself. *In the Pentagon? I thought those were for battle, not bureaucracy.* Wondering at first glance who this older man was since a soldier in fatigues looked the same whether a private or a general, Conrad soon noticed a cloth tag with four embroidered stars on it attached to his shirt. Seeing his confusion, the man stated, "Welcome. I'm General Casey."

Conrad felt like a fan meeting a celebrity as he shook the hand of the Chief of the Army.

"You're here to see the Vice Chief. His office is at the other end of our suite," General Casey stated as he pointed to the left of reception. "Thanks," Conrad whispered, a bit too stunned to voice his response aloud.

Conrad then turned around as Sergeant Williams addressed the soldier-in-charge at the reception desk for the Chief and Vice Chief. "This is Dr. Conrad, to see Vice Chief Morelli."

The soldier-receptionist looked at the schedule and said, "Have a seat. I'll tell General Morelli you're here."

Conrad's escort did an about-face and exited. Moments like this made Conrad think about having a drink to calm his nerves and keep him from erupting in anger. In the distant past he'd tried more destructive solutions, but that was another story. Candy was his drug of choice now. Just then, a tall, fit man in his mid-40s moved toward him with rapid, fluid motions, sporting one star on each shoulder. As he entered the reception area, he commanded, "Right this way." Conrad noted the man's rod-straight military bearing, as the brigadier general made a gesture towards the open door of the Vice Chief of the Army. Conrad walked up to the man with his own hand extended, and the general responded by shaking his hand dismissively and silently with only a glimpse of eye contact. The general then gestured once again towards the door, Conrad noted, much as a maître d' in a restaurant would lead you towards your dinner table. *Maybe more like leading the lambs to the slaughter,* Conrad thought to himself. He then entered the Vice Chief's office, followed by the escorting general, into a large dark vault ahead. As the door shut, Conrad, feeling somewhat overwhelmed, slipped a piece of candy into his mouth and suddenly could not get over the sinking feeling he was walking into an ambush.

Chapter 5

ON THE WESTERN FRONT, FRANCE, AUTUMN OF 1915:

"I can't take it! God help me," Murphy screamed next to Jennings in the trench, sending a wave of shock right up Jennings' spine. Private Murphy mentioned a scratchy throat yesterday right after they'd all been gassed by the Germans for the first time. Today Murphy began howling without stop from pain in his eyes. Yesterday, he and Jennings had both gone "over the top" again and both had fought valiantly for the fifth time in a week. As if anything could be worse than the unrelenting machine gunfire and mortar shells, they were all gassed in "no man's land." Jennings' eyes got runny, but Murphy didn't have it so easy.

"Don't be pitiful, soldier, no one else is whining," Lieutenant Robbins barked at Murphy after they had returned to their trench. Neither Murphy nor Jennings replied to the lieutenant, but Jennings was worried about his fellow infantryman, apparently more than their officer was.

Later that day, when Jennings went to the latrine with Murphy, Jennings recoiled as he saw Murphy pulling up his pants. "What the hell is that?"

Burns were erupting on Murphy's skin and yellow sacks of blisters had appeared in his groin area. Jennings felt his skin crawling and his own groin aching in sympathy at the gross and disgusting sight.

"You need to get that looked at right away. I'll take you to the dressing station."

"Doesn't hurt. I'll see the doc tomorrow if it starts bothering me."

Against his better judgment, Jennings relented and they both tried to get some sleep as night fell.

JENNINGS AWOKE AT DAWN and discovered to his horror that he should've forced his comrade to get medical attention the previous day. Now, it was too late for that. Jennings almost vomited when he saw Murphy's face had liquefied into slime overnight. White foaming bubbles and blood were coming out of Murphy's mouth. He had obviously drowned in his own froth last night. The eyes of his friend had turned bright red and remained open, unnerving Jennings, as he felt himself shake terribly on the inside. Those dead eyes seemed to move and follow Jennings everywhere until the medics finally came and closed Murphy's eyelids and took his tired, poisoned body away.

Nobody in the trenches had gotten any real sleep the past fortnight. Jennings was beyond exhausted, feeling almost like a zombie. Relentless bombing the whole time kept them all up for days without any break in the action.

Shell after shell after shell. First, there was the detonation. Then the flash, followed by heat. After a beat came a pulse of air—the wind of the shell. Then the explosion and the ground erupted. Pungent fumes stung your face. All the senses violated time and again beating you into submission until you couldn't stand it anymore but had to keep taking it anyway. Then, that last shell.

Lieutenant Robbins noticed all four of Jennings' limbs beginning to shake even before Jennings noticed it himself.

Chapter 6

THE PENTAGON, WASHINGTON, D.C.:

Upon entering the Vice Chief's office, Conrad immediately realized he was ensconced inside more of a bunker than an office. No windows. No natural light. Somber but expensive-looking mahogany furniture throughout accentuated the darkness of the place. A huge, unmanned desk sat at the far end of the office with empty overstuffed chairs facing it. To the left of the desk was a coffee table of fine wood on which sat a purple football helmet with a white "W" on both sides.

As Conrad eyed it, a voice from the end of the table boomed proudly, "University of Washington Huskies. Got my master's there." To the man's right stood an enlisted soldier at attention, ready to serve coffee or tea. To the man's left stood a pleasant-looking woman in her early 40s with lieutenant colonel insignias on her uniform. The emotionless brigadier general who had greeted him in the outer office stood across from Conrad on the other side of the conference table, and nervously paced up and down. Suddenly Conrad realized the brigadier general who had already greeted him so perfunctorily, was not the Vice Chief of the Army, but rather one of his staff.

Wow. The Vice Chief is so exalted by the army he gave himself a brigadier general for his lackey, Conrad thought to himself.

Conrad responded to the man at the head of the conference table, "Yes, I recognized it. I'm a Pac-12 man myself. Stanford."

"That means we're rivals," the general said with a broad smile. "I hope it'll prove to be our only rivalry," he added, his face now turning into a cryptic expression.

As Conrad made his way toward the resonant voice at the head of the long, elegant conference table, he noticed the man sitting there was a handsomely cut, graying, fit officer in full-dress uniform with four stars crowded onto each shoulder's epaulet. The seated figure speaking to him finally stood to shake his hand firmly, rising to the same six-foot height as Conrad, and said, "General Pete Morelli, doctor," and then motioned to an empty seat, "please have a seat. Anything to drink?"

"Thanks. I'm Dr. Gus Conrad. Pleased to meet you, General Morelli. I'll take some coffee. Black, please," Conrad replied as he sat, feeling more than a bit intimidated by the surroundings. The enlisted soldier literally jumped to pour Conrad and the Vice Chief each a cup of coffee. General Rossi and Colonel Richards, both still standing and not joining them for coffee, looked on as Conrad sat and began to sip nervously.

Plasma screens occupied every square inch of space on the walls all around the bunker. One had the red CNN logo in the corner. Another revealed a camera shot from somewhere in a desert with "Zulu time" pasted in the lower right-hand corner while a black and white flag of the Islamic State of Iraq and Syria—ISIS—flapped in a light breeze in the middle of the screen. A third screen had "Fox News" in the lower left-hand corner. Conrad smiled and mused, *I wonder what MSNBC would think of that?*

As soon as Conrad sat, General Morelli said, "I see you've met my head of intelligence, Brigadier General Andreas Rossi."

"Yes, I had the pleasure in the outer office," said Conrad as Rossi nodded yes with a barely audible grunt.

Conrad decided not to mention Rossi had appeared brusque and inhospitable. Meanwhile, Conrad could not help but have his attention drawn to General Morelli's four stars on each of his shoulders twinkling impressively in the artificial light that illuminated his dark cave.

"Thanks for coming on such short notice."

"Thank you for fetching me on your jet and helicopter. It was quite an experience."

Ignoring that, General Morelli began, "We have a bit of a situation here." He then paused and waited as he sipped his hot coffee. The coffee-serving soldier stood at attention again to Morelli's right as Rossi continued pacing on the other side of the room and the female lieutenant colonel remained standing and watching to General Morelli's left.

"Let me explain, if I can," said the voice standing to General Morelli's left. Conrad turned in his seat to look at the woman who was speaking. "Colonel Ellen Richards here, Dr. Conrad. I'm head of army psychiatry. I've certainly heard a lot about you and I've read all your textbooks during my training." Dr. Richards extended her hand to shake Conrad's as he stood, giving him intense eye contact. As their hands met, she pulled him toward her, tipping him off balance and making him take a step forward while her hand was still shaking his, bringing him involuntarily closer to her so their eyes were within inches of each other as she then clasped his hand with both of hers. Looking up at him from her five-foot-two stature in army dress pumps, she continued admiringly, "You're a real rock star to me, Dr. Conrad. I never thought I'd get the chance to meet you in person. You've contributed so much to psychiatry."

Conrad blushed briefly and stammered as he stepped back, "Uh, well, thanks. You're too kind."

Colonel Richards beamed with excitement as she took a step towards Conrad, narrowing his retreat so they continued standing close together until he sat back down. All the while, Richards never lost intense eye contact with him, giving him an uninterrupted and inviting smile. *Is this chick trying to come on to me or knock me off-center to unsettle me?* Conrad asked himself.

"Anyway," Colonel Richards continued, remaining standing, "we're taking a lot of flak from the news media regarding the various shootings at Fort Hood and our recent epidemic of army suicides."

"Yes, I've heard. As I'm sure you're well aware, before the Iraq and Afghanistan conflicts, the army had a lower suicide rate than civilians, but it now has twice the rate of civilians."

"You don't need to lecture us," Rossi spit. "Let's get to the point. We're concerned about your preliminary report from Fort Hood. It places army behavioral health services in an unfavorable light."

"That's not my intent. I'm only reporting my observations."

"We've looked into your observations and it appears they're not valid, so we want to talk to you about modifying your report," oozed Colonel Richards. Now at a more comfortable distance, Conrad noticed she was all military in appearance, hair bundled professionally away from her face, moderately attractive and a bit pudgy in her tight army-issue women's dress uniform.

"What do you mean?" asked Conrad.

"For starters, you say army psychiatrists prescribe too many drugs. That's not true. We simply follow published guidelines, including some of those from your own books," Colonel Richards said, never breaking eye contact and continuing to hold her radiant smile.

"My findings don't support that," Conrad returned. "Although admittedly, I only interviewed about thirty soldiers in the Warrior Transition Unit out of about 650, all of them were taking about a dozen drugs each, some as many as fifteen. That's not how we'd treat the same cases in civilian psychiatry, even at VA hospitals," Conrad continued firmly.

Ignoring Conrad's response, Rossi took over. "You assert army primary-care doctors prescribe too many addicting pain killers. We've looked into that and can demonstrate we specifically have a policy prohibiting this." Rossi continued, "You also report the cadre—our line commanders at Fort Hood—think PTSD isn't a mental illness. 'Bullshit.' We've ordered the cadre to treat PTSD as a legitimate wound, and have also issued orders commanding all army personnel to stop committing suicide."

Conrad was blown away, astonished at the breadth of ignorance on display. "You ordered them not to commit suicide? Exactly how do you manage that?"

Unfazed, Rossi forged ahead. "Here's another one of your invalid assertions. And I quote," Reading from Conrad's draft report, Rossi continued ...

> "The nurses are confused about the diagnosis of PTSD since they cannot use those words or write them in the soldiers' charts unless a psychiatrist has first made the diagnosis. Nurses are not allowed to diagnose PTSD. This leads to an inappropriate lack of diagnosing that condition in certain soldiers who in fact do have PTSD."

Colonel Richards interrupted. "Dr. Conrad, the reason why psychiatrists diagnose PTSD is not just because they're the experts, but also because we don't want the medical records to have inaccurate statements that could lead to unjustified pension claims at a later date."

Rossi bludgeoned on without regard for any sense of propriety. "You say that primary-care doctors and nurses don't have adequate access to psychiatric records. I've researched your allegation and specifically found we have a strict policy that mandates adequate access to psychiatric records for all medical personnel, so this can't be true."

Conrad's expression changed from attention to concern. Then for a nanosecond, his focus turned to Libby sitting in the outer office. *I'd rather be out there with her,* he thought.

Rossi continued. "You also say your review of serious incident reports of all suicide attempts on base at Fort Hood for the past year indicates that in every case, they involve excessive alcohol intake combined with overdoses of pain killers prescribed by army doctors. How can that be accurate when we have a policy against prescribing too many pain killers? Bottom line, Dr. Conrad, given our inability to verify your claims, we think you should correct these errors in your report before you submit the final draft."

"They're not errors," Conrad fired back. "You may have policies intended to prevent these things, but they're simply not working."

Pressing his attack, Rossi spouted, "How many times do I have to state it? We see no evidence to back you up. In fact, all our other reports say that army mental health procedures at Fort Hood are in full compliance with army regulations."

"Well, that may be in your reports, but I've just seen the contrary in person and as you say, 'on the ground,' as recently as yesterday."

No one was smiling. Colonel Richards tried once again. This time her eye contact became an icy stare. In an intimidating gesture, she sat down next to Conrad at the conference table, between him and General Morelli, and audibly thumped the papers on the table in front of her with her index finger, never losing eye contact. "We simply don't believe your preliminary report, and ask you again, firmly, and with respect, to reconsider how you present things in your final report."

Simply flabbergasted, and before he could help himself, Conrad looked at General Morelli, and said with no hint of his being intimidated at this point, "As a scientist, I can't change my report to suit you, but only to suit the data and the real observations. You're certainly free not to believe my report and be fooled into thinking having a policy means it's being followed or it's the right policy."

Pausing to collect himself, Conrad noticed the Vice Chief's posture: slightly slumped forward, almost hugging himself with his own arms while rubbing the four stars on his right shoulder with the fingers of his left hand. Conrad wondered to himself, *is this guy unconsciously reassuring himself of his God-like status in the military? or trying to intimidate me? or both?* Shaking his head, Conrad decided to give it one last try. "The U.S. Army is simply not equipped for 21st century warfare. The modern army needs modern psychiatry, not just modern equipment and state-of-the-art battlefield medicine for blast wounds. The truth is the army is fighting last century's wars with its current medical priorities."

Without realizing he was lecturing the man who ran the army's entire operations, including the wars in both Iraq and Afghanistan, Conrad continued to shoot his unsolicited analysis at the Vice Chief. "A century ago in World War I, *shell shock* was first identified, with 80,000 cases in the British infantry, accompanying two million battlefield deaths. In contrast, a hundred years later during Operation Iraqi Freedom, about 4,500 soldiers died, some 40,000 were wounded—about 10,000 seriously—but with a staggering 400,000 plus psychiatric casualties. A veritable explosion of PTSD in modern warfare. However, there are fewer psychiatrists for the entire U.S. Army than there are in the Palo Alto phone book."

The generals and Lieutenant Colonel Richards were being schooled and it was obvious from their facial expressions and postures they didn't like it. Before Rossi could find the words, Conrad continued his verbal fusillade.

"Almost all the army's medical resources go toward the 10,000 or so seriously wounded. Scant attention is paid to the 400,000 with PTSD, substance abuse, depression and suicide, and it shows. Although the best place on earth to be after you get a blast injury is inside an army hospital, the worst place on earth to be if you get PTSD is inside an army hospital."

The Vice Chief's eyes continued to ignore Conrad, as he seemed to be smoldering inside. With one last burst of effort, Conrad pointed his finger at the Vice Chief, who was now obviously taken aback by Conrad's sudden act of bravado and recoiled in his chair, finally locking eyes with Conrad. Conrad failed to realize no one had ever talked to the Vice Chief this way and he noticed the eyes blowing wide open on General Rossi's face and the jaw dropping on Colonel Richards' face. He nevertheless continued, leaning forward in his chair. "With all due respect, sir, I believe you need to get on top of this situation and equip the army for warfare in the 21st century, which means giving high priority to 'psychological' war wounds."

On a roll now, and despite his coaching by Libby, Conrad couldn't help himself as he reverted to his self-righteous style under pressure and blurted out, "Whether you realize it or not, sir, you have a potential national security issue in front of you, not just a mental health issue."

Conrad certainly had the Vice Chief's full attention now. "If the word ever got out to the patriotic families of our country, many in small towns all across America, and many with generations of service to their country in uniform, that the most likely thing to happen to their sons or daughters in modern military service was not death, nor even a horrible injury, but a psychiatric wound, and that such a wound would be denied, dismissed and dumped unceremoniously onto a VA waiting list without a pension, then you'd no longer be able to sustain your volunteer army. That's a national security emergency if there ever was one."

A long pause ensued as the Vice Chief, Rossi and Richards all appeared momentarily stunned. Finally, General Morelli said, while looking again at the conference table and without eye contact, "That will be all."

Conrad was unceremoniously escorted out of the E-Ring by the enlisted soldier standing next to General Morelli and without a word until he exited the sprawling building silently with Libby. As they boarded the helicopter for their return to Andrews Air Force Base and their plane back to Fort Hood, Conrad remained silent and Libby patted his hand on his knee reassuringly as they lifted off in the helicopter.

"How'd it go?" she finally asked nervously, trying to be understood above the roar of the rotor's massive blades and screaming jet engine.

"I think I may have stepped over the line," Conrad said barely and with resignation.

Trying to be sympathetic, Libby finally said, "Something horrible must have happened in there. You look *shell shocked*."

Chapter 7

ON THE WESTERN FRONT, FRANCE, AUTUMN OF 1915:

"Sergeant Anthony, Jennings is on the twitch!" Lieutenant Robbins shouted and then turned his back and walked away as Sergeant Anthony rumbled by. "Handle this," the lieutenant barked over his shoulder.

Jennings' battle buddy Private Harry Simpson looked on in dismay.

Sergeant Anthony walked up, assessed the situation for a moment silently and then ordered, "Jennings, get the hell off your backside. Bugger you, Jennings, don't be a shirker."

"I ... I ... I can't help it," Jennings pleaded.

"Christ, another mental," Sergeant Anthony said under his breath. "Jennings, go see the doctor. Simpson, take Jennings to the dressing station and get yourself back here fast or no rations for you this morning."

Jennings felt humiliated as he stumbled along the muddy trench, detritus all around, on his hands and knees until he found a broken piece of duckboard serving as a crude floor for the trench, and started using it as a crutch. Arms and legs trembling, he wished he could just melt away, aware of the spectacle he was causing and hearing the snickering of the others as he made his way with Simpson to the nearest dressing station about a hundred yards away.

Once he was there, he and Simpson entered a large white tent. Jennings noted the makeshift hospital, intensely overcrowded today, drew a press of bodies into its belly. Reeking, bleeding men. Stretchers blocked the floors, the battered entrance, the approaches outside. At the crude dressing tables doctors were feverishly at work. Nurses—called sisters by nearly anyone who was British—were ministering to some of the men still lying on the ground half-manacled to stretchers. Working space was quite limited—everyone got in each other's way. A constant movement of bearers shuffled in and staggered out with stretchers, seeking bare space to deposit their burdens. Overwhelmed and frightened as he waited in silence with Simpson for several hours, Jennings would occasionally hear a man gasp and die as he lay on his stretcher. Although Jennings recoiled in disgust, to others this seemed part of the routine. The waiting crowd looked on unconcerned. No one spoke.

Jennings and Simpson sat for a long time on a bench in triage giving Jennings time to once again wonder how he'd gotten here. It was still a puzzle to him. Seemed like nearly all important things in his life just *happened* rather than being events he shaped in any way. As a *Donny*, raised on a farm near Doncaster in Yorkshire, England, he followed the custom of many other working-class boys from the North, enlisting rather thoughtlessly in the British Army as soon as he dropped out of school a few years after the turn of the century. Jennings had even exaggerated his age, claiming to be eighteen when he was only sixteen so he'd be accepted into the service early. It was still amazing to him the army had allowed him to enlist at the time. With his short stature and slight build, he knew even now he was at times mistaken for a boy.

His plan—to the extent he had one—had been to join the military for some adventure, then marry and build a family in good Yorkshire tradition. Indeed, just a year ago he married Sarah, the love of his life. A stable, no-nonsense girl, Sarah had also grown-up on a farm, and was part of a large extended family in the Yorkshire countryside. She was his bedrock, filled with common sense and was the salt of the earth. She loved children and was eager to start a family of her own, so she was thrilled beyond words when she discovered she was pregnant a few months ago.

Abruptly bringing Jennings back to the present, a clerk finally shouted at him from the desk, "What do you blokes want?"

Simpson told the clerk, "He needs to see a doctor."

"I don't see blood. You hit?"

Jennings just stared back at the clerk. There was no thought in his head. Just blank.

Simpson answered for him. "No, he just can't walk. Shaking all over.

All of a sudden. Just this morning. He was normal yesterday."

"Can't walk? Are you sure? You weren't riding here on a stretcher, now were you? So how'd you get here if you can't walk?"

Jennings' arms and legs continuously shook as he sat. He pointed at his duckboard crutch, feeling foolish for being here. He didn't know what was happening to his body. Like so many other things in his life he didn't understand, he tried to accept it as one more thing he didn't cause and over which he had no control.

Simpson replied for him, "With that crutch," pointing to the makeshift support fashioned out of duckboard at Jennings' side.

The clerk then yelled to a figure standing about halfway up the long tent, "Hey doc, another mental up here."

Up strode the casualty doctor: tall, vigorous, with an upper-class bearing in a crisp uniform of the Royal Army Medical Corp with its RAMC insignia.

He asked, "Name, soldier?"

Simpson answered, "This one is Simon Jennings."

"Can't speak for himself, hey?"

Simpson ignored the question.

"Very well then, rank?"

"He's a private, like me."

"Regiment?"

"We're both in the 1st, West Yorkshire."

"Complaint? Soldier, this time you answer my question."

Jennings heard and understood, but couldn't form the words.

"His nerves have been on the twitch since dawn, and his arms and legs can't keep still," Simpson remarked.

The young doctor looked at Jennings—four limbs in constant motion. "Take a few steps. I want to see you walk."

Embarrassed, but trying hard, Jennings stood unsteadily, leaning on the duckboard crutch, and lurched forward, swaying wildly but not falling.

"That's enough. Now stretch your hands and arms out in front like this," he said as he demonstrated what he wanted.

Jennings tried, dropping the crutch, his arms trembling as his body jerked side to side, but remaining on his feet.

"Say something, soldier."

Jennings sputtered what came into his head as he looked blankly at the floor. "Heavy rain. Had a shock. Can't keep still. Red eyes. Had a shock."

The doctor wrote on Jennings' chart:

Incoherent. Temporarily deranged.
Treatment: rest for two days and then back to the Front.

"Sister, get this man cleaned-up and fed, and let him rest today and tomorrow," the RAMC doctor barked. "I'll see him again tomorrow."

The nurse obediently came over to Jennings. "Let's get these boots off. Is it Private Jennings?"

Jennings nodded, feeling kindness coming from the sister. As his damp boots peeled off rather than dropped off, an acrid odor from his exposed feet assaulted his nostrils.

"Let's get your feet dry. We must get these feet clean and tepid," the nurse said to Jennings, ministering to him tenderly with a soft, warm cloth. Beneath the caked mud his feet were red, and as they plunged into a pan of warm water, they began to reveal scaling green blisters.

"You have trench foot," announced the sister. "These hooves of yours will be all better in a couple of days. Now, off with those clothes."

Jennings gave the nurse a quizzical stare, then obeyed her order. As his pants and jacket dropped to the floor, a battalion of lice scampered away across the dried mud floor.

"We'll wash these feet and you'll be good as new, especially after we shave your head to keep your little critters from coming back."

Jennings was oblivious to it all. Sitting now on the edge of a bed, he just stared at the ground, feeling both awkward and inadequate.

"After a cuppa tea, you just lie down here and rest. In a day or two, you'll be a fine young man again. Yes, you will."

He so strongly wanted to believe her.

Chapter 8

AIRBORNE EN ROUTE TO TEXAS:

As Libby and Conrad tried to relax after transferring from the helicopter to the military jet returning them to Fort Hood, Conrad asked Libby, "How about dinner tonight when we get back? The least I can do is feed you after today."

"Would you mind if we asked Adam to come along? He and I haven't had a chance to catch up since he got back from leave. He went to visit relatives in England."

"No problem. Let's have him meet us at your favorite 'greasy spoon' diner."

"Yea. Lester's, 'Home of the world's largest cup of coffee.' I'll call Adam when we land. You know, he's not doing too well. Before going on leave, he had just got back from his fourth deployment."

"Sorry to hear that. What's wrong?"

"Everything. Not responding to treatment for his PTSD. Addiction to pain pills continues. Now thinking more than ever about suicide. Maybe you can do your psychiatrist thing gently over our meal and give me some suggestions about what you think we should be doing for him at the Warrior Transition Unit at Fort Hood."

"Back on duty, Nurse Warburton," said Conrad as he gave her a mock salute. "Not a problem at all."

The two sat in silence. Sipping a cold beverage, Libby looked out at the late afternoon clouds below them. Conrad just stared at his computer screen perched on the tray in front of him.

"Why so glum?" Libby asked.

"You know, they're gonna bury this report and ignore it."

"Unfortunately, there's little you can do if that's what they decide to do."

"Not exactly true. I could publish it. I'm the editor of a psychiatric journal, *CNS Spectrums*, and I'm sure our readers would be interested in learning what the army 'cadre' thinks about mental illness."

"Since the cadre chain of command sees PTSD as an excuse for cowardice and weakness, its treatment is just a farce?"

"Exactly. They'd also be shocked to learn how the mental health professionals treating these soldiers perceive the quality of mental health care at Fort Hood: namely—abysmal."

"I'd have to agree."

"Look, here's the data I collected that dispute Morelli and his mob's view of the world."

"You can't send that off for publication. The army would be furious."

Conrad returned to his silent brooding, then, he finally said aloud, "Watch me," as he hit a key on his keyboard. With warp speed the E-mail left his laptop, and would soon start a cascade of events he could never have predicted.

Chapter 9

THE PENTAGON, WASHINGTON, D.C.:

"Gee, that went well," Richards said to Rossi in a biting tone dripping with sarcasm, which he hated. The two entered his office in the Pentagon down the hall from General Morelli's bunker following their meeting with Conrad and the Vice Chief.

"Big fuckin' deal. Conrad's a self-righteous asshole," Rossi said as he ran his tense hands through his military-cut hair.

"Maybe so. But one with a lot of credibility in psychiatry," Richards added.

"So what. More importantly, he's a traitor to my army. I'm glad I put the son-of-a-bitch under surveillance. I don't trust him."

"I agree, but we need to be careful. He could be influential with the press."

"Speaking of the lame-stream media, have you read this yet?" Rossi tossed the day's *Washington Post* onto the table in front of Richards.

"That article in today's *Post* by Jennifer Roberts?"

"Yeah. Piece of shit reporter for a piece of shit news rag."

"Well, there have been a series of shootings and suicides with firearms on army bases, not just at Fort Hood. And the various shooters were receiving mental health treatment. Sort of."

"So what?"

"And soldier abuse of opiates and alcohol and overdoses on them are at an all-time high." Picking up the newspaper, Richards read for a moment and then said, "Roberts reports details on several of the shootings over the recent past. She says here that when our second Fort Hood shooter was refused leave to go home, that's what set him off."

"Oh, that makes sense," Rossi shot back sarcastically. "Just because he has to stay on duty instead of going home to mommy's funeral, he has the right to go postal? Freeloader was never even deployed, but everyone still blames incidents like this on the army and on combat. Hard to get a combat wound without combat."

"True enough. But we did refuse him leave to go home for his mother's funeral. How did Roberts find all this out for her article, anyway?"

"Same way she weaseled information out of the Brits for her Pulitzer. By finding insiders willing to betray the very military that protects them day and night."

"Brits. That reminds me, how about our talks for the upcoming Annual Meeting on Military Psychiatry at Madingley Hall in the U.K.? Anything we need to discuss before we leave for London Heathrow Airport tomorrow night?"

"Naw. I have my talk on resilience training all ready to go. How about you?"

"Still putting the data together on military suicides."

"The ones we cause or the ones they do to themselves?"

"Very funny. I've got to dress up our statistics so they don't blame all these deaths on poor mental health care in the U.S. Army."

"Speaking of dressing or rather undressing, I need you to come back here at the end of the day to finish up some business."

Both of them knew what that meant.

Chapter 10

ON THE WESTERN FRONT, FRANCE, AUTUMN OF 1915:

After Jennings had two days of rest, his RAMC doctor stopped at the foot of his bed.

"How're we doing, soldier?"

Jennings looked back blankly. Trembling in each of his four limbs, he sputtered, but said nothing coherent. He then looked at the floor, ashamed at his lack of progress.

"I see from your chart you're not sleeping. Stand up and take a few steps."

Jennings lurched left and right, catching himself on the beds as he stumbled by, but did not fall. The RAMC doctor wrote in the chart:

> Hysterical gait.
> *Astasia abasia.*

Jennings sat on the edge of his well-worn bed, dejected and wearing sagging shoulders. Next to his athletic mates in casualty, he felt ashamed of his small, boy-like frame. Jennings thought his size and his shaking exposed to everyone that he was the only one amongst them who couldn't bear the weight of the horrifying memories common to all of them.

Jennings was not a large man, humble in presentation, slight in build, average height, honest face, and unremarkable in every way. Nevertheless, he was the man who stole Sarah's heart and married her more than a year ago, and who would be a father in the New Year. Sorry to admit it to himself, but it appeared to him that in the conflict between his need for self-preservation and his duty to stay and fight, self-preservation had easily won.

"You're in no shape to go back to the Front yet. I'll have to send you to Le Havre for more treatment," the doctor announced.

Feeling somewhat relieved, Jennings began to get ready for the overland trip to the rear lines in Le Havre, France, and the base hospital there. Meanwhile, his doctor wrote in his medical records words that would haunt Jennings and his family for the next century.

Diagnosis: *"Shell Shock."*

Chapter 11

NEAR FORT HOOD ARMY BASE, KILLEEN, TEXAS:

Conrad, Libby, and her son Adam all exchanged greetings and sat down to eat at Lester's Diner, "Home of the world's biggest cup of coffee," just off base in the town of Killeen, Texas. Conrad looked around and said, "This is truly an army town."

"Yes, Dr. Conrad. Killeen has little reason for existence other than to support the army and their families at Fort Hood," Adam replied politely and then added, "and to serve them big-ass cups of coffee."

Libby smiled and said, "Good, decent Americans."

"Call me Gus, Adam. Evidently no high end restaurants in Killeen. And no Tiffany's," he said, razzing them.

"Yep. The only millionaires here are the senators who breeze in and out of the Commanding General's office and leave as quickly as they arrive," Adam contributed in a sarcastic tone.

"Adam, I've been eager to hear, how'd your visit with Papa Geoff go?" Libby said, getting straight to the point.

"He was nice enough to me." Silence.

"That's it?" Libby responded. "Why so gloomy? Cat got your tongue?" After no response and a brief pause, she continued, looking at Conrad. "My grandfather—Adam's great-grandfather Geoffrey Warburton—is past ninety-years-old, and a World War II hero who served in the British infantry. We call him Papa Geoff. He's always been my lifeline, and

I thought a visit to see him would be good for Adam. Doesn't seem to have worked out that way," she added now looking over at Adam.

Adam then blurted, "Basically, we have a pretty screwed up family, and I'm just another freak in our tribe ... the misbegotten child of a single mother whose parents kicked her out when she got pregnant as a teenager, then moved in with her grandfather, whose own father was a World War I coward and committed suicide just like I probably will."

"Adam, that's enough. Just because you're twenty-one now and an army sergeant doesn't mean you can talk to me like that."

"Sorry, mom, but it's true."

"For the record, now that you so tactlessly brought it up, Adam, yes, I did get pregnant as a teenager and got kicked out by my parents. And yes, I did move in with my grandparents to raise you while I went to nursing school. They were my salvation. Without their support, I could've never become a nurse, nor immigrated to the States with you."

Locking eyes with Adam, she continued, "And that's no way to talk about your great-great-grandfather, Papa Nigel."

"Look, Mom. I went there to learn about *all* the military men in the family, not just the hero. And the more I learn, the more I realize I'm more like our family's World War I coward, than our World War II hero."

"Papa Nigel was not a coward, Adam," Libby fired back, looking embarrassed by the conversation Conrad was witnessing.

"Well, according to Papa Geoff, both his father and I developed the very same symptoms ... nightmares, can't sleep, flashbacks, drink too much, get into fights, and now I'm doing Papa Nigel one better, because I'm also addicted to pain pills."

No one noticed as Conrad's own bad memories caused him to cringe with the words "pain pills." Just then, a cute waitress, who was all eyes for Adam, came up to the table and took their order.

"Mom, my trip to England convinced me I'm a soul mate of Papa Nigel," Adam continued. "Maybe I'll even kill myself like he did."

"Adam. I said that'll be enough. Let me explain for Dr. Conrad. My great-grandfather—Adam's great-great-grandfather—whom we call Papa Nigel, was an officer in the British Expeditionary Force in World War I, and was evacuated back to Britain to be treated in a military hospital. It was all hush-hush, but we suspect it was for *shell shock*. He died under suspicious circumstances at the Maudsley Hospital in south London shortly thereafter. Papa Geoff, my grandfather, told us the army treated Papa

Nigel's death as a suicide. Our family never believed it, but we've always been denied access to his military records to find out for sure."

"For your information, Papa Geoff told me the British Parliament has now made the government's World War I secret archives public after seventy-five years. Evidently it's Parliamentary policy to keep state secrets for only seventy-five years and then release them to the public. So I applied online to get those records for myself. I wanna find out if cowardice and suicide run in the family," Adam said.

"Papa Nigel was not a coward, Adam," Libby insisted. "Stop such terrible talk."

"Then what do you call somebody who goes to not one but two looney bins during the middle of a world war? They haven't locked me up yet but they have me in the modern equivalent, the 'losers brigade' at Fort Hood for slackers who are too weak to make it as soldiers. No purple heart for me."

"Gus, can you please help here?" Libby pleaded.

Clanking the plates onto the table, their waitress served the salads and winked at Adam who blushed and looked away from her.

Conrad shifted comfortably into "professor" mode. "Adam, I hate to tell you, but the military ideal of the warrior is just a myth, namely that combat is always noble, heroes are never afraid, and if you're traumatized by war, you're not a man, but a coward."

"What've you been smoking, doc? If you ever spent fifteen minutes with a group of enlisted guys, you'll find out we all still believe in the military ideal. Any losers like me assigned to the Warrior Transition Brigade with post-traumatic stress are weak-willed and an embarrassment to the army."

"Adam, it's a natural human reaction to become traumatized by atrocities like combat. Your mom and I are working hard to support rather than blame our psychologically wounded warriors."

"Good thing those of us with PTSD are only blamed now. Papa Geoff told me that in his father's time, they used firing squads to execute soldiers with *shell shock*."

"What?" Libby said as she brought her hands to her mouth. "Is that true?"

"I'm afraid it is," Conrad replied in his detached, lecturing style. "In World War I the British Army had a special unit—decorated for bravery—who court-martialed and then executed hundreds if not thousands of their own troops with *shell shock* as cowards."

"Yeah, according to Papa Geoff, his Papa Nigel ranted and raved about firing squads in France when family visited him at the Maudsley Hospital in London before he died. Everybody thought Papa Nigel was nuts. Especially after he killed himself."

"That's enough," Libby fumed.

"Sounds like you need to learn what really happened to your Papa Nigel," Conrad continued. "If you want, I'd be willing to help. I have an old mentor in Cambridge, where I studied, who's a world famous historian. His name is Professor Trevor Chamberlain. He always gets privileged access to archival materials for his academic studies. I can ask him to help you look into your great-great-grandfather and his death if you'd like. I think it'd be of great interest to you and be helpful as well to Adam."

"I'm way ahead of you, doc. I already made a friend over there who's researching the archives for me. In fact, it's your professor friend's granddaughter, Victoria, a student at Cambridge."

"Small world," Conrad replied. "I haven't had contact with Professor Chamberlain for over twenty years. What do they say about six degrees of separation? Seems it's a lot less than that now-a-days."

"And when you contact your Cambridge professor, try and find out what this thing is," Adam said as he pulled out a solid gold Medallion and handed it to Conrad.

Chapter 12

LE HAVRE, FRANCE, AUTUMN OF 1915:

As the train drew up to the Casualty Depot in Le Havre, France, Jennings noticed the sounds of warfare had completely faded. The lack of hearing shells being fired already calmed him. He no longer felt like he was trembling on the inside, although all four of his limbs kept shaking without relief. He'd been here before, several months ago when he first disembarked with the British Expeditionary Force, but it was a different place now. He remembered it as a sleepy French port; one look around revealed Le Havre was now the hub of British Imperial efficiency. Hustle and bustle was everywhere; human misery was ferried about in various ambulances, stretchers, wheel chairs; and doctors, sisters, and important-looking officers were all going about their day in a hurried, businesslike atmosphere.

Hundreds of wounded soldiers made the 135 mile train journey from the Front along with Jennings. Not knowing what to expect, he noted one of the first soldiers to get off the train was so exhausted he could not stand without assistance. Jennings watched as that soldier, clothes saturated with urine, was put on a stretcher and given brandy. Unable to speak, the man muttered occasionally, eyes sunken. Looking scared, he was fidgety and restive, sinking from physical depletion.

Jennings was mortified. Still with his rudimentary duckboard crutch, he then hobbled himself onto the platform of the train depot, and began to weave his way towards the hospital intake area just off the receiving platform. Stepping alongside him, a soldier grabbed his arm, almost pulling both of them over. "Where are we? Help me find intake."

Jennings responded with, "You mean where we're admitted? It's right in front of you, plain as day."

"I can't see."

"Your eyes are open. You sure you can't see?"

"No, ever since that shell exploded in my face, I've been blind." Looking over the top of Jennings' head with eyes wide open but no eye contact, the soldier offered his other hand in greeting. "Lance Sergeant Trevor Wickings, 9th Battalion, Rifle Brigade."

"Private Simon Jennings with the 1st Yorkshire," Jennings replied as they shook hands. "This is Le Havre and we're right in front of convalescent intake for the hospital."

"Thanks, Jennings. My lieutenant told me Le Havre has been our number one base ever since we took it over from the Frogs."

"Ah, the incomparable French. If you can't see, I can tell you it looks like we made this place into a bit of British decency on their side of the Channel."

"British decency my arse. Looks more like the number one base for fresh cannon fodder, dead bodies and the maimed." Up strutted another soldier after clambering onto the train platform. "Gunner Frederick Wills, 50th Trench Mortar Battery, Royal Field Artillery," he said with a smile while shaking Jennings hand. "You blokes got *blighty* wounds? Or are you going back to the Front?"

Jennings' face screwed-up into a question mark. "What's a blighty wound?"

"Something that gets you back to England. Don't you think you better know that?" Wills spouted off.

"I'm not sure what fits with that but I have the shakes and this fellow is blind. What's wrong with you?"

"Hip wound. Hit by a sniper." Looking around, Wills said, "There're supposed to be four convalescent depots, three general hospitals and two stationary hospitals here."

"My wife wrote me and told me to do whatever I could to get back to England," said Wickings. "She heard they'll send about half of the wounded back to the Front from Le Havre, but almost nobody goes back to the Front if we get shipped home."

"Maybe so, but there's no honor in a blighty wound," Wills announced. He then picked up a newspaper on the ground by the ambulance. "Here's one who'll not get shipped back to the Front." Wills read aloud:

> *"Sergeant William Herbert Waring, VC, MM, 25th*
> *Battalion (Montgomery and Welch Horse Yeomanry),*
> *Royal Welch Fusiliers, age 33, led an attack against enemy*
> *machine guns and, in the face of devastating fire from the*
> *flank and front, rushed a strong point single handed,*
> *bayoneting four of the garrison and capturing twenty others*
> *with their guns; then under heavy shell and machine gun*
> *fire, he reorganized his men, led and inspired them for*
> *another 400 yards, when he fell mortally wounded."*

"A fucking hero," Wills spit and then tossed the paper back on the ground.

"That's the bugger who's getting the Victoria Cross," Jennings exclaimed.

"A helluva lot of good that does him now," Wills snarled.

Chapter 13

THE PENTAGON, WASHINGTON, D.C.:

"Colonel Richards?" the army's chief psychiatrist heard as she picked up the phone in her office at the Pentagon.

"Yes, who's calling?"

"This is Dr. Jorgensen from Johns Hopkins University Emergency Department in Baltimore calling about your brother."

"Brother? I don't have a brother."

"Well, we have a man here in our emergency department who has your contact information as someone to call in case of emergency. He says you're his sister."

"Oh, yes," replied Colonel Richards nervously. "There's a man who's stalked me over the years, is delusional and thinks I'm his sister, but I have no brother. Is his name Jordan Davis?"

"Ah, yes it is."

"You see, we don't even have the same last name and I'm single. He's an unwelcome stalker."

"It's happened to me before as well," Dr. Jorgensen said. "Stalking's an occupational hazard for us in psychiatry. We're just trying to find a family member to contact, as he came into the emergency department intoxicated and apparently manic after getting in a fight at a local bar. We're gonna have him admitted on an involuntary hold."

"Good. Make sure you keep him there for a long time. Tell him to stay out of my life. I never want to see him again. I don't want to be forced to get the police involved and issue a restraining order."

"Understood, Dr. Richards. Sorry for the intrusion."

As she hung up, Colonel Richards thought to herself, *not as sorry as that son-of-a-bitch brother of mine will be if he ever tries to contact me again.*

Chapter 14

The next week was a blur for Jennings. Wills' hip wound was dressed and he'd already been sent back to the Front. Wickings suddenly regained his vision and was going back to the Front today. But Jennings could still not walk and his trembling arms and legs were no better.

Two RAMC doctors strolled up to Jennings. "Walk, soldier. And put that damned stick down," demanded the senior doctor.

Jennings had received no crutches or canes, as he was expected to get better and not need them. He rose up, lurched left and right, then collapsed to his knees and crawled back to his bed.

"He's gone entirely off the rails," the senior doctor said to his colleague.

Jennings' doctors always discussed his case in front of him as though he weren't there. That made him feel insignificant and like a number and not an individual. The doctors often insulted him this way, but Jennings didn't feel like he could respond, since they were upper-class and he was just a working-class lout. Although the doctors weren't talking directly to him, they had to know he could hear them.

"I agree. A disgrace to the service. But I don't think he's daft, just weak-willed, morally inferior and showing a shameful dissolution of manly virtues. Might respond to some toughening," the junior officer replied.

"Yeah. We'll have to send him to Netley," the senior doctor stated.

"Netley? Back home?"

"Yeah. The Royal Victoria Hospital in Netley, Hampshire, has been converted to a ward for *shell shock*ed soldiers. Actually, only for 'other ranks.' Officers with *shell shock* go to a different hospital. You know, you can't mix working-class 'other rank' soldiers with upper-class officers."

Preoccupied with their discussion, both doctors missed the smile on Jennings' face, appearing despite their harsh words. Home! Jennings would now be going home with his blighty wound.

Chapter 15

NEAR FORT HOOD ARMY BASE, KILLEEN, TEXAS:

As Conrad took the Medallion from Adam, he noted it was quite heavy, about the size of a silver dollar and attached to a thick gold chain. Staring up at him was the image of Perseus on the Medallion's obverse and that of Medusa on the reverse. "Perseus, the god of heroes, who vanquished the enemy goddess Medusa. Number 59 engraved under the head of Perseus. Wow. I wonder what this is?" Conrad asked.

"Papa Geoff said his father gave it to him when he was only two-years-old, but he doesn't remember. It happened when his mom brought him to visit his dad in that looney bin in London."

"Adam, that's not necessary," Libby fired at Adam.

He continued, ignoring her. "Papa Geoff told me, according to his mom, the conversation giving them the Medallion was the last time they ever saw Papa Nigel alive."

"Amazing story. So what is it?" Libby asked as she took the Medallion from Conrad and examined it.

"That's not the whole story. Papa Geoff said he has no memory of these things because he was too young. But his mom told him officials from the British Army came by after Papa Nigel's death. Evidently they were real jerks right while everybody was mourning. They demanded to go through Papa Nigel's personal effects, insisting there was a gold Medallion in his possession and it was the property of the British Expeditionary

Force and must be returned under the penalty of death."

"So why do we still have the Medallion?" questioned Libby.

"His mom was so upset, she didn't cooperate. Instead, she hid it for many years until she was near her own death. That's when she gave it to Papa Geoff. Papa Geoff kept it as a memento of his father but told nobody about it until he gave it to me during my visit."

Looking at the Medallion in Libby's hand, Conrad asked, "What do you suppose it means? It's made of solid gold, so it has to be worth a lot. The chain itself must be worth a fortune, what with the price of gold these days. Why do you suppose there was all that fuss by the British Army to get it back all those years ago?"

"Well, that's an interesting story. I think I might have started to blow some old secret wide open myself," said Adam excitedly. "While I was over there, I got an E-mail response to my online request from the database manager of the British World War I archives. That's how I hooked up with Victoria."

The pretty waitress delivered their main courses and purposely brushed Adam's shoulder as she left. He smiled at her and then looked sheepishly at his mom, who returned his look with an approving one of her own—one eyebrow elevated.

"Victoria found mention of a Lieutenant Nigel Warburton in the files of the firing squads for various soldiers executed by the British military. He was one of the officers in charge of several execution teams—but there were no military records for him individually at all."

"Omigod," Libby interjected, feeling horrified.

"Yep. Looks like Papa Nigel was an assassin."

"Maybe that made him feel guilty and caused him to commit suicide when he was hospitalized in England," Conrad suggested.

"Probably did feel guilty. But, Victoria thinks they murdered him," Adam remarked.

"What? Why would anybody want to kill Papa Nigel if he was just doing his duty?" Libby asked, looking shaken.

"Well, for one thing, Victoria found out those assassinations by Papa Nigel's firing squads were a secret at the time and everybody in the army lied to the public, the press and to the Parliament about their existence," Adam answered. "They kept it a dirty little secret for over seventy-five years until they opened their archives and could no longer deny it."

"Amazing," Libby said shaking her head.

Their fetching young waitress played with her pencil and pad as she waited for them to pause their conversation and then took their dessert and coffee orders.

Adam pressed on. "Victoria and I texted quite a bit while I was there and I got her interested in Papa Nigel and the Medallion."

"Did you get Victoria interested in Sergeant Warburton as well?" Libby teased.

"Naw. Anyway, we didn't find Papa Nigel's hospital records or his death records. Quite strange, according to Victoria, they haven't been found yet. She originally thought it was possible they were misfiled within the original archives still being held at the Imperial War Museum storage in London, or that some of his medical records might still be on file at the hospital. Although Papa Nigel was hospitalized at the Maudsley Hospital, Victoria found out the old hospital records are actually kept at an affiliated hospital, the Bethlem Royal Hospital in Kent."

"The Bethlem Royal Hospital?" Conrad interjected with great interest. In full "professorial" mode again, he elaborated, unable to help himself. "That place is the oldest known psychiatric facility in the world, founded way back in the 1200s. That's why it houses old records. Although a leading psychiatric center today, it has quite a shameful past."

"Maybe Papa Nigel's medical records are there," Libby added hopefully.

"We did find out more than a hundred British soldiers had Perseus Medallions in World War I. They were called *Patrons of Perseus* and they had a leader they called the Commandant. However, any list identifying who they were or any information about what the Medallion signified are still marked as *C-L-A-S-S-I-F-I-E-D*. Victoria thought that was funny, since all British World War I files are supposedly in the public domain now. She tried to get information from Parliament's oversight committee, but was referred to U.S. Army Intelligence," Adam said.

"U.S.?" Conrad asked, surprised.

"Yep. Seems like any secrets the British didn't want to release from their archives are now U.S. classified information. Victoria thinks it's a cute little trick. Lets the British government say they've come clean while still conveniently able to hide any secrets they want."

"I agree, she's probably right," Conrad agreed.

"Well, they better watch out because Victoria is one of the world's premier hackers. She's also friends with many of the world's best, and they give special recognition and respect to anybody who can penetrate the most secure computers. There's even a point system that rates the values for hacking the toughest computers. All the geeks in that gang compete for the highest points. Victoria just got to the top."

"That's awful," said Libby.

"That's illegal," said Conrad.

"Victoria says that's what makes it fun," Adam shot back at them. "Don't have a cow. These geeks just break in, deposit proof they were there and then leave without messing anything up or taking any information. It's about penetrating and outsmarting the best computer programmers' defenses, not about harm. Victoria says the highest points go for various countries' intelligence operations."

"Now that's asking for big trouble."

"That's why the points are so high. Victoria's wanted to go after one of these high-point targets for a while now, and she found out U.S. Army Intelligence was easier to hack than the NSA. She got in and that's why she now has the highest hacking points of anyone."

"Adam, this is no game," Libby said with a concerned look on her face.

"Get real, Mom," Adam replied rolling his eyes. "Victoria already found some old records of the Patrons of Perseus in U.S. Army Intelligence files."

"Incredible," Libby said, shaking her head in obvious disbelief and Conrad confirmed with a nod of his head.

"She's now looking for files on Papa Nigel, on the Medallion, or anything that would help us understand why they wanted it back from Papa Nigel or why they still want it back."

"They still want it back?" Libby asked.

"As a matter of fact, yeah. Today, I was talking to my army psychiatrist about my trip to England and told him about the Medallion and he almost flipped out. He tried to get me to give it to him. Fortunately, I didn't have it with me. He told me—no ordered me—not to tell anyone about it, not even you. He said anyone with unauthorized possession of one of these Medallions is in danger of his life. What a drama queen. Anyway, I don't want it with me on the army base so I'm giving it to you now for safekeeping, Mom."

"Uh, you don't suppose it's dangerous to be in possession of one of these?"

"No better way to find out than to hack the answer out of Army

Intelligence computers. I'm sure they'll just ignore the public request I made online to Army Intelligence to find out what a Perseus Medallion from World War I signified. I also told my psychiatrist today I'd made that online request and he blew another gasket. He acted like the Medallion was some big secret. I guess we'll all find out if that's true, assuming Victoria's as good a hacker as I think she is. Watch out, Wikileaks, you're about to be bested."

"That's a dangerous game Victoria is playing," Conrad interjected.

"Don't you get it? That's why it's so much fun."

"Adam, I don't think you see how serious this is," Libby said with a furrowed brow and an intensely worried look on her face.

"Well, if you'd rather talk about public information, one thing Victoria found in public records is the fact Papa Nigel informed the Parliament Select Committee on the treatment of *shell shock* during the war and about the assassination squads that killed cowards. He got in a lot of trouble for it. But his statements came to nothing, since Parliament ignored him."

Conrad noticed Libby's eyes gaping wide in amazement.

"Hey. Maybe that's why he died," Adam speculated. "He was becoming a threat to expose these assassinations."

"Maybe Papa Nigel was trying to make amends," Libby offered.

"Oh, yeah. One more thing. Look at this weird note Papa Geoff gave me. Papa Nigel gave it to his mom when he gave her the Medallion, but she kept it hidden and Papa Geoff never got it until they went through his mom's things after her death." Adam took out a crumbling note on yellowing paper written in fading ink.

I am so sorry for what I did and for what I have become.
I realize the Patrons will make me pay for becoming unworthy,
but whatever comes, will come. I can bear the secret no longer.
I have only one request. If my death were to be caused before
my acts are made known, whoever reads this message, please
tell the public or the Parliament about the Patrons, show them my
Medallion and beg on my behalf for my forgiveness. My
soul will never be at rest until somebody does this.

Conrad and Libby sat in stunned silence for a long while. Clearly uncomfortable, Conrad stood to signal they should depart, leaving money for the check. As their waitress walked by, she picked it up and handed Adam a slip of paper with her phone number.

Conrad smiled at Adam, but Libby was oblivious.

"See, Papa Nigel was feeling guilty and was trying to do the right thing." Libby reflected out loud. "I hope that's not why he killed himself."

Conrad mused, "Sounds more like a man who thinks he's about to be murdered to me, not a suicide note."

Chapter 16

D BLOCK, ROYAL VICTORIA HOSPITAL, AUTUMN OF 1915:

Arriving in Netley, England, Jennings came off the hospital ship from Le Havre, France, and onto docks directly across from the Royal Victoria Hospital. Looking around, he thought the Royal Victoria looked like an enlarged version of an archdeacon's country villa surrounded by a grass tennis court and swimming pool instead of a hospital.

Little did Jennings know what awaited him inside. He was assigned to D Block of the Netley Lunatic Asylum, a section of the larger general hospital. He was met at the dock by the ward corporal for D Block and clumped along with his silly crutch until finally ushered to his bed in a crowded line of about forty beds that looked like a parade of horizontal warriors.

No hero's welcome, that's for sure, Jennings observed silently upon his arrival at Netley. *But it sure is good to get out of a tent and inside for a change.*

After months of trench warfare and living outside, things were getting better and better for Jennings. First, a couple of days at the dressing station near the frontlines, and then a week in a four-man tent in the stationary hospital in Le Havre. Now inside D Block of the Royal Victoria Hospital in Netley, there were real floors, men milling about, smoking, playing cards. Some men were resting on their beds. How bad could this be? He sorely missed his wife and baby, but maybe they could visit him here. At least it's England!

Chapter 17

D BLOCK, ROYAL VICTORIA HOSPITAL, DECEMBER OF 1915:

Several weeks passed as Jennings settled into the routine at D Block, Netley. One of the nurses was kind enough to transcribe letters to his wife each week, as he continued to shake too much to write them for himself. He'd learned D Block had recently been converted by the army from a lunatic asylum and warehouse for the insane and mentally incurable to a military ward for *shell shock* victims. Some of the old lunatics were still about to staff the kitchen, the laundry and the farm. He'd heard the sisters say thousands of men with *shell shock* were filling casualty stations in France, and now room had to be made for them in England. Rumor was the French and Germans had just as many. Doctors had never seen anything like this in past wars and feared the rapid advance of technology was the cause. D Block at Netley was the result of all this, and now housed about 350 patients, most in their 20s, with four doctors in total.

For treatment, Jennings was provided with rest assisted with either morphine or Veronal—a heavy duty barbiturate tranquilizer—along with a milk diet and massage. They tried all kinds of hydrotherapy at D Block, including showers, semi-baths and moist wrappings around his tremulous arms and legs. All to no avail. He had hot baths in sealed body chambers, administered as various types of "balneotherapy," namely, baths of tar, bran and pine needle extract as well as carbonate baths.

On one occasion, they tried to give him a sulphur bath. However, as soon as Jennings smelled sulphur, it triggered the sensation in his nostrils of shells exploding. He panicked and jumped out of the tub in the midst of a terrible flashback. Jennings yelled and screamed in horror as if he had just witnessed the death of his battle buddy next to him in the trenches.

"Heavy rain. Had a shock. Can't keep still. Red eyes. Had a shock. Red eyes following me everywhere. Had a shock." Afterwards his tremors were worse than ever.

When all these types of therapy didn't work, they kept him in luke-warm baths for long periods of time; first for a few hours, then longer; he'd just finished one that lasted a few weeks. Between baths they tried a new breathing treatment called "pneumatotherapy" with various kinds of in-haling apparatuses; and also "thermotherapy" with electrical light appara-tuses. But the shakes continued all the same. The whole time doctors, sis-ters and reconstruction aides constantly told him he'd get better and he should try harder to help himself. Some of the men in D Block called it the "cheery chap" school of medicine. The doctors called it "reeducation" to strengthen the will.

Strange cases continued to arrive daily at D Block. The army got them out of the trenches as quickly as possible because their symptoms were contagious and could cause whole battalions to come down with the same symptoms if these men were not isolated. Arriving soldiers were not wounded, yet they could not see, smell, taste, speak, urinate, or defecate. Some even lost their memories; and still others vomited uncontrollably. Many like Jennings suffered from the shakes and couldn't walk. It was a motley crowd the doctors said had weak minds and low spirits. Most of the doctors also thought the men arriving were all morally degraded idiots and pitiable beings. There was the strong expectation all of them should get well and rejoin the war in France. They were expected to stop being clearly lamentable failures as soldiers.

The total lack of privacy didn't bother Jennings. As was his nature, he just took things in stride. By listening unobtrusively to the doctors and sisters as they came by, he was actually able to learn a lot about the men around him. Beds were crammed into as small a space as possible, with just one partition down the middle of forty beds on each site, with scarce room to pass between them, so it was easy for him to see many of his fellow pa-tients and to overhear the doctors talking.

The man next to Jennings periodically shouted "Francine," but de-clined to reveal who that was. He constantly made a mess next to Jennings' bed, spitting on the floor to rid himself of the poison the Germans had put into him, and complaining he could smell foul odors all around him.

When the doctors came by to see that man, the junior officer reported to the senior officer, "He will not obey orders, has no manners, and walks away when questioned. Family history bad. Uncle died in an asylum; sister suffers from hysteria; another sister attempted suicide by means of 'spirits of salts;' and his father died of tuberculosis. Ignorant and has a nervous demeanor; he does not know what he is afraid of; is extremely nervous and apprehensive. Appears to be a low class 'defective.' As you can see, his features are asymmetrical; he squints; he has a stammer; is plaintive, intensely dull and stupid; and possessed of a thick speech. Hydrotherapy still ineffective."

They passed along to the next bed. The junior officer continued, "As you can see, this one wears a heavy, dull, stupid and bloated appearance; does not know how long he's been in the hospital; and will not answer questions or give any account of himself. Knows where he is; knows he's barmy; says he doesn't know his drill; and has never done any work since joining the army. Truculent and disrespectful. Much of this is put on. Appears to be malingering."

For the third in line he stated, "This man's papers state that under shell fire in the trenches; he had a fit, before losing consciousness for a time; spending the rest of the day just sitting around; unable to fire his rifle while feeling pains in his head and reporting sick in the evening. Went into shock because his mate's head was blown off by a shell close to where he had been standing. Here he has been wandering around more or less half-dressed; up and down in an excited state. He's been forgetful, and has begun to wear a rather wild look; draws attention to himself. The only words he's uttered since admission are, 'Don't hurt me, sir.' Ravenously hungry all the time; keeps pointing to his mouth; spends the day crawling about under his bed and playing with the springs. Will not answer questions. Goes through a pantomimic action to answer questions. Gait spastic and dragging."

All of a sudden the man threw himself on the floor before the doctors declaring, "I want to do my duty; let me kill myself."

The senior doctor, unmoved, said, "Obvious case of confusional insanity caused by *shell shock*. Possibly salvageable. Have you tried hypnosis or faradization yet?"

The junior doctor responded, "Not yet. Some others who are not responding to treatment are scheduled ahead of him."

Having been here a long time, Jennings knew that meant him.

Chapter 18

THE PENTAGON, WASHINGTON, D.C.:

General Rossi looked up from the papers on his desk as soon as he heard a gentle knock on the door of his office for the army chief of intelligence. He glanced at his watch, noting it was almost nine P.M., and knew no one would be on duty any longer in his outer office, and the E-Ring would be mostly deserted this time of night. Relishing the treat he was about to demand for himself, he stood and shouted, "Come in!"

The door opened halfway, revealing Colonel Richards with her coat on and a computer strapped to one shoulder and her purse in the opposite hand. "Just stopping by to say goodnight on my way out. It's been a long day, and I need to get home and get these shoes off. I still have to go over my slides for my lecture before we leave tomorrow."

"What's the hurry? Come on over here and have a drink with me."

"Maybe once we get to the U.K. I'm really tired."

"Now, is that any way to treat your superior officer, especially since he was the one to have you promoted to one of the youngest lieutenant colonels in the U.S. Army? And put you on the fast track for promotion to full-bird colonel despite your problems when you promoted Major Hasan?"

"Not tonight, Andy. And what about your wife?"

"The bitch threw me out. I thought you knew that. I've been living on my own and away from her and the kids in an apartment while we try and work it out."

"Monogamy never was your style."

"Speaking of that, I also had a hard day and want to see how badly you need these special operation requests of yours signed off," Rossi said as he picked up some papers on his desk and pointed them at her, feeling important and powerful, relaxed and fully in control. "You know, your use of Special Forces doesn't happen unless I authorize it and pay for it outta my budget."

"Yeah, I know, and for that I am eternally grateful. I couldn't really be effective in my job without all your help."

"Then come over here and show me how grateful you can be."

"Andy. ..."

Rossi pointed the papers at her once again. "You want these signed off or not?"

Richards dropped her coat and computer along with her purse in the chair just inside Rossi's office and shut the door as she did so. Walking over to Rossi, she stood on tip toes and kissed his neck, then his lips. Sliding to her knees, she unbuckled his pants, as Rossi took her head in both hands, stroking rambunctious strands of blonde hair behind both of her ears with his own fingers, thinking of how she tormented him with that motion all day long. Slowly, she took his member in her mouth until he climaxed.

Chapter 19

D BLOCK, NETLEY HOSPITAL, WINTER OF 1916:

"Jennings, fall out!" the ward corporal shouted. "Time for therapy. Something new today. Sister, take him to Room 8 and Dr. Brown."

Jennings entered Room 8 of Netley Hospital. The room was warm, inviting, and somewhat dark, even though it was morning. With the window shades closed, a cozy fire in the doctor's fireplace served a purpose, since it was now the dead of winter. A couch appeared in the middle of the room and a light was shining on it; the doctor's desk was muddled with papers; and the chair where he was sitting was next to the couch. Jennings hadn't sat on a couch in over a year. Word was Dr. Gordon Brown came from a prosperous London family and a long line of physicians. He was short and stout. According to the others receiving his new treatment, Dr. Brown supposedly had a positive, even sunny disposition, and was highly energetic. His office revealed he was also cultured in the arts.

"Take a seat on the couch, soldier. I shall stop your trembling and restore your walking in a few minutes, if you do exactly what I say," Dr. Brown said in a tone of strong conviction. "You believe in the power of the mind over the body, don't you soldier?"

Jennings, feeling reassured with such a famous expert willing to work with him as his doctor, but a bit afraid to address an upper-class doctor out loud, nodded yes.

"You know you shake because your nerves are exhausted and your mind is telling you shaking is the way to survive. You've been told by all of us this is the wrong thing to let your mind do to your body, right soldier? I'm sure you also know you can reverse your shakes by using your mind's power over your body, by strengthening your will today, and that shall happen now, if you just listen and obey me."

Although the doctor was upper-class, Jennings was beginning to feel comfortable in his presence and thought it would be okay to respond to him verbally. "The doctors have given me that explanation, and I'll try."

"No, soldier, you shall not try. You shall obey and be successful."

Jennings winced; worried he had already angered or disappointed his important doctor. "Yes, sir. I shall obey."

"To be clear, are you absolutely confident in my ability to make this happen?"

"Yes, sir."

"I remind you, you're in the army and need to be completely obedient to me as an officer giving you commands."

"Yes, sir, I know. I'm a good soldier and shall obey your orders."

"Finally, everyone here knows you're going to be cured today and is expecting your arms and legs to stop shaking when we're done here. Don't let us down. Are you ready to proceed?"

Jennings nodded affirmatively. His baby girl had just been born in Yorkshire, and he thought if he got well, they might allow his love Sarah to visit with his newborn buttercup Gertie.

"Now, lie back on the couch, close your eyes and think of sleep. Relax. Give yourself up to sleep, let sleep come to you as it assuredly will. You're getting drowsy. Your limbs are getting heavy with sleep and are stopping to shake."

Jennings did as he was told. But he knew he didn't tremble in his sleep, so he couldn't figure what good this would do if he fell asleep.

"All your muscles are now relaxed," the doctor continued. "You are breathing more and more slowly, more and more deeply. Your eyelids are getting heavy. Heavy as lead. You cannot open them however hard you try. You must be obedient. When I put my hand on your forehead, you will seem to be back again in the trenches. There is absolutely not the slightest shadow of possibility of my words not coming true. You are certain of this."

Jennings did understand and respect authority, so he tried to be-lieve what he was being told by Dr. Brown. He was too sleepy to speak or nod or even open his eyes.

"Now I'm placing my hand on your forehead. You are back in the trench in France. You see shell after shell explode. You see the red eyes of one soldier next to you, dead from nerve gas. Then the last shell lands. It blows another poor fellow next to you to bits, with his body parts all over you. The breath has been blown out of your body. Your head is split and your hair is torn by the vicious blast and the whizz of the shells. You are gasping and reeling, you gradually adjust yourself. You see the last shell explode, you feel the wind of it, smell the burning earth." Despite the ominous nature of his words, the doctor spoke soothingly. He paused for a moment.

"Are you there soldier? What is happening?"

Jennings suddenly started writhing on the couch, twisting, turn-ing, and shouting out in a terror-stricken voice, experiencing a flashback of one of his battle buddies being blown to bits right next to him in the trenches. "Oh, my god, get this off me. Hot blood on my face. Eeeeeeeeek! Pungent smell of burning brains. Pungent smell of burning brains. Get it off. I can smell but I can't see. I can't hear. Ringing in my ears but no sounds." Jennings continued squirming on the couch, eyes closed, his face flushing, sweating copiously. He was shaking all over. "I can't stop my arms and legs from shaking. I can't find my face with my hands to get this off. I can't stand up."

Jennings fell silent and after a pause, his shaking miraculously stopped.

Dr. Brown continued. "Now you see it was a terrible scare, but you were not hit, you did not bleed. You witnessed a horrible thing. But once you were cleaned up, you knew you were not really wounded. You no longer need to tremble. When I tell you to wake up, I will put my hand on your forehead again, and you will be cured. I command you to stop trembling." Dr. Brown gently put his hand on Jennings forehead. "Now wake up."

Jennings opened his eyes.

"See, you are no longer shaking."

Jennings was amazed.

"You are cured. Good work soldier."

Jennings stood gingerly, but did not sway from side to side, and was now without the support of his crutch. With a smile, the sister took his hand and led him tentatively but most assuredly back to his bed. Finally, he was cured. Now he would surely get a visit from Sarah and Gertie. It was a marvelous wonder.

TUESDAY

Chapter 20

AT "THE WASHINGTON POST," WASHINGTON, D.C.:

Jennifer Roberts' nimble fingers barraged the keyboard in front of her, clacking out her story in rapid-fire sequence as one of *The Washington Post's* editorial assistants handed her a hard copy of a medical article. Roberts swiveled rapidly in her chair to take the papers with a deft move. Everything she did was agile and energetic, and she liked to live her entire life at ninety-miles an hour. Her speech was animated, her walking pace was brisk, and her thoughts occurred at breakneck speed. Jennifer also tried to juggle multiple activities simultaneously whenever possible to maximize her productivity as a reporter— which was her raison d'être. One problem with all of this, she knew, was men didn't like to be just one element of her constant multi-tasking, so relationships so far were not deep or sustained, which was all right with her for now. Her priority was to throw all her kinetic energy headlong into her work.

"Editor thinks you should take a look at this," the young man said. Roberts was working from her modest cubicle. Despite being offered an office with a window after winning her Pulitzer Prize, she preferred being in the center of the action in the middle of the enormous newsroom. Working there also had the added benefit of reducing the envy of her colleagues for the fame the prize had brought her almost a decade ago when she was only a cub reporter.

"Thanks, Bert," Roberts said as she picked up the report with one hand and grabbed her early morning Marko Mocha with the other. Skinny iced venti decaf, four pumps of mocha, float the last shot and no whip. Her ex-boyfriend got her addicted to these. The mocha was now gone, but Jennifer knew there'd soon be another one she would coddle in her hand —for as long as it lasted—it was her daily routine. Looking at the title, "Crisis in Army Psychopharmacology and Mental Health Care at Fort Hood" by Dr. Augustus Conrad from Stanford University, she quickly scanned the article and after a beat shouted, "Bert, get me the Pentagon on the phone. Tell them I want their comment on Dr. Conrad's findings. Interrupt whatever I'm doing when they call back. And see if you can get Conrad on the phone as well. Pleeeease?"

"Yes, ma'am."

"Thaaaaank-you, Bert," Jennifer purred as she purposely slowed down the pace of her praise for emphasis; her way of indicating sincerity.

Just then, Roberts' cell phone rang. Immediately recognizing the call as coming from the U.K., she answered, "Jennifer Roberts."

A young voice at the other end responded, "Hello, this is Victoria Chamberlain from Cambridge. Thanks for taking my call."

"No problem. I got your E-mail earlier today requesting the call. Your grandfather's a hero of mine. It's the least I could do."

"Don't know if you heard, but I'm working part-time for Gramps these days."

"Really? You're all grown up now, I guess. You were just a schoolgirl when your grandfather and I worked on the 'Shot at Dawn' scandal several years ago."

"Not completely grown up. Just an undergraduate at Cambridge, and a geek organizing the database of the Great War Archives for Gramps. We're following up your and Gramps' work that uncovered the scandal of the British military executing its own soldiers as cowards when they really had *shell shock*. Anyway, you wouldn't believe what I've found."

"I'm all ears."

"I don't think your 'Shot at Dawn' project is inactive."

"Yes, I'm aware there's research ongoing by several academic historians."

"Everybody knows that. I'm talking about the U.S. Army taking over the Patrons of Perseus and keeping it going."

"As a research project?"

"No, no, no. As an assassination unit to rid the army of cowards."

"Well, we did find evidence the U.S. helped the British assassinate soldiers during World War I and might have continued it into World War II."

"You're missing the point. They're doing it now."

Roberts bolted straight upright in her chair. "That's a pretty wild accusation."

"That's why I'm calling. I wanna see if you're interested in checking this out from the leads I have. I'm a computer hacker, not an investigative reporter."

"What evidence do you have?" Roberts asked as she wedged her cell phone between her shoulder and ear so fingers on both hands could fly across the keyboard as she listened to Victoria.

"I came across some information recently on a British soldier who's the relative of one of your current U.S. soldiers. The young soldier just visited me in Cambridge on leave from the U.S. Army. If you can believe it, his great-great-grandfather is the very officer who led the firing squad that executed the British soldier whose personal story you documented in your exposé."

"Really? Very interesting." Roberts switched ears with her phone. "But what does that have to do with the U.S. Army today?"

"Funny thing. I can't find the military records of his great-great-grandfather in the Great War Files, although his name shows up in the files of other soldiers. The dude died at the Bethlem Royal Hospital during the war of an apparent suicide."

"Was that officially confirmed?"

"Dunno. His great-great-grandson wants to find out. That's why I was looking for the records. As I dug, I found out those records were given to the U.S. Army around the time of the Second World War, and they remain classified by U.S. Army Intelligence."

"That's weird. Why would the Americans want to classify those records? They're old news and we published over 306 such victims in my 'Shot at Dawn' exposé already. Looks like you're at a dead end. You'll never get a look at those files if they're classified by the U.S. Army."

"Not exactly true," Victoria shot back.

"Well, yes. An act of Congress could de-classify them."

"Hacking's a lot easier and faster."

"What? You want to hack into U.S. Army Intelligence files?" Roberts said incredulously.

"Not exactly. I already did."

"Whoa. That's illegal."

"But heady stuff. You get lots of *geek cred* for penetrating any government intelligence network."

"This is no game, Victoria. It's serious business. Have you ever heard of Edward Snowden? Do you want to move to Russia?"

"Not to worry, Ms. Roberts."

"Call me Jennifer." Roberts shifted nervously in her seat.

"Okay, Jennifer. I must say in reality it was easier than I thought. Over here we say your 'U.S. Army Intelligence' is an oxymoron. The NSA is the hard one to hack. They've got the smartest programmers. Army programmers and contractors are oftentimes just plain stupid, so I could easily find my way into Army Intelligence files. I now have a list of the assassins in the Patrons of Perseus and guess what? The young U.S. soldier's great-great-grandfather is on the list."

"So, he was an assassin for the Patrons in World War I. Have you told the young soldier yet?"

"Yes, he knows. But I wanted to get to you first with some other findings."

"Fire away."

"I also found the list for all the victims executed by the Patrons. It includes all the names you exposed of course, and quite a few more from that era."

"Damn. Where were you hackers when I wrote 'Shot at Dawn?' I had to find those names the old-fashioned way, with informants and hard copy. Must not have gotten all of 'em."

"Yeah, that was Neanderthal-style searching then. Sorry. But you're not going to believe who's on the list now. "

Suddenly feeling old, Jennifer flung back, "Try me."

"Not just British World War I soldiers. I also found names of current American Iraq and Afghanistan War soldiers at the end of that list. Lots of 'em."

Bolting straight upright and onto her feet, Jennifer asked, "Are you saying what I think you're saying?"

"Yep. If the last names on the list mean the same thing as those on the list starting about a hundred years ago in the British Army, I may have found actual indications the U.S. Army is still executing cowards."

"That would be atrocious if true," she said incredulously. "That would be murder. That would be illegal. But surely you must be mistaken. And we would certainly need independent confirmation of what this list means, or at least copies of the files to verify this. What do you have?"

"So, like I said, I think the U.S. Army is now executing its own soldiers with a re-activated Patrons of Perseus. But not by firing squad, like in World War I. No, instead, I think they're trying to make 'em look like suicide, an accident or murder by somebody else."

"Unbelievable. What's your evidence for that?" Jennifer was getting all riled-up and ready for a new hunt, still clacking away in a frenzy at the keyboard as naturally as if it were an extension of her own body.

"Well, I've downloaded a list of all names of apparent suicides from Iraq and Afghanistan servicemen and women since the beginning of the wars there. A couple of thousand now and growing every day," Victoria answered.

"Uggh. You know, there's such a crisis now with increased numbers of suicides by army soldiers these days."

"Yep, but they may not all be real suicides. Maybe the spike you're seeing is due to the Patrons of Perseus."

"Wow. I have a hard time believing that."

"Well, then, listen on. I looked to see if any of the names at the end of the list of the Patrons of Perseus corresponded to soldiers listed as present-day suicides. And guess what?"

"Afraid to ask," Jennifer remarked.

"They match."

"Omigod. That means some of those suicides were actually assassinations by a modern Patrons of Perseus organization. Why the hell would the U.S. Army want to assassinate its own soldiers?"

"You're asking *me* that? I thought *you* were the one who figured out why our British Army assassinated its own soldiers in the Great War."

"*Shell shock*, ovvvv coursssse," Jennifer said slowly as she realized she was experiencing a dawning realization of something truly horrible. Something other-worldly.

"Exactly. Suppose the U.S. Army is trying to get rid of some of its soldiers with PTSD?"

"That would be outrageous. Has no one learned that soldiers with PTSD aren't cowards any more than soldiers with *shell shock* were? Is there no lesson learned from 'Shot at Dawn?'"

"I'm not done."

"Now I really am afraid to listen. But go on," Jennifer said.

"There are asterisks next to several names on the Army Intelligence list of all suicides from the Iraq and Afghanistan soldiers. These are the same names that are on the list of the Patrons of Perseus, so they're probably assassinations, not suicides. Next to the asterisks are three-digit numbers."

"Hmmm. What do you think those numbers mean?"

"I was going to ask you. Didn't the Patrons of Perseus each receive an individually numbered Medallion?"

"Yes, of course," Jennifer said emphatically. "And there were more than a hundred Medallions documented to have been given out during the Great War."

"So, maybe that's the Medallion number of the Patron who's currently assassinating U.S. soldiers. If so, it means the U.S. Army's started issuing Medallions again. I'm still looking for the names of who are current Patrons and the name of their current Commandant and the military files of their victims but can't find any of these files online."

"Maybe one of their smarter programmers managed to hide this successfully from you."

"Ha!"

"This is all important and interesting, Victoria, but I can't condone your hacking the U.S. Army Intelligence database any further to find them."

"Don't think that's where the military records are anyway."

"What? Why not and where would they be? Certainly those records exist somewhere?"

"Well, I have a hunch. I think they might be here."

"What makes you think U.S. Army Intelligence records would be in England and not online?"

"You should also know that at the bottom of the list with asterisks is a footnote with another asterisk and the name 'Madingley,' seeming to indicate that those with an asterisk have something to do with Madingley Hall."

"What's Madingley Hall?"

"It's a famous stately home several centuries old, here in Cambridge. Now owned by the University of Cambridge. Queen Victoria once rented it for her son Prince Edward as a place to stay while he was a student at Cambridge."

"You're kidding."

"Nope. Three stories, acres and acres of manicured grounds, massive dining hall, stables, rooms for staff and servants—the whole works."

"Just for one prince? Some dormitory."

"Well, he *was* first-in-line to the throne, and eventually *did* become

King Edward the Seventh once his mum Queen Victoria died. And the local story here is that the young Prince Edward was betrothed to some German Princess but had girlfriends he used to sneak in-and-out of Madingley through a secret turret staircase."

"Great story, but what could possibly be the connection of Madingley Hall to the U.S. Army and the Patrons of Perseus?"

"Dunno, but it's suspicious that the only American Cemetery for U.S. soldiers in the entire U.K., is located right next door to Madingley Hall. And the U.S. and British Armies hold regular meetings there on combat stress and various psychiatric issues."

"Whatever in the world for?"

"I think that's what I have to find out next. Madingley is just outside of the city of Cambridge, so I'm gonna go down there and check it out in person. Dunno why the Americans would keep an ongoing relationship with the British at Madingley, but I wonder if they might be keeping the top-secret records of the names of the Patrons that I can't find in the Army Intelligence database on file there. Just a wild idea."

"Well, come to think of it, if there really is an illegal and monstrous operations unit like the continuation of the Patrons of Perseus under U.S. command, it would make sense to hide the records not only outside usual online databases, but also offshore as hard copies with our best ally in the U.K."

"So, maybe you can look into things at your end and I'll get back to you with anything I find out from Madingley."

"I can see your apple's not fallen far from your grandfather's tree," Jennifer said.

"Gramps'll get a kick outta that one. Ya know Sir Isaac Newton, the guy who discovered gravity by seeing an apple fall from a tree? He did his work here in Cambridge."

"Doesn't surprise me. It's probably the world's most famous university. Anyway, be careful. If there's an active assassination squad in the U.S. Army, it'd be explosive if uncovered, and they would certainly target anybody who threatens to expose them."

"Don't worry. I'm learning that scandal can be exhilarating."

"I said, be careful."

Chapter 21

THE PENTAGON, WASHINGTON, D.C.:

Brigadier General Andreas Rossi burst into the Vice Chief's office first thing in the morning. "That son-of-a-bitch published it. Can you believe that? He gawddammed published it."

"Slow down, Rossi. Who published what?" cooed Colonel Richards calmly from her seat in front of the Vice Chief's massive mahogany desk—a holdover from the Vietnam Era.

The Vice Chief looked back at him from behind his desk, and sat silently. Rossi thought the Vice was looking at him as a king from his throne, anticipating a response from one of his royal courtiers. General Morelli and Richards were both sipping their early morning coffee and Rossi suddenly realized he had interrupted General Morelli holding court with Richards.

"Your boy, that arrogant shrink Conrad, not only didn't change his report, he published it in the fucking medical literature," Rossi complained. He threw down the print-out, felt a pain in his stomach as he stewed, and paced up and down aside the Vice Chief's intimidating desk attempting to calm himself down. "The news media saw Conrad's publication of his report this morning when it was released online in the medical literature, and they're already asking questions about it. That worthless slut from *The Washington Post*, Jennifer Roberts, called this morning and wants an official reaction from the army," he spewed.

"Settle down, Rossi," General Morelli growled. In his usual manner, Morelli looked down at the desk in front of him, wrapping his arms around himself, touching the four stars on each of his shoulders with the fingers of both hands. "Stop grousing like a little girl. We're gonna have to handle this situation with Conrad's report and Roberts delicately, not with rage and bluster. We don't need Roberts retaliating against us and making a Pulitzer Prize scandal out of this one, too. She has real power to cause us problems. Already thinks the army doesn't know the difference between cowardice and mental illness, so don't give her any ammunition to shoot back at us."

"That's for sure, sir," Richards added with a deferential look. "Remember, General Rossi, Roberts is the reporter who broke the story about the British Army using firing squads to execute its own soldiers for cowardice in World War I. She has huge credibility and an enormous public following."

"I know that already," Rossi responded, trying to deescalate—ratcheted down his defensiveness a notch or two. "Roberts' original exposé displayed deserters, cowards, and insubordinates in World War I, as really British heroes suffering from fucking *shell shock*, whatever that is. And surprise, surprise, the lame-stream media has entirely bought her revisionist account of things."

"Right," Richards agreed. "And we don't need Roberts getting the public thinking we're abusing today's soldiers because weaklings in our ranks get some form of 21st century *shell shock* we call PTSD instead."

"You guys need to be careful here," General Morelli interjected and then sat in silence, escalating the tension in the room as Rossi and Richards waited for him to continue. "We don't want the same repercussions from our problems now as occurred in the U.K., after their scandal broke. Remember, the modern backlash about the execution of British World War I cowards got so bad the Brits even erected a monument in the U.K., for the three hundred or so men with *shell shock* that Roberts supposedly documented as having been executed."

"I know, I know," Rossi acquiesced. "I heard Roberts seduced her way into the British World War I Archives once those records were opened to the public seventy-five years after the war. We don't need her snooping around our own records of this war."

"She's a potentially dangerous woman to the interests of the army, and since she's a reporter, we have to handle her more carefully than other civilians," Richards added.

"That means I want Army Intelligence to monitor her, but otherwise be hands-off," General Morelli ordered.

"Yes, sir," Rossi responded quickly. "With pleasure. We're already 'monitoring' that bastard Conrad."

"Remember, General Rossi, Roberts already has her own statue erected to herself," Richards warned. "It's called the Pulitzer Prize, and none of us want her to get another one at our expense by criticizing our work with weak warriors who claim psychological war wounds in the modern era."

"Don't worry," Rossi responded as he unfolded his pursed lips into a wry smile. "I'll make sure Roberts won't be able to report on our activities as a 21st century version of her 'Shot at Dawn' exposé. Fortunately, we lock up our actions as 'Top Secret' and 'Classified,' so no one'll ever know."

"That's assuming Congress doesn't reclassify your records as public information," General Morelli said, shooting Rossi a concerned look. "I have to testify before that bunch of grandstanding idiots this afternoon. Don't give them the scent to come after us any more than they already are."

"And there's always another Edward Snowden out there," Richards chimed in. As she stroked a rude curl behind her ear in a delectable motion, Rossi audibly groaned as fond memories of last night took hold of his mind. "In the meantime," Richards continued, "I just had a thought. Isn't the information in Conrad's report based upon confidential materials belonging to the army? If so, I think the Department of Justice might be interested in what Conrad just did by making his report public," Richards said with a devious smile aimed at Rossi.

"Brilliant," Rossi said, as he stopped mid-pace and the issue at hand began to compete successfully with his salacious thoughts. Tension left his face, and a wicked smile replaced his worry. "As a matter of fact, it *is* already confidential. Let's even make it *classified*."

"Meanwhile, if you agree, General Morelli, let me handle Jennifer Roberts and give her an official response for the media," Richards offered as General Morelli nodded in agreement.

Rossi, thinking aloud, and feeling great delight, muttered so General Morelli and Colonel Richards could hear, "Conrad just put his own ass in a wringer. I'll notify DOJ immediately and have them handle this on behalf of Army Intelligence." Rossi then relaxed and smiling gleefully, said to himself, *I'm gonna ruin that son-of-a-bitch. Just watch me.*

Chapter 22

D BLOCK, NETLEY HOSPITAL, WINTER OF 1916:

The wonder of Jennings' cure by hypnosis lasted all of forty-eight hours. By the start of the second day following his hypnosis session, Jennings' legs began to tremble again, slowly at first, but he was still able to walk. By the end of the second day, his arms and legs were trembling full-force like never before. Jennings was heart- broken. Anguished, he thought, now *I'll never see my wife and daughter.* He was also feeling guilty not just for losing the opportunity to get a family pass, but also for wasting Dr. Brown's valuable time. Loss of his cure just reconfirmed to Jennings he had no control over his life and things just continued to happen to him.

His doctors stopped by again. The senior one addressed Jennings. "Dr. Brown will surely be disappointed in you, soldier. He has an almost hundred-percent cure rate and you'll make his work look bad. You must try harder to get well. I guess you must be weaker than we thought."

"Sir, how about 'faradization?'" asked the junior doctor.

"Ah, the miraculous new electric treatment that is astounding us all. Yes, this man needs the full treatment and lucky for us, Dr. Holmes is here this week for demonstrations and he's the best in the army."

Jennings was dumbfounded, wondering what they had in store for him next. He then realized there was nothing he could do, so

might as well try and not get upset—*stay calm; carry on*, he thought
to himself.

"Sister," the senior doctor ordered, "take this man to Room 4 as
soon as Dr. Holmes is ready for him."

Chapter 23

D BLOCK, NETLEY HOSPITAL, WINTER OF 1916:

As Jennings left his sleeping quarters and stepped outside into the midday weather, he was greeted with another cloudy, dark day and no sunshine. It was so bleak at midday that the time could easily have been mistaken for early evening. Trudging into a dreary winter rainstorm, rain was whipped about by a swirling wind. Jennings' aide tried without success to shelter both of them with a makeshift umbrella as Jennings used both arms to lean on his duckboard crutch, slopping along slowly in the mud on his way to the new treatment pavilion within D Block.

These days, Jennings rarely got beyond D Block, which had several buildings cordoned off for the 350 or so soldiers with *shell shock* housed there. In addition to the sleeping quarters, which he was now leaving, he next passed a detached dining room with its own self-contained kitchen and food preparation area. Those buildings had been converted from these same uses by the former lunatic asylum to serve military personnel now. Another building housed the doctors' offices, a small surgery area, and various administrative offices.

As Jennings shuddered from the penetrating cold, he entered a different building from all of these—the new nerve treatment pavilion of D Block. Soaking wet with muddy feet, he noted there could not have been a greater contrast with Dr. Brown's room and his hypnosis session in the doctors' offices a few days earlier. Reluctantly entering the treatment room in the new building, Jennings felt a great deal of apprehension and really had no idea what was about to happen to him. He had heard about his new doctor from the sisters and now saw him inside the treatment room, turned away from the door.

Dr. Charles Holmes was tall and athletic, impersonal and brusque. A choleric Irishman, he was all business, and had the reputation of treating patients like objects without empathy or even eye contact. At one end of the large treatment room Jennings saw an ominous looking heavy chair with numerous leather straps. Medical equipment was set out on a stand next to the chair, and an intimidating jangle of wires emerged from a modern looking, big black machine with dials and switches all over it, standing next to the medical equipment.

"You shall be doing this session in a state of dishabille, young man," Dr. Holmes smirked.

Jennings just stood there with a quizzical expression, having no idea of what Dr. Holmes had just said.

"Undressed. Naked. Have you no cultivation, soldier?"

Jennings continued to stand there and look blankly at the doctor. *What does he want me to do?* he asked himself, afraid to say anything to the upper-class doctor.

"Do you need an engraved invitation? Take your bloody clothes off."

Hoping to get some warm, dry clothes in exchange for his rain-drenched patient gown, Jennings readily complied, shivering a bit as it was now winter and the room was not well-heated and he was wet and cold from the brief walk to the new pavilion.

"Might be a bit nippy in here, but that will help make you work hard with me to finish this quickly. Now walk over there and take a seat," Dr. Holmes commanded as he pointed to the massive chair. "And this will be the last time you will ever need to use that shameful crutch of yours."

Jennings was dumbfounded. *I think he's going to treat me without letting me put any dry clothes on,* he thought with alarm. However, acting passively as was his nature, Jennings walked without objection or any word to the end of the room with the assistance of his makeshift duckboard crutch. As he did so, he looked up and noticed an ominous apparatus overhead—a sort of a trolley carrying long connecting wires the whole length of the room on a track mounted on the ceiling. *Looks like an animal's harness*, Jennings thought to himself.

Dr. Holmes saw Jennings looking at it. "That's to keep you from being able to escape the current when you're up from the chair. You cannot leave the room once we have you hooked-up until you are cured." Dr. Holmes then turned and locked all the doors leading into the room, and removed the keys. He then drew the blinds. The only light in the room came from the resistance bulbs of the batteries feeding the large black machine with all the dials.

"First, we shall try the chair. One way or another, you shall be walking and your shakes shall be gone before you can leave the room. Let's get started. Before I strap you in, I must ask, what do you think ails you, lad?"

Jennings noted the doctor had not used his name nor given him any reassurance and barely even looked at him yet. "*Shell shock.*"

"That could be anything from a lunatic to a malingerer. Be more specific, boy."

"I tremble all over, and I can't walk."

"Caused by weak nerves and cowardice. Cured by me and my magic current. You see, we can strengthen your willpower by putting electrical current through your affected parts. The plan today is to keep the galvanic current flogging until your shakes are gone and you can walk normally again. With this technique and enough shocks administered, the deaf hear, the blind see, the dumb speak and those who believe themselves incapable of moving certain groups of muscles begin to move them freely."

Using electrical shocks to treat shell shock? Jennings asked himself, gripped with the irony of the situation. *Seems pretty far-fetched to me.*

Dr, Holmes continued. "In all cases, one treatment suffices."

One treatment? Jennings thought in disbelief. *That hardly seems possible.* Now totally nonplussed, Jennings began to realize Dr. Holmes was approaching this more as a showman or even a con-man than a doctor. But as a good soldier, he decided to remain silent, cooperate and obey.

"Now it's time for me to strap your arms and legs into this chair." Dr. Holmes fastened heavy leather straps around all four of Jennings' limbs. "Next, we apply the electrodes."

Whoa, Jennings thought. *I'm not sure I should let him do this.* He began to wonder if this was going to be therapy or punishment, but once again, decided to comply passively. *Seems like Dr. Holmes is making things worse, not better,* Jennings thought, since he now had the quivers from the cold on top of his shaking.

First, Dr. Holmes doused several small areas on each of Jennings' four limbs with a cold liquid, presumably alcohol. Then he placed several flat pieces of metal on top of each wet area at multiple sites all over Jennings' limbs, and tied them all down with cotton bandage strips. Jennings continued to comply passively.

"Now, there we are. Ready-to-go. Through these electrodes I shall deliver an increasingly powerful galvanic current to your weak nerves, thereby feeding your limbs until they are restored to normal. We shall not leave here today until our job is complete. I am prepared to stay here as long as it takes."

Jennings now wondered what he had got himself into with this doctor today.

"You are about to experience a form of divine healing by the royal touch, if I must say so myself." Dr. Holmes laughed to himself as he said that. "Ready, soldier? Let's hope this is a brief healing procedure. Most with your condition are cured in twenty minutes. Now, let's apply some light current to your trembling arms and legs." Dr. Holmes started to move the dials. "Feel the tingle?"

Jennings nodded.

"Now, stop trembling. I know you can do it."

Jennings looked at his limbs and nothing changed. His arms and legs moved like always. He looked quizzically at the doctor. He decided neither to expend any effort nor to resist, only to sit passively for now and see what happened.

"Let's try a bit more current," Dr. Holmes said as he moved the dials up.

Jennings now felt a light shock moving into each limb. Not painful, but shaking movements still occurred without any voluntary input from Jennings.

"Stop trembling. Don't you wish to be cured? You are a young man with a wife and daughter at home and you owe it to them if not to yourself and certainly to your country to make every effort to restore yourself. Show me some of that courage and resolve and don't be a disgrace to the service by displaying such mental weakness. You can certainly pull yourself together with a little more effort."

Jennings didn't know what he was supposed to do, but felt the doctor was trying to intimidate him with mention of his family. He looked down at his body and watched with fright as his limbs ignored the electricity.

"Are you indifferent, soldier? That will not do in these times when we need every man at the Front and cannot afford for you to continue to be wastage. Let's increase the current some more." Dr. Holmes moved the dials up more, acting as if he were a mad Victorian scientist.

Jennings began to get worried. He now felt uncomfortable; there was pain, especially at the points where the various electrodes touched his skin. However, it was bearable, so he decided to accede to Dr. Holmes' authority and go along with the program.

"We shall leave this on for several minutes now," Dr. Holmes declared.

They both sat in the dark in silence for several minutes, but the pain was getting worse and worse for Jennings. Finally, he hurt so badly he had to say something.

"Can you turn that down?" Jennings pleaded.

"How can I do that if you keep trembling? If you persist in your shaking, we shall not allow you to receive your post from the Royal Mail nor hear from your family any more, and you shall lose your rights to have visitors or a furlough. Are you sure you don't want to stop this shaking?"

"I'm trying, sir." *Now Jennings was getting angry. Don't you dare threaten to cut-off correspondence with my family,* he thought. *That's the only thing that's keeping me going. That, plus the prospect of a visit from them if I get better.* This doctor was now threatening to withhold his chance to see his Sarah and Gertie. *That's not playing fair,* Jennings thought silently.

There was still no change in the tremors in his limbs. Jennings closed his eyes and tried to bear the pain for several more minutes. Without warning, a sudden jolt of electricity passed through each limb, and all four limbs extended fully, straight as a stick, while his back arched and his head drew back with his chin high in the air. The pain was excruciating. He writhed in the chair and howled in agony.

Dr. Holmes observed, "Aha! Now the trembling has stopped."

"Please turn it off, it's unbearable," Jennings pleaded.

"Nonsense. Don't be a weeper." After a cruel pause, Dr. Holmes said, "All right, let's see what happens when we turn it down." Dr. Holmes then turned down the current, but the trembling returned. "See, with enough electricity the trembling stops, but with too little, you still shake. We can keep it off for good once the trembling subsides permanently."

Jennings was dubious and somewhat trepidatious at this point. *This man is performing torture, not therapy,* he thought. *How can I get out of here?*

Again and without warning, Dr. Holmes dialed the gauges up high. Jennings shrieked and out shot his limbs into full extension, back arched and chin up. Due to the spasms caused by the electricity, there was no trembling of any of his limbs as long as the strong painful current was on. Dr. Holmes stopped it again, and this time Jennings' legs and arms remained still.

Jennings just sat there and looked at his limbs. Motionless. *Amazing*, he thought. *I wonder if it'll last.*

"Great work, soldier!" Dr. Holmes then wrote in Jennings' medical chart:

> *This hitherto intractable case received four hours continuous treatment.*
> *Harsh and merciless, but savagely effective.*

Chapter 24

THE PENTAGON, WASHINGTON, D.C.:

"Ellen?" the caller asked as Colonel Richards picked up the phone in her Pentagon office.

Richards seethed as she immediately recognized his voice from that single word. "How'd you get this number? Never call me here."

"With your new high profile job, you keep making the news, so all I had to do to track you down was go through the Pentagon's Web site. Chief of Army psychiatry. Sweet. And quite an irony."

"I don't know what you want, but I told you I want you out of my life. As far as I'm concerned, you don't even exist," she said angrily.

"Oh, but I do exist. And I need your help."

"That means you want more money."

"Money is help," he chuckled out loud. "I need a few Benjamins for my meds and for food."

"I've had it with you. No more. Never contact me again or else there'll be consequences and they won't be pretty."

"I wonder how the army would feel if they knew about your juvenile past, and the problems of your loving brother? And how would the press feel about your relationship with a certain general in the Pentagon? Suppose you'd keep that sweet career of yours moving along?"

"I've put in too much blood, sweat and tears to get this far, and I'll not let secrets ruin it for me," railed Richards spitting the words out. "Don't threaten me, Jordan. I have access to ways of silencing you now, so don't test me on this," she threatened as she slammed the phone down.

Chapter 25

FORT HOOD ARMY BASE, KILLEEN, TEXAS:

After their dinner last night, Libby was quite upset with Adam as she left Lester's Diner. Conrad went his separate way to his hotel. But this morning was another day, and she greeted Conrad with a smile in the all-purpose room at Fort Hood, ready to co-chair the mental health course today for nurses in the morning and cadre in the afternoon. No sooner had the audience of 150 nurses got settled in the massive room with noisy, beat-up linoleum floors and converted bingo tables used for note taking by the nurses, than two athletic-looking men in dark suits and sunglasses, earpieces mounted in one ear, barged through the side door at the front of the room. They interrupted proceedings as they came right up to the chairman's table where Conrad and Libby were sitting. Conrad laughed to himself at how comical they looked and couldn't decide whether they were *Men in Black* or *Saturday Night Live's* take on the Blues Brothers.

The smile vanished off Conrad's face when they announced: "Federal agents." They shouted, "Dr. Augustus Conrad? You're under arrest for violating the U.S. Federal Espionage Act of 1917. You have the right to remain silent ..."

Chapter 26

Back from the coffee kiosk with her signature Marko Mocha in hand, Jennifer Roberts noticed the flashing red light on her desk phone in her cubicle at The Post. Punching the code to retrieve her voicemail, she listened and took notes as the recorded message declared:

> *"This is for Jennifer Roberts, that reporter who writes about the army and its mental health problems, like that article on the last shooter at Fort Hood. I'm close to the chief of army psychiatry, Colonel Ellen Richards, and there're some things I think you should know about her. She's the wrong person for the job and only got promoted because she's having an affair with a married officer at the Pentagon. Nobody there knows about that or about her past or about her family. She'd lose that job if anybody found out. I know because I'm her brother. If you want to speak, let me know when I can call back. I don't have a cell phone."*

"Bert," Roberts called out.

"Yeah, Jennifer." His reply filtered over the partitions of her cubicle.

"I want you to check out Colonel Ellen Richards at the Pentagon. And see what you can find out about her brother as well. Thaaaaaank-you, Bert."

Chapter 27

THE PENTAGON, WASHINGTON, D.C.:

Following his conversation with Colonel Richards and Vice Chief Morelli, General Rossi remained in the Vice Chief's office with Richards to watch their boss testify live to the Senate Armed Services Committee across town at the Capitol Building. C-Span beamed out of a huge plasma screen on the wall of the Vice Chief's bunker.

"Look who's grilling the Vice," Rossi complained as he rolled his eyes. "That brassy bitch from California, Benham. Always on our case."

"Senator Barbara Benham. She's chair of the Senate Armed Services Committee, so the Vice must play nice with her. Remember, she pays our salaries and all the army's bills," countered Richards.

"Now she wants us to waste funds on psychiatric services for slackers with PTSD, and divert resources away from what we really need, like properly armored vehicles and body armor. IEDs are always maiming our guys in theatre, and those wounded warriors certainly aren't slackers," fumed Rossi.

Senator Barbara Benham presided over the committee hearing from her high perch with a microphone in front of her and a gavel in her right hand as she looked down upon the seated witnesses in front of her committee. A lineup of several heavily decorated three- and four-star generals, including General Morelli, sat next to each other down in the "pit" serving as the witnesses' arena, each at his own microphone. This layout required the witnesses to look up at the Senate committee members who surrounded them all in an intimidating semi-circle. The balance of power was evident from this seating arrangement and the Senate liked its hearings conducted this way, especially when cameras were rolling. In the middle of the high semi-circle and in the position of greatest authority sat Senator Benham. The senator appeared to be in her mid-to-late forties, was short, good looking, dressed to the nines in expensive designer clothes with "don't fuck with me" jewelry adorning her powerful, fit little body.

Benham's just a pontificating powermonger, Rossi thought to himself. Then, speaking aloud, he complained to Richards, "That Senate bitch is acting disrespectfully to the man who runs her army. Who the hell does she think she is?"

"Settle down, Andy," Colonel Richards said, sitting down at the conference table to view the broadcast. "Come sit by me and rest your bones," she said, patting the seat at the table next to her.

"I prefer to stand and pace," he fired back.

Senator Benham continued from the plasma screen. ... "So, you have no explanation for these increases in suicides among your soldiers?"

Rossi just then thought the Vice Chief looked like a deer caught in the headlights, frozen in awkward silence.

Senator Benham scowled as she raised her voice, "General, do you need me to repeat the question?"

General Morelli looked like he was trying to get his bearings and then answered, "No, that won't be necessary. Pardon me. Um, well, um, what we do know is that army suicides are not due to the stress of combat or repeated deployments. We've found just as many of our troops kill themselves who've never been in combat after deployment, as those who have been in combat after deployment. In fact, the suicide rate of soldiers who have never deployed at all is just as high."

"I'm sorry, General Morelli, but that just doesn't make a lot of sense. You're saying the stress of combat, the number of deployments, the length of deployment have nothing to do with this new epidemic of suicide in the army?"

Rossi now thought General Morelli looked flustered and seemed to be scrambling for an answer. The Vice Chief finally replied to the senator, "I'm sure deployments must have something to do with it, but we believe the real issue is that the quality of the soldiers entering the service has deteriorated over recent years. More and more young people are bringing their pre-existing problems into the military, and due to their own deficiencies, and not to their army experiences, they just happen to commit suicide when they are in the service but not because they're in the service. We think they would have committed suicide anyway even if they hadn't joined the army."

"Sounds fanciful. If true, what are you doing about that?" the senator fired back.

"We're trying not to recruit weak soldiers with poor coping skills, and we've developed strict policies telling soldiers who have been recruited they are not to commit suicide but are to report their problems to their battle buddy or up the line-of-command. We're also trying to make them less psychiatric by giving them resilience training."

"'Less psychiatric?' I'm not sure what that means. So you think you can train people not to commit suicide?"

Rossi thought the Vice was gaining confidence, so he finally took a deep breath and decided to sit down beside Richards as she smiled back at him. Meanwhile, General Morelli seemed to sit more erect and to lean forward into his microphone, looking more self-assured as he continued, "Yes, resilience can toughen up certain pre-existing weaknesses and we think that's the best path to reducing suicide."

"General Morelli, I realize you're spending millions on resilience training at the expense of putting those resources into mental health care. Top civilian mental health experts say the way to reduce suicides is not resilience training, but improving mental health care in the army while reducing the stigma the army has towards psychological problems that develop in those serving in uniform for our country."

"We're doing all of that, too. We have great policies about how to treat PTSD and traumatic brain injuries. And we have the best guidelines for which medications to give and policies of access to medical records for our medical and psychiatric personnel to allow rapid and full communication of psychological issues for individual patients among all medical personnel."

"That sounds good, but what you contend is just not true according to many outside experts. In fact, general, but we have evidence. ..." Senator Benham paused as she waved papers at General Morelli before she continued, "... that the army's not learned much in the past hundred years since the days of *shell shock* in World War I."

Rossi, watching from the Pentagon wished he could be there to warn General Morelli, becoming alarmed and pounding the conference table as he thought, *omigod. She's got Conrad's report.*

The senator continued, "Experts say PTSD is a 21st century version of *shell shock*, and instead of *treating* those soldiers, in those days many were executed as *cowards*. Don't you think that shaming today's soldiers who get PTSD, fostering the warrior mentality that such individuals are cowardly weaklings unworthy of serving in the military and neglecting to provide adequate psychiatric care is just a 21st century version of symbolically beheading our present-day soldiers?"

General Morelli looked stunned. Even on television Rossi could see the Vice-Chief's face flush red in anger. He looked like he was about to explode into a purple rage.

"With all due respect—"

"I'm not finished, general," Senator Benham interrupted. "Wait till I yield the floor." Waving Conrad's report again, Benham pressed on, looking self-assured and like a cat now toying with her cornered prey, biding her time before deciding to pounce and finish him off. "We have evidence you're still mired in providing psychiatric care that's outdated by a hundred years, including the fact your very own policies are not even being followed, and your soldiers hide their symptoms from medical personnel and their line-of-command due to fear it'll compromise their military career and make them appear weak."

"Don't let that bitch talk to you that way," Rossi said aloud, shooting once again to his feet and feeling like tearing the plasma screen from the wall of the Vice Chief's office. Rossi thought General Morelli began to reassume a rather defeated posture. "Be a man and give her some of her own medicine," Rossi shouted like a fan rooting at a Washington Redskins game.

"Andy, he can't hear you," Richards said in a soothing tone. "Please sit back down." But Rossi ignored her and began to pace furiously.

The senator rolled on with, "Surveys show fewer than one in four soldiers who need mental health care seek it because of the culture of the army. When they do, we have evidence of excessive prescribing of pain pills—opiates—by your medical personnel."

"That's false evidence," General Morelli countered as he looked like he was getting his bearings, brushing his fingers lightly across the numerous citation ribbons on his chest.

The ranking member of the committee interrupted Senator Benham.

"Please, senator, you don't need to badger the witness."

Senator Benham turned to the ranking member and said, "Senator, I'm not badgering the witness, I'm trying to get to the bottom of this horrific situation of suicides we have in the United States Army. It can't go on, so if you'll please, permit me to continue."

The ranking member of the committee slinked back into his cozy leather chair.

Don't know if he's reassuring himself or trying to intimidate the senator, but go for it, sir, Rossi thought silently.

"General, please respond," the senator demanded.

"We have policies that prevent prescription opiate abuse. As you know, civilians of the same age are suffering an epidemic of prescription opiate abuse, so it's not surprising this might occasionally occur in the army, but it's not a big problem."

"Do you think the cadre line-of-command has confidence in mental health treatment in the army?"

"Certainly," the general answered now forcefully.

"Do you think cadre line-of-command has an understanding of the difference between PTSD and cowardice, general?" the senator pushed.

"Of course," Morelli responded through clenched teeth.

"General Morelli. Do you think heroism is manly, and cowardice is not manly? Even womanly?"

"No, ma'am. Of course not," Morelli spewed out with his face once again colored in anger.

"What did you just say?"

"No, ma'am," Morelli repeated just as hotly.

"Don't call me ma'am. General, you will call me *Senator*. Do you understand?" Senator Benham pointed the handle of her gavel directly at Morelli while leering at him forcefully with the confidence of one who knew she had the upper hand. "I worked very hard for the title of United States Senator."

Morelli was nonplussed, and looked foolish and like a schoolboy being scolded by his school marm. After hesitating and swallowing hard, he replied, "Yes, m ... , Yes. Senator."

"What was that again, General Morelli?"

"Yes, Senator Benham."

The ranking member of the committee was seething, but held his fire. He was no match for Senator Benham.

Rossi laughed nervously as he watched, trying to substitute trou-
bled mirth for the anger welling up in him as Senator Benham threatened
his army with ridicule. "Now that's ridiculous and disrespectful to my army's leader," he said aloud to Richards. "The Vice didn't manage to wiggle
so well out of this grilling from the chairman did he, or shall I say from the
'chairperson'?" he added sarcastically.

"Ooo, you're so politically correct, Andy," Richard clucked as she
rose to her feet, sat on the edge of the conference table and crossed her legs
sensuously. "I'm really impressed. You're becoming quite the feminist," she
teased.

Rossi groaned in torment as she stroked her sassy curls.

Chapter 28

"Hey, Roberts. Pentagon on line three," shouted Bert halfway across the newsroom.

"Thanks," Jennifer shot back as she picked up the line and answered, "Jennifer Roberts here."

"Hello, Ms. Roberts. This is Colonel Ellen Richards, Chief of Army Psychiatry, returning your call to the Pentagon. I've been designated as the official spokesperson for your questions on Dr. Conrad's report. How might I help you?"

Jennifer wondered if she could knock Richards out of that sickening and syrupy singsong tone. It dripped with insincerity. "Yes, thanks. I'd like to get your reaction to his findings uncovering deficiencies in mental health programs at Fort Hood."

"The U.S. Army is concerned that our soldiers get all the mental health services they need at Fort Hood and that they're all of the highest quality," Richards purred. "We're working to extend every benefit available to our brave wounded warriors."

Roberts felt like throwing up after being force-fed this bullshit by Richards, but continued now with more of a bite. "That's nice, Colonel Richards, but not specific. I'm after your particular reaction to Conrad's findings that soldiers are given too many medications, especially prescription opiates, and that medical professionals at Fort Hood don't have adequate access to psychiatric records."

"You should know we've already met with Dr. Conrad here at the Pentagon and have been unable to confirm his findings. To the contrary, we have strict policies on medications, drugs of abuse and access to medical records that we've already documented are being followed appropriately."

Roberts rolled her eyes and fired back in a disbelieving tone, "So, it's 'he said, she said,' is it? Is that the army's game? What about the findings that patients at Fort Hood have to wait a long time to get evaluated for PTSD by psychiatry, are frustrated with the bureaucracy, and generally feel unsupported by the command there that thinks PTSD is not a medical condition, but a weakness?"

"Surely Dr. Conrad's been greatly misinformed. We spend vast time and resources training our commanders and enhancing our services. We simply do not know what Dr. Conrad is talking about," Colonel Richards said with an edge.

"For real, Colonel Richards? With all due respect, your responses strike me as unresponsive platitudes. Seems like army psychiatry needs a skilled spokesperson these days since you're constantly under fire, what with this unflattering report from Fort Hood, the two mass murders there by your own soldiers, and an epidemic of suicides, drug and alcohol abuse. How is it that someone so young became head of army psychiatry when you were responsible for promoting, instead of firing, the psychiatrist who became the first Fort Hood mass murderer? Are you really personally equipped to turn things around and what's your plan for doing so?"

There was a long pause at the other end of the line. *Gotcha*, Roberts thought to herself.

Richards continued, now with a wavering voice. "I have the full support of my superiors and have been given the resources to maintain and improve psychiatry not only at Fort Hood but throughout the army. I've only been in this position for a couple of years, and deserve a chance to make things even better."

"So, you don't think your early promotion at such a young age had anything to do with your close association with a superior officer at the Pentagon?"

Richards' tone suddenly turned edgy again and defensive as she shot back, "I resent the implication of your question."

"Just doin' my job, Colonel Richards. We received an anonymous tip today regarding your relationship with a senior officer in the U.S. Army. Are you denying that relationship or stating that it's not inappropriate?"

No response.

"And you don't think your problems as a juvenile should be a potential deterrent to your serving in such an important position?"

Richards now broke her silence, retaliating with hostility. "With whom have you been speaking? You need to get your facts straight before you start throwing out slanderous innuendos. This conversation is now over." Richards slammed the phone in its receiver.

Chapter 29

WASHINGTON, D.C.:

The Department of Psychiatry and Behavioral Health unit at Fort Hood Army Base in Texas was notorious. It was where Major Nidal Hasan, an army psychiatrist, had once worked when he shot up dozens of his own soldiers, mostly mental health professionals working in the behavioral health unit, while killing more than a dozen of them as he was about to deploy to Iraq. It was also where Private Ivan Lopez was a patient when he, too, went berserk, killing three, wounding sixteen and then committing suicide.

As Sergeant Adam Warburton left his psychiatrist's office in that same facility after his behavioral health appointment with his army psychiatrist treating him for PTSD and opiate addiction, his psychiatrist accessed a secret phone number with a password given to him to call in case of emergency. He dialed and when he heard a click stated, "This is Major Benson, head of psychiatry at Fort Hood."

"You've reached the Commandant."

"Great. Then I have the right connection. I was instructed to call this number in case of any threat to our unit."

Major Benson knew he was about to betray doctor-patient confidentiality with this call. He also knew that patient confidentiality in army psychiatry was a joke. Army psychiatrists worked for the army's interests and not for the patient's. It took Major Benson a while to get used to that because it contradicted, if not eradicated, his Hippocratic *oath*. Other specialties like surgeons were able to be patient advocates. However, psychiatry had always been different in the military. For over a hundred years the army used psychiatrists as agents to protect the interests of military cohesion against the scourges of weakness, cowardice and mental illness in soldiers as a priority over treating mental illness in those very same soldiers because mental illness was in most cases considered to be cowardice under another name.

As such, we psychiatrists are noble army warriors in our own way, Benson thought, trying to reassure himself he was doing the right thing.

Continuing, he said to the Commandant, "Today a young soldier who's a patient of mine returned from leave visiting family in England and brought back an actual Medallion."

"Are you sure it's authentic?"

"Didn't see it, but he said it was owned by his great-great-grandfather, a British Army officer during World War I. My patient found out he was one the original Patrons of Perseus, an officer who commanded firing squads executing cowards in France."

"No harm, no foul. He could've found that out from the newspapers. It's ancient history."

"True, but I'm calling because the young soldier wants to know more about the Medallion and about his British great-great-grandfather and is digging online and in the British Great War Archives overseas."

"That's not so good. Does he have any inkling of our current operations?"

"Don't think so."

"Good enough. By the way, why was the young soldier seeing you in the psychiatry department?"

Benson hesitated, feeling creepy about betraying Sergeant Warburton's psychiatric confidentiality. "PTSD. Opiate addiction. And seems about ready to kill himself. A real basket case."

"How convenient. Is his name Warburton by any chance?"

Benson was stunned. "How'd you know that?"

"Let me just say I'm way ahead of you."

The Commandant had received notification just an hour ago from contacts in Britain that a request had been submitted for the records of one Lieutenant Nigel Warburton of the World War I British Expeditionary Force and also an inquiry about a Medallion of Perseus Number 59 by a current Sergeant Adam Warburton of the U.S. Army.

Hanging up, the Commandant concluded, *I know exactly what has to be done next.*

Chapter 30

D BLOCK, NETLEY HOSPITAL, SUMMER OF 1916:

Having lost his symptoms, Private Simon Jennings was given rest for a few days and then "systematic exercises" by an instructor. He prepared next for an assignment working outside on the farm that fed the hospital. He also had the stunning good news that his wife and daughter would be visiting in a fortnight. Jennings called Sarah his "petal dust" and his daughter Gertie his "cherub," in the odd language of a genuine Yorkshireman. The army had granted them a visitor's pass and even provided money for the train tickets and accommodations. What a blessing. He was so excited he could hardly sleep, also hoping the army would soon be discharging him as they did almost everybody with a blighty wound.

Jennings' electrical treatment had a profound impact on D Block, as many heard his screams and the rumors of his "faradizations" circulated all around. In fact, right after that, several soldiers who had hysterical paralyses for quite some time lost their symptoms on their way from D Block to the nerve treatment pavilion.

Chapter 31

With a pencil clenched lightly between her teeth and her eyes bearing down on the monitor, Jennifer Roberts was engaged in her futile mission to have her fingers keep up with her thoughts. Her cell phone rang and she answered it before checking the incoming phone number.

"Jennifer Roberts."

"Hold for the senator."

After a brief pause, a familiar voice greeted her, "Hi, Jennifer. It's Senator Benham. How're ya doing?"

"I'm great. To what can I credit a call from such a busy woman?"

"No busier than you. As I'm sure you're aware, activity in the senate rarely translates into productivity. I wanted to give you a heads-up we're looking into problems with mental health care in the military in general and at the army base at Fort Hood in particular."

"Doesn't surprise me. Now two mass murderers there are linked to problems with their mental health unit. Suicides skyrocketing. I've been reporting on all of that," Jennifer added.

"Yes, I know. And well done, by the way."

"Thanks."

"I'm calling because I've been informed the army's arrested and charged one of their own civilian psychiatrists working at Fort Hood with espionage."

"Yes, I'm aware of that. A famous Stanford psychiatrist by the name of Conrad. You think there's any basis to it?"

"Not at all. Turns out Dr. Conrad's an old friend of mine. You could say an old beau. We used to date at Stanford when we were undergraduates there before he went his way and I went mine. We've stayed in contact and he's also been one of my most loyal campaign donors. There's absolutely no way he could've committed espionage. He can't find his own keys half the time. No way he could've organized treason. And he has no motive to do so."

"Then why do suppose they'd accused him?"

"Likely to shut him up. Gus, I mean Dr. Conrad, has a way of antagonizing people with his strong convictions. And he doesn't think highly of army psychiatry to begin with. He's probably angered some important people in the army."

"Maybe the army is hiding something and he's getting too close."

"Good point, and just what I was thinking. I have to be careful in my position not to be seen as advocating too strongly for him in public. I'll have to do my thing behind the scenes which is why I'm calling you. If he's too close to something for the army's comfort, I'm sure there's a story in it for you, if you find out what it is."

"It wouldn't take a rocket scientist to guess if he's a psychiatrist and they're calling the publishing of an academic article a form of treason, there's something about the way the army is dealing with PTSD they don't want him to get any closer to discovering."

"Bingo. It's a trumped up charge for sure. Pisses me off, pardon my French, and don't quote me on that. I'd appreciate it if you'd look into the matter as only you can."

"Sounds like a great lead, and I'll certainly follow-up with you as soon as I have something solid."

"I've also got this really bad feeling things are not likely to get better for wounded warriors with psychological problems unless we can put pressure on the army by shaping the public's perception that PTSD is a war wound and not voluntary frailty. I think the right publicity might be just what we need," the senator said with real conviction.

"I agree and I'm beginning to wonder if the army is treating its soldiers today not any differently than the British did in World War I."

"Well, at least we aren't shooting our own as cowards."

"Senator Benham, I wouldn't be so sure of that."

Chapter 32

D BLOCK, NETLEY HOSPITAL, LATE SUMMER OF 1916:

As British days go, Jennings knew that this one was glorious in more ways than one, after all, there was the sunshine as he walked outside his dormitory towards the visitors' center. A few clouds but warm enough for shirt sleeves with the grass flickering bright green and not a bit of gloom. An appropriate welcome for Sarah and precious wee Gertie, Jennings thought. He would finally be seeing his family in just a moment. Striding confidently into the reception area on his own two feet and without any need for crutches, Jennings shouted, "Sarah," and they ran to meet and hug in the middle of the room.

"Don't you look the army venturer," Sarah exclaimed with a beaming smile once they separated from numerous kisses. "I'm so proud. And look who's here to see daddy."

Jennings scooped his little one out of her pram. "Hello, blossom. Now aren't you daddy's little nipper? She's beautiful, Sarah."

"We're so glad to be here," Sarah said as a lovely smile grew on her kind-looking face.

"How long's it been? Over a year?"

"Four hundred eighty-days to be exact."

"And exactly how old is Gertie now?"

"Can't you figure it out? Seven months."

"Of course, born right after the new year."

"Yes, the product of your last visit home. You left a fatherly touch last time and look what the good Lord's given us."

"Ah, my little angel, soon you'll be walking. And soon daddy will be home, maybe in time to see you take your first steps."

"Simon, that would be wonderful, but the Great War's still raging. I don't see how that can happen. So many men and boys are now leaving for duty."

"I know, I know, but I've been recovering and almost everyone with a blighty wound goes home with a medical discharge."

"That would be wonderful. When do you expect to know?"

"Any week now. A whole group of us here expect to receive orders before the end of summer. But this is so splendid, let's just enjoy our time today. When do you have to go back?"

"Tonight. They only let us have this brief visit. If you don't get discharged, maybe they'll at least grant you a furlough so you can visit home for a short time before you go back to France."

"I'm not going back to France," Jennings said flatly.

Just then a rude voice yelled from the doorway of reception. "Jennings, time's up."

"Can't we have some more time, Sarge?" he pleaded.

"Not possible. Got a whole queue of visitors today, so that's it. Need to make way for the next one. Now on your way missus."

"Don't worry, Sarah. I'll be home soon."

Chapter 33

FEDERAL COURTHOUSE, DALLAS, TEXAS:

Exiting the courthouse with both his lawyers but without his dignity on a hot, muggy Texas day, and after getting a haircut of two million bucks for bail, Conrad was incensed over his treatment over the past twenty-four hours, but glad to be going back to Palo Alto tonight.

"This is bullshit," Conrad spouted, as he left the courthouse. "I hate being treated like this. And the humidity here is not making me any less disagreeable. Let's get the hell out of Texas and back to California."

"What with the Bradley Manning Wikileaks case and the Edward Snowden NSA case, you're lucky to bond out at any price," said John McLaughlin, Conrad's federal criminal defense lawyer.

"You can afford it," reassured Alan Poors, Conrad's longtime family lawyer and financial advisor from California. Poors handled the transfer of his parents' considerable estate, including the proceeds of his father's business sale, to Conrad's mother when his father died, and later to Conrad when his mother died. Poors now managed the investments in Conrad's eight-figure trust fund.

"That's not the point. Publishing the truth about psychiatric care at Fort Hood in a medical journal hardly rates an accusation of treason."

"I know. But you obviously pissed off the army and they're gonna show you who's boss. Now unless you want to get a GPS strapped to your leg, or spend your time in jail preparing for trial instead of practicing medicine at Stanford, once we get back to California, don't leave the state until this is resolved," McLaughlin warned.

"Yeah, yeah, yeah. I get it," Conrad admitted reluctantly. "Anyway, I have to make a call."

With that, they got into their stretch limousine and were whisked off to the airport.

AT "THE WASHINGTON POST," WASHINGTON, D.C.:

JENNIFER ROBERTS WAS SITTING at her desk in her yoga clothes, ready to leave work for her nightly workout. The office was mostly deserted and she was heading to the door when the phone on the desk in her cubicle rang. Her lithe dancer's legs beat a hasty retreat back to the desk, and with a graceful arabesque, Jennifer grabbed the phone before the third ring and announced, "Roberts here."

"Hello, this is Gus Conrad from Stanford returning your call. I think you might have some questions about the report I just published on Fort Hood."

"Ah, Dr. Conrad, thanks for returning my call. That would be a yes. Seems like you've stirred up a hornets' nest at the Pentagon, and they're denying the accuracy of your findings. What's your response to their rebuttal of your report?"

"The data in my report were objectively and scientifically collected on keypads. They're not my opinions, they're those of the nurses and the cadre—you know, their term for the line-of-command—at Fort Hood. Maybe their perceptions are incorrect, but I stated that. However, their perceptions are their own, not mine. I happen to agree with them based on what I saw there, but that isn't the point."

"You certainly have had an eventful day. What do you think of the espionage charge against you?"

"I better be careful here. It's been a very long day, and I'm on my way to the airport here in Dallas ready to take off for Palo Alto after being released on bond. Shall I just say I think the government is over-reaching here?"

"Tactfully done, Dr. Conrad. Senator Benham had some saltier words for it when she called me earlier today. I remain interested in the treatment of soldiers and veterans with PTSD. I'd appreciate it if you'd keep me apprised of your findings on these matters. Can I call you in the future as a potential source for my stories?"

"Yes, but until this case is resolved, I'd prefer my statements to be on background as well as off the record."

"Understood."

"Hope this matter becomes resolved and you don't have to cover my espionage trial," Conrad said half-jokingly.

"Well said. With all due respect, I think the army has much bigger problems to tackle than trying you for espionage, like rectifying the crisis in its behavioral health programs."

"They can't keep a lid on their problems forever. At some point, they're gonna have to fix 'em. It's becoming a national scandal."

"Get me the proof, Dr. Conrad, and I'll do my very best to make it one."

Chapter 34

D BLOCK, NETLEY HOSPITAL, SUMMER OF 1916:

Following his permanent miracle cure, and after his glorious but short visit from Sarah and his dear Gertie, Jennings was assigned to work on the farm while he awaited his discharge orders. This allowed him to get outside and start using his newly functional limbs. Working on the farm was natural to him as he had done it as a boy in Yorkshire. Here, he learned the workers farmed crops, tended gardens of vegetables and took care of different animals. Farming was considered a form of occupational therapy for the newly cured and Jennings worked alongside other soldiers cured of *shell shock* as well as some of the old lunatics who stayed at the hospital to help staff the farm after D Block was converted into a ward for the treatment of war neuroses. The patients were supervised by reconstruction aides, mostly civilian women hired for the war effort by the army. Jennings rarely saw doctors anymore.

"You shall work on the farm to continue the strengthening of your will, and also to serve your country. It shall also get you ready to be a soldier again," his doctor said as outdoor duty began for Jennings.

Jennings cringed at the thought of being a soldier again. As far as he was concerned, he was all done with that. He knew most soldiers with blighty wounds never got sent back to France.

Up at dawn, Jennings and his fellow *shell shock* patients planted, hoed, harvested and prepared food. He knew this was not just a form of therapy, but also a way to reinforce to the men that their *shell shock* had been unmanly. Their psychiatrists developed a number of work therapies based upon traditional women's work. Thus, after farm chores were done at midday, Jennings and his fellow D Block patients busied themselves until sunset in decidedly unmanly activities such as rug making, basket weaving and poultry farming. Jennings didn't care. It occupied his time and relaxed him. The other soldiers from the general hospital sneered at him and his fellow *shell shock* patients as the "new womanly men in action."

While awaiting further orders, Jennings was able to write to his wife by himself, now that his shaking had stopped. He also heard that the army had just banned any official use of the diagnosis, *shell shock*. You were either NYDN (W) which meant Not Yet Diagnosed Nervous (Wounded), and awarded a wound stripe and eligible for a war pension because you were considered to have been wounded due to combat; or NYDN (S), Not Yet Diagnosed Nervous (Sick), with no wound stripe, not eligible for a war pension and not considered to have been wounded by combat. NYDN (S) was just a fancy term for *shell shock* and everybody knew it.

On this warm summer day, several of the men working on the farm got official notices from the army. Eleven of them were being discharged and sent home; eight were being removed to asylums; and three were being removed to other war hospitals. Jennings opened his orders.

Diagnosis: NYDN (S).
Return to the Front.

Chapter 35

PALO ALTO, CALIFORNIA:

M aster Sergeant Jason Bowie, Army Special Forces, retired, never prepared for a mission in such a pastoral setting. The psychiatry offices
at Stanford were not in the main medical center building with its majestic
fountain in front, but were banished to an out-of-the way building a few
hundred yards away. Bowie walked the perimeter of the building, made
convenient by the peaceful Spanish architecture, with arched cloisters
providing passageways, gardens and benches around the entire building.
Bowie thought, *this will be easier than I thought*, as he stood for a moment
outside of Conrad's ground floor office. Several large windows were there,
one propped open for ventilation. Bowie broke-off the latch and pushed
the window shut without latching it.

Chapter 36

EN ROUTE TO THE AIRPORT IN DALLAS:

No sooner had Conrad hung up with Jennifer Roberts at *The Wash-ington Post* than his phone rang. "Please hold for the senator," a voice announced. Conrad had called his old beau last night after his arrest to see if she could pull some strings for him.

"Barb? Fantastic to hear from you. Thanks so much for calling me back. I know how busy you are."

"Anything for an old boyfriend and current campaign donor. Gus, what the hell have you done now?" Senator Benham sighed.

"Long story, but I'm gonna need your help, Barb."

"There's only so much I can do, Gus. I see from the papers you have yourself in another ringer. Maybe the worst one yet. Can't you keep your-self in check? Same old Gus."

"Yeah, but the army has slapped a totally bogus espionage charge on me."

"I assumed it was bogus. However, the army doesn't do that unless somebody really frosts their rear ends. What the hell did you do to them?"

"As you probably know, I released a report on deficiencies in psychi-atric care at Fort Hood. I have every right to release that information be-cause it was from an educational activity accredited by Stanford and the university owns the data, not the government."

"That's not the point, Gus. Your report was inflammatory. I guess

I'm never going to be able to nominate you for a diplomatic post."

"Wait a minute. That's not entirely fair. After I had a meeting with the Army Vice Chief, in which I was critical of mental health care at Fort Hood, the army decided to make the report classified so they could come after me, I think to silence me."

"Sometimes that means it would be a good idea to be silent, Gus."

"You know I can't do that."

Senator Benham gave an audible sigh and continued, "You do have a point, no matter how self-destructively you've decided to make it. Mental health care in the military is a grave concern these days for my committee."

"I knew your heart was in the right place. I'm only trying to help in my own way."

"We all know about the problems of doing things that way. By the way, how're you doing with all this ruckus?"

"As good as could be expected. I have good legal representation."

"That's a start," the senator said.

"But I fear the army is covering up their problems rather than addressing them with a culture change that would equip them to take care of predictable needs of soldiers for the rest of this century."

"Couldn't agree more. The army's leadership is too male, too pale and too frail, if you ask me, and when it comes to PTSD, they see it as a moral deficiency and not a combat wound."

"Psychiatric care is as bad now as it's been for the past century, only now they know how to dress it up for Congress and the press. Current warriors are still stereotypically male, macho, and psychologically resilient. Anybody in combat who's sensitive, female, gay or psychologically traumatized by combat is seen as a coward. That must change but there's no sign of it at this time," Conrad concluded.

"I'll make some calls and see if I can help behind the scenes. Gus, I'll need more proof of army incompetence in the delivery of mental health care for this to break as the scandal that it truly is. If we can corroborate and verify what you say, I even have contacts at *The Washington Post* to blow this wide open, but for now, please do try to stay out of the paper, will you?"

"The papers are actually on my side. Early reports of this make the army look like bullies. Sort of like David and Goliath."

"We all know what Goliath can do to David most of the time, so be careful."

"Yes, ma'am. I mean, yes, Senator Benham," Conrad joked, knowing it was a pet peeve of hers to be called ma'am. "Seriously, I can't thank you enough. I'm going to need your help to get through this."

As the limo pulled right onto the tarmac with no security gauntlet to run at Love Field outside of Dallas, they opened the door of the air-conditioned limo to a blast of heavy, unbearable heat.

"The atmosphere today is awful," Conrad complained. "How do people stand it here?"

"We're so spoiled in Palo Alto," his lawyer Poors responded. "They call it ninety-ninety breath here."

"What?"

"Ninety degrees, ninety percent humidity."

"Lovely. Let's get on the jet where I hope they've already cranked up the air."

The three of them then boarded the leased NetJet for the trip back to Palo Alto.

"Amazing what thirty grand will buy you," said Poors.

"Is that what this cost?" asked Conrad.

"I chartered it to get you out of Dodge as quickly as possible and avoid the press. You can afford it."

Before Conrad could comment, the jet engines spooled up as the pilot released the brakes. Lift-off was achieved faster than a scalded dog running home.

Chapter 37

AT THE FRONT LINES, ON THE SOMME, FRANCE, AUTUMN OF 1916:

It was almost a year since Jennings had seen the trenches and things were worse than ever once he returned to France. Rejoining the 1st Yorkshire, he was instantly miserable as he suddenly found himself in the middle of the bloodiest battle in military history. He simply could not believe he wasn't discharged home with his blighty wound. Another example of life just happening to him and out of his control.

Although Jennings had returned to France in August of 1916, the long battle had already begun in June. Reports were on the first day of the Battle of the Somme, June 24, there were more than 60,000 British casualties, with over 20,000 killed and another 40,000 wounded. It was the worst day in the history of British warfare. And that was just the "first" day.

The Somme offensive continued to rage as it would for almost five months, eventually killing or wounding over 600,000 British soldiers. In the end, the Germans would suffer the same number of casualties. The "butcher" General Douglas Haig, Commander-in-Chief of the British Infantry on the Western Front, was determined to break the two-year stalemate with the Germans. His strategy was now to throw more men at the Germans than the Germans could replace, and win a battle of attrition. The side whose entire population of males was depleted first would be the loser, and Haig decided to bet that in the end the British would prevail, even if it was several hundred thousand to a couple of million dead soldiers later, depending upon whether you counted the projected casualties on both sides.

The Battle of the Somme started with seven days of bombardment—which Jennings had missed. There were an estimated 15,000 British guns amassed along twenty miles of front on the Somme River. The battle had already raged for weeks with Jennings arriving in the middle of this massacre. Since returning to the Front, he and the other soldiers along the Somme had been subjected to several days of continuous shelling. Jennings and his comrades had bravely fought the past several days by going "over the top" and into "no man's land." Those in the trench with him now were among the lucky few to return alive against the odds.

This dreary September morning Jennings was not able to awaken fully and was taken aback as he eventually realized ... *my mind has gone blank*. He didn't go through his morning's preparations but waited in the trench to be rescued. He couldn't concentrate. Fewer and fewer of those who went "over the top" into "no man's land" came back alive at the end of each day's fighting, and the danger of battle was getting to Jennings again. To make matters worse, sustained shelling day and night by the Germans in retaliation to the British shelling was resulting in increasing deaths in the trenches as well, horrific injuries—dismemberments, blast wounds, and blood all mixed with mud and flesh.

"Permission to fall out, sir," Jennings asked as his sergeant walked by in the trench in front of him.

"What the hell for, private? In case you need a lesson in the obvious, it's not exactly a good time for that. We need every able-bodied man we can spare for combat," his sergeant replied.

"Not feeling well, sir," Jennings pleaded.

"Not feeling well? Neither is any other bloke in these damned trenches. Suck it up and quit whining."

More shrieks passed by and then a nearby explosion occurred, just missing the trench where Jennings sat passively.

"Sir, permission to fall out, sir," Jennings persisted.

"Don't tell me you're gonna be a blighter again, Jennings? Didn't you just get back from your holiday at Netley?"

"Can't climb the fire step any more. I need to see the doctor," Jennings tried to explain.

Giving up, the sergeant groaned, "Then get your ass to casualty and be back in time for rations."

"Yes, sir." Jennings, feeling unsteady on his legs but only wobbly and not needing a crutch again, made his way to the dressing station.

Arriving at the medical dressing station, he was greeted by a doctor. "What do you want, soldier?" he asked.

"I just can't fight anymore," Jennings said.

Another mortar hit near Jennings and the doctor, spraying mud and debris but causing no injury.

"Have you been hit? What's the matter?" asked the doctor.

"I'm afraid, sir."

Not another one of these, the doctor sighed. "We have no time for anything but *real physical injuries*. In case you haven't noticed, there's a major offensive going on. Nobody's getting out of battle because of weakness or fear. Don't be a poltroon. Get back to the trenches, soldier."

Jennings left the dressing station but didn't return to his position in the trench. Later that night he was found wandering aimlessly by himself and still at the rear. An officer saw him and ordered, "Get your bloody rear-end back to the trenches."

"I can't stand it there, sir," he said, looking dejected and rudderless.

Jennings was brought to Regimental Sergeant Major Hastings. "Please let me have some rest. I'm still recovering from *shell shock*," Jennings appealed.

Sergeant Major Hastings replied with venomous anger, "You are a fucking coward and you will go to the trenches. I give fuck all for my life and I give fuck all for yours and I'll get you fucking well shot."

Jennings began to move forward but then ducked behind a shed of horses and momentarily out of sight.

Later in the day, Sergeant Major Hastings found Jennings again. "What the sod are you still doing here, private?" Shouting over his shoulder, the Sergeant Major barked, "MacGregor, Stephens, get over here and escort this invertebrate forward."

As MacGregor and Stephens escorted him, one on each side, Jennings felt more and more wobbly. *If I don't get away now, I'll lose control of my legs again*, he thought. Before they had traversed even a hundred yards, Jennings decided to make a run for it. A fracas broke out between Jennings and his escorts, but they let him run away. However, the following morning, Jennings was found in the shed with the horses.

"Private, you're under arrest," Sergeant Major Hastings spat out in contempt.

"Does that mean I can see the doctor now?" asked Jennings hopefully.

"A real jokester, we have here. I give sod all for this gutless milksop. You're going to be charged with showing cowardice in the face of the enemy."

"What about my nerves?"

"Tell that to the Presiding Officer at your court-martial."

"Court-martial? I have *shell shock!*"

Chapter 38

STANFORD MEDICAL CENTER, STANFORD, CALIFORNIA:

After landing near Palo Alto in an unexpected down pour, Conrad went directly to his office. Going through paper work and checking E-mails, he got a call from Libby.

"How're you doing?" she asked. "They're really playing hardball, aren't they?"

"Nothing a couple of $800 an hour lawyers can't fix. I hope. How're you and Adam?"

"Truth be told, I'm more concerned than ever about him." Libby sounded shaky and a bit desperate to Conrad. "Will you see him again and do a formal evaluation? Adam said he really liked you after our dinner. For him to really get better, I think he desperately needs you to give the army your recommendations for treatment. He's getting worse rather than better."

Conrad wondered whether this was a smart thing to do given his *persona non grata* status with army psychiatry, but sensed her urgency. "Adam has a funny way of showing he likes somebody, but if you really want to travel all the way to California from Texas, I can see him tomorrow." Conrad glanced at his watch and continued, "There're flights out of Dallas/Fort Worth that can get you into San Francisco International tonight. If you can book one of those, you guys could be at my office for an 8 A.M. appointment."

"Great!" The tension left her voice as she exhaled in agreement. "As you know, I'm now between contracts for the army, so this is a good time for us to come. Adam's still officially on leave for a couple more days." Her voice then ramped back up in an ominous note. "I have to tell you I'm petrified he's gonna try and commit suicide."

"Did he threaten to harm himself?" Conrad suddenly reached for the crystal candy jar and retrieved a raspberry jawbreaker as he listened.

"Well, actually, no. Other than mentioning it to us over dinner last night when he talked about Papa Geoff." She paused, and Conrad sensed her shame. "Adam's convinced he's tainted by his family heritage and by his diagnosis of PTSD. I thought his visit to England would help him get his head together, but it seems to have made things even worse. I'm sorry now I encouraged him to go."

"Don't lose hope because these things usually get better with treatment. We can talk more tomorrow after you arrive."

"Oh, Gus, that'd be so terrific. I just don't know what to do. I feel I'm slowly losing my only son."

"Okay, I'm here to help. I'd like to see him alone for an hour, and then see the two of you together, so we'll make a two hour appointment."

"I'm counting on you, Gus."

Conrad knew there was more to wanting to help Libby's son than his duty as a doctor.

Chapter 39

LOS ALTOS HILLS, CALIFORNIA:

Late in the afternoon, Special Operator Bowie pulled his fake cable television service van into the stately driveway of an estate where nobody was home, in the countryside of Los Altos Hills, a few miles from the Stanford University campus. Slipping around the back, Bowie cut the security wires, picked the lock to the secluded back door and entered. Finding what he was looking for, he easily cracked the lock to Conrad's gun cabinet, and removed a Glock 9mm handgun. Then he entered Conrad's bedroom, took a bottle of pills out of his pocket and placed it in the night stand next to Conrad's bed. Finally, he left the property in his fake cable van.

So far, so good, said Bowie to himself. *So far, so good.*

Chapter 40

AT THE REAR LINES, ON THE SOMME, FRANCE, AUTUMN OF 1916:

Jennings spent two weeks in a rudimentary stockade at the rear, about a mile from the trenches. One morning, without notice, he was pulled from his cell by two armed guards who dragged him to a court-martial proceeding in another part of the building. As Jennings entered the courtroom, he saw four soldiers at the prosecution table ready to give evidence against him. All four of them took part in the attack against the Germans the day after Jennings went "off the rails" again. All four of them survived without injury despite their battalion losing 150 out of its 600 men. All four of them had friends who didn't survive. It was common knowledge on the night Jennings became afraid, their battalion was to go into action the following dawn, as indeed it did. And it was common knowledge it would be costly, as indeed it was. Refusal to go to the trenches that night meant sending his comrades into battle while saving his own skin.

Across the aisle from the witnesses against him and the prosecution table was an empty defense table. There was no "prisoner's friend" at the defense table to represent him. Jennings knew this meant he was to speak in his own defense. He had no witnesses to testify on his behalf, given the gravity of the situation on the battlefield and how his colleagues all felt about him abandoning his post. Also, there were no psychiatrists or doctors there to testify about his condition or any mitigating circumstances. When the needs of the army conflicted with the needs of a patient,

Jennings had learned a long time ago there was no doubt on whose side the medical officer was going to be.

The President of the Court—an army colonel—entered the courtroom, took his seat, and shouted "at ease" as he rapped his gavel on the huge desk in front of him. After all were seated, he snarled, "Private Jennings, you're accused of contravening section 4 (7) of the Army Act—showing cowardice in the face of the enemy."

Jennings blinked hard over eyes nearly popping out of their sockets.

"Do you have an opening statement?" the President of the Court continued.

Jennings swallowed hard as he turned his hands into tight fists. He looked over at the blustery old army colonel with the gavel and then back to the prosecution table where several witnesses were obviously lined up against him. Jennings hated speaking to a group, and despite the butterflies in his stomach, decided it would be a good idea to explain his situation the best he could.

"I joined the British Army in 1911. I was very proud to become a soldier because it was something I had wanted to do for a long time. To be honest with you, I was only sixteen then. They should have never allowed me to join the army, but I pretended to be eighteen, and they wanted to believe me—so I became a soldier. I've always enjoyed serving my country."

Those in the room focused on Jennings with a look of disgust on their faces.

"In 1914, the war with Germany began and I was sent to France in November of that year. I fought with pride of country alongside my comrades from the 1st Yorkshire for many months. However, in the autumn of 1915, I had to leave the trenches because I was suffering from *shell shock*. I didn't go back to the trenches for several months, because my nerves were so bad. I've had a relapse since getting back to France as well."

The President of the Court, acknowledging Jennings' statement said, "Thank you, Private Jennings. Now, Sergeant Major Hastings, what can you tell us about the events in question here?"

A tall, good looking man in his mid-30s stood. Jennings cringed when he saw Hastings. That was the man who said he gave "fuck all" for him. Jennings was sure he would be bad news for him now.

Sergeant Major Hastings then proceeded with "Yes, sir. On the 17th of September, 1916, at 9 A.M., I saw Private Simon Jennings turn up. He said he was feeling sick and he had not stayed with his company when they had returned to the trenches the previous evening. I told Private Jennings to report sick, but he returned later saying the doctor had refused him an examination because he wasn't wounded. At about 8 P.M., I sent Private Jennings with a ration party going up to the frontline. By the time the ration party had returned, Private Jennings was missing again."

"Do you have anything to add, private?" asked the President of the Court.

"He's right," Jennings said, reassured that so far Hastings' testimony against him didn't seem to be too damning. "At about 1 P.M. the sergeant saw me standing near a fire. He asked me what I was doing standing there. I told him I couldn't take it anymore. The sergeant asked me 'what did I mean?' Once again I said, I couldn't take it anymore. He swore at me and called me a coward."

"May I respond, your honor?" asked Sergeant Hastings.

The judge nodded yes as Jennings braced himself for some damning testimony. "Certainly. Go ahead."

"I didn't know what he was talking about," Hastings added. "I told him he'd have to go to the trenches that night. He told me he wouldn't go."

"Is that so, private?" asked the President of the Court.

"Some soldiers tried to drag me towards the trenches," Jennings answered. "I screamed and struggled with them. I was desperate not to go to the trenches because I was very much afraid. I said I was sick enough as it was. If the soldiers had left me alone, I would have gone up to the trenches on my own accord."

"If I may, sir, that's a bit of a stretch," interjected Sergeant Hastings. "I had no choice but to put Private Jennings under arrest."

"Thank you, Sergeant Hastings," the President of the Court said. "Now, Sergeant Andrews, I understand you're Private Jennings' platoon leader at the Front. What can you add?"

Andrews stood as Hastings sat. Jennings felt Andrews would be a sympathetic witness towards him. Jennings thought Hastings even liked him and had acted sympathetic to his *shell shock*. "Sir, Jennings had reported sick with nerves soon after he returned to the trenches, about a week after he got to France. He'd been kept back by the doctors for two weeks then. He'd reported sick again with bad nerves about a week before the incident in question. Then he just 'lost the plot' again on the night in question."

"You mean, Jennings went 'off the rails,' became confused, acted crazy? Private MacGregor, do you have anything to add?" asked the President of the Court.

Jennings didn't think things were going too badly so far and now MacGregor stood to testify. Jennings and MacGregor both knew MacGregor was just a pawn in this whole thing and he probably wouldn't say anything.

"No, sir. I was just Private Jennings' escort. I agree with everything that's been said here," MacGregor answered nervously.

"Lieutenant Jones," the President of the Court continued. "I believe you're the commanding officer here. What's your statement?"

Now this could be my turning point, Jennings thought with the first real hope he'd felt since the beginning of these proceedings. *Lieutenant Jones likes me and he has the highest rank here. I'm sure this'll be good for my case.*

"Yes, sir. Simon Jennings joined the regiment and was sent down with *shell shock* in September of 1915. I can't say what's destroyed this man's nerves, but he's proved himself incapable of keeping his head in action and is likely to cause a panic. Apart from his behavior under fire, his conduct and character are quite good," Lieutenant Jones said.

The President of the Court then asked, "Private Jennings, you seem to have developed the bad habit of reporting sick ever since you joined His Majesty King George's Army. Did you have the opportunity to report sick yet again between the night of the offense and now?"

"Yes, sir. But I didn't."

"And why not, I must ask, when you report sick so often and so many other times?"

"Because being away from the shell fire, I felt better."

"What? That's a preposterous excuse. Everybody feels better away from the shell fire."

"But I have a history of *shell shock*," Jennings pleaded.

"Yes, I've heard all about that. You should listen to Lord Gort, VC, who informed our command that *shell shock* is really a regrettable weakness and not found in good units. The Parliamentary Commission back in the U.K., concluded recently that good soldiers, properly led, with good morale and good training, should not break down. All we know about this *shell shock* nonsense is it is also contagious and hence a threat to fighting spirit. Young man, this isn't mere scrimshanking you've done—you're not

here merely for breaking the rules this time so you could get better treatment like you've done in the past. No, this time it's cowardice. You've let
your mates down and left them all in danger. *Shell shock* is your disreputable
excuse. You should be ashamed to try to use that convenient medical label
for yourself to avoid your duties." The President of the Court then looked
down at the papers in front of him in disgust. "Enough of this. I've made
my decision."

Taking this as a cue, the sergeant-at-arms for the court shouted, "All
rise. Attennn-shun."

Glaring at Private Jennings, the President of the Court began, "Since
these events of a fortnight ago took place 'in the face of the enemy,' I find
you guilty of violating section 4 (7) of the Army Act, failing to take your
place in the frontline when so ordered and showing cowardice in the face
of the enemy."

The prosecution witnesses all smiled and nodded in agreement.

"I have also determined your punishment," the President of the Court
continued ominously.

The room fell silent. Those in the room focused on Jennings, then
the President of the Court.

"You're hereby sentenced to death by execution."

Gasps were heard about the room from some as Jennings sank to his
chair and sat there in stunned silence. He didn't know what to think, but
here again, as seemed to be the pattern for his entire life, events happened
to him rather than him making events happen. As his foggy mind began to
clear and he started to re-enter the here-and-now, he suddenly realized it
had taken only twenty minutes for his court-martial to find him guilty of
cowardice and give him the death penalty. He had originally thought he
would be sent back to a hospital, but now he faced execution. *Could the
verdict actually be true?* he questioned himself in silence.

Slowly, a more optimistic notion bubbled into his blank head and
then into his consciousness. Jennings realized there was hope as he tried to
comfort himself with the knowledge he was in fact unlikely to be executed. Everyone knew almost all the death sentences from a court-martial
were commuted by the commanding general once the soldier had been
made into an example. So, all he could do now was to wait and hope. In
any event, no execution could take place until it had been confirmed by
General Haig and in nine out of ten occasions he commuted any death
sentence coming to his desk.

Chapter 41

AIRBORNE EN ROUTE TO LONDON HEATHROW:

Airborne after a hard day at the Pentagon, Rossi and Richards sat next to each other in business class for the trip from Dulles Airport in Washington, D.C., to London Heathrow Airport.

"You looking forward to the conference?" Rossi asked Richards.

"I certainly need to get away. We also can use the trip to Madingley to talk to our allies about the increasing threats being leveled against the army in the form of criticism of psychiatry. And get some suggestions about what they think we should do about it," Richards responded.

"Everywhere we turn, someone wants to expose our covert operations. We need to protect the army. Psychiatry is its soft underbelly," Rossi said matter-of-factly.

"Agreed. We also need to go through the list of recent operations and anything in progress."

"Okay, and once that's done, we can talk about how to use the Patrons strategically. We need to use them to help us eliminate the threat of turning PTSD into some bullshit form of heroism."

"Yep. Now, let's get some shuteye. I hate flying civilian. Damned budget cuts. We land at about ten in the morning local time. After we take a cab to Madingley, check in and get an early dinner, I think we'll be shattered and need to make an early night of it. The conference starts at 9:30 Thursday morning. See you when we land. Tell the flight attendant I'm skipping dinner."

With that, Richards pushed the button to make her seat lie flat, unwrapped her blanket covered in a plastic wrap, fluffed her pillow and was out like a light.

Rossi gave her one last look then faded off himself.

Chapter 42

"General Haig, some paperwork for you to sign," announced the general's adjutant, handing over a sheaf of papers as he walked into the general's office in British expeditionary headquarters at the rear lines in France.

"What's it now?" General Haig asked while exhaling in frustration and not giving his adjutant the courtesy of eye contact. Haig was a powerfully built, balding man who projected arrogance and self-importance. He was aware he was a man of great influence and wielded it like the rapier of an 18th century European count.

"An execution order to sign," answered the adjutant.

"What, more cowards?"

"I'm afraid so, sir. I don't think we can let this one go. Given the situation on the Somme right now, we really can't afford any quitters getting off scot-free. My recommendation is we make an example of this one to prevent fear from infecting the entire corps."

Jennings didn't know it, but he chose possibly the worst day in the war to expect the general to commute any sentence. He'd also chosen the wrong battle for his *shell shock* to return, namely one of the most horrible battles of the Somme offensive. The day Jennings could stand it no longer was the Battle of Flers-Courcelette.

Jennings' West Yorks were due to join this battle the following morning as part of the 6th Division's assault against the notorious fortified German position known as the "Quadrilateral." He and the West Yorks had been moving through what was known as "Chimpanzee Valley" where his unit was forming up for an assault against the Germans. It was a particularly unpleasant location because of the proximity to the British artillery laying down the barrage for the attack the following day. It was the British guns, and not the German guns, that so disturbed Jennings and brought back his *shell shock*.

General Haig thought for a moment and responded to his adjutant. "Good point," he said, nodding his head in agreement. "We're losing men as fast as we can bring in new recruits across the Channel. I know we'll prevail, but I don't know how long we can continue to withstand the strain of the Western Front if we allow shirkers to go unpunished. The Frogs are already deserting like rats. Italian morale has collapsed at Caporetto. The Russians are disintegrating and losing discipline. Alas, most of our regular army is now dead or injured. Those men were the great and noble 'Old Contemptibles' of the regular army who were in service before this horrible war started," General Haig said nostalgically.

"Actually, the one sentenced to be executed is one of our regulars," replied the adjutant.

"Yeee-gods, man, he's supposed to provide an example for our detestable citizen army," said the general, wincing noticeably.

"Ah, all we now have is a beggarly 'Kitchener Army' of miserable conscripts. Not fit to be soldiers, but if they can stand upright and carry a rifle, they're fit to feed the beast in no man's land until we wipe out the Jerries," said the adjutant.

"Bollocks. We're going to have to make them into a real army if we're to win this war. There's no way we can afford any reduction in morale. We must stop once and for all this *shell shock* nonsense. It's causing too many of our soldiers to be derelict in their duties and get away with it. We're potentially on the verge of a catastrophic collapse or mutiny just like those of our allies and our enemies. So, let's teach our boys a lesson. If patriotism, sense of duty, leadership and local *esprit de corps* aren't working on their own, never hurts to use a bit of the *stick* as well. Has General Cavan of the GOC 4th division reviewed this yet?"

"As a matter of fact he has. See that message on the top of your papers?" the adjutant pointed out.

The General read it aloud:

"The charge of 'cowardice' seems to be clearly proved and the Sgt. Major's opinion of the man is definitely bad to say the least of it. The GOC 6th div informs me that the men know Jennings is no good. I therefore recommend that the sentence in this case be carried out."

"Well, I guess that seals it for the old boy. Give me that pen." With that, Haig signed the order in front of him:

Execution by firing squad. To be shot at dawn.

WEDNESDAY

Chapter 43

WASHINGTON, D.C.:

Jennifer Roberts was clacking out a draft of her column for Friday morning's *Washington Post* as a follow-up to her past investigation a few years ago regarding the second Fort Hood shooting and the continuing controversy about psychiatric care in the army.

"You should get a quieter keyboard, Jennifer," her assistant Bert joked as he sat down on a stack of file boxes in her cubicle next to her desk. "Always sounds like you're making popcorn in here."

Without missing a beat and without taking her eyes off the monitor, Jennifer responded, "Whatcha got for me, Bert?"

"Some follow-up on that Pentagon psychiatrist Colonel Richards and her brother."

"Great. Whatcha find out?" Jennifer asked taking her attention away from the monitor, and directing it instead to her smartphone to check her texts and E-mails, all the while never making eye contact with Bert.

"Lieutenant Colonel Ellen Richards, graduate of Useless U and got specialty training in psychiatry at Walter Reed," Bert began.

"Ah, yes, Uniformed Services University of Health Science or USUHS, not useless. The army's medical school," Jennifer said while thumbing a text response on her phone.

"Whatever," Bert said, rolling his eyes. "After psychiatry training, she was embedded in Iraq as a psychiatrist and after deployment, she served at Fort Hood as chief of psychiatry there. Then a faculty position at Useless U in Washington, D.C., came her way, and at the same time was at Walter Reed Hospital, where she supervised the first Fort Hood shooter Major Nidal Hasan. Remember, he was in training there as a psychiatrist."

"Ouch. That should've been a career-ender," Jennifer said, finally looking up at Bert.

"Didn't turn out that way. After Walter Reed, Richards went on to the Pentagon and then has had a rapid ascent to the head of army psychiatry and a lieutenant bird rank."

"What's her claim to fame?"

"Dunno. Seems she's good at worming her way into great assignments. Good politician. Smart enough to hire Conrad to try and dress up army psychiatry to the outside world."

"Still, seems like the first Fort Hood shooting should have derailed her career. Maybe we're missing something, Bert."

"You're right. I think she's probably been sleeping her way to the top."

"Careful there, Bert. Just because a woman gets to the top rapidly doesn't mean she's a tramp, you male chauvinist pig," Jennifer said, throwing her pen at him.

"Incoming," Bert shouted, using his arms to feign protection of his head. "But the current head of psychiatry training at Walter Reed told me he thought Colonel Richards had an inappropriate relationship with her married supervisor who was head of psychiatry training at Walter Reed at the time."

"Whatever."

"But he also told me to check out rumors that Richards spent a lot of time travelling with the former Surgeon General of the U.S. Army, who appointed her to her current position."

"Your contact at Walter Reed is probably just jealous of her. You guys are all the same," remarked Jennifer.

"Could be. But put those two stories together with the message on your recorder from the brother claiming she now has an inappropriate relationship with her current married supervisor at the Pentagon, and you begin to wonder if there's a pattern here."

"Who's her married supervisor?"

"A guy by the name of Andreas Rossi, a brigadier general and now head of the Army's Military Intelligence Corps."

"Wow. Head of Army Intelligence?"

"Yep. And one helluva dickhead."

"Whoa, what do you mean by that?"

"West Point grad. Gung ho to the extreme, narcissistic, grandiose sense of self-importance, and loyal to the army to a fault. Don't cross him or the army or he'll bear a grudge against you for a lifetime and will attack you and ruin your career according to past associates I've interviewed. He's preoccupied with doubts about the loyalty of soldiers around him and constantly purging his command of subordinates he suspects are attacking his reputation. Mostly, he has wildly exaggerated responses to perceived threats that are all in his head. A real paranoid about anybody who doesn't blindly support the army," Bert said, as if he knew the man personally.

"What's his relationship with Colonel Richards?"

"Male chauvinist pig, rumored to be exploiting her for sex, apparently in exchange for rapidly moving her through the ranks, most recently promoting her to one of the youngest lieutenant colonels in the army, now assigned to the office of the Vice Chief of the Army as head of all army psychiatry."

"Lovely man," Jennifer said sarcastically. "What about the brother?" she asked, looking intently again at her monitor as her fingers danced atop the familiar keyboard in front of her.

"There's an older brother. An Iraq war veteran with four deployments who got PTSD and was hospitalized with acute mania, then discharged from the army. Supposedly homeless now."

"Tragic," Jennifer mused out loud but without looking up at Bert. "And what an irony. The head of army psychiatry has a brother with psychiatric problems. What's his name?"

"Jordan Davis."

"Davis?" Jennifer continued, keyboard erupting in chatter.

"Yeah, Richards is her married name, Davis her maiden name."

"So that means she has a husband."

"Ex-husband."

"Can you check him out?"

"I'm already on it, boss," Bert smiled. "She was married for something like twenty minutes. I've got some calls in, and I'll get back to you when I have more details."

Jennifer was beginning to get a horrible feeling. For once, pausing her relentless typing, she thought to herself, *this Ellen Richards and Andreas Rossi are turning out to be real pieces of work. They're beginning to look like one helluva diabolical team.*

Chapter 44

STANFORD MEDICAL CENTER, STANFORD, CALIFORNIA:

Having taken the late flight from Dallas/Fort Worth to San Francisco International Airport last night, Adam and his mother Libby arrived bright and early for their 8 A.M appointment at Stanford Medical Center, and pulled their rental car into the visitors' parking lot. The psychiatry clinic was on the edge of the beautiful, palm-tree lined campus of Stanford University—a world-class school of higher learning founded by the railroad baron and U.S. Senator, Leland Stanford. The sun was shining as it always did in Palo Alto, with a splendid 72 degrees, no wind and low humidity.

"No wonder people like living here," Libby said to Adam as they walked into the psychiatry clinic to meet Dr. Conrad. "The weather is perfect."

"Maybe the army should ship all of us misfits here so we can be cured by fresh air and sunshine," Adam groused.

"More importantly, let me remind you that you're about to see one of the world's premier psychiatrists. You've met him and know he's a good guy as well."

"And doesn't work for the army. Maybe I'll finally find somebody who's working for me."

"Point well-taken," his mother said.

After registering in reception and taking seats in the waiting area, one of the assistants at reception came over to them. "Adam Warburton? To see Dr. Conrad? Come right this way. Just Adam at first. Dr. Conrad will come to get you for the second hour, Mrs. Warburton."

"It's Libby. I'll be right here waiting," she said and then pulled out the current issue of *Martha Stewart Living* and began leafing through it while she waited.

Entering Dr. Conrad's office after a long walk down a well-lighted hallway, Adam saw Conrad sitting behind a huge wooden desk. As Conrad stood to greet him, they shook hands and Conrad said, "Have a seat, Adam," and motioned to an overstuffed chair facing the desk. "I'm so glad you could come and see me today."

"Thanks, doc. Same here."

"A bit different setting than our first meeting at Lester's in Killeen. Reminds me. Want a cup of coffee? Sorry, but it won't be the world's biggest cup here."

Adam smiled and relaxed. "No thanks. Already got tanked up on caffeine on the drive over here."

"So, your mom asked me to look into your case and see if I could help. She tells me you're getting pretty desperate. Is that true?"

"There's part of me that wants to get better, but I'm so discouraged I mostly feel like quitting."

Conrad cringed with Adam's use of the word "quitting," and knew he had to approach delicately the ultimate question, namely suicide. Laying the ground for that, Conrad continued the interview and eventually got to the heart of the matter. "So, Adam, it's clear your PTSD symptoms have been a huge burden for you and you feel guilty about not being back on deployment with your buddies. All of us, your mother included, have tried to reassure you these symptoms are not your fault and with time and treatment, you'll begin to get better."

"I know you and Mom have been trying to sell me on that way of thinking, but it's just not the way a soldier thinks. I feel weak and worthless. Despite trying to get better for months now, I see no progress. So, I'm losing hope."

"But Adam, you haven't really been getting adequate treatment. It's still very possible you could get much better with the proper treatment."

"Maybe, but in case you forgot, not all of you shrinks are trying to help me. My own army psychiatrist, Major Benson, is more concerned with that damned Medallion I got from Papa Geoff in England than he is with my PTSD. He's shown me no respect and doesn't keep my matters confidential, spilling what I tell him in our sessions to others in the army. Can't trust the bastard, so I'm not going back to him."

"I don't blame you. Did you tell your mother that Major Benson was betraying your privacy?"

"For sure and boy was she pissed. I even told Victoria in Cambridge. She couldn't believe my shrink ratted me out to authorities about that damned Medallion—my albatross. Wish I'd never seen it. I guess you get what you pay for. Free care in the army is worthless."

"Adam, there are some difficult issues in play here. I need to ask, do you ever get so discouraged that you think of killing yourself?"

"Not really."

"Do you have a plan to end your life?"

"Wish I was just dead."

"Can you make a promise to yourself that you won't do anything to harm yourself for at least a few more months so some new treatment might have the chance to start working?"

"That all depends on my crotch rocket."

"What?"

"You know, my souped-up high-speed motorcycle. The man's way of dying."

"Just exactly what do you mean by that?"

"Well, lots of us losers in the Warrior Transition Unit have one of these beautiful machines and driving fast reminds us of the thrill we got in combat, and makes us forget about our problems for a while."

"Sounds dangerous."

"That's the whole point of it. Some of us want the glory of death by crotch rocket."

"What?" Conrad asked, dumbfounded.

"You know. Drink to dull the pain, then lose the helmet, rev' it to a thousand miles an hour on the highway at night—you know how fast those babies can go?—and see what happens. If you come back home, it wasn't your time yet. Not really suicide, just fate."

"Adam, that's what we call thoughts of suicide, or 'suicidal ideation.' It's serious. Tempting fate is an indirect form of committing suicide. I'm amazed that you're not on an antidepressant, so I'm gonna prescribe one for you. I want you to see somebody daily for the next few days, then weekly for the indefinite future. If you're in town, I'll see you myself. If you're going back to Fort Hood, I'll arrange for somebody in the private sector to see you off base in Killeen."

"Who's gonna pay for this? Not the army."

"I'm not charging you and I'm gonna pay for your meds and therapy for a while. Let's just call it my donation to the wounded warriors cause."

"Now I'm a charity case."

"How about we make a deal?"

"What's that?"

"You take an oath to yourself, to me and to your mother, not to do anything dangerous with motorcycles or your handgun that could potentially lead to your death. Stop drinking and see these professionals, and I'll make sure you get therapy, have a safe sleeping pill and an antidepressant that'll help your pain. Deal?"

"You're an all right guy, doc." Adam had tears in his eyes. "Thanks ... if you're willing to invest in me maybe there's hope."

"I knew you'd get it, Adam," Conrad replied with his own emotions catching in his throat. "Now how about I go and get your mom and we fill her in on our plan?"

"Sure."

"Just stay here. I'll fetch her from the waiting area and be right back."

When Conrad finished his hour with Adam, he left his office to retrieve Libby from the waiting room to join them, but halfway down the hall he heard a single "pop" behind him. Startled clinic staff turned to stare down the hall in the direction where the sound came from as Conrad rushed back to his office to find Adam slumped over in his chair, blood trickling from his mouth and from the side of his head. A handgun lay on the floor. *Obviously dropped from his outstretched right hand,* Conrad reasoned. His body was slumped forward from the waist, looking like a marionette puppet no longer supported by its strings.

"No! No! No!" Conrad shouted. "Code blue! Code blue! Code blue!"

The hospital staff wheeled in the crash cart with defibrillator. Conrad initiated advanced CPR as Libby raced into the room and had to be restrained. A half-hour later, Adam was officially pronounced dead on the floor of Conrad's office.

Emotionally, as well as physically depleted from the desperate administration of CPR, Conrad turned to comfort Libby, but she wasn't there and Conrad realized she must be outside in the hallway waiting to see what had happened. Conrad suddenly noted the swaying of the blinds from a breeze entering the ground floor window of his office. *I don't remember opening the window this morning,* he said to himself.

Looking for the first time beyond the lifeless body of Adam, with tubes everywhere, expended syringes strewn on the floor and beeping sounds all about, Conrad was taken aback as he recognized the handgun on the floor as one of his own. A horrific sinking feeling descended upon him as it dawned on him, *that's the gun that was missing after the break-in at my home yesterday. Suppose that's how Adam got it?*

Unable to move away from the scene, he took a jawbreaker candy out of his pocket and slowly put it in his mouth.

Chapter 45

IN THE FOREST AT THE REAR LINES, NEAR CARNOY, FRANCE, OCTOBER 6, 1916:

It was always cold just before dawn. But it was chilling to the bone when you pulled duty on the firing squad. A sense of foreboding descended upon Lieutenant Nigel Warburton, tormenting his sleep and violating any chance of last minute slumber before he had to get up. Seemed like the middle of the night, but dawn was less than an hour away. Giving up on finding any composure, he finally decided to get out of bed early. As he stretched and grabbed for his uniform, Lieutenant Warburton, an officer in the British Expeditionary Force stationed on the Western Front, wondered who the idiot was who started the tradition of executions at dawn. He strapped on his officer's sidearm thinking, *I hope I don't have to use this*.

Tall and lean, with an officer's proud bearing, Lieutenant Warburton joined the army before the outbreak of the Great War, continuing a long tradition of military service in his family. From the "officer class," Warburton was the third of three brothers, the eldest of whom would inherit the responsibilities for managing their family estate in Hertfordshire, and the middle of whom was predictably and according to tradition, an Anglican priest. It fell to the third son to make his career in the military, as upper-class sons had done for centuries. The three of them had enjoyed a privileged upbringing, and were part of the landed gentry—the riding, shooting, hunting, polo-playing class. Lieutenant Warburton had attended the elite Royal Military Academy Sandhurst—the British "West Point"—prior to getting his commission before the outbreak of the war in France. Married for two years now, he had a baby boy back home in Hertfordshire waiting for him with his wife and extended family.

Down the hall, Warburton could hear his twelve riflemen stirring. Evidently, they couldn't sleep either. *How'd we all get assigned this miserable duty?* Although it was still dark, he thought to himself, *might as well get on with it.*

"Jones, go get the prisoner," Lieutenant Warburton barked. The tension of anticipation eased a bit within him once the action had been initiated. However, the idea of shooting one of your own seemed unnatural and certainly not right.

There were lots of threats of execution, but this one was really going to happen. Executing deserters was a longstanding military practice for centuries, but executing cowards with *shell shock*? *My first, ... and hopefully my last,* Lieutenant Warburton reflected to himself. He was ambivalent as to whether today's orders were a good idea or even fair, but he was a loyal soldier and intent upon following orders, not analyzing them. Military tradition had the officer in charge loading the guns and not the shooters, with one of the twelve sharpshooters firing a blank so everyone shooting had some doubt whether they were the one delivering the *kill shot*. Lieutenant Warburton had completed this task last night before trying to get some sleep.

Convicted soldier, twenty-two-year-old Private Simon Jennings of the 1st Battalion, West Yorkshire Regiment, appeared in shackles as his platoon leader escorted him indelicately outside the barracks. An Anglican priest was present, along with the platoon leader and a second sergeant, all three acting as escorts of the prisoner, and the dozen shooters. "Fall in," the platoon leader shouted.

The men grabbed their rifles and scrambled into formation. "All present and accounted for, sir," the platoon leader offered with a crisp salute.

Warburton returned his salute and noted the gloom all around, the lifting bank of fog, and the forlorn bare trees in the direction they were to head.

He then barked, "Right shoulder. Arms!" Slap, slap, the sound of hands on rifles retorted.

"Left face." Stomp, stomp.

The squad's movements further violated the somber quiet.

"Permission to speak, sir," Jennings interrupted unexpectedly.

Surprised, Lieutenant Warburton decided to allow it. "Go ahead soldier."

"Request a second jacket, sir."

"What? You want to be comfortable before your execution?" asked Lieutenant Warburton quizzically.

"No, sir. I don't want to shiver in the cold, and have it be mistaken for cowardice."

It was a somber moment just before dawn, with a chill in the air, and Lieutenant Warburton and his riflemen felt it as well, compounded by the beastly task they were about to perform. Still, Warburton was dumbfounded by this odd request, but responded, "MacDonald, get this man a second jacket." At just that moment, Lieutenant Warburton felt a sudden bond with the slight man, more of a boy actually, who looked back at him with sincere eyes. Warburton was sure that Jennings must have reciprocated the bond. In other circumstances, their roles might easily have been reversed. Jennings was not so much pleading with his eyes, but showing understanding, even forgiveness for the horrible act his fellow soldiers were about to commit against him. *A bigger man than I,* Warburton thought to himself with a shudder he knew that no amount of clothing could suppress. Once the second jacket was in place on Jennings, he continued, "Forward, march."

The formation marched Jennings about one-hundred yards into the nearby forest. In front of a massive oak tree now lit by the early dawn sunrise, Lieutenant Warburton growled, "Halt." After a pause, he shouted, "Prepare the prisoner for execution." Standing in the breaking sunlight, he noticed that despite the current bleak briskness of dawn, it promised to become a fine autumn day, at least for everyone but Jennings.

The platoon leader and second sergeant tied Jennings to an immense old-growth oak tree, encircling his upper body with ties so he wouldn't collapse to the ground after execution. His lower legs were bound so he couldn't move until the execution was completed. Meanwhile, the priest was muttering reassurance and reciting prayers but Jennings seemed to ignore him. "Have you anything to say, soldier? Any last request?" asked Lieutenant Warburton.

"Yes, sir. No blindfold, please."

"No blindfold? You want to see this happen?"

"Yes, sir. I want to look the firing squad in the eye when they do this.

I'm a proud soldier, not a shirker."

Jennings looked at Lieutenant Warburton with his sincere eyes and Warburton thought he saw deep into the young man's soul for a moment and found no coward there, but an injured waif he was about to brutally destroy. Lieutenant Warburton took a deep breath, finally was able to pull his eyes away from Jennings and then told the men preparing him, "No blindfold." As the men stepped away, he pursued the task at hand. "Right Face." Stomp, stomp. "Order arms." Slap, whack. "Ready. Aim."

Jennings looked calm, proud, and even defiant. He caught Warburton's eyes with his final forgiving gaze, this time Warburton thinking that Jennings was looking into his own dark soul, trying to tell Warburton that it was okay what was happening here and not to be upset. Appearing little older than a boy, the slight figure standing against the oak tree stared at his executioners with a demeanor that could only be described as *brave*.

"... fire!"

A splintering burst of gunfire punctured the quiet of the dawn and delivered the verdict to Jennings.

"Order arms," Lieutenant Warburton commanded, as smoke from the barrels of eleven guilty rifles plus one exonerated weapon wafted upward in dreary silence. To the shock of all, they could see that Jennings was still alive. Several guns had missed him entirely at point blank range, and Jennings only showed nonfatal wounds in his left thigh and right shoulder. *Unbelievable,* he thought. *Nobody fired a kill shot? They all missed landing one?* With a wave of anguish overtaking him, Lieutenant Warburton knew immediately what he had to do.

Chapter 46

Conrad slowly exited his office as Libby tried to enter. He grabbed her softly and pulled her towards him in a hug and whispered, "He's gone, Libby, he's gone."

Libby wailed with her face into Conrad's chest, "No. Oh my God, no, no!"

Breaking away, she tried to enter his office to see her son, but Conrad drew her gently back into his arms. "You don't want to see him like this. Later. Let the authorities do what they have to do."

Oh, no, Conrad thought. He suddenly realized he was covered in blood and making a mess on Libby's clothes as he hugged her. Then it happened. The sight of blood triggered it. All of a sudden, Conrad heard the screech of tires, explosion of glass, grating of metal, while smelling noxious gas and flaming rubber. *Here we go again,* he thought as the flashback gripped him for the millionth time, tearing apart the fabric of his body while terror seared his guts. Waiting for it to pass, it ended like it always did with deafening silence and the devastating sense of loss of both his wife and daughter as though it had just happened. Willing himself back to the present as he always did as these things passed, he quickly shut himself down emotionally, feeling numb. *There will be nightmares tonight,* he thought.

Collecting his wits, but feeling a bit detached from the reality of the moment, Conrad abruptly noticed that the chief of campus security, Don Armstrong, a longtime acquaintance of Conrad's, came over and put a big beefy hand of support on his shoulder. Libby slumped into a chair against the wall in the hallway outside of Conrad's office, sobbing uncontrollably to herself. Meanwhile, Conrad stared painfully through the open door into his office at the shocking scene. "Sorry about this, doc," Armstrong said. A tough cop who handled Stanford University Medical Center affairs with tact and good taste, he had worked with Conrad over the years on various security matters and they had mutual respect for each other.

Conrad nodded but said nothing.

"I already called Santa Clara County Coroner and Palo Alto P.D. Should be here momentarily," said the chief.

"Of course. Routine for a suicide. Guess I'll clean up from the CPR and be right back." A few minutes later Conrad emerged wearing surgical scrubs and a fresh white coat and sat down at his desk in his office, head in his hands.

Blasting through the door of Conrad's office, Detective Jack Monday, Palo Alto P.D., barked, "What're you doing sitting there? Get the hell out of my crime scene. I need to talk to you outside." Monday was a seasoned officer, twenty-year veteran of Palo Alto P.D. A toothpick protruded from one side of his mouth, and he was wearing a cheap suit, showing a badge flopping out of his belt, and a bulge under one arm where his gun obviously rested.

Conrad looked up quizzically, "Crime scene? This is my office."

"Out! It belongs to me now."

Conrad sheepishly left his office. *What an asshole,* he thought. *Just because there's a crisis doesn't mean you have to be a jerk about it.*

"You're presumably Dr. Conrad?" asked Detective Monday.

Conrad nodded yes.

"This your office and your patient? What can you tell me about your visit with him today?"

"I guess there's no need for confidentiality now," he said as he looked down at Adam's lifeless body. "Truth is, he was thinking about suicide but told me he had no plan and no intent of acting on it now. I certainly had no idea he was going to do something this desperate today and just as soon as my back was turned. After meeting with him for an hour, I'd just left him for a minute while I went to get his mother from the waiting area to join us. That's when he shot himself—a complete tragedy. My fault for not recognizing how close he was to doing this and for leaving him alone."

"That's all for now, doc. But don't leave town. I'm gonna need you to come down to the station for a formal interview as soon as I get some more information here. Oh, one more thing. Any suicide note?"

"I didn't see one," Conrad answered.

The detective walked up to Libby, who was sitting on a padded bench in the hallway outside Conrad's office, sobbing softly but inconsolably. "I understand you're the mother? Sorry for your loss. Were you aware he was thinking of killing himself?"

Struggling to gain her composure, Libby said, "Truth be told, yes. In fact, that's why I brought Adam here, because I was worried something just like this would happen. He was so upset having gotten PTSD in Iraq. He felt like he was a coward, especially after being put into the Wounded Warrior Brigade labeling him as mentally ill. I think he felt he had no other option."

"So he's active duty?"

"Yes." She hesitated, then revised her answer and sadly said, "Was."

"We'll have to get Army Criminal Investigation Command involved."

Libby looked at him quizzically. "Why? Is this a crime?" asked Libby now in a firm voice without any signs of crying.
"Just routine until we have an official cause of death. You just flew here from Fort Hood?"

"Yesterday."

"How'd he get a gun? Did he pack it in his luggage?"

"I've no idea."

"If you feel up to it, I'd like you to come to the police station as soon as army investigators are finished here."

Libby was stunned but replied automatically, "Sure," not realizing she faced a confrontation, not an interview.

Chapter 47

YORKSHIRE, ENGLAND, OCTOBER OF 1916:

Sarah Jennings was having a cuppa tea in her cozy kitchen on a crisp autumn day in her modest home. Her infant daughter Gertie played at her feet as she opened the day's post, a letter from the War Office. Sarah slumped to her knees in disbelief as soon as she read the letter.

> *Dear Madam:*
> *We regret to inform you that your husband has died.*
> *He was sentenced for cowardice and shot at dawn on*
> *16th October.*

What? This can't be true. I just saw Simon a month ago. He told me he was coming home. I didn't even know they'd sent him back to France.

Sarah turned the letter over. Nothing there. *That's all it says?* she asked herself.

Gertie looked up at her mum sitting on the floor next to her wondering what was wrong as she saw her break into tears and hide her face in her hands.

SIX MONTHS AFTER receiving the first letter, Sarah Jennings, just beginning to recover from her grief and shame, went to the post office to get her war allowance as she had every month since her husband Simon had left for war.

"There's no money for you this week," the lady behind the counter said.

"Why not?" asked Sarah.

"Dunno. The allowance has been stopped."

Sarah had no other source of income. Money was tight and she had a baby to feed. *What is going on? Must be some sort of mistake,* she thought.

A WEEK LATER, Sarah got another letter from the War Office.

> *Dear Madam:*
> *Owing to the death of your husband and owing to the way*
> *your husband died, you are not eligible for the allowance*
> *any more.*

Sarah was shocked. She was now broke and her meager pantry was almost out of food. *The only thing I can do now is move back in with mum,* she figured. *I can't tell her why. I'm humiliated.*

SEVENTY YEARS LATER, on her deathbed, Sarah would recount for her daughter Gertie exactly what had happened. "I had a blouse on at the time I got the first letter from the War Office and pushed it right down my blouse in case anybody saw it. I was so affected by it."

Mentioning the second letter to Gertie as well, Sarah went on to explain, "I felt so ashamed. I couldn't tell anyone what had happened. I thought it was terrible, I suppose. It was all on my shoulders, that stigma. That's how I felt. My dear mother didn't know; neither did his."

Sarah never knew the stampede of events her revelation to Gertie would set loose.

Chapter 48

PALO ALTO, CALIFORNIA:

While waiting in the reception area of the Palo Alto Police Department, Libby's cell phone rang. Still numb from what had just happened in Conrad's office, she hesitated to answer, not recognizing the incoming number. Answering anyway, she stood and walked outside the police building to take the call.

"Hello. This is Libby Warburton."

"Mrs. Warburton, Adam's mother? Hi, this is Victoria Chamberlain calling from Cambridge. I'm Adam's friend."

Libby hesitated a beat, then said, "Oh, yes, Adam mentioned you." "You can call me Libby," she added without emotion.

"I've been trying to reach him for the past twenty-four hours. Texting and E-mailing Adam—no answer. He left me your cell in case I needed to contact him through you. I think he's in danger and I've been trying to warn him."

Libby was dumbfounded and just stood there in silence.

"Hello, Libby?"

"Victoria, Adam is dead."

"Omigod. I'm too late."

"Gunshot wound to the head. Apparent suicide."

"Libby, I don't know, but I don't think so. Oh, no. I'm too late, I'm too late. This is just awful."

"What are you trying to say, Victoria?"

Trying to compose herself, Victoria continued. "I've been hacking around the Army Intelligence computers and looked at the list of victims of the Patrons of Perseus. Since the last time I checked, I saw Adam's name on it as the last entry."

"No. It can't be. That's crazy. That group was active a hundred years ago. Not now. And on another continent. How could that be?"

"Libby, I think it's possible he was murdered by a modern-day reactivation of the Patrons by the U.S. Army. Maybe Adam was killed because he had that stupid Medallion."

"That just seems so incredible. I don't know what to say, Victoria. Everything's happening so fast. I need some time to process this. I have your number. Can I call you back later?"

"Sure, sure. Omigod. Sure."

Chapter 49

PALO ALTO, CALIFORNIA:

Entering the interrogation room at the Palo Alto Police Department, it was clear that army investigators had already gotten there. "Thanks for coming in this morning, Ms. Warburton," Detective Monday said as he greeted Libby at the station. "Meet Army CID investigator Major Molson, who's just arrived."

A dour man with a pocked face, and a disinterested manner, Major Molson shook her hand and Libby nodded, remaining silent, fighting to hold back the tears.

"Today has obviously been horrible for you," Detective Monday continued. "Are you up to answering a few more questions?"

Libby nodded yes and said through a controlled sobbing sound, "I'll do my best."

"To begin, did you find a suicide note from your son?"

"No. His suicide was a complete shock," said Libby with painful resignation.

"How well do you know Dr. Conrad?" asked Detective Monday.

"I met with him several times when he came to Fort Hood to teach. I was the nurse contractor assigned to help him deliver mental health courses there for the cadre line-of-command and for the nurses. I also accompanied him on a trip to the Pentagon. Why do you ask?"

"How well did your son Adam know Dr. Conrad?"

"Well, he met Dr. Conrad a couple of days ago in Texas over dinner with me."

"Did you ever go to Dr. Conrad's home here in Los Altos Hills?"

"No, never."

"Did your son ever go to Dr. Conrad's house?"

"No. Of course not. Why would either one of us go there?"

"Did Dr. Conrad ever mention that he owned guns?"

"He's a psychiatrist. We talked about treating mental illness, not guns for heaven's sake."

"Did you ever see Dr. Conrad in an intoxicated or drugged state?"

"Of course not. That's ridiculous. What sort of question is that? The only thing I ever saw him take was candy," she fired back.

"Candy, huh? Did he ever mention that he was a prescription opiate abuser?" Monday asked as he put a copy of a reprimand of Conrad from the Medical Board of California in front of her.

"No, but it looks like that was twelve years ago according to what you have here. I know he had a bad back injury years ago that still gives him lots of pain."

"Did your son also have a prescription opiate problem?"

"Yes. He has—I mean had a shoulder injury and headaches, and was taking more pain pills than he was prescribed. What's the point of all of this?" she asked, frazzled by all the questions.

"I have a few questions, Ms. Warburton," interrupted Major Molson. "Did your son deal in opiates in order to feed his habit?"

"Of course not. Stop insulting Adam or this interview is over," Libby fumed.

"Then would it surprise you to find out we discovered a bottle of prescription pain pills from your son's psychiatrist, with your son's name on the label, in Conrad's home?" Major Molson continued tactlessly.

Libby was stunned.

Molson continued, "Army CID received an anonymous tip, and we got a search warrant for Conrad's home. We found this bottle of OxyContin with his fingerprints on it; so are Adam's. Looks like Adam was selling drugs to Conrad."

"We're done here," Libby spouted.

"One last thing," Major Molson continued, ignoring her. "Are you aware that Adam was killed with a handgun registered to Dr. Conrad. Only Conrad's fingerprints were on it but not Adam's. Adam had no gunshot residue on him. And did you know that Conrad washed up and tossed his white coat in the laundry after he killed Adam and unfortunately it's been cleaned so we couldn't test him for gunshot residue?"

Libby was blown away.

"If you're interested in finding your son's killer, you might be a bit more cooperative instead of denying the facts."

"There's something terribly wrong here. Your facts don't add up," Libby said and ran from the interview room.

Monday looked at Major Molson, nodded and said, "That's all I need. We have our killer. Let's roll."

Chapter 50

AT "THE WASHINGTON POST," WASHINGTON, D.C.:

"Hey, Roberts," yelled Bert from across the noisy newsroom at *The Washington Post*. "Fort Hood PIO on line three."

Jennifer Roberts pushed her noisy computer keyboard under her monitor and picked up her landline. "Jennifer Roberts here."

"Yes, this is Major Donahue, Public Information Officer at Fort Hood. I understand you want some information about our psychiatry programs here for an article you're writing. How can I help you?"

"Well, for one thing, you can let me talk to your head psychiatrist, Major Benson."

"As a veteran reporter, Ms. Roberts, I'm sure you're well aware the army handles all press inquiries centrally. Major Benson is too busy to talk to reporters. Also, your earlier article on the most recent Fort Hood shooting was highly critical and it's best for you to get your information from an official source. Major Benson is not authorized to talk to you."

"Not trying to hide anything now are you, Major Donahue? I only want to ask him as the senior mental health professional in charge there about your policies and procedures for giving appointments for PTSD evaluations, for granting leave and for treating soldiers there with PTSD."

"We're certainly not hiding anything. I can answer any questions you may have on those matters. We know how important it is to keep in good communication with the press."

Jennifer felt like throwing up, hearing that drivel.

"I also have information from a confidential source that Major Benson has violated the privacy of one of his patients. I'd like to ask him about that."

Major Donahue continued, "Doctor-patient matters are between doctors and patients and I can't answer any questions related to that. However, I'm fully briefed on other matters and can answer all your other questions."

Roberts took a long draw on her cup of ice-cold Marko Mocha and said, "Remember Private Lopez? Our sources inform us that your second Fort Hood mass murderer Private Lopez is a good example of failed army mental health policies. Official Army reports of the investigations of this event have finally been released and I have some questions about their findings. They seem to confirm that this soldier, like many in the army now, was denied speedy access to a PTSD evaluation, and that contributed to his decision to shoot those he felt were responsible."

"Not true. We have a policy of providing a preliminary PTSD evaluation within forty-eight hours of receiving a soldier's request or the cadre's request. Private Lopez received that. Moreover, all our active duty soldiers receive the same evaluation."

"My understanding is that in most cases the army only performs a preliminary screening evaluation, namely a form being filled out and a brief interview with a nurse case-manager. Most soldiers don't see a psychiatrist quickly. In Private Lopez's case, he never saw a psychiatrist. Since psychiatrists are the only ones who can diagnose PTSD, how can a soldier get this diagnosis and appropriate treatment for it if soldiers have limited access to psychiatrists?" Roberts asked.

"Our screenings all lead to formal psychiatric evaluations at a later time. In the meantime, we can diagnose and start treatment for post-traumatic stress, which everyone experiences in deployment and many experience during active duty in the army even when not deployed."

"That's an interesting twist on things, Major Donahue. How do you respond to mental health experts who say that the army is using the term 'post-traumatic stress' rather than the accepted psychiatric diagnosis of PTSD—post-traumatic stress D-I-S-O-R-D-E-R—just as a ruse to make stress appear normal and thus not an illness caused by events occurring while on duty and therefore ineligible for a pension?"

"That's a very cynical point of view."

"Those same mental health experts say that you use the term 'post-traumatic stress' while soldiers are on active duty in order to discharge them and dump them into an overburdened VA system."

"Now that's really unfair, Ms. Roberts. The army recognizes all legitimate illnesses. And the VA takes fine care of our discharged veterans, especially recently discharged veterans with mental health problems."

"Are you serious? Have you read about the waiting list scandal at all the VAs out there that's been going on for years?"

"Mistaken perceptions fueled by domestic politics. Soldiers and veterans are our priority."

Getting nowhere and feeling like this man was only giving platitudes for public consumption while answering none of her questions, she caught herself before she groaned audibly. Trying once again, Jennifer asked, "Well then, why do you think the army's screening process failed to identify Private Lopez's dangerousness?"

"Danger and violence are almost impossible to predict, and only past violence predicts future violence. Private Lopez had no past history of violence."

"We have reports from his family that Private Lopez felt neglected in terms of experiencing significant delays in getting psychiatric treatment, and then became enraged when he was denied leave to attend his mother's funeral."

"Well, there was a bit of an administrative foul-up about his leave, but if he had just been patient, we would've worked it all out. Being a psychiatric patient or having to experience army bureaucracy is no excuse for mass murder and suicide. Anybody that close to the edge and who kills himself, clearly had problems not of the army's making, but from his own personal inadequacies."

This time Jennifer groaned audibly. "Private Lopez's treatment seems oddly consistent with the criticism recently published by Dr. Augustus Conrad, your outside psychiatric consultant at Fort Hood. Do you have any response to Dr. Conrad's report?"

"I think Dr. Conrad is seriously misguided and his work is flawed. I refer you for further details to the Pentagon. I have nothing more to say about it."

"With all due respect, I think you're giving me the runaround and are failing to admit systemic deficiencies in the army or are unaware of them. Either way, it's bad."

"That is unjust criticism, but everyone is entitled to his or her own opinion. This interview is now over." And with that, Major Donahue hung up on Jennifer.

Chapter 51

ON THE SOMME, FRANCE, WINTER OF 1916:

Lieutenant Warburton couldn't get it out of his head. Images of the execution invaded his thoughts night and day, whether his eyes were open or closed. He relived it during the day as flashbacks intruding into his daily routine; he experienced it at night as nightmares. Each experience was burdened with terror, sweating, and a racing heart. His actions had an entirely different effect upon upper command. He was heartily congratulated again and again by his superiors. Today he was to meet with a special envoy from General Haig.

However, Lieutenant Warburton didn't feel good about it. On one hand, he was just doing his duty. He'd killed before, so it shouldn't have been a big deal. But that was always the enemy, and men he didn't know. He hadn't expected it to be so different killing a comrade, especially at close range. Churning it over and over in his brain, he kept wondering, *how could it be a noble act of warfare when it felt like murder?*

Entering a rudimentary officers' quarters in the rear lines, Lieutenant Warburton snapped to attention, saluting and announcing, "Lieutenant Nigel Warburton reporting, sir."

"At ease, lieutenant," said the colonel sitting at a desk, returning the salute from his chair. "Have a seat."

As Lieutenant Warburton took his seat in front of the desk, the colonel continued. "We're very appreciative of your leadership of the firing squad last week. Nasty business finishing it for them, for sure, but necessary when we have such a serious internal threat that must be removed."

"Yes, sir." Lieutenant Warburton could see the face of wounded Private Jennings where the colonel's face should have been. Jennings was alive, clear-eyed with a steady but not angry gaze, still bound to the oak tree, not looking at all like an internal threat but like an innocent victim. Warburton literally shook his head like a hound doing a wet-dog shake in a futile attempt to jolt the image out of his brain and get the face of the colonel to register.

"We want to recognize special service such as yours," the colonel continued.

"Ready ... aim ... " The echoing of his own words was competing with those of the colonel in his ears.

"You see," the colonel said as he pressed on, oblivious to what Lieutenant Warburton was experiencing, "we have an elite unit in the army." He leaned forward and lowered his voice as he said, "Actually, a very special detachment." Then, leaning back in his chair, he continued, "Which counts as its members only special officers such as yourself who perform exceptional duties that require especially heroic service, such as you've already demonstrated."

Warburton, far from appearing spellbound, looked back at the colonel blankly. He then shifted mindlessly in his chair, and involuntarily felt for his sidearm with his right hand, which began to shake as he touched the holster and gun at his side.

"Can I trust you to keep this in strictest confidence?" asked the colonel.

"Of course," Lieutenant Warburton replied automatically.

"We call ourselves the Patrons of Perseus. You remember the story of Perseus, lieutenant?"

Realizing he was hesitating too long before answering, Lieutenant Warburton quickly replied. "Sorry, sir. Yes, sir. Perseus. Warrior of heroes. Slayed the evil Goddess Medusa, if I remember my mythology correctly." His hand felt hotspots of fire all over it. Suddenly, the smell of sizzling brains mixed with splinters of skull assaulted his nose as the sensation of a splatter of rancid—yet strangely sweetly sickening—hot blood coated part of his face and neck.

"We have a little something here for you." With that the colonel passed Lieutenant Warburton a Medallion. You are now officially but secretly a member of our special detachment, known as the Patrons of Perseus. You are now a Patron. Number 59. We thank you for your duty, and welcome you into our brotherhood, dedicated to celebrating heroism and destroying cowardice."

Every time thoughts of Private Jennings' execution intruded, Warburton felt like he was experiencing the sensations associated with the execution for the first time. But they'd already come hundreds, if not thousands of times since the execution. He had burned his uniform to rid himself of the stains and washed his gun hand and face until they were raw. But he still couldn't get rid of the smell or the burning feeling. He waited a week before he even tried to clean Jennings' blood and brains from the barrel of his sidearm, but couldn't bring himself to finish the task. The weapon was mostly ceremonial. Now it was disgraced with the blemish of having killed a fellow British soldier, having pressed it to the back of Jennings' head and making direct contact with Jennings' skull before pulling the trigger. Lieutenant Warburton knew removing the taint was now futile. The gun could never be cleaned. "I guess I should say thank you. And I'm honored, but I don't feel like a hero. Instead, I have a lot of guilt."

"Real heroes always do the first time. Not to worry. You'll get over it. We have great plans for you. You've been appointed to lead firing squads all up and down the Western Front to implement formal orders." Smiling, he said *sotto voce* as he leaned forward, "Patrons also act on authority to summarily execute cowards in the trenches or in no man's land without a firing squad as long as it's done with no witnesses." The colonel winked at him.

"... fire!" Innocent eyes stared back at him. Friendly eyes. Forgiving eyes. Eyes that tormented him. Still alive, job not finished. Then ... thwack. Private Jennings' eyes remained open as his head ricocheted forward, then back, then slumping forward finally dead. *Was that a smile on his face as his brains issued out the back of his head?* Lieutenant Warburton kept asking himself. He coughed unwillingly and almost sneezed as the sensation of bits of bone mixed with hot blood rose in his nostrils. "I'm honored, but are you sure you have the right man?"

"We've looked into your pedigree and you come from the right kind of family. There's a potential promotion to major in it for you, and if you ever want one of these," he said pointing to the bird insignia of his rank as colonel, "this is a good path forward for you. One more thing. Protect that Medallion with your life. It's only given to Patrons of Perseus and cannot fall into the wrong hands. Although we have *top-secret* clearance from the War Committee of Parliament, most do not know about us, not even in the British Army and certainly not any but select members of Parliament. You can imagine we've got quite a few enemies, even back home. They think shirkers have this psychological condition called *shell shock*. Surely our domestic enemies would object to our activities, which could become a scandal if uncovered. I know I can trust you."

Mercifully, Jennings' face faded from Lieutenant Warburton's eyes as his pulse escalated and his skin crawled over the entire upper part of his body, while beginning to sweat profusely. *Could the colonel see his flushing and sweating?* he wondered to himself. Warburton couldn't suppress the wave of dread arising from his gut to his face. It was all he could do to suppress vomiting as he said, "Thank you, sir. I'm honored." He jumped to his feet, saluted, did a rapid about-face, and exited the room, finally retching just outside the door.

Chapter 52

EAST PALO ALTO, CALIFORNIA:

A shattered and traumatized Libby got into her rental car outside the police department and just started to drive. She didn't know what to think. *Adam dealing drugs? To Dr. Conrad? Blackmailing him? Dr. Conrad killing Adam, and making it look like a suicide? Maybe so he wouldn't lose his medical license?* It all seemed surreal. Things just didn't compute.

Suddenly, she remembered a conversation she had with Adam on the plane trip to California about the Medallion she now had in her purse. *Somebody didn't want Adam to find out what this Medallion is. Did they kill him for it? Am I now in danger since I have it?*

With resolve she never knew she had, she turned her car into the parking lot of the psychiatry building on the Stanford campus and was determined to trust her instincts. Walking up to reception, she asked for Dr. Conrad.

"Yes, he's in his office now that they've just taken down the yellow crime scene tape," explained the receptionist. "Let me buzz him for you. ... Dr. Conrad, Adam Warburton's mother to see you. Yes, I'll send her right in." Looking up, she said, "You can go in now. He's expecting you."

Libby walked down the hallway and into the room where Conrad was sitting at his desk. She closed the door behind her and locked it.

"Libby! How are you? ..." Conrad seemed happy to see her, even under such tragic circumstances. He had yet to be formally questioned himself.

"I have just one question for you," Libby interrupted. Pointing her index finger at him while narrowing her eyes, she asked forcefully, "Did you kill my only son Adam with your own gun to silence him because he was supplying you with pain pills?"

"Wha ... wha ... what?"

She could see the pain on his face and knew right then and there that he was not Adam's killer.

"Didn't think so. Either I'm about to make the biggest mistake of my life, or do the right thing for Adam." Trusting her instincts, Libby said, "We've gotta get outta here before the police arrest—"

The buzzer on Conrad's phone growled. "Dr. Conrad, I just sent the police down the hallway to your office," the receptionist said.

"What?"

Within seconds, there was pounding at the door. "Palo Alto Police, Dr. Conrad. Open up. We need for you to go with us to the police department for questioning."

Conrad froze for a moment. "Libby," he whispered, pointing to the window where the blinds were swaying in the breeze after they found Adam's body yesterday. Then, putting his forefinger to his lips to indicate silence, he pushed it wide open, and motioned for Libby to crawl out. Another rap of knuckles on the door made Conrad move faster. After he'd helped her, he followed, and said under his breath as his feet reached the ground outside his office window, "Well, I guess we found out how they got in here to kill Adam yesterday."

At that moment the police broke into Conrad's office and saw Conrad and Libby fleeing on foot.

"Get them!" yelled Detective Monday.

"This way," Libby said, and in a flash they both got into her rental car. Libby whipped it out of the parking lot with the police losing visual contact. As large, chubby men, they had no real option to follow them out a skinny window gap. So, the police turned to run headlong out the entrance at the other end of the building.

"Great, we've got a head start," said Conrad. "But we've gotta change cars. They'll be able to trace your rental. Turn left here and then exit on Embarcadero."

Quickly Libby found herself in an industrial area of East Palo Alto as they pulled up to a long garage. Conrad hopped out of the car and worked on a combination lock on the door to open it. "This' where I keep my toys. I'm a bit of an Anglophile ever since my year at Cambridge. I've got a collection of exotic British cars including several Aston Martins." As he opened one of the garage doors, he said, "Let's take this one; it's the least conspicuous." He motioned to a black on black convertible with the top up, and quickly backed it out of the garage. "Most people don't even know what this is, especially since it's all black," he said to Libby out the open window. "I think the red one might be a bit much."

Libby wheeled her rental car into its place, grabbed her overnight bag and purse, and Conrad shut the garage door. He then gunned the enormous V12 engine, raising the most beautiful throated sound in all of auto-land, and started down Highway 101. Still not hearing sirens behind them, Conrad relaxed a beat. He loved driving the Aston Martin Virage Volante, oftentimes called a race car in a tuxedo. The police had no link to this car yet, so Conrad figured they had a couple of hours. "I think I know where we can go to sort this out. I have a home high-up in the San Bernardino Mountains at Lake Arrowhead where we can collect our thoughts and figure out the next step."

"Where's that?" Libby asked.

"It's in Southern California, about six hours away. Unless of course, you're in an Aston Martin on the back roads, in which case it's more like four hours, even with a stopover at Burger King. And that's without the assistance of my James Bond rockets."

At first, Libby thought Conrad's comments odd. Then she realized it just might be his way of coping with the moment. And after all, it was a really spectacular car.

Chapter 53

Dialing the secret number given to him for such an occasion, special operator Bowman waited for the Commandant to answer. "Commandant. This is special operator Bowman. The police know that the target was a murder now and not a suicide. However, Conrad went on the lam with that nurse girlfriend of his before they could arrest him."

"Don't worry. They won't get far."

"We've searched the Stanford campus, his home, her hotel. His car's in the university parking lot, but her rental car's gone. The police have a BOLO out on them and her car. They've notified all the area airports and have officers on site. Police and Feds are tracking credit cards and cell phones. Chances are he might just go to his lawyer and turn himself in, so there are eyes on the lawyer's office as well. Should have them both in custody within twenty-four hours."

"Keep me posted," the Commandant demanded.

Chapter 54

MADINGLEY HALL, OUTSIDE OF CAMBRIDGE, ENGLAND:

Jolted out of a deep sleep, General Rossi sat bolt-upright in bed. His cell phone was ringing. Grabbing it clumsily, he answered, still drunk with sleep, "Hello."

"Sorry to wake you, sir. This is Army Intelligence officer Colonel John Salingway. I have some important news for you."

Rossi's brain was slowly turning on, but was not all the way there yet. *Salingway*, he thought. Trying to get his bearings, he finally realized he was in the U.K., sitting in a bed in the hotel room attached to Madingley Hall in Cambridge. "Yes, Salingway, I remember. Sorry, just getting awake."

"Not a problem. We've received notification from Palo Alto Police and the U.S. Army Criminal Investigation Command that one of our soldiers has just been killed."

"Why are you calling me about that? This happens all the time," Rossi barked.

"His name is Sergeant Adam Warburton, stationed at Fort Hood."

"Fort Hood? Good gawd. Just what I need. Another death at Fort Hood. Murder or suicide?"

"Not at Fort Hood, sir. Sergeant Warburton is stationed there but at the time of his death was seeing a Dr. Conrad at Stanford."

"Well at least that's good news. How did he die? Natural causes, murder, suicide?"

"At first it looked like a suicide, but now we have proof that it was murder."

"Any idea who did it?"

"Conrad."

"What, the doctor?" Rossi asked with a smile.

"Yes, he's being questioned as we speak. Should be arrested soon."

"Any idea of motive?"

"Evidently the doc is a junkie and our soldier was dealing him prescription Oxys. Maybe he threatened to expose the doc, so he got knocked off."

Now fully awake, Rossi was clearly feeling elated and enjoying the news. *Gonna be a good day today. Gonna be a good day indeed,* he said to himself.

Chapter 55

ON THE SOMME, FRANCE, WINTER OF 1917:

Over the next few weeks, in addition to his usual duties, Lieutenant Warburton travelled up and down the Western Front, commanding a number of firing squads, executing cowards—one at a time. He hated it. However, he felt obliged to follow orders. He was tasked with killing soldiers designated as cowards by the British infantry. As such, he was now an involuntary member of the Patrons of Perseus and had this damned Medallion. Not a medal to Lieutenant Warburton, but a curse.

In the several executions following his first one—Private Jennings—the riflemen were able to fire kill shots, mercifully releasing Lieutenant Warburton from the necessity of using his sidearm again. In the past weeks, he had become increasingly sleepless. Hearing rifle fire in the trenches gave him a new chill down his spine, as it now reminded him of the sound of being shot at dawn.

Whiskey was of little help. Lieutenant Warburton nevertheless resorted to heavy doses of it nightly. Drinking could put him to sleep but he'd wake up in only an hour or two, often mercilessly drenched in a cold sweat, feeling the pungent smell of burning brains and sharp skull splinters mixed with hot blood splattering on his right hand, his face, his neck and up his nostrils. Often he woke-up suddenly, highly aroused after such nightmares and couldn't get back to sleep. He became more and more irritable, with frequent angry outbursts that were out of character.

"You look like bloody shit, Warburton," said Major Kennedy, one of his fellow officers and roommate as they were getting ready for another day of action.

"Thanks for that, Kennedy. Then I look like I feel." Warburton had sunken eyes from weeks of little sleep. His once impeccable grooming had gone to the dogs. His hair was disheveled and he had taken to shaving only intermittently. His uniform was now crumpled. Hard for him to believe he was the same man who used to wear crisply laundered shirts and pants. He was gaunt from weight loss and his clothes no longer fit. Lieutenant Warburton hadn't even bothered to finish cleaning his sidearm after he executed Jennings—'hit-man' style to the back of the head. In fact, he couldn't even look at his gun or its holster. He tried never to touch the gun when he had to buckle it on.

"You're becoming a real bastard, Warburton, what's wrong?"

"Nothing's wrong. Mind your own business."

Ka-bam! Just then, a huge German shell exploded somewhere outside their quarters. Warburton immediately hit the floor, lying flat with his hands folded behind his head.

"Jesus, Warburton. That one wasn't even close. What's up with you?"

"Go fuck yourself, Kennedy."

"Have it your way, then," Major Kennedy shot back.

"I'm going back to bed," Lieutenant Warburton said as he got to his feet and moved to his bed. "I got no sleep again last night. Haven't slept for weeks. I'm in no shape to travel to Carnoy today."

"Haven't you missed duty a bit much recently? Why don't you report to casualty?" asked Kennedy.

"I just need some rest. I've got to get back to my normal self. Can't concentrate. Doctors can't be trusted. My whole nervous system's ruined. There's nothing they can do about it." *I should be taken out and shot myself,* he said to himself. *If I had an ounce of courage, I'd find a time and place to do it.*

Chapter 56

WASHINGTON, D.C.:

Bert ran over to Roberts' cubicle in the middle of the newsroom, dodging another reporter and nearly tripping over an assistant delivering the mail. Finally reaching her nest—inside the maze of cubicles—and out of breath, Bert said hurriedly, "Jennifer you're not gonna believe this. I tracked down Colonel Richards' ex and he's willing to talk to you. Line two."

"Two gold stars for you, Bert," Jennifer said as she swiveled her chair away from her monitor and picked up her landline. "Jennifer Roberts here. Is this Mr. Richards?"

"Yes, this is Joe Richards. I believe you wanted to talk to me."

Jennifer was surprised at his voice, which seemed like it was coming from an older man. "Thanks for speaking with me. I understand you were once married to Ellen Richards?"

"Yes, twenty years ago, and I've often wondered why no one's ever contacted me about her."

"Why do you say that, Mr. Richards?"

"Because she's a highly exploitative woman."

"Sorry to hear that. Can you be more specific?"

"Yeah, sure. I met Ellen when she was a teenager, just after she'd dropped out of high school."

"Dropped out?"

"Yes. I managed a fast food restaurant and she worked there part time. We struck up a romance even though I'm twenty years her senior, ashamed to say. She seemed so needy and I took pity on her. At first I just tried to help her, but before I knew it, we'd moved in together and soon she became pregnant. It's then that I asked her to marry me."

"Sounds like she had a rough life up to then."

"That's what I thought at first and it's why I wanted to rescue her. She seemed so distressed by life and so sweet. But I was just one big sucker. She repeatedly lied about her past. She was congenitally incapable of empathy. Ellen had this way of taking another person's goodness as her opportunity to take advantage of them. You see, she was only using me to get a place to stay and to be able to quit work and get her GED."

"Would you say she was manipulative?"

"That's not the half of it. No sooner did we get married than she got an abortion without my knowledge or consent. Told her doctor she wasn't married. Within weeks after that, I realized what a mistake I made marrying her. Caught her with another man. She said she'd only give me a divorce if I helped pay for her to move out and start college. I was very much manipulated like the fool that I am."

"Very cunning indeed."

"She had a mask of sanity. It just took several months to slip and show me the real Ellen," Joe Richards said with a tone of resignation.

"Sounds like a classic psychopath."

"That's what I've been told."

"You also said you wondered why no one had ever contacted you about her. Although a failed relationship from a teen marriage and pregnancy is tragic, is there anything else you wanted to tell me?"

"Yes, of course. Lots of us have breakups, but she has a past that hardly makes her eligible to be a doctor, let alone a psychiatrist."

"Why do you say that, Mr. Richards?"

"Talk to her brother. If you could ever find him, he'll confirm what I'm telling you and would probably be able to provide even more details about her past, since he was around her before I was. What I learned from Ellen herself is that she has a long criminal history as a juvenile, from shoplifting to destroying property to drug abuse."

"A full-blown juvenile delinquent? And a psychopath in the making?"

"For sure. Ellen was ruthless in trying to get ahead and pull herself out of her circumstances. Absentee alcoholic father. Her mother committed suicide. Had bipolar disorder. Her mom's suicide happened before Ellen and I met."

"At some level, didn't you admire her for trying to escape her past and trying to get ahead?" Jennifer asked.

"Yes, at first. But the means she employed and how she exploited me and others was calculating and brutal. She has no conscience, no empathy and exploits people like tools to be used and discarded."

"Again, classical psychopath."

"Ellen was not only ashamed of her mother's suicide but was enraged by the fact that she was hospitalized several times herself in psychiatric facilities as an adolescent."

"Really?"

"Yep. Two suicide attempts and one nervous breakdown, probably from drugs. Ellen told me during our divorce proceedings that she only married me to get away from her past and to change her name so that no one could ever connect her to her adolescent record."

"Clever. With juvenile records generally expunged and a change in her last name, it would be easy to move on and keep her past from catching up with her."

"Not sure I believed her at the time, but she also told me that she would kill me if I ever told anybody what I knew about her past, so do not tell her I gave you this information."

"What?" Jennifer asked, brutalizing her keyboard on autopilot as she listened. "Thanks for being so brave, Mr. Richards. Rest assured I'll never disclose you as a source for this information. I have no interest in exposing you to any further danger from a psychopath."

"Thanks. That's reassuring. I was pretty sure that somebody like you would do the right thing. When I saw in the papers that Ellen became a hot-shot and got that big appointment to chief of psychiatry for the whole U.S. Army, I just couldn't believe it. I imagine she's more paranoid than ever about having her past discovered, especially by the army. Maybe her past could interfere with her all-important career."

"Well, given the army's attitude toward mental illness, it would likely ruin her career for sure. A shame because lots of people are sympathetic to those who can turn their lives around after experiencing psychiatric problems."

"So now you understand. If the head of army psychiatry is seen to be a psychopath who comes from a family full of mental illness and with a history of her own psychiatric problems, everything she has worked for could be shot down. Maybe that's exactly what should happen. Do you think Ellen is the type of person who should be a doctor, let alone a psychiatrist, particularly one in charge of all psychiatry in the army?"

A sinking feeling came over Jennifer, as she said, "I'm beginning to think that Colonel Richards is not at all fit for her current position, Mr. Richards. Not at all."

Chapter 57

THE PINNACLES, CALIFORNIA, ON HIGHWAY 25:

Speeding south down Interstate 5, no sirens within earshot, Conrad slowed his Aston Martin to ninety-miles per hour, and breathed a sigh of relief. He looked over at Libby, sitting silently, somber and looking at her hands in her lap. "Libby, I think you should take the battery out of your cell phone."

"Why?" she asked.

"So they can't track us."

"Okay. You've done this before?" Libby said, now with a bit of her usual sparkle, still not looking up.

"Run from the cops? No, but I watch a lot of cop shows," Conrad quipped, trying gently to cheer her up a bit. "Seriously, you took such a huge risk coming with me. I'm so sorry about this whole mess that's put us on the run. And right after Adam's death. But honestly, I had nothing to do with Adam's death."

Conrad slowed down to seventy-five, not wanting to get picked up for speeding and to avoid the main highways. He decided to take the turn off for the Pinnacles onto Highway 25. Conrad knew the area well, as he and his wife Emily used to come here in one of his exotic toys with the top down, to see the beautiful scenery and sample some of the local wines before her tragic death. Seeing the lush green countryside also reminded him of his honeymoon in New Zealand and the beautiful scenes he and his new bride drove through many years ago on the South Island en route to Queenstown. Saddened by those memories, Conrad thought better of mentioning his thoughts or anything about his family tragedy to Libby, so they both sat for a while longer in silence as he raced along the winding roads to avoid traffic.

Eventually, Libby turned her downcast gaze of red and swollen eyes slowly towards Conrad. "I know you had nothing to do with Adam's death," she said softly. After sitting in silence for a few more minutes, Libby sat upright, as though she remembered something. "Gus, I forgot to mention something to you. Victoria Chamberlain called me while I was waiting for my interrogation at the police department with a confusing message. I was so messed up I didn't get it all, but it was something about a list of victims of the Patrons that Adam was on. She was trying to get a hold of him to warn him that he was in danger." Libby paused again, then added, "Too late, sadly," choking back tears so she could talk.

"What list? Why did that mean Adam was in danger?"

"I'm not clear, either, but whatever it means, I quickly figured out Adam didn't commit suicide, and that you weren't the one who killed him," Libby said. "The police were making Adam out to be a drug dealer and you a drug addict and murderer. That's just wrong."

A long silence, then Conrad said, "I have to tell you I did have a prescription pain pill problem about a decade ago, following a back injury from a bad car accident." Conrad's back felt a twinge just at that moment as he remembered the horrible night. "I was reprimanded for writing myself a prescription of OxyContin. That's illegal, and I was reported to the state licensing board. Soon after that, I finally entered rehab and I've been fine for many years. As you know, candy is my only drug of *abuse* now. Actually, I love jawbreakers."

"I think somebody framed you. Somebody working for the Patrons, I bet," Libby said.

"Well, somebody broke into my home, planted the pills, and lifted my Glock. But why kill Adam? And why try and pin it on me?"

"I think you've made some very dangerous enemies within the army, Gus."

"They don't kill U.S. civilians. Or at least I don't think they do. And they don't kill their own soldiers."

"Wait a minute. I think that was what Victoria was saying. Yes, I remember now. She thinks the list means the U.S. Army is now killing its own soldiers."

"What?" he said disbelievingly.

"I think you pushed the wrong person's buttons, Gus. And Adam must've also known something he wasn't supposed to know."

"You suppose Adam's death is linked to your Papa Nigel's Medallion?" Conrad asked.

"I was thinking the same thing, especially after talking with Adam on the flight out here from Texas last night. He told me about a very peculiar conversation he had with his psychiatrist just before we left. Remember how Adam told us he posted a picture of the Medallion on Facebook and asked if anybody knew what it was?"

"Yeah. Adam's psychiatrist supposedly freaked-out and demanded he take down the picture. Remember, we talked about that at Lester's diner that night in Killeen. Didn't he also tell Adam that having the Medallion was threatening U.S. Army security?"

"Yes, he did. What Adam told me on the plane and didn't mention at our dinner was his psychiatrist told him he was going to report this information about the Medallion to Army Intelligence.

"That's outrageous and completely unethical," Conrad said as he bristled. "What you tell your psychiatrist is supposed to be confidential. Even if you're in the army. His psychiatrist has no right to tell anybody the things Adam disclosed in their sessions."

"I thought so, too."

"Sounds more like he was working against Adam's interests and confidentiality because Adam stumbled onto something he shouldn't have and the psychiatrist knew the army would want to keep him from knowing why."

"Maybe this is how Adam's name got posted on the list Victoria hacked. This is just too overwhelming. I'm not thinking straight. Gus, my son is dead!"

Conrad was silent. After a moment, he touched her hand with his briefly and finally said, "Would it make you feel any better if we called Victoria and got some more information?"

Libby wiped the tears from her eyes and her face and told Conrad the answer.

"We need some gas anyway. Astons are gas hogs, especially racing around these curves. We can drive through and grab something at Burger King, and then pick up a couple of burners and supplies at Walmart right next to the gas station at the next exit. Okay?"

"Burners?"

"Yeah, disposable cell phones."

"Now I know you watch too much television."

"We can get a couple, one with an international package if we can buy it quickly. Then you can call Victoria when we hit the road after our quick pit stop."

"Burners? What's next?" Libby mumbled to herself.

Chapter 58

ON THE SOMME, FRANCE, SPRING OF 1917:

Spring was in full flower outside, birds chirping, flowers blooming. Sunshine on the fields belied the grief they had witnessed in the past year. After two days of failing to report for duty, Sergeant Dawkins came to Lieutenant Warburton's sleeping quarters at dawn to rouse him, on orders from the unit commander, Colonel Hastings. "Sir, you're to get dressed and come to Colonel Hastings' office forthwith," Sergeant Dawkins informed Lieutenant Warburton with authority.

Lieutenant Warburton rolled over and put the pillow on his head.

Sergeant Dawkins walked over to him and lifted the pillow. Warburton quickly shot to his feet in a fury, hands around Dawkins' neck strangling him as he knocked the sergeant to the floor and sat atop of him, squeezing the life out of him. Suddenly, Lieutenant Warburton felt peaceful, calm, like he was somewhere else, like he was in a dream. Everything seemed surreal. He wasn't in France. He didn't have his hands around Sergeant Dawkins, choking him by the throat. It wasn't him. It was someone else. Slowly, he rose above his body and looked down at himself sitting on top of Dawkins, but then was rudely jolted back to the here and now. He quickly released Sergeant Dawkins as he coughed and sputtered and twisted out from under him.

"You're a fucking lunatic, Warburton," Sergeant Dawkins said as he fled the officer's bedroom.

Chapter 59

SOUTHBOUND ON 395 TO LAKE ARROWHEAD:

Conrad and Libby were in luck. He was able to buy two disposable cell phones—paid for in cash—and added an international package to one of them. He made sure one had a speakerphone, that it was fully charged and got back on the road in less than twenty minutes. Conrad had already shot across the state on Highway 198 past the state hospital in Coalinga that housed sexually violent predators and where he consulted several times a year, and down Highway 99. He had also purchased enough fuel to fill the bellies of all three of them: himself, Libby and Aston. Now bearing down on Highway 58, continuing to avoid the interstates and keeping his speed at a reasonable clip, he decided to take 395 south to Lake Arrowhead as soon as it came up ahead.

"Now, let's see. How's this gonna work?" Libby asked as she took out one of the burners.

"You'll have to get Victoria's number off your own cell phone, so try to turn it on for just a second, get her number and turn it right back off. I hope this doesn't hang us."

"I'll be quick," Libby said as she fished her cell phone out of her purse, replaced its battery and quickly copied down Victoria's number, removing the battery in the blink-of-the-eye. "Done."

"Now dial Victoria in the U.K.—plus sign first, then 44 country code, then the Cambridge exchange 1223, and then her number. When she answers, can you put it on speakerphone so I can hear as I drive?

"Sure ... it's ringing."

After several rings, Victoria picked up, a bit groggy. "Hello?"

"Hello, Victoria?"

"Yeah, who's this?"

"Libby Warburton calling from the States. Sorry to wake you, but I'd like to get some more details of what you were saying to me earlier today."

"Oh, Libby. I've been crying my heart out. I can't imagine how you must be feeling. I'm so sorry for your loss. If I'd just acted a few hours earlier, I might've been able to save Adam's life."

Libby paused, her eyes swelling again, but she seemed to Conrad to be out of tears. She then replied into the phone, "Thanks so much for your support, but this isn't the time to be blaming yourself. We have to find out who killed Adam. You know, they're trying to frame Dr. Conrad for his death."

"It's much worse than that. I've been desperately trying to call you for hours, but your mobile's been off. I'm so glad you called. I think I may be able to save your and Dr. Conrad's lives even though I couldn't save Adam."

"Whatever are you talking about?"

"You and Dr. Conrad have just been put on the list."

"List? What list?"

"The list I told you about on our earlier call. You and Dr. Conrad are now in great danger. Real danger."

"I'm not following you. Being on a list is dangerous?"

"You're targets for assassination by the Patrons of Perseus."

Libby and Conrad looked at each other, both stunned with this news. "Victoria, slow down. Start from the top. I wasn't thinking all that clearly the first time you called. What exactly is going on?"

"I hacked U.S. Army Intelligence data and came across files on the Patrons of Perseus. At the end of World War I, the British gave the files to the Americans they never wanted to be made public, including a list of all the victims of the Patrons of Perseus."

"What does that have to do with us?"

"You're on that list now. And so is Adam." Libby and Conrad were stunned as Victoria continued. "I talked to Jennifer Roberts at *The Washington Post* and told her there are many recent names on the list, almost all of which correspond with official army suicides of active duty soldiers. We think if the last names on the list mean the same thing as those on the list starting about a hundred years ago in the British Army, the U.S. Army is still executing cowards and making it look like suicide. They may also be assassinating anybody who threatens to uncover their secret operations."

The revelation was too much. Conrad and Libby were shocked.

Libby gulped. "Like Adam, Gus and me."

"Exactly. And with Adam's death, that means you and Dr. Conrad are in very grave danger. I'm working with Jennifer Roberts to find the evidence we need to blow this scandal sky high. Until then, you better go into hiding."

"How long until you think you have the evidence to expose this?"

"Hard to say, but both Jennifer and I are on it. She's working her contacts in the States. I'm looking for secret files I think might be stored at Madingley Hall here in Cambridge. I'll go there to snoop around later today once the sun's up."

"What makes you think U.S. Army Intelligence records would be in England?"

"Modern names on the list have asterisks next to them as well as a three digit number, such as 869. Jennifer and I think this might correspond to the Medallion number of the active Patron of Perseus responsible for those deaths. And at the bottom of the list next to another asterisk are the words, 'Madingley Hall.' We think there's some connection of this case to this stately home owned by the University of Cambridge. It's a conference center that sits next door to the only American Cemetery for U.S. soldiers in the entire U.K."

Conrad interrupted. "Madingley? That rings a bell. I think there're some psychiatric conferences there every year."

"Right you are, Dr. Conrad. Didn't realize you were listening in. In fact, a two-day psychiatric conference starts tomorrow. It's jointly sponsored by the U.S. and British military."

"Wow," Libby exclaimed. "Before you go, did you find anything about Papa Nigel in the files? Anything that could link his Medallion to Adam's death?"

"I did confirm that Adam's great-great-grandfather is listed both as a member of the Patrons of Perseus and as a victim of the Patrons of Perseus."

Libby thought for a beat. "You suppose that means they killed him?"

"That's my assumption. He was hospitalized with *shell shock*, so maybe they thought he was a coward. Made his death look like a suicide."

"Omigod."

"It's possible that his records are at the Bethlem Royal Hospital, which stores old medical records from the Maudsley Hospital where he was actually hospitalized. Jennifer and I think it's also possible that his records are at Madingley. That's what I intend to find out today," Victoria said.

"We have to go Victoria. Things are happening so fast, and I must process all of this. Be careful and keep me posted. This is one of those 'burner' cell phones, so you can call us without it being traced if there're any developments. Bye."

Libby sat with downcast eyes, looking at the phone in her lap. Conrad sped along in silence, the melodic roar of the Aston's V12, the only sound. He was lucky that the back roads seemed all but deserted. Finally, Libby broke the silence. "If the army knew Adam had Papa Nigel's Medallion, maybe they decided to execute him before he could figure out that the Patrons were still active."

"Sounds like the story starts with your Papa Nigel, and leads to Adam," Conrad concluded.

"Let's hope it doesn't end with us."

"Let's hope it doesn't end us."

After zooming about twenty minutes up a winding mountain road, they arrived at the entrance to the village of Lake Arrowhead. The air had become crisp and clear and the dark sky was illuminated by twinkling stars. They were welcomed by the beauty and tranquility of the mountains at night. Conrad always relaxed when he met these environs, and this time was no different, even though he knew it was only on the surface. Roiling beneath was the fact that both federal espionage agents and homicide police were on the hunt for him. He had dragged Libby into it. Now they were both targets of the army's assassination squad. Likely they both had only hours until they would be found. Maybe only hours to live. Conrad pulled in front of his garage, looked out on the calm, moonlit alpine lake, and said to Libby, "We flew here in record time. I should say 'drove' here."

"No, flew here is right. Except it was less than six inches off the ground."

As they walked up the front steps of his house, the full moon illuminated the calmness of the lake nearby. Conrad could tell that the dogwoods were blooming in white while the jacaranda trees were blushing a magnificent lavender in the light of the moon. Before entering the house, a strong scent of pine caused Libby to stop and enjoy a smell foreign to her. A few more steps and the two were at the threshold.

Entering his home, Conrad said, "Have a seat. I'm going to put on some coffee. Milk or sugar?"

"Bourbon," she replied. "This has been a long day.

"It's not over yet."

THURSDAY

Chapter 60

ON THE SOMME, FRANCE, SPRING OF 1917:

Lieutenant Warburton entered the colonel's office as he was commanded to do.

"Lieutenant Warburton, reporting as ordered, sir."

The colonel did not order him "at ease" nor did he offer him a seat. "I want you to go to casualty today and see a doctor."

"Please no, sir."

"That's not a request. It's an order. You've been acting dodgy for weeks, can't be trusted to do your duty, and we want you evaluated for a trip to Craiglockhart."

"Where the hell is that?"

"Scotland."

"Why'm I going there?"

"That's where we treat officers with *shell shock*."

Chapter 61

CRAIGLOCKHART, SCOTLAND, SPRING OF 1917:

The day was one of those glorious, if rare occasions, where golden sunshine penetrated the clouds and shone upon the Scottish hills carpeted in rich green hues and dotted with lavender heather—seen only in a place with so much rain. Nasty weather almost all the time, all year around, seemed like a small price to pay for these precious glimpses of majestic color. Slateford Military Hospital at Craiglockhart, Scotland, was exclusively for the treatment of British infantry officers with shattered nerves. Craiglockhart was a huge campus of structures built in the 1880s, an Italianate pile that served as a private clinic for rich invalids. Not particularly successful commercially, it featured the use of various water cures of the day—hydrotherapy—and prescribed rest amidst stirring views of the Pentland Hills on the outskirts of Edinburgh. The War Office took it over in the summer of 1917, and soon filled it with *shell shocked* officers traumatized by the worst battle in the history of war—the Battle of the Somme. Lieutenant Warburton had already been a patient here for almost a year now, and wasn't getting any better. Today, as he and his friend Lieutenant Siegfried Sassoon were sitting in the officers' club having a drink, a new patient walked in.

"Come on over and have a drink with us," Warburton offered. "Nigel Warburton, here. And this is Siegfried Sassoon. We call him 'Sieg.' Don't shoot him, he's not a Kraut. His mother liked operas, so named him after Wagner."

Reluctantly, Owen joined them. "Second Lieutenant Wilfred Owen, Manchester regiment. Call me Wills." Owen was in his late 20s, handsome, with a small wisp of a moustache trying to emerge from his upper lip and a full head of hair parted in the middle and grown a bit too long for military standards. Both eyes blinked closed nervously again and again as he spoke.

"Welcome to the home for damaged officers and political prisoners, Wills," Sassoon added. Sassoon was also in his late 20s, with a prominent forehead and a generous nose. Thin and lanky, he moved gracefully, with effeminate gestures as he caressed his cigarette while he smoked it.

"You have *shell shock*, too?" Lieutenant Warburton asked Owen.

"I thought we were supposed to avoid that term," replied Owen, both eyes blinking shut again.

"That is indeed the idea these days," agreed Warburton. "Whatever you have, consider yourself lucky to find yourself here at officers' quarters rather than at a converted asylum for the 'other ranks.'"

"Yes, my psychiatrist has explained it to me this way. We 'upper-class twits' have the condition of genteel 'neurasthenia' requiring rest, whereas working class soldiers in the lower ranks are afflicted with 'hysteria' requiring strengthening of the will, learning manly virtues, and electrotherapy," interjected Sassoon sarcastically. "Evidently nobody has *shell shock* anymore and never did. The whole thing has turned into a stupid word game to our government. Believe me, I know that with what I've been through."

"Yes, old man, disagree with the government and you're crazy. You'll get put in an asylum," Warburton added.

"Exactly," Sassoon said, continuing on his rant. "This whole war is just a matter of playing a lethal game to our government at this point. There's actually nothing wrong with me except something I wrote that offended persons in power."

Warburton had to chuckle to himself. It was absurd that a controversial poet who was well-known, and had plenty of political connections through his wealthy family, would be declared mental and sent to Craiglockhart rather than forced back into combat or shot at dawn like a coward. He had too much visibility for the British Army to do anything with him but hide him away in remote Scotland.

"You were sent here because of what you wrote? That's a bit scary. I'm a writer, too, actually more of a poet, although no one seems to read my poems," said Owen.

"Truth be told," continued Sassoon, "I was naively patriotic when I joined up at the start of the war. Since then, they've even called me a hero on a good day, but I threw the ribbon from my Military Cross into the River Mersey when I figured out what was really going on. Now, according to the army, I'm a coward or worse. After convalescing from the last time I was wounded, I decided not to return to duty as ordered."

"Coward? What's a coward? I've been trying to figure that out ever since they told me I was coming here," said Owen blinking furiously.

"Listen to this, then," Sassoon continued. "Instead of going back to duty, I sent my commanding officer a letter, and at the same time forwarded it to the press. My MP, stupid bugger, actually read it out loud in Parliament, trying to be supportive, but some there said it was treasonous. I condemned this government's motives as not being 'liberation and defense' as they claim, but 'aggression and conquest,' which is morally corrupt and wrong."

"Incredible. Seems your Member of Parliament opened a can of worms for you. What did they do to you and how did you get here?" asked Owen, now showing growing interest in his new friend, seeming to relax and blinking much less as he spoke.

"Rather than send me to court-martial which is what I deserve, 'Old Mac' proclaimed me to be a lunatic unfit for service and sent me here to be treated for *shell shock*," continued Sassoon irreverently. "Disagree with the government and they'll give you that label. I'm here until I agree to return to the Front."

"Ah, yes, Under Secretary of State for War Ian Macpherson. Warmonger number one," added Warburton, as he sipped his warm ale and then wiped some froth clinging to his moustache.

"You see, it's not shattered nerves that got me sent to this place, how about you?" asked Sassoon.

"I got wonky after being buried alive in an explosion on top of a half-dozen of my dead men. I guess it's *shell shock*, too, but a different form than yours for sure," Owen said smiling, blinking now completely gone.

Sassoon returned the smile. "Well put, Owen. You must show me some of your work soon."

"Maybe if I get up the courage to share it," Owen replied, a quick blink returning. "My poems aren't really any good, but writing them makes me feel better. Maybe they'll let me write poetry as my therapy here?"

"That's a new one for the treatment of *shell shock*. They make Sieg here *stop* writing poems as *his* therapy," quipped Warburton.

"Amazing, this *shell shock*," Sassoon added. "Officers, soldiers, the 'man on the street,' poets and government critics all still use this forbidden term. It's as though everyone knows what it is, yet everyone has his own definition of it—from madness to sheer funk, neurasthenia to hysteria, or a metaphor for an unjustifiable war," Sassoon announced.

"What's the treatment here?" Owen seemed a bit pensive and concerned as he expressed this question and blinked again furiously.

"Ah, treatment. At Craiglockhart, we 'rest' in our serene country house, and drink in the stunning views, lofty trees, green spaces and tranquil old-world charm appropriate for us young, well-educated martial elites," Sassoon continued scornfully. "To prevent utter boredom, we play billiards, badminton, bowling, croquet, cricket, golf, tennis and even water polo in the pool—which is heated, by the way. In addition, we have individual therapy with our psychiatrist. Basically, we tell our doctor about our dreams."

"Sounds tough," Owen said bitingly while rolling his eyes. "Enough of this *shell shock* nonsense. Tell me more about this place."

"I guess I'm the resident expert, having been here the longest, the most hopeless dreg of this place," interjected Warburton. "You likely already know that Craiglockhart is one of six special hospitals for officers with nerve problems. All of them serve only officers, not any regular soldiers. Those blokes—the 'other ranks'—go to places like the Royal Victoria Hospital at Netley. I hear tell that D Block at Netley is organized as huge wards of eighty beds side by side. Here at Craiglockhart, we're fortunate to all have single rooms. Have you been assigned yours yet?"

"Yes, I suppose I should go there now and unpack," said Owen as he stood, looking like he aimed to please.

"You'll find it's not too bad," said Sassoon. "I suppose it's just a matter of what you were used to before you joined the army. Separating the officers from 'other ranks' was originally based on the idea that we officers are all upper middleclass or aristocratic, well-educated, and considered highly imaginative with artistic temperaments and thus need different treatment from that given to 'other ranks.' This idea persists despite the fact that many officers are now drawn from the 'other ranks' as we have killed off most of the professional officers in France. If you go off the rails and are an officer, you come to Craiglockhart for the 'rest cure' in our single rooms and our secluded residences. Same treatment as members of our class have received for years for anyone becoming deranged. Just like sending one of our barmy relatives to the country for fresh air and sunshine. Well, here we are, all of us, barmy officers," Sassoon spat out derisively, toasting onlookers with his glass of ale.

Chapter 62

WASHINGTON, D.C.:

Jennifer Roberts was jolted awake after midnight having fallen asleep in front of the late night news on the couch in her home. Almost knocking over an empty wine glass, she grabbed blindly for her trusted cell phone, never kept more than an arm's length away. She punched it "on" and mumbled, "Yeah, what is it?"

"Jennifer, its Victoria Chamberlain calling from Cambridge. Did you hear?"

Jennifer's usual lightning fast brain had not warmed up to full take-off speed yet. "Now that's an open ended question. Hear what?"

"My friend Adam is dead."

"Adam? The soldier who visited you in Cambridge? Isn't he the same one whose great-great-grandfather headed firing squads in World War I?"

"Yeah, that's him."

"How horrible."

"I've never experienced someone that I know die like that."

"Well, it does happen and I'm so sorry for you." Jennifer's brain slowly gaining cruising altitude, she suddenly realized she didn't understand what she had just heard and asked Victoria, "Died like what?"

"Adam was murdered."

"That's terrible. No wonder you're upset."

"And they want that Stanford doctor for questioning."

"Conrad?"

"Yep. But it's a ruse. He didn't do it. I think the Patrons did it. No, I know they did it."

Now fully engaged, Roberts transferred the cell phone to her other hand as she sat up and brushed her hair back out of her face with her free hand. She hated taking important calls without a keyboard in front of her. *And where was her Marko Mocha when she needed it?* she asked herself. Coming directly to the point, Jennifer questioned, "How do you know all of this?"

Victoria continued. "The list. You know, that list of names from the Army Intelligence files of all the victims of the Patrons of Perseus. I told you about it last time."

"Of course."

"I have more evidence to prove the Patrons are re-activated as an assassination unit. But I blew it."

"Blew it? What on earth do you mean?"

Victoria began sobbing. "I should've called you before. I might've been able to save Adam's life. It's all my fault. I should've called and pre-vented this."

"Slow down, Victoria. What do you mean you could have prevented this?"

"That list of victims of the Patrons of Perseus that I found in U.S. Army Intelligence file ..."

"Yes. ... "

"Well, I went back to those files ... "

"Victoria, I told you not to do that."

"... and found another name added to the list about twenty four hours ago. The name was Adam Warburton."

"Wow. It really does sound like the Patrons have ongoing opera-tions. Somebody decided to make him the next target of the Patrons and added him to the end of the list—diabolical."

"I tried to call Adam to warn him, and he wouldn't respond. By the time I got hold of his mum to warn her, she told me that Adam was already dead. The police think Dr. Conrad murdered Adam in his office at Stanford."

"Whoa. That doesn't make any sense."

"As I said, Dr. Conrad's wanted for questioning and seems to be on the run."

"Victoria, if there's truly an undercover assassination unit of the U.S. Army targeting those they think are cowards with PTSD, maybe they made it look like a murder by Conrad to cover it up. There's probably nothing you could've done to prevent Adam's death."

"It doesn't feel that way. I'm devastated."

Understandable."

"There's more."

"I hesitate to ask. But, hit me."

"I hacked into Army Intelligence files again a few hours ago ..."

"Victoria. ... "

"... and discovered that Dr. Conrad and Libby have bigger problems than evading the Feds for espionage and the State cops for his trumped up murder charge. I found something far worse."

"What is it?"

Pausing for a beat, Victoria finally blurted out, "Libby and Dr. Conrad's names appeared just hours ago on the Patrons' hit list."

Now Jennifer halted for a beat.

Not receiving the usual rapid-fire response from Jennifer, Victoria repeated, "Libby and Dr. Conrad are next in line for assassination by the Patrons."

Finally, Jennifer was able to process what Victoria was saying. "That's devastating. What an unbelievable catastrophe you've uncovered. At this point, their lives depend on them getting into hiding and you and I exposing this travesty. We've got to get the good parts of our government to shut it down."

"How're they gonna do that?"

"Don't know but we have to help them. The new Patrons of Perseus obviously will do whatever they need to do to keep their current activities from being uncovered."

"One more thing."

"I'm not sure I can take any more," Jennifer exclaimed.

"Libby and Dr. Conrad called me from somewhere in California just a little while ago. I told them they're targets and should hide."

"How'd they take the news?"

"Took them a while to wrap their heads around it, that's for sure. I told them exactly how much danger I think they're in, and to go into hiding."

"Good call. You think they'll follow your advice?"

"Who knows? This is Dr. Conrad we're dealing with here."

"Let's hope he uses his head and gives us enough time to find solid proof to expose the Patrons and shut them down before he and Libby are assassinated like Adam."

"I've never played for stakes so high. It's very frightening."

"I told you, Victoria, this is no game."

"I believe you now. I have to focus. You said you need records of the modern Patrons of Perseus, including operational plans, names of assassins, victims, dates, and the Army Intelligence files of operatives in the present day."

"Yes. That proof has to be in the form of sources inside current operations—which I'm working on—or copies of actual documents—which is where I hope you can come in."

"I don't think any of the information you want is online. I can't find it anywhere. Isn't my list of names downloaded from the Army Intelligence files enough?"

"Nope. Not for something this hot. The best way to get the proof we need is to find an informant or whistle blower on the inside. Do you know anybody who could help corroborate your findings and provide further information and documents on the Patrons?"

"Not really. Maybe we're gonna have to go Neanderthal like you usually do, so we can find hard copies of the proof we need."

Jennifer cringed, feeling very old again. Victoria had a way of doing that to her.

Victoria continued. "If you need documents or copies of them, and they're not online, I think the best way to get the corroboration you need is for me to go after the documents myself."

"But where are they stored?"

"That's a little problem I still have to solve. Don't know. But I have a hunch. I'm gonna snoop around Madingley Hall here in Cambridge later today and find out what the U.S. Army's doing there."

"Victoria, Neanderthal may be old-fashioned, but it can still be very dangerous. I think finding an informant is safer."

Ignoring her, Victoria rattled on, nearly matching the high speed thoughts and speech of her colleague at the other end of the line. "All those names on the current list of the Patrons that match the army's official list of suicides have an asterisk next to them referring to 'Madingley.' I've looked and looked online and can't find anything in the army database on the Patrons or their current activities other than that list of victims. However, the list does seem to be continuously updated online."

"Maybe we should get the British authorities involved in this—MI5 and London Metro. It could be too dangerous for you to do yourself."

"Not until we know which authorities are involved with the Patrons and which aren't. We don't want to tip our hand about our suspicions to the very people we're trying to undercover."

"Good point. But this is very, very dangerous. Not just for Libby and Conrad, but for you, too. I think I should contact a senior government official over here, and see if I can get some action on this matter with people we can trust. I'm gonna say it again. Keep me posted. And be careful."

"I will. This isn't fun anymore," Victoria said.

Chapter 63

EN ROUTE TO TIJUANA, MEXICO:

Trying to get his bearings on the situation while decompressing for a moment at his Lake Arrowhead home, Conrad spiked Libby's coffee with Bourbon at her request, while drinking his own coffee black. "Let's regroup. We know why Adam was killed. We know why we're targeted. It's that damned Medallion. The army knows we have it and is afraid we know they've reactivated the Patrons of Perseus. Somebody there's trying very hard to keep us from exposing that."

"This whole thing is unbelievable," Libby said shaking her head, the pain of her son's death seeming to consume her soul.

"The U.S. Army killing its soldiers deemed cowards. Making it look like suicide. Haven't we learned anything in the past century?"

"The army's also killing its own soldiers and making it look like murder," Libby said, eyes downcast again and beginning to fill with tears. "What an outrage."

Libby's tears brought Conrad back to the present and he responded in a supportive tone, "This must be horrible for you. We've gotta do something. Can't stay here for long—I'm sure they'll look for us here within hours. What a jam." Conrad paced up and down, combed his fingers through his thick hair again and again, and then popped a piece of candy into his mouth. Without thought, he chomped it right down and popped another piece, stewing and sorting possible actions in his mind, trying to find a plan that made sense.

Finally, Libby said aloud, "Nobody's gonna believe all of this without solid proof."

"That's for sure. Good thing Jennifer Roberts and Victoria Chamberlain are working on that."

"Meanwhile, we need to keep our heads down and try to survive until they tell us it's safe. What're we gonna do?"

"Sorry, but it's just not my style to hunker down and wait," Conrad replied. "I think we need to go to England and help Victoria find the proof."

"Oh, yeah. Go to the U.K. And exactly how're we gonna get there?"

Conrad ignored her and continued. "Without proof, we're trapped. We don't have much time until they find us. Might as well spend that time trying to save ourselves. There's no other way out for us."

"Gus, we have no idea where the current-day records are kept. Without those, this scandal won't be exposed."

"I say we start with your Papa Nigel's military records and his Medallion. I bet that evidence will lead us to Adam's murderers and the records of present-day operations."

"We're not detectives."

Continuing to ignore her, Conrad started to pace up and down, and remained intensively preoccupied and self-absorbed while hatching his plan. "Probably, we should start with documents from the Great War Archive ... and try to find where Papa Nigel's own military records are stored."

"They're evidently not in U.S. Army files online. Victoria couldn't find 'em."

"Right. The only way to investigate other sources is to visit the Great War archives in England in person. The Imperial War Museum in London has many important military records. Maybe Papa Nigel's are buried or misfiled there."

"Or at Maudsley Hospital in London," Libby added. "Papa Nigel was hospitalized and died there."

"You mean the Bethlem Royal Hospital—old Bedlam—where the Maudsley World War I records are supposedly stored."

"Right. But Jennifer thinks classified U.S. Army Intelligence records could be in Madingley Hall outside of Cambridge. Possibly the modern records are there, too."

"It's beginning to look like we've got no alternative but to go to several sites in the U.K., in order to find out who killed Adam and why."

"You mean Victoria needs to do that," Libby shot back.

"I have a creepy feeling that evidence of this horrible secret operation is being hidden somewhere in the U.K., by the U.S. Army with the cooperation of the Brits. We should be able to get the help of my Cambridge mentor, Professor Trevor Chamberlain, as well as Victoria, to search the archives there and find out what's going on."

"Earth to Gus. How're we gonna get there?" asked Libby. "Surely they'll be able to track us before we board any international flight. Did you forget you're a double fugitive from the Feds for espionage and from California for murder? That's one up on me."

"Believe me, I haven't forgotten. It's just that we could get there if we take a private plane."

"How're you gonna pull that off? And don't they have to file a flight plan anyway?"

"Yes, but it takes a while to get that information back to the U.S. from Mexico. The government there is slow and corrupt, if not useless."

"Mexico?"

"Yes, we are less than two hours from the Tijuana airport the way I drive. And, we need to switch cars. Going down to the border and leaving a car there that looks like the Aston will draw too much attention."

"You have another car we can go in?" Libby asked.

Conrad shot her a look.

Libby then said, with a chuckle, "Why of course you do."

"Yep. I've got an old SUV in the garage. An ordinary Mercedes, nothing flashy," said Conrad dismissively. "My stepbrother comes up here sometimes and uses it when he stays."

"There's nothing ordinary about a Mercedes SUV," replied Libby. "You have a step brother?"

"Yeah, don't know him very well, though. He was born in Germany right after World War II. He's twenty-years older than me."

"Your mother was German?"

"Yes, so was my stepfather, but I never met him. Mom remarried after my stepbrother left home, so we grew up separately. Never been close. Anyway, he'll never miss the car. He won't be coming up here again till next year. We'll take it to Tijuana and park it there."

"And what about credit card transactions? Won't they be traced?"

"Not if you've already paid." Conrad took a NetJets card out of his billfold. "You put $100,000 increments on these cards at a time, in advance, and NetJets just deducts it from the prepaid card when you get to the airport. Sort of like a prepaid debit card."

"Some debit card. A hundred grand at a time?"

"Do you have your passport? I got mine."

"In fact, I have both of them," Libby answered.

"You mean yours and Adam's?"

"No, I mean both my British and American passports. I have dual citizenship," Libby explained.

"Oh, that's what you meant by being an American. Anyway, for the outbound trip, use your British passport. You may need the other one to get home," Conrad suggested. "Finish your drink, and I'll use my burner to charter a plane."

"I don't know about this. Are you sure this is gonna work?"

"It'll take a while for the authorities to figure out what we've done, and by then we'll be through customs in the U.K., especially if we go to a secondary airport."

"Stansted is a secondary airport in England, and very close to Cambridge," Libby suggested.

"Exactly what I was thinking. In the meantime, you can take a quick shower if you want, and I'll arrange the plane. Then you can cook up these eggs and bacon we picked up at Walmart and make us an after midnight breakfast while I take my shower. We can then wolf it down and get outta here."

As Libby emerged from the bathroom looking fresh and relaxed, almost radiant despite it being the middle of the night, she said, "That shower was just what I needed. It gave me some energy. Now I'm starving."

Conrad was already on a desktop computer, searching the Internet for news and for driving instructions to the General Abelardo L. Rodríguez International Airport in Tijuana. "We made the local news in the San Francisco Bay Area, but not the national news yet. Any luck at all and we'll squeeze out of the U.S., to Mexico and then England before the authorities are alerted."

"Now I'm worried again. We have to stay ahead of the story or we're going right back to Palo Alto in handcuffs."

"Yeah, yeah, but the point is, it has not even reached the news here in Southern California. Meanwhile, I already booked the plane. Will you make us some breakfast while I shower?"

At just that moment, Conrad felt her energy, noticed the attractiveness of her blonde hair and blue eyes, and appreciated her sense of purpose in the midst of all the chaos. The quiet serenity of the lake in the presence of Libby ignited his anticipation as they prepared to depart for the border.

Chapter 64

AT "THE WASHINGTON POST," WASHINGTON, D.C.:

Turning on the lights in the newsroom, Jennifer Roberts noticed that things were just beginning to stir at *The Washington Post* as dawn was breaking outside. Slumping down in her chair, grasping double-fisted Marko Mochas—one in each hand, the one on the right nearly drained, she yelled. "Bert, are you here yet? Get over here, I need your help already."

A voice from the other end of the room wafted over the cubicle dividers, "And a pleasant good morning to you, too, Ms. Roberts." Arriving at her work station, Bert thrust his bald head into the opening to her compartment. Jennifer noted out of the corner of her eye that Bert had an imploring look on his face with those dark puppy dog eyes of his. Giving him the benefit of only the most transient eye contact, Jennifer remained preoccupied with organizing her work space and multitasking on her smart phone.

Bert then said, "Boy, you look like crap. With those dark semi-circles under your eyes, sure you weren't punched last night? And before you say anything, maybe I should wait to talk with you until the grump awakens." Looking down at the untouched second iced-mocha, Bert then pointed to it and said, "Think I'll come back after you get that second jolt of rocket fuel inside you. This still looks like a no-fly zone over here."

"Very funny, smart ass. I need to talk to several people today. See if you can get Senator Benham on the line as soon as she gets into her office. I also need to talk to that Colonel Richards over at the Pentagon. And tell our managing editor Samuelson I need a slot on the front page of the Sunday paper for a blockbuster scandal for him to print as long as you're able to help me get all my ducks in a row by deadline Saturday. Move. And tell him I want the story above the fold. Move."

"I'm movin' ma'am. But be gentle. It's early," Bert joked.

"Grr," Roberts growled.

Chapter 65

AIRBORNE EN ROUTE TO STANSTED AIRPORT, ENGLAND:

Conrad and Libby were fortunate to procure the services of a Gulfstream G550 with the range to get them nonstop to Stansted Airport from Tijuana.

"What do you think of our little rocket ship here? Probably last used by a member of the Mexican drug cartel," Conrad chortled.

"Amazing! I've never even seen one of these, let alone flown on one."

"Blew a hole right clean through my hundred thousand dollar NetJets card, but I don't care. We gotta get there to figure things out."

"And fast. I can't believe Adam's gone," Libby said sadly.

"Let's expose the bastards who did this so no other soldiers or their mothers will ever have to deal with something like this again."

The tears in Libby's eyes stopped flowing as Conrad saw her set her jaw with resolve. "You've got that right. We don't have anything to lose. We need to put this right and stop the abuse of soldiers with PTSD."

"You betcha," Conrad said as he settled back in his plush seat after takeoff and tried unsuccessfully to relax for the first time in many hours. Instead, stewing with worry, he added, "I looked on the Internet again in the lounge just before we took off, and we still haven't gone global, although there's quite a bit on the news in Northern California. Meanwhile, we've been making incredible time since leaving Palo Alto. Should be landing in nine to ten hours, maybe sooner. The pilot said we've got strong tail winds to blow us to England."

"Let's just hope we blow in before Interpol notifies British immigration services."

"It's gonna be close. We should arrive early morning local time in the U.K., just after sunrise there. So, there'll be plenty of time to rest on the plane."

"That's not gonna be easy."

"I know, but we'd better try and get ourselves somewhat re-charged. We've got a really big day as soon as we land, chasing records all over London and Cambridge, hopefully evading capture by the authorities or *something worse*, by the Patrons."

"You didn't really need to say that again."

Conrad winced, reminding himself he was the one who had dragged Libby into all of this. Trying to be helpful, he said, "Plenty of food aboard and the seats lie flat if you want to try and sleep a bit. We can't go two nights in a row without sleep."

"I'm too wired to sleep right now," Libby responded. "Maybe I can eventually unwind enough to get some rest. But now, I can't turn my mind off—and can't wrap my head around Adam's death."

Conrad felt bad about Libby's situation and what he'd done to complicate it, but knew it was out of his control. The only thing he could do now was to try and bring this travesty to an end. "It certainly wasn't my plan to make your life miserable. So sorry for all this."

"I understand." As Libby was about to continue her thought the plane lurched as it hit turbulence, triggering the "fasten seatbelt" sign.

"These little planes can get thrown around a bit, so let's keep our seatbelts on."

"Things are happening so fast, I'm not sure what we should do once we land. Maybe this isn't such a good idea to be going to England."

"Nonsense. All we need is a little help from our friends in Cambridge once we land."

"Sounds good in theory, but just how do you suppose they're gonna help us find Papa Nigel's records?" Libby asked.

"I think that might be the easy part. What we really need is for them to help us start from those records and trace the evidence to the records of the Patrons' current operations."

"That's the proof we need to save our own skins."

"You got that right."

"Can you believe all the trouble that a century's old piece of jewelry from World War I Britain is causing us?"

Despite a bit of buffeting from the turbulence, the flight attendant on wide spaced legs delivered their plates with an amazing gourmet dinner and without spilling anything.

"The significance of that Medallion is certainly part of the mystery," Conrad agreed.

"Ever since this whole catastrophe began, I've been wondering: what's the difference between a *hero* and a *coward*? Or the difference between being a *coward* and being *mentally ill*?"

"If you figure that one out, you'd need to give a lecture to the Pentagon, I think," Conrad quipped sarcastically.

"Seems like the army thinks PTSD and *shell shock* are the opposite of heroism."

"That's why they want to eliminate PTSD."

"Even to the point of murder." Libby started to tear up again. After a brief pause, and looking fully engaged despite the rocky ride, she continued. "Next question. What's the difference between *shell shock*, which Papa Nigel apparently had, and PTSD, which Adam had? How can one family have three generation of soldiers, one *shell shocked*, another a hero and a third with PTSD? Two cowards and a hero? I just don't get it."

"In the days of your Papa Nigel, psychiatry provided a scientific front to help the army label *shell shock* as cowardice," Conrad informed.

"Today, psychiatry's doing the same thing for PTSD."

"No overt firing squads today, only covert assassination squads."

"Some progress," Libby said sarcastically.

He looked over to Libby's body, now motionless and asked, "Are you asleep yet?"

"Not yet. I'm too worried to sleep. We're on the run, if you remember, and I'm not sure we'll even get through customs and immigration at Stansted."

"Don't worry. I think we're still ahead of the news in the U.K."

"One last thing," Libby added. "I think we go directly to my Papa Geoff's home in Little Hadham as soon as we land, and borrow his car. With no advanced notice, he'll be surprised to see us, but it shouldn't be a problem."

"Good idea. I have several grand in U.S. dollars—Jacksons and Franklins—so we can convert to Sterling and take a cab from Stansted when we land. So, we have a plan. First to your Papa Geoff's place in Hertfordshire, not far from Stansted, and then we need to get to Cambridge to see Professor Chamberlain, which isn't far from Hertfordshire."

"Good idea."

"We need to use cash and our burners to give us the best chance of escaping detection for a while."

"When do we land?"

"With this strong tailwind, we should be landing at sunrise, like the pilot said. We'll have all day to investigate matters. Better get some shut-eye if we can, so we're fresh as daisies as soon as we arrive." With that, Conrad turned off his seat light, flattened his seat and arranged his bedding and then fell-off to sleep as he said, "We can still try and get a bit of rest."

Chapter 66

CRAIGLOCKHART, SCOTLAND, SUMMER OF 1917:

Lieutenant Warburton knew he was going downhill fast ever since coming to Craiglockhart. Gaunt from significant weight loss due to no appetite and neglecting his meals, as well as weak from lack of exercise, he was getting tired of everybody telling him he looked terrible. Now the staff was on him about his hygiene as he was too indifferent to shave, bathe or even change his clothes for days in a row.

Nevertheless, Warburton was trying to do his bit to play the "hail fellow, well met" routine for Owen. Sassoon also played the game as well as he could, but as was his style, he cloaked his friendly responses in genial ridicule and tepid contempt for the place. For all the banter, Lieutenant Warburton knew that the truth, however, was far different than the "cheery chap" act of forced masculine conviviality. In reality, residents of Craiglockhart were coerced to display that as a matter of therapeutic military policy. Warburton thought all this false camaraderie did was mask the terror of the nights during the hours of the day. Unable to penetrate the nights, the atmosphere instead attempted to make the days appear as contrived pleasure.

Awake during the day, Warburton noticed the officer-patients and their psychiatrists tried to counter the gloom of the place. They did all they could to hide the seriousness of why they were here. However, their various stupid activities failed to get them to ignore the wrecked faces amongst themselves. Cheerful conversation attempted to blunt the aura of melancholy and weariness that was Craiglockhart by day.

By night, it was far worse, especially tonight. The sky was black and foggy while thick sheets of rain continued to fall. Warburton lay awake in his single room, encased in the smell of stale cigarette smoke and the rising dampness issuing from the rotting bones of the building. Meanwhile, the sound of shuffling feet penetrated the quiet from the passages of the old place.

Warburton thought the sounds were the most wretched thing about the night. An unrelenting chorus of morbid muttering and droning all night long, emitted from the men around him and continuing throughout the night. Continuous moaning punctuated at regular intervals by screams of terror emerging from their shared underworld of suppressed memories. These reflections may have been submerged during the day for the men, but came out to play at night. There was no respite at night for any of the men, only torment. The sounds dared Lieutenant Warburton to fall asleep and re-experience his own demons. He anticipated them nightly amidst the predictable shocks and self-lacerating persecution he could not avoid.

Chapter 67

AT "THE WASHINGTON POST," WASHINGTON, D.C.:

Jennifer Roberts' cell phone rang at her desk. Punching her phone to answer, she heard, "Jennifer Roberts? Hold for the senator."

After a long pause, "Hello, Jennifer, this is Senator Benham returning your call. Must be important for you to get back to me so soon, and so early in the day. What's up?"

"Did you hear Dr. Conrad has been accused of murdering one of his patients, an active duty soldier seeing him for a psychiatric consultation at Stanford?"

"Wow. What has Gus done now? No, I haven't heard it from official sources yet or the news, but wouldn't believe it if I heard it. As you know, I've known Gus Conrad since college and would have a hard time believing anything like that about him."

"In fact, I'm calling because the accusation indeed seems bogus."

"Agreed."

"The deceased soldier Conrad is accused of killing is someone he met at Fort Hood. He's working with the soldier's mother, a civilian nurse practitioner contracted to work for the Warrior Transition Unit at the base. My investigation has been stonewalled by Fort Hood, by the Pentagon and by army psychiatry."

"Well, army psychiatry is certainly under fire these days, what with the rash of suicides they're experiencing among soldiers, with two incidents of mass murder-suicide at Fort Hood and other shootings and suicides at additional army bases in the U.S. When criticized, the army circles the wagons, denies everything and hopes the issue blows over. Then it's back to business as usual."

"Exactly what I fear is happening now. But this time they may be hiding an explosive secret. If so, I'm gonna need your help."

"Shoot. Sorry, bad metaphor. Tell me more."

"Well here it is. I have a contact from the U.K. who tells me that the Patrons of Perseus, the assassination unit of the British Army from World War I that I uncovered for my Pulitzer, may have been taken over by the U.S. Army and may still be in operation, targeting soldiers with PTSD who served in Iraq and Afghanistan.

"What!"

"We've discovered a list of names of victims of the Patrons of Perseus dating back to World War I, but with an ominous group of contemporary names added in recent months that match those names on the official list of recent army suicides."

"I don't know what to say. How'd you get the list of the victims of the Patrons of Perseus?

"A young hacker from the U.K. found the list online."

"Oh, no, not another Edward Snowden. And why target soldiers with PTSD?"

"As far as why, it looks like the army may be trying to silence or eliminate its worst examples of the ravages of war to discredit the notion of PTSD."

"Aha. Probably also to keep people like me from diverting resources for weapons to psychiatric care and pensions for those injured with PTSD by these wars. Has our hacker released the findings to the public or the press?"

"Well, she's released this information to the press through me, and as far as I know, only me. I'm looking to you as a highly placed but anonymous government source to confirm the existence of an ongoing military operation sanctioned by U.S. Army Intelligence to kill their own soldiers with PTSD as cowards. Can you help?"

"Sounds too incredible to be true. I'm not only head of the Armed Services Committee of the Senate, but also on the Senate Select Committee on Intelligence, and I've never heard anything about this. I would've been briefed if that were true. So, no, I cannot confirm this story of yours."

"I think it's possible the spike in suicides the army is experiencing may be due in part to a modern Patrons of Perseus operation assassinating soldiers and making it look like suicide."

"Hard to believe the army would be doing that," the senator fired back.

"After investigating the head of Army Intelligence and the head of army psychiatry, I think it's simply the most gruesome aspect of some in army leadership as well as their inability to grasp the difference between true cowardice and legitimate psychological reactions to serving in the armed services, especially in combat. And I have something else to tell you."

"I'm afraid to ask what that is."

"I think it's possible the Patrons killed Conrad's patient and framed him for it."

"Omigod. Why would they do that?"

"The young soldier was about to discover the existence of the Patrons because it turns out his own great-great-grandfather was a member of the Patrons back in World War I. Plus Conrad is a real pain to army psychiatry with his very public criticisms of their mental health programs."

"That's true, but frame him for murder? Hard to believe."

"Wait. One more thing."

"I'm not liking this conversation. Go ahead, I think."

"My hacker found that the list of targets of the Patrons of Perseus contains the name of the patient Conrad is accused of killing."

"I'm really not liking this conversation. That finding is consistent with the Patrons killing Conrad's patient and then framing him for it."

"Exactly what I've been thinking."

"I don't need this problem right now. What a horrific mess."

"Sorry, but you have one more piece of bad news you still have to hear."

"Uggh."

"Adam is not the last name on the list. Dr. Conrad and Adam's mother have just been added. I think they're now in grave danger, and will be assassinated imminently by the Patrons."

"I'm on it. Looks like I'm gonna have to call for a special investigation. Let's see if I can get that started and keep it under wraps for a bit."

"If you can confirm the existence of an active assassination unit, I'll expose it. And you can shut it down. Meanwhile, you can help get your friend Conrad out of quite a jam."

"'Quite a jam' doesn't describe what Gus has stumbled into this time."

"Hurry, Senator. Hurry. We're counting on you."

"Like I said, I'm on it."

Chapter 68

MADINGLEY HALL, CAMBRIDGE, ENGLAND:

B rigadier General Andreas Rossi walked into the breakfast room and
sat down at the table for two where Richards was already seated and
sipping her morning coffee.

"Good morning," she said with a hoarse voice.

"Good morning. A little ragged around the edges to start the day
are we? How about some good news to brighten your dreary English
morning?"

"Sure, my body always arrives ahead of my brain whenever I travel to
Europe. My brain won't arrive until later today. Anyway, go ahead and
brighten things for me, sunshine."

"Take another sip of coffee and let me get some food first." Rossi
walked over to the buffet and grabbed a traditional English breakfast for
himself. *English style bacon, scrambled eggs, mushrooms and tomato would
do just fine,* he thought.

Returning to the table with Richards, Rossi said, "I got a call in the
middle of the night from one of our operatives. Conrad just killed one of
his patients."

"What? Did I hear you correctly? Conrad killed a patient?"

"And get this. It was one of our soldiers seeing him as a patient in his
office in California. Can you believe it?"

"Who was the soldier?"

"Don't remember his name. But he was stationed at Fort Hood. We should be able to duck any bad press and nail his ass now. He's as good as toast. By the way, can you pass me some toast?"

Richards handed over the tray of toast and asked, "Well, that should make you happy."

"Some slacker with PTSD evidently. Seems your fucking psychiatrist friend Conrad is evidently addicted to pain pills and our guy was supplying dope to him when Conrad would come around to Fort Hood to teach. Musta gotten greedy, maybe tried to blackmail the doc, and pow, he's yesterday's news. Anyway, Conrad is discredited and he'll no longer be a thorn in our side."

"Or a pain in the neck."

"I was thinking he was a pain somewhere lower down on the anatomy. Goes to show that your psychiatrist colleagues and their leftwing political friends are useless and there's no place for psychiatry in the military. We shouldn't 'treat' cowardly bums, but just throw them out of the army before they infect everyone else."

"Settle down, Andy," Richards meowed as she stroked Rossi's upper arm with her hand reaching across the table. "That's more or less what we're already doing by isolating psychiatric complainers in Warrior Transition Units, then discharging them, letting the VA deal with them. I'm seeing to that."

"Meanwhile, I can't wait to see Conrad arrested for violating his parole on our Federal espionage charge once the California cops slam his ass in jail."

"No, I think we keep a low profile and let the California police handle it all by themselves for now. Murder with state jurisdiction trumps our bogus Federal espionage charge. We can keep tabs on the murder investigation by insisting on a joint task force with army criminal investigation command. Once they have Conrad in custody, we can take over whenever we want."

"You've got a point there, Colonel Richards. Not bad for a psychiatrist." Rossi took a deep breath and a wicked smile came across his face as he thought about it.

Richards continued, "Watching Conrad sink into so much trouble is turning out to be more fun than tearing wings off a fly. Let's see him slowly get crushed, maximizing his defeat and demoralization. That's what he deserves. Nobody threatens your army or mine."

"Why, Ellen. I couldn't have said it better myself. I think I'm in love. Talk like that really turns me on."

Chapter 69

SCOTLAND TO LONDON, SUMMER OF 1917:

The next morning Lieutenant Warburton left his room and walked to his psychiatrist's office. A brief jaunt between buildings exposed him to ominous clouds above, promising another wet and blustery Scottish day. He was going to his regular session with his psychiatrist Dr. W.R.H. Rivers, a kindly man with a professorial bearing that he came by honestly. Dr. Rivers had entered the Royal Army Medical Corp to support the war effort by interrupting his teaching at Cambridge University. He had substituted his academic "uniform" of a three-piece suit, traditional waist-coat with pocket watch and fob for a proper senior officer's uniform with riding boots, jodhpurs, and walking stick. His kind face was graced by wire-rimmed glasses and a handlebar mustache. Dr. Rivers had tried for many months now to assist Lieutenant Warburton out of his funk and deep hole at Craiglockhart. But it was to no avail. Warburton really had no interest in continuing to interrupt his daytime by purposely dwelling on the same sick memories that intruded involuntarily into his sleep.

Why rehearse it over and again? Warburton asked himself as he walked into the medical building for his appointment. It was always the same thing, namely that fateful execution in France. Jennings' face looking peaceful and accepting, and not angry. No fearful coward at all. Elegant dignity snuffed out by a gunshot strategically placed to the back of his head—center mass. Not an execution. Murder. Ricocheting blood, brains and bones all over Lieutenant Warburton's shooting hand, his face and his neck, never to be washed away from his thoughts.

"So, how was your night, lieutenant?" Dr. Rivers asked.

"Same as always."

"Can we talk about your dream?"

"Again?" Warburton questioned.

"Yes. Eventually you will become desensitized to it."

"Nice theory, doc, but no signs of that. I'm a hopeless case. I should be shot or maybe I should shoot myself."

"I'm growing increasingly concerned by those statements as well as your lack of progress here. You're certainly not on course yet to return to duty after about a year of treatment, so I've decided to send you to another hospital a bit closer to home. There's a new place receiving officers now that was just constructed for *shell shock* patients, and I think that's your best chance of recovering. They have some of the new therapies there like faradization we don't do here and might be helpful to you."

"Giving up on me, huh, Doc?" asked Warburton.

"Not at all. Just a change of scenery and some new hope."

"Where's this miracle place?"

"In South London. I know you live in Hertfordshire north of London, but it's readily reachable by train for your family to visit you there," said Dr. Rivers.

"Thanks, Doc. Oh, by the way. What's it called, this new hospital?"

"The Maudsley Hospital named after Sir Henry Maudsley, the famous psychiatrist."

"I'd rather go to Bedlam with the lunatics."

"The Bethlem Hospital is for incurables and the mad. Your *shell shock* is still quite treatable."

Lieutenant Warburton had a bad feeling about just how wrong that prediction would prove to be.

Chapter 70

MADINGLEY HALL, CAMBRIDGE, ENGLAND:

" ...So in conclusion, resilience training is the most effective intervention known today to prevent combat related stress reactions. Combat stress should be prevented, not treated. Thank you very much," Rossi said, finishing his lecture with a flourish.

The conference room held about fifty behavioral health experts as participants in the meeting from the U.S., and U.K. The audience responded with polite applause as Rossi ended. The Joint Conference on Combat Related Stress was sponsored every year by the Behavioral Health Services of both the U.S. and British Armies. Rossi loved "telling it as it is" at these conferences, and especially enjoyed being the center of attention. He could see many admiring faces in the audience, including that of Richards in the front row. She sat next to the civilian psychiatric expert on British military psychiatry from the Bethlem Royal Hospital in London, Sir Simon Bessely. The audience was full of Rossi's people—the right kind of psychiatrists and mental health workers, almost all active-duty military, who toiled loyally in the armies of two great allies, the Americans and the British. *If only the leftwing radicals in Congress and the press understood things as well as everyone did in this room, there'd be no epidemic of PTSD or suicide,* Rossi told himself. Only heroes should be allowed in the army and losers should be excluded or expelled.

Richards had given her talk earlier that morning on the spike in army suicides of recent months, attributing them to the poor quality of recruits and their pre-existing psychiatric problems. It was now time for their closed breakout session and working lunch with the half dozen U.S. Army officers and similar number of British Army officers who worked covertly out of Madingley Hall on joint behavioral health projects, sharing ideas and resources.

Rossi and his counterpart, who was a British Army general and also head of Army Intelligence for the U.K., sat at opposite ends of the conference table. Just as they were about to start, Rossi's cell phone summoned him. He left the room and then came storming back in a few minutes, taking Richards aside while the others waited for him to begin the proceedings. "That bastard Conrad eluded Palo Alto P.D. They have a BOLO out on him and that nurse friend of his, but no results yet. Sealed his mother fucking guilt, for sure," Rossi spouted as he began pacing, all the while launching spittle as he fumed and spoke.

"Settle down, Andy. We'll get him. Let's focus on the business at hand, then we'll get more follow-up details after this meeting," Richards said in a reassuring tone.

"Lousy yellow-bellied invertebrate, that Conrad. Too chicken to face the music like a man."

"Andy, we're all waiting for you," Richards said in a low voice, pointing towards the conference table.

Rossi stopped pacing, tried to compose himself, sat at one head of the table and took a long drink of water. "Let's begin. General MacDoogle, any opening comments?"

"Thank you General Rossi. And thanks to all of you who've come to our quarterly review of joint activities. I welcome you all on behalf of behavioral health programs shared by our great and historic alliance. First on the agenda are our public programs. Then we go on to covert activities. Colonel Raddison, can you dispense with the public programs? Or shall we call this our smoke screen?" he said, as nervous laughter filled the room.

Dr. Raddison, a lanky U.S. Army colonel, with short-cropped hair and an awkward bearing took her cue and began. "I'd be delighted, General MacDoogle. As you can see from the handout in front of you, we continue to provide for public consumption a number of programs aimed at showing the sensitivity and caring of the military for its psychologically compromised warriors. Community outreach. Publications in the medical literature. Dog therapy. ..."

"Dog therapy?" Rossi interrupted, "Now you're telling me we've gone to the dogs?" More nervous laughter.

"Yes, we've found that troops who claim psychological problems from their army service complain less if they have a dog as a pet—we call it dog-assisted therapy—and it also gets us tremendous positive publicity," Colonel Raddison replied.

"Unbelievable," Rossi continued, shaking his head in disbelief. "What else is in your little bag of tricks, or shall I say, what are the other elements of our little façade for the public here?"

"The list is on page six. You'll see programs for failed relationships, spousal support, financial troubles, substance abuse, legal entanglements, acupuncture, yoga, mindfulness, exercise, diet, vitamins, and chaplains. Details you can read later."

"No fresh air and sunshine therapy?" Rossi asked, sure that he was impressing everyone as being clever and humorous.

"Not per se," Colonel Raddison responded. "But we do tell our psychological complainants that they will get better as soon as they go home and rest."

"Does it work?" asked one of the American army majors at the table.

"Of course not," Colonel Raddison answered. "This type of soldier brought his problems into the army and he also takes them home with him when he leaves the army. It just sounds good and mollifies some of those who are grousing all the time about their service in the army."

"Works for us too," agreed an officer from the British Army with a nod.

"Related to that, we're also publishing articles showing that if you kill yourself and haven't been deployed that it's not the army's fault, but yours. It also seems to be effective in blunting criticism about lots of our suicides," Raddison said. "Major Benson, can you mention our new pilot program, not included in the handout?"

"Sure," responded the young U.S. Army psychiatrist eagerly. "We're also seeding into the public consciousness the notion of moral injury. This is a contribution from the British side of our partnership and we've implemented it to see if it works. It seems to be a good one."

"What's moral injury?" asked a British officer.

"It means you've been morally injured with feelings of guilt and shame instead of pride. Brings to mind moral deficiency, which is something the army doesn't cause, of course, but you bring with you into the army if you have it. Helps exonerate the army from blame for everything that goes wrong with a soldier's life," Major Benson said, beaming with pride and apparently happy for his moment of attention from all around the table.

"Okay," Rossi interjected. "I see from the feedback you document here in our handout from families, affected soldiers and the press that this notion is indeed de-fusing the issue where we've used it. Seems also to be keeping things on a low-boil until the whiners get sent home and booted out of the army. Might be worth expanding. Now, how about the covert operations? See now the folder labeled classified. Colonel Richards, can you take the lead here?"

"Yes, thank you General Rossi. And thank you, members of this joint task force. I appreciate all your support so far getting me up to speed and moving ahead with the covert operations. On top of your folder is the list of veterans groups, wounded warrior charities, etc., that we are infiltrating with operatives who disrupt the proceedings when their purpose is to generate adverse publicity for the army or to influence their local members of congress to take action increasing psychiatric services or pensions for psychiatric problems.

"Is it successful? We don't do much of that here in the U.K.," the British general asked Rossi.

"Big time," Richards responded. "But we're unfortunately having less success infiltrating professional organizations of psychiatrists and psychologists, including our attempts to infiltrate the committees working on diagnostic criteria for PTSD. This is probably going to take some more time to identify and recruit operatives who are trained as psychiatrists or psychologists since these individuals in the civilian world tend to be left leaning and adverse to our point of view."

"Same problem here," the British general nodded.

"Finally, the United States has numerous operatives who are former military, now working in civilian law enforcement, who let us know about murders and suicides of active duty soldiers off base. They're also our eyes and ears for adverse events that various individuals and groups try to blame on psychiatric problems coming from military service. These operatives live in local communities and attempt to keep negative stories out of their local press while working to prevent bad stories from gaining national attention. They also plant 'feel good' stories in small local newspapers that tend to be more patriotic than left wing. Any questions?" Richards asked as she finished.

One of the British officers then asked, "Will we be discussing our programs that plant stories of heroism in the press, and our success in developing stories that discredit those who commit suicide or get PTSD?"

"It's on the agenda for our meeting next quarter," Richards responded. "By the way," she continued, "those of you involved with covert 'Special Operations' will meet with me tomorrow at 1000 hours in the underground conference room in the tunnel connecting Madingley Hall with the American Cemetery next door. Meeting adjourned."

Only a few of the most elite among them knew this meeting was for planning the modern activities of the Patrons of Perseus.

Rossi smiled as he observed his attractive protégé take her assignment seriously and impress the entire team with her performance. *Tonight I'm going to get some well-deserved appreciation,* Rossi thought to himself. After all, he was a *goddamn* general!

Chapter 71

Jennifer Roberts filed her story for the Friday morning *Washington Post* well ahead of deadline.

Inadequate Psychiatric Care at Fort Hood
Just the Tip of the Iceberg for the Army

The article contained quotes from Conrad and others claiming problems in obtaining timely psychiatric evaluations for PTSD for active duty soldiers, not only at Fort Hood, but throughout the entire U.S. Army. Jennifer also hit the army hard on their attempt to separate "post-traumatic stress" from a bad day of combat from PTSD and cowardice. The army was saying that real warriors might get post-traumatic stress, but would certainly not develop into any psychiatric disorder—taking the "D" out of PTSD. A clever attempt to distinguish acceptable short term reactions to war from unacceptable psychiatric disorders. Also included in the story were the standard and expected denials and disavowals from the army via Colonel Richards at the Pentagon, Major Donahue at Fort Hood and others.

Jennifer was pleased with the article, but disturbed she didn't have enough information yet to break the really big story brewing under the surface. Could she prove the Patrons of Perseus were an active unit of the modern U.S. Army? Did the army really reactivate a century-old assassination unit to rid itself of soldiers with mental illness it mistook for cowardice?

Deep into developing the story, now with critical tips from Victoria Chamberlain, Jennifer tried to reassure herself she was going to get the documentation she needed in time to publish an exposé on the army's handling of mental illness for the front page of Sunday's *Washington Post*. Her fingers dug words out of her trusty keyboard as her eyes hunted for the truth on her computer's monitor, pencil clenched between her teeth, Marko Mocha at the ready.

Let's see where I am, she said aloud. Reading her notes on the monitor to herself:

> *1. Evidence the army misunderstands mental illness as cowardice.*
> > *Check.*
>
> *2. Evidence the army does not put a priority on diagnosing or treating mental illness.*
> > *Check.*
>
> *3. Evidence the army covers up its anti-psychiatry warrior mentality with platitudes about all the good things they are doing for soldiers, and by blaming the soldiers for their own mental illnesses rather than combat.*
> > *Double check.*
>
> *4. Evidence the army took over the Patrons of Perseus from the British and is continuing to use them as assassins to kill cowards.*
> > *One source, no confirmation; no primary documents to substantiate.*
>
> *5. Evidence the Patrons killed Adam Warburton to keep him from discovering their secret operations, and to frame Conrad for the murder.*
> > *Same as above*

I need to find a contact inside army operations. Or have Victoria get me those files or I've got no story. Meanwhile, I think I should dig deeper into Colonel Ellen Richards and General Andreas Rossi to see if there's some sort of collusion there.

Just then, Bert's voice came booming over her office partition again. "Hey, sunshine, Jordan Davis on line one. Colonel Richards' brother."

Jennifer couldn't believe her good luck. "Hello, this is Jennifer Roberts."

"You that reporter who writes about the army and psychiatry and PTSD and stuff?"

"Yes, that's me. Are you Colonel Ellen Richards' brother?"

"Yeah."

"Would you be willing to answer some questions I have about your sister?"

"Not on the phone."

"Do you want to come to *The Washington Post* to talk?"

"You kidding? I'm homeless and dirty. I usually hang out under the Whitchurst Freeway along 'K' street. And I'm hungry."

"I'll buy you a meal then. Where?"

"How about over at Au Pied de Cochon off 'K' street?"

"A fancy French restaurant?"

"C'mon, Ms. Richards. How long you worked in D.C.? It's a greasy spoon that's been there for decades, although rumor is they're going out of business soon. How fancy can a place be that's where the homeless live and is called 'the foot of a pig?' Meet you there at one o'clock tomorrow afternoon." And with that, he hung up.

Chapter 72

SOUTH LONDON, AUTUMN OF 1917:

Lieutenant Warburton, feeling low, given the long time he had already spent at Craiglockhart, sank to new depths once he arrived at the Maudsley Hospital. London was just a different type of gloom than Scotland, he noted. More fog, more stench. Same clouds and lack of sunshine.

Accepting his transfer to London as a sign of defeat and a sign he was incurable, he figured he would probably spend the rest of the war at the Maudsley, if not the rest of his life. His nightmares continued at the newly built hospital. He lost his temper frequently. Whenever he could get extra alcohol, usually wine from the officers' mess, he'd get drunk, and when intoxicated, he'd get into arguments and occasionally fights.

Warburton learned that the Maudsley, in south London, was designed as a civilian hospital, but taken over by the army as soon as it opened in early 1916. The army ran it as a *shell shock* subsidiary of No.4 London General Hospital—King's College Hospital—across the street. Officially, it was a "neurological clearing hospital" but different from other facilities with that designation in that the Maudsley treated both officers and "other ranks." However, treatment was not equal, with up-market lounges and individual rooms for neurasthenic officers but crowded wards of many beds side by side for hysterical "other ranks."

It was not many weeks after arriving at the Maudsley that Warburton received a visitor who arranged to meet him alone in the officers' lounge. He stood to attention as the man entered. "Colonel Gregory Reed. I assume you're Lieutenant Warburton," he said returning Warburton's salute.

"Yes, sir."

"As you were, soldier," the colonel responded and they both sat down as the visiting colonel adjusted his tie and lightly burnished his war ribbons. Colonel Reed then took a Medallion out of his pocket. "I understand you were given one of these, because of your service in France. I am the current Commandant for our organization."

Lieutenant Warburton looked down, avoiding Reed's gaze.

"If you're one of us," Reed continued, "then why on earth are you making trouble for the Patrons with Parliament? As a member of the Patrons of Perseus, you have an honored position and obligations to uphold, my man. This is a secret society of the most heroic and noble warriors in the entire fighting force of Britain, as well as the most trusted. We simply can't afford to have one of our own betray the group. We have things under control at the moment, but your letter to your MP has the potential to bollocks things up for all of us. Whose side are you on anyway?"

Warburton continued to look down silently. He knew the importance of the Commandant to the Patrons of Perseus. A visit from someone so exalted and also secret felt ominous to him.

"We've successfully fobbed off Snowdon's inquiries with general reassurances, and they still have no idea that we're executing cowards," Reed explained.

"Snowdon?"

"That whining Member of Parliament from Labour, Philip Snowdon, who's leading an inquiry into whether the army is executing cowards," snarled Reed contemptuously. "Let me read some of the nonsense from your letter to your own MP which was given to Snowdon about our Field Court-Martials and which is damaging to us:

> *"... the stilted brevity of the evidence, the haphazard presentation of the defense, and the perfunctory enquiries which are usually made into the character and record of a convicted soldier."*

"What the hell were you thinking sending this? Good thing they don't believe it."

"But it's true," Warburton finally said.

"What's that got to do with anything?" Reed said, pressing him. "The point is the army cannot suffer cowards in its ranks and yet it's not acceptable to the public or the government to have a public policy of executing cowards who use *shell shock* as an excuse for not fighting. Most of the public is poorly informed and think these men are sick or wounded. Idiots," he spat out in contempt.

"But *shell shock* is a psychological wound, not cowardice or just some excuse. It should be abundantly clear to all by this point in the war that even the bravest man can break down," argued Warburton, finally showing a bit of spunk.

"Don't go down that road, Lieutenant Warburton. And we're now more than a bit suspicious of you. Since you've gone off the rails, we've been wondering whether you've turned coward on us, are a traitor or both."

"Nonsense. You're not going to intimidate me with that," Warburton fired back, now fully piqued. "It's wrong to execute our own men as cowards when they have *shell shock*. And you know it. There's a difference between a man who's been psychologically wounded by war and a deserter. And there's a difference between execution and murder. God knows, there's a difference," he said as the face of Jennings appeared in front of his eyes.

"It's clear I'm getting nowhere with you today, lieutenant. Let me say emphatically, 'don't rock the boat any further.' We still have 'Old Mac' plugging for us in the Commons, but if your stuff gets into the press, you never know what could happen. We have policies that are honorable but we must preserve as a state secret what we really practice so the government and our military leaders can deny those practices in public. That's why the Patrons are so critical to our army's success. We do the necessary dirty work to keep up the morale of our troops so we can win this gawd-dammed war."

"Yes, sir," Warburton said unconvincingly.

"You hardly seem enthusiastic, Lieutenant Warburton. A piece of advice. Keep your mouth shut. You need to get well and back into action for us. And if not, let me give you another word to the wise. Now, how shall I put it? Let's just say it would not be good for your health if you send any more of these," the colonel said glaringly as he stuffed Warburton's letter to Parliament back into his pocket, turned around and strutted out.

Chapter 73

MADINGLEY HALL, CAMBRIDGE, ENGLAND:

Rossi knocked on Richards' hotel room door. "Ellen, it's me. I need to speak with you about tomorrow."

Richards was in her sweats as she answered the door. "Can't it wait until breakfast? I'd like to get some rest."

"It'll just take a minute," Rossi said as he pushed into the room and closed the door behind himself. "Since I'm gonna chair the sessions tomorrow and introduce the speakers, I won't be going over to the underground conference room tomorrow, so you'll have to handle that meeting on your own, okay."

"Not a problem. I was expecting that. We can discuss more over breakfast in the morning before our meetings begin. Goodnight."

Rossi turned to leave reluctantly. "By the way, I've got some more Special Forces requests from you, my dear," Rossi said with a wicked smile. "You know what that means if you want 'em signed."

"How about tomorrow?"

"I need some relief of my tension now—if you get the drift. This won't take long. Just lay down and be quiet."

With that, Rossi firmly pushed Richards onto the bed, climbed on top of her, and experiencing no resistance from her, took advantage of the situation until all the stress and strain of the day drained away for him.

Chapter 74

SOUTH LONDON, AUTUMN OF 1917:

The morning following his disturbing visit from the Commandant, Lieutenant Warburton felt all washed out. Sleep last night was even more tormented than usual. However, mercifully, morning had come and his demons seemed to recede into the warm sunlight. Not for long today, however. Reading the paper this morning, he became more disturbed than ever. *The Times* of London reported on page one the ongoing Parliamentary inquiry into accusations that the army was killing its own soldiers who had *shell shock*, considering them cowards.

Inquiring on the record, Conservative backbencher Geoffrey Hazelton addressed "Old Mac"—Undersecretary of War, Ian Macpherson—as Warburton read:

> *Is it not universal practice for a most complete and exhaustive report to be called for in every case after a death sentence has been awarded and that, under those circumstances, it is practically impossible for any man to be executed who has suffered from shell shock, because the fact that he has so suffered is certain to be included in the report?*

As the article continued, Macpherson replied:

I am assured of all these facts and in the cases
personally brought to my notice the Court had
given them the most serious consideration. In
fact, when a prisoner on trial had suffered from
shock, that fact was always disclosed. Indeed,
\I have not come across a single case where
any soldier has been executed without being
examined, before trial, and before sentence,
by a medical officer.

The article reported that Members of Parliament continued to press with more questions. Four days after the initial inquiry by the Conservative backbencher, the article reported that "Old Mac" was asked again, this time by Snowdon:

Despite your reassurances, what can you say
about the reports we are getting from the
executioners of our own soldiers? There
is no question among the people as a whole
today upon which they feel more concerned
and more strongly than the carrying out of
death sentences, not because of anything
said in the House of Commons, but because
of statements made by the men who have to
carry out these death sentences—the horror
of them.

Lieutenant Warburton knew—and so did the Commandant—that this referred, without naming him, to his own letter and probably letters from others like him. He bristled as he read Macpherson's reply, a lie now polished as his ritual reassurance:

I have not come across a single case where a man
was proved in the past to have suffered shell shock
or was proved to have been wounded, who had
suffered the death penalty.

Warburton felt sickened. The face of Jennings—just as it looked when he delivered the kill shot—now peered up at him from the newspaper and he was unable to read further. As was his habit when Jennings' face appeared before him, he shook his head like a hound doing a wet-dog shake to try and rid himself of the excruciating image. He stood and got himself another cup of tea while his breakfast dishes were being cleared away. As the face of Jennings receded, he was able to read more of *The Times* of London again, which now quoted from a letter from the butcher himself, Field Marshall General Douglas Haig.

> *When a man has been sentenced to death, if at any*
> *time any doubt has been raised as to his responsibility*
> *for his actions, or if the suggestion has been advanced*
> *that he has suffered from neurasthenia or shell shock,*
> *orders are issued for him to be examined by a medical*
> *board which expresses an opinion as to his sanity, and*
> *as to whether he should be held responsible for his actions.*
> *One of the members of the board is always a medical officer*
> *of neurological experience. The sentence of death is not*
> *carried out in the case of such a man unless the medical*
> *board expresses the positive opinion that he is to be held*
> *responsible for his actions.*

Haig was clearly lying, and Warburton was stunned at the deception. Private Jennings had none of the considerations the Undersecretary of War or the Supreme Military Commander was claiming. Their statements were all lies for public consumption, while the fact remained that the army continued to operate according to their dirty little secret, and the Patrons were key to having one policy and another practice.

The lies piled-up in Warburton's head. *Court-martials where shell shock was always brought up as evidence? Always examined by a psychiatrist? Who worked for the soldier-patient's interests and not the army's? No one with shell shock ever executed?*

Warburton not only knew the truth from the firing squads that he had led, but also he had learned while on the Western Front there were many instances in which another member of the Patrons would summarily execute cowards in "no man's land," without so much as a court-martial when that was more expeditious than going through the ruse of one.

Warburton also knew he could not allow these lies to remain un-challenged or these practices to continue.

FRIDAY

Chapter 75

LITTLE HADHAM, HERTFORDSHIRE, ENGLAND:

As the Gulfstream was on final approach to Stansted Airport north of London just before sunrise, Libby and Conrad were still rubbing the sleep out of their eyes and taking their last sips of morning coffee as their seatbelts were about to come off. Conrad fidgeted in his seat, looking out the window, clicking open and closed the ballpoint pen in his hand, again and again.

Libby finally said, "Calm down, Gus. You've been back and forth, up and down the aisle, in and out of the toilet for the past hour. There's nothing we can do anymore but go through U.K. immigration and hope Interpol doesn't have our names from Mexico or the U.S. yet as fugitives."

"I suppose you're right. We're essentially rolling the dice on being able to get into the U.K. without being arrested. How'd you sleep?"

"Well, considering I didn't sleep the night before during our late run to Lake Arrowhead and then Tijuana, I actually slept like a rock," Libby remarked.

"Amazing how a hundred grand is all it takes to buy you a good night's sleep these days," laughed Conrad.

"I don't suppose you fared as well," Libby said looking at the rumpled blanket and pillow on the floor in front of Conrad's seat.

"Tossed and turned mostly. Planning and organizing our day today and wondering if we'll be able to find the proof we need in the U.K. before we're arrested."

"Or shot like Adam was," Libby said, wincing as she said it.

"Yeah, or shot," Conrad echoed. "Even assuming we're not killed, I'm really leery of what it's gonna be like once we're eventually arrested. I keep obsessing about how I'm gonna get us out of this jam. Surviving alone isn't gonna hack it."

"Here, have one of these," Libby said, passing a mint over to Conrad.

"Thanks. Haven't had my fix this morning yet," Conrad said as he chomped it down. "Can I have another?"

Conrad grabbed the tote bag he packed with a few things from Lake Arrowhead and then heard a curious rattling sound coming from inside the bag, but chose to ignore it. Libby hoisted her own carry-on over her shoulder and they walked down the jet bridge into the Stansted arrivals terminal. Both travelled light, Libby having rescued her bag from her rental car in Palo Alto before they fled in Conrad's Aston Martin.

Outside it was dreary, dark, and before sunrise, with moisture on the tarmac and in the air but not actually raining. It put a chill through Libby as she bounded into the terminal, saying, "Nippy out there this morning. Hope it warms up a bit later. Jolly good ol' England—you can always count on bad weather," she said rather bright-eyed.

"Once inside, Conrad noted they were in a large receiving area with empty mazes of guide-belts with signage that read: this line for "U.K. and E.U. citizens" and this for "non-E.U. citizens."

"You go in the U.K. line and use your U.K. passport, and I'll go over there in the visitors' line for non-European Union citizens. Keep your fingers crossed." Libby slipped Conrad another mint, and then they split into their separate queues. Not really queues, Conrad thought, since both of them were able to go directly to the front of their respective lines as the cavernous terminal was only now beginning to stir for the day. No commercial airline arrivals had yet occurred.

Presenting himself in front of a uniformed official, Conrad noted "Her Majesty's Customs and Immigration" was indicated both on the desk and on a badge across the man's breast pocket. In a disinterested manner, continuing to look down at his copy of *Hello* magazine, the man motioned with one hand for Conrad to come forward—no eye contact made. Conrad offered the immigration officer his passport and landing card.

"Business or pleasure?"

Conrad hesitated. "A bit of both, I guess."

"Where're you staying?"

Conrad's mind went blank. He suddenly realized he had no hotel reservation, and no documentation of any invitation to give a talk as he usually had when travelling abroad. He hoped the immigration officer didn't notice the hesitation in his voice or his quickened pulse causing a bit of facial flushing as he searched for a good answer to the question. *Will he demand documentation?* Conrad asked himself as his own cross-examiner.

"Staying with friends in Hertfordshire," Conrad finally answered. Just then a bolt of terror penetrated right through his midsection as he noted the official scanning his passport through a digital reader and then searching with his eyes up and down the computer screen in front of him. Conrad almost dropped to his knees as the man squinted to read the information on the monitor with more interest than he had expressed yet for anything this morning, as Conrad thought, *I'm a goner for sure.*

With that, the immigration official reached for something under the desk. Conrad wondered if it was an alarm to summon the police or even a gun. Feeling his heart rise up into his throat, and unable to speak, he saw a rapid movement that startled him as the immigration official took an object in his right hand and banged it on a pad and then banged it on Conrad's passport. As it registered to Conrad this was simply an entry stamp the official inked and then entered into his passport—he breathed a huge sigh of relief. The official then proceeded to shove the stamped passport back towards Conrad and said nothing, looking again down at his magazine.

Conrad couldn't believe his good luck as he slinked away, trying not to attract the official's attention again. Catching up with him, Libby said, "That was easy," as she glided quickly and effortlessly through customs and immigration and into the terminal of Stansted airport.

"I agree," Conrad lied. "Immigration is always less of a hassle at private jet terminals. Especially early in the morning before the regular staff arrives. If the authorities back home have reported us to Interpol, the computers from Mexico have obviously not caught up with us yet. Finally some good luck for a change," Conrad said with noticeable relief.

"Let's get a taxi to Little Hadham after you exchange some dollars for pounds, and then I need to get a few things at the sundries shop," Libby suggested.

As they entered a taxi waiting in a queue at airport arrivals, they carried only hand luggage and a few items they purchased at the airport terminal. As the two exited the terminal, they were greeted outside with the continuation of their dreary, overcast English morning. "We're so spoiled in California. We have this thing called the sun there," quipped Conrad.

"If you don't like the weather, you know what we Brits always say, don't you? Just wait fifteen minutes and it'll change for you," joked Libby. Then to the cabbie, "We're going to Little Hadham in Hertfordshire, about a half hour or so from here. Do you know where it is?"

"West of Bishop's Stortford, I believe," the cab driver responded.

"Yes, take the A120 West to the Nag's Head Pub, turn left at the light, then an immediate right and follow the road to Westland Green. We're going to Harley House on Pig Lane."

"Right-o, young lady. Just north of Much Hadham as I recall, where Sir Henry Moore used to live. Some of those big sculptures are still there," the cabbie added, trying to be friendly.

Settling into the back seat with Libby, Conrad said, "I hate not to alert your grandfather before we get there, but I'd rather not use our burners except when absolutely necessary."

"I'm sure Papa Geoff won't mind," Libby agreed.

"So, according to our plan, we'll try to find out what we can about Adam's recent visit here, and also see what Papa Geoff knows about his father—your Papa Nigel—and the Medallion. We've got to figure out how to get what Jennifer Roberts needs to prove the link between that Medallion and Adam's murder. It's probably only a matter of hours before the authorities discover we're here and track us down."

"If they haven't found out about us already," Libby agreed, barely listening as she was clearly admiring the view outside their car window. "Oh, look at those fields. A single splash of yellow oilseed rape. What a colorful interruption of those green meadows. Reminds me of my youth growing up here. I just love the beauty of the English countryside, especially scenes like this. It's spectacular how the colors become so vivid now when they catch a glimpse of the fickle sun. See it there?" she said happily as she pointed to a suspicious sun in the distance. "I guess we must have all that rain for moments of glory like this. Yes, I just love it."

Conrad thought the scene must be providing Libby with an emotional break for an instant from the horrible loss of her son. He was pleased as he observed her getting a brief respite from the tragedy. "I must admit, so do I," said Conrad, pausing his nervous planning to appreciate the moment. "I remember these incredible, if transient glimpses of sunshine glory from the days when I was a student at Cambridge up the road a bit. Great when the sun shines. Should last, what, about fifteen minutes?" Conrad joked.

"Very funny," said Libby. Turning serious, she added, "Let's keep on task. I think we've got to confirm whether Papa Nigel had *shell shock*, in order to figure out why he was murdered by the Patrons."

"My guess is he did have *shell shock*."

"This is so horrible," Libby said with sad eyes looking down again at her hands in her lap. "I can only imagine what the British Army must have thought at that time if one of their officers with a Perseus Medallion got this condition."

"And to think that Adam, you and I have all gotten caught up in this a hundred years later."

"I'm afraid I'm gonna have to face how Papa Nigel got that Medallion in the first place—commanding firing squads. I'm overwhelmed with questions. Including this one—I still don't get the difference between Papa Nigel's *shell shock* a century ago and Adam's PTSD."

"Best explanation is that both are psychological reactions to warfare, with different symptoms conditioned by the social circumstances of the times. The major point for us is that armies have confused both of these with cowardice."

"And armies hate cowards enough to assassinate them."

"Including those with psychological war wounds they mistakenly think are cowards."

"Such incredible injustice. Hard for me to comprehend why the modern army still has this tragic blind spot."

Just then, Conrad looked nervously at his dark smartphone screen, wondering if there was anything about their escape in the news yet, but didn't dare turn it on to find out. "I sure hope we can check the news once we get to Papa Geoff's."

"Gus, we're almost there," Libby said, patting his thigh with her hand and smiling with anticipation as they turned right at the Nag's Head Pub and made their way up Pig Lane to Westland Green and stopped directly in front of Harley House.

Chapter 76

LITTLE HADHAM, HERTFORDSHIRE, ENGLAND:

"Thanks, gov'nor," the cab driver said as Conrad paid him. "Very generous, very generous indeed."

"I can't believe how much the area around our old house has developed since the last time I was here," Libby exclaimed.

"Impressive digs. When's the last time you were here?" Conrad asked.

"Gee, I think it's been almost five years. But I keep in touch with Papa Geoff by phone almost every Sunday, especially since he became a widower last year."

"Your parents still in the area?"

"No, they sold out after the property crash in the late 1980s and immigrated to Canada. Papa Geoff is the last of the Hertfordshire Warburtons."

As Libby came up to the front door, she lifted a heavy metal knocker hanging at about eye level and admired it briefly before she banged it on the metallic plate. Conrad was feeling anxious and wanted her to get on with it, so he could check out the news, but thought it best not to say anything just yet.

"This is a Grade II listed property," Libby said, stepping back and admiring the home.

"What's that?"

"It means the house has some historical significance. Harley House was originally a 17th century cottage built to house farm workers on the local estate, and then a huge addition was built in the 1920s by a famous cricketer."

Conrad felt better as Libby rapped on the door again, and a woman in her mid-40s, cooking spoon in hand and sporting an apron, opened it.

"Libby," she exclaimed in surprise, hugging her with her free hand as Libby hugged back. "I had no idea you were coming for a visit. And who's this handsome gentleman with you?" the woman asked with a wink and a big smile.

"Emma, meet Dr. Gus Conrad, famous American psychiatrist and my boss."

"Boss, you say now?" Emma asked with a skeptical grin.

Ignoring her, Libby continued with her introductions. "Gus, meet Emma, Papa Geoff's long time housekeeper. She lives in the nanny flat next door with her husband Graham. He tends to the property. Emma, we decided to come at the last minute to checkout Papa Geoff and find out more about Adam's recent visit here. Is Papa up yet?"

"Right this way. Mr. Warburton's in the kitchen warming himself by the AGA and getting ready to have breakfast. Want to join him?"

"Sure," Gus said almost too quickly, suddenly aware of the hunger rumbling in his stomach. "I love English breakfasts. By the way, what's an AGA?"

"You haven't lived until you've seen an AGA," said Libby. "It's the most important status symbol of country living by the upper-middle class in England."

Emma added, "An AGA is just a big, old iron cooking stove most admired because it traps heat all day long and makes the kitchen incredibly cozy, keeping your toes toasty any time of the year."

"A stove as a status symbol? You've got to be kidding," Conrad said shaking his head.

"Have you forgotten our horrible weather and how chilly a house can get in England?" Libby responded. "For an Anglophile who plays polo, drives British race cars and went to Cambridge, you're certainly more than a bit deficient in your class education. If you're not careful, we'll take away your hunting-shooting-riding-polo-playing license," Libby said bewitchingly.

"Come along now, kids," Emma prodded.

Conrad looked again at his own dark smartphone, about to jump out of his skin waiting to find out if the news of him had caught up with the British media yet. "That would be the least of my problems right now," he mumbled as they made their way through the front door, and into the enclosed porch at the front of the property.

Following Emma through a second door and then inside the cottage itself, Libby took the second door from Emma and held it open for Conrad. "You see this old door?" Libby asked. "It's the original door for the cottage from the 17th century. Papa Geoff acquired Harley House about sixty years ago, raised his sons, including my father here, and has lived here ever since. It's also where I came to live with Adam while attending nursing school."

Passing through the cottage door, Libby pointed up at the dark, well-hewn oak beams throughout the ceiling of the sitting room as they passed them by. Dark with centuries of aging, they were about a foot wide and a foot deep and twenty or more feet long. "These notches are where the beams were once connected to make up the hull of some late 16th or early 17th century English ship before the ship was dismantled and the wooden parts sent to the countryside for constructing this cottage. Maybe that ship would have even sailed to America shortly after Columbus."

"Now that's old," Conrad said, following Emma to the kitchen. "I always found it interesting that in England what some call a cottage would be called a rather large house or even a mansion in the U.S."

Libby continued with, "And look here," as she pointed. "This is the original Inglenook fireplace. See how it's open so it forms a wall between two rooms, the sitting room and the formal parlor, and big enough not only to cook in, but literally to sit inside to warm yourself?"

"Very cool."

"No, very hot," Libby smiled as they entered the small kitchen at the back of the original cottage and saw Papa Geoff sitting at a table next to the AGA, with a blanket across his lap.

"Look who just blew in, Mr. Warburton," Emma said as they came into the kitchen. The smell of eggs frying, with crackling bacon, tomato and mushrooms all in the skillet on top of the AGA made Conrad's mouth water.

"Well, saints be praised, what're you doing here, Libby?" asked Papa Geoff, taking her hand and kissing her on both cheeks.

Papa Geoff had a few wisps of long dark hair combed back on his head, wobbly jowls and a wrinkled neck, but sharp, alert, piercing blue eyes. He remained seated as Conrad came up to him and extended his hand.

"I'm Gus Conrad, and I'm accompanying your granddaughter on this trip," Conrad said as they shook hands a bit stiffly. Papa Geoff still remained seated.

"Glad to meet you, and take a load off. Emma, can you pour these fine people some coffee and serve them some breakfast with mine?" Fixing his faded-blue eyes on the two, he asked, "You kids hungry?"

"We just got off the plane from the West Coast of America. I'll bet Dr. Conrad is famished," Libby replied eagerly. "Taxi from Stansted dropped us just now. Sorry we didn't call to let you know, but we really couldn't. I'll explain in a minute."

"First things first," Papa Geoff said. "Please sit down here with me. Let's eat." Emma handed Conrad a heaping plate of hot English breakfast and he began wolfing it down in big bites.

"I can't eat. I'm too shattered, Papa," Libby said softly.

"We have some very bad news for you, I'm afraid," Conrad said between bites.

Libby's hands gripped the end of the tabletop trying to hold her emotions in check. Tears welled up in her eyes and she looked down to avoid eye contact with Papa Geoff. "Adam is dead."

"What? What? He was just here a few weeks ago, kicking and sassy. Whatever in the world happened?" Papa Geoff waved his hands in protest.

"He's been murdered."

"Murdered? It can't be true. Libby, how can you bear it? Come here and let me comfort you," Papa Geoff said. As Libby hugged him tight, he whispered, "Mothers aren't supposed to bury their sons. I'm so sorry."

After a long pause, crackling bacon in the background the only sound, Papa Geoff broke the silence and said. "My god. Such a fine young man and with such promise. What a tragedy,"

"Yes, and that's why we're here, to figure out what happened," Libby said.

"In fact, we'd like to get the most recent news. Can you turn on the television?" Conrad asked nervously.

"Sure, young man," Papa Geoff replied and walked out of the kitchen into the sitting room and turned on the BBC News while Conrad and Libby followed. "You still watch the tellie? Most of us modern folks get our news online these days," he said with a smirk as he fished a new iPhone out of the pocket of his robe and handed it to Conrad.

"Papa," Libby asked, "You have a smartphone?"

"Of course, dear. Never underestimate an old man. I even plan to get on Facebook."

"Thanks," Conrad interrupted. *No mention of us on the BBC yet,* Conrad said to himself as he watched the news out of the corner of his eye while he simultaneously thumbed through newsfeeds on Papa Geoff's smartphone. Conrad began to freak out by what he was seeing on the Internet, but decided to remain silent.

"Papa, we don't really have time to explain, but we've got to go snooping around a few places in London," Libby said. "Can we borrow your car?"

"You mean Sally?"

"You still have that thing? You were driving it when I was last here."

"She's still going full gun, thank you very much. She may need a bit of petrol, though. Wellies and Barbour in the back as you would expect. Here're the keys. Have you been gone so long you've forgotten no self-respecting Englishman at his country home would be without his proper Range Rover?"

"Or his AGA?" Conrad interjected.

"Thanks Papa, but I just hope Sally will be able to hold up for whatever adventures lay ahead of us today."

Chapter 77

BRITISH MILITARY HEADQUARTERS, FRANCE, AUTUMN OF 1917:

Across the channel at British Headquarters in France, not long after his visit to see Lieutenant Warburton, Colonel Reed met with the infamous General Haig as part of a larger meeting with several of his staff. The agenda was to discuss an action plan to handle the controversy being stirred-up in the House of Commons about the army executing cowards with *shell shock*. As Reed walked into the meeting room, he saw Haig sitting at the head of the table with his new chief neurologist for the 4th Army, Dr. H.W. Hills, who had recently replaced Dr. William Brown. Also attending the meeting, as always, was the general's adjutant.

"Dr. Hills, how goes it in your new position?" General Haig began.

"Just fine, sir," Dr. Hills replied. "The psychiatrists in the RAMC of the 4th are all on board with the new policy, but we're getting some resistance from the line-officers commanding the troops."

"An order is an order, Dr. Hills, and I insist it be followed," blurted the general forcefully. "And given the pressure from home, we need a policy that in the future, all of our own men arrested as prisoners for cowardice, shall be referred to the neurologist in charge for a medical report."

"With all due respect, sir, there's considerable resistance to this," Dr. Hills tried again. "You should know what the situation is within the officer corps. I don't agree with it, but it's happening nevertheless. Just today in the officers' mess one of the line commanders told me, 'Dr. Hills, we like you but we don't like your circus. We think they ought to be shut up or better still, shot.'"

"I'm hearing much the same thing," the adjutant interjected. "We may have a good policy of referring soldiers to psychiatrists on the books, but you should be aware the 'old stagers' amongst our officer corps are unhappy with this change of policy. As an 'old stager' myself, I can't help but agree with the position out there if a man lets his comrades down he ought to be shot. And, if he's a looney, so much the better."

"Gentlemen, gentlemen. Not a problem here. Not a problem," Colonel Reed butted in. "We have our policy for public consumption, but ways of not letting this *shell shock* nonsense destroy any chance we have of winning the war, as you well know," the colonel said with a smile and a wink. He was proud of creating a policy that deceived the public—a policy that kept the public from knowing the truth about how military psychiatrists really treated *shell shock* and war torn nerves. Indeed, it was a policy that might be admired and followed by armies for the next century.

Chapter 78

CAMBRIDGE, ENGLAND:

As Libby and Conrad gulped down the last bit of coffee, Conrad turned on one of his burner phones and texted Victoria. Almost immediately he received a text back. She was shocked they'd come to England but agreed to meet them in a half hour at the Three Horseshoes Pub near Madingley Hall just outside of Cambridge.

"Thanks for the breakfast, Papa Geoff." Conrad said. "Libby, let's roll."

As they walked outside, Libby asked Conrad, "Wanna drive?" flipping him the keys.

Conrad approached the left-hand side of the car and opened the front door of the faded-silver 1993 Range Rover on the wrong side. "Oops." Flipping the keys back, he said, "Maybe you'd better drive. I don't seem to even know which side the steering wheel is on these days."

"I'm sure this old girl can get us anywhere from Cambridge to London, including across a few muddy fields and streams if necessary with the four-wheel-drive."

Which old girl, you or the car?"

Libby slapped Conrad on the arm playfully. "That's enough out of you, Dr. Smart Aleck. I can see you've had too much coffee this morning."

Libby sped down the back roads, quickly entering the M11 for a trip that usually took forty-five minutes, pushing to make it in thirty or so.

"Gus, do you still have Papa Geoff's smartphone?

"Whoops. Yes, I didn't give it back to him."

"Actually, that's good. Put the Three Horseshoes Pub into Papa's Google maps and tell me where to get off the M11. I've never been there. It's out of the way in a small village on the outskirts of Cambridge. Wonder why Victoria's having us meet there?"

"I guess we'll find out soon enough," Conrad added.

Conrad observed the dew was drying on Sally's windshield as they continued down the road. The sun was playing hide and seek with the clouds, and the day promised to be clear at times, if not cloudy at others.

"So, 'Professor' Augustus Conrad, finish the story. Please explain why psychological wounds between the Great War and the present changed from *shell shock* to PTSD. How can a soldier's reaction to war change so much in different wars and over time?"

"By the way, we need to watch for the exit for the Three Horseshoes off the M11 in about twenty miles. And the answer to your question is that soldiers with combat related psychological injuries have always experienced discrimination, and the experts keep changing the name of this condition as different political forces have come to pass. As you know, the British banned the term *shell shock* during World War I in favor of 'hysteria' or 'neurasthenia,' but by the time we got to World War II, psychological trauma from combat began to be called 'battle fatigue.' The notion during World War II was that everybody had his—"

Libby interrupted, "I notice you didn't say *her.*"

"Exactly true. Everybody had *his* breaking point after too many days of combat. Although one in three casualties of World War II were psychological, you rarely hear that when history glorifies the Greatest Generation."

"Why?"

"Shame. Plus everybody believed at the time there were no long term cases of psychological problems after getting rest."

"Incredible." Libby flipped her hair behind her ear as she was listening and bore down aggressively in traffic, passing anyone she could on the right.

"Yep. We just passed the A428. Next left is The Avenue," Conrad interjected.

"What avenue?"

"Just 'The Avenue.' Turns into High Street after you cross Dry

Drayton Road in a couple of miles. Then the pub's on the left."

"Thanks."

"Anyway, it's not entirely clear in retrospect whether World War II psychiatrists actually believed there were no long-term psychological problems from combat."

"Were they cynical or just stupid?"

"The question is, did they miss what we would call PTSD today, or were they acting as instruments of the army to denigrate cowardice as mental illness and to prevent having to pay pensions?"

"I must admit I've become more than a bit cynical myself."

"I actually think they just missed it. However, when you hear the story of how psychiatrists diagnosed combat related psychological reactions in Vietnam, you'll become an incurable cynic."

"Go on. I can handle it."

"So, right after World War II psychiatrists thought that soldiers could suffer psychological damages due to war, and called it 'gross stress reaction.' Not *shell shock*, not 'battle fatigue,' but 'gross stress reaction.'"

"What's the difference?"

"'Gross stress reaction' was described as a temporary condition caused by exceptionally stressful situations such as war, namely a normal reaction to abnormal events that would go away with rest once the war or catastrophe ended."

"What if it didn't go away?"

"Incredible now in retrospect, but psychiatrists and military commanders thought then they were able to return to active duty almost every soldier who had suffered a psychological breakdown in that war. It was not until much later that it became apparent to everyone just how wrong this was."

"Maybe 'gross stress reaction' was conceptualized just in order to preserve the notion of the warrior as hero."

"And manly," Conrad said with a wicked smile.

"It fits with the idea only those with pre-existing moral deficiencies, weak spirits, or cowards could get mentally ill during combat," Libby reflected.

"True enough," Conrad confirmed.

The sounds of loose gravel crunching under the trusty Range Rover's tires reached their ears as they pulled into the car park of the Three Horseshoes Pub. A thatched white building with three brick chimneys, obviously recently renovated, freshly painted and beckoning as only a century's old village pub can beckon.

"My saga is not complete, but as we are here, that's a story for another time."

"Story indeed. Sounds like a lousy work of fiction if you ask me."

Chapter 79

MADINGLEY, ENGLAND, OUTSIDE OF CAMBRIDGE:

Libby shivered as she pulled her sweater tight against herself while exiting the Range Rover at the Three Horseshoes Pub. "A bit nippy now, with the sun hiding again," she said to Conrad. They entered the pub, bustling with the breakfast crowd as it was still early. Brick fireplaces at each end of the seating area both roared with flames, immediately cutting the cold and announcing this pub as a cozy place to gather. A skinny young woman with a boyish face and long brown hair tied behind her head shot up nervously and waved them over. She appeared dejected and weary with a pair of puffy eyes that had obviously been working overtime crying.

"You Adam's mom? Mrs. Warburton?"

"Yes, call me Libby."

"And I'm Victoria."

"And this is my boss, Dr. Augustus Conrad."

All shook hands and took a table. They sat in silence, Victoria nursing her tea with a nervous spoon.

"By the way, you want a drink or something to eat?" Victoria finally said, motioning to a waitress.

"No, but thanks for seeing us on such short notice," said Libby. "Want another coffee, Gus?"

"No thanks."

Without looking up from her cup of tea, Victoria spoke. "I don't know how I can even face you, Libby. I'm so, so, sorry. Adam's death is my fault. I just didn't act fast enough." Tears welled up in Victoria's eyes as she struck the table with both fists. She had something of a "gentle genius" demeanor about her gawky, unrefined and at the same time innocent and vulnerable. She combed her fingers through unkempt bangs hiding her forehead, saying, "Those bastards running the Patrons must be taught a lesson."

"Thanks for caring so much Victoria. When you're young and someone your same age dies, it's especially hard."

"It's the first time anybody I really knew has died. It's unfathomable."

Stretching across the pub table, Libby took both of Victoria's hands into hers. As their eyes met, tears spilled over in both women. Libby said gently, "Victoria, you did what you could. It's not your fault. What we need to do now is prove who murdered Adam."

After another awkward silence, Victoria took a deep breath, and replied, "You can bet I'll do whatever's in my power to get those bastards."

"But we have to act fast," Conrad said, nervously looking at his watch. "We may only have a few hours before we're caught or worse. Victoria, can you check Interpol for me on your phone and see if we're mentioned as fugitives? We're already on the Internet."

"Sure. I'll do it now as we're talking," said Victoria, multitasking effortlessly. Continuing while punching into her smartphone, Victoria said, "So, if we split-up and each of us pursues a different area, we should be able to meet up again here tonight. You guys could go down to the Bethlem Royal Hospital and double-check to see if Lieutenant Warburton's war records got mixed up with his hospital records since we know he was at the Maudsley Hospital when he died."

Looking down, and suddenly jerking back in her seat, still holding her smartphone in front of her, Victoria continued, "Bad news. Yeah, Interpol has you guys listed as fugitives from California, and wanted for questioning in the murder of Adam in Palo Alto. No indication yet they have any idea you are in the U.K."

Conrad continued, "I was afraid of that. We'd better get this show on the road as we likely have only a few hours of evading detection. There're more security cameras in London than anywhere on earth. If Libby and I go to the Bethlem Royal, maybe Professor Chamberlain could go to the Imperial War Museum and keep checking out those records," Conrad suggested.

"Great plan," Victoria said, now appearing enthusiastic. "He's planning to go to the museum today anyway. One way or another we have to find Lieutenant Warburton's records as well as communiqués and military orders for all the suicides on the current list of victims for the Patrons of Perseus. Gramps'll have to go back and check the relevant un-scanned original files at the museum. He's an old hardcopy Neanderthal."

"I guess I know where that puts me," said Conrad.

"We've gotta breach the Patrons' records and find proof of their current operations, but I've exhausted all I can do online."

"So, what're you gonna do today, Victoria?" Libby asked.

Ignoring her, Victoria said, "I suggest you catch Gramps in his university office for a minute on your way out. Sort out your plans for today. He's in his office now. I'll text him you're on your way. Remember where he works, Dr. Conrad?"

"Yes, I do. Clare College. We're on it."

Repeating herself, Libby asked, "What're you going to do, Victoria?"

"I have a cemetery within walking distance of here I need to visit."

Chapter 80

IN THE TUNNEL UNDER MADINGLEY HALL:

The Commandant took the 18th century oak staircase from Stair Hall down to the underground passageway connecting Madingley Hall to the American Cemetery about a half mile away. Walking over the flagged floor and past wooden Ionic columns dating from 1757, the Commandant briefly glanced at the coat of arms of Colonel Harding—one of the past owners of Madingley Hall—in a large stained-glass window overlooking the stairs. An immense display case on the wall opposite of the staircase contained an 18th century patchwork counterpane the Commandant always liked. The porter at Madingley Hall said it had been donated by another past owner and had been made in 1790. It consisted of pieces of printed cotton material as well as embroidered panels of animals—elephants, tabby cats, golden fish—mythical creatures and flowers, all worked by hand. Upon reaching the tunnel, motion-sensing lights blew pale orange illumination onto the pathway of the Commandant below. After walking a few hundred yards, storage rooms shot off to the sides of a central passageway, where the Commandant's arrival was awaited by several operatives.

Entering the conference room, all stood, and the Commandant snarled, "At ease, gentlemen. Let's get right to work."

Around the small conference table were a dozen or so civilian operators from the U.S., and the U.K., along with high ranking U.S. Army officers.

The operatives were all retired former members of military Special Forces units. The U.S. Army officers all worked in the Pentagon. The Commandant began. "888, can we review the target list?"

"Yes, I have it, 912," a big burly operative with huge biceps and maybe twenty pounds more than he needed around his midriff replied. His belly spilled over a belt holding a handgun in a holster on his right side and a hunting knife in a sheath on his left. "Over the past six months, we've had fifty-two successful mock suicides, all in the U.S. None are being investigated for any other cause of death. Plus one other that was an execution that framed a doctor for murder. I believe we're caught up."

"Not so fast, 888. I need to inform you that twenty-four hours ago, I added two more names for action."

"Who are they?"

"Dr. Augustus Conrad and Libby Warburton. You know what that means. I'm authorizing action now. Meeting adjourned."

Chapter 81

UNIVERSITY OF CAMBRIDGE:

Tooling down Madingley Road towards Cambridge, Libby heard Conrad tell her to hang a right onto Queens Road, and then passing Trinity College on their left, take another right into Clare College. A small car park squeezed behind iron gates was still empty due to the early hour. Libby wheeled her faded silver Range Rover into the space next to where Professor Chamberlain's car was already sitting in the slot reserved for the "Master." She shut off the engine, pulled up the parking break with a harsh ratcheting sound and hopped out of Sally.

"I need one of those signs for me at Stanford," Conrad quipped as he launched himself onto the loose gravel on the ground outside his door.

"Very funny, 'Master.' We'll park here for a moment even though we don't have a permit."

Conrad led the way up the stone stairs to the entrance of Clare College, taking two steps at a time. Reaching the top of the stairs, he entered the portal up to the porter's lodge on the left just inside the massive gray stone building that served as the entrance to Clare College. Today was looking very gray indeed in the absence of any sunshine. "We're here to see Professor Chamberlain," Conrad announced to the porter.

"Just missed him," the porter said disinterestedly without looking up from his morning paper. "He's just walked over to a Syndicate meeting for the University Press."

"Cambridge University Press? Over at the Pitt Building?"

"Yes, gov'nor."

A chill went up Conrad's spine as he saw his picture on the front page of the morning paper, facing him as the porter looked at the page three girl inside. Conrad pulled his collar up alongside his face and moved quickly back to Sally to get a baseball cap to serve as a partial disguise. "Let's walk, or rather, let's jog. Too hard to park again. Pitt Building's just a couple of colleges away."

"This is an amazing place," Libby said, looking awestruck as she tried to keep up with Conrad while taking in the Fellows Garden as they crossed Queens Road. Soon they came upon the River Cam. "All Brits know about Cambridge, but very few ever get to attend."

"Ah, look at them 'punting' already this morning on the river."

"It's the namesake of this ancient city—The bridge over the River Cam—Cambridge. The city's been here since the Stone Age. Romans held it for four centuries. Clare College is the second oldest college of the university. Founded 1326."

"That's old. I didn't know Professor Chamberlain was Master of Clare College."

"Yep, Top Dog. And Professor of Imperial History. A major figure on campus and in his field worldwide."

Conrad and Libby could hear the famous boys' choir rehearsing in the majestic chapel of King's College as they passed by.

"Makes me shiver with emotion hearing that sound," Conrad said. "Fond memories."

Walking at a fast pace, they came past the famous sign in five languages to stay off the grass at King's College. "I'm a fellow here. We're the only ones allowed to walk on the grass, so I don't want to get you into trouble taking a shortcut across the grass."

"A vestige of the old class system."

"Not bad if you're a fellow."

Continuing along King's Parade, they passed by several shops, including the Cambridge Chop House.

"Good steaks in there," Conrad said as they walked by briskly. "This whole city is alive with centuries of heritage and significant events. I really feel invigorated every time I visit."

"My I.Q. feels like it goes up by just walking through these streets."

"Some of the smartest people on earth have studied and taught here, and some are still here. First religious scholars, then notables like the architect Sir Christopher Wren, the writer Samuel Pepys, the poet Lord Byron, and later Sylvia Plath and Virginia Woolf, not to mention the King Kong of Intellect, Sir Isaac Newton. More than ninety Nobel Prizes from Cambridge. Including the discovery of electrons, the nucleus of atoms, neutrons and DNA. Famous economist John Maynard Keynes did his work here."

"Amazing. Who's here now besides Professor Chamberlain?"

Continuing at their fast pace, they passed by without inspecting the entrances to Corpus Christi College and St Catherine's College, then shot onto Trumpington Road, finally arriving at the Pitt Building on their right.

"World famous theoretical physicist Stephen Hawking is here in the post once held by Sir Isaac Newton. You might have heard of the actors Emma Thompson and the Monty Python comedian John Cleese who studied here as well as Shakespearean star Ian McKellen, most recently famous for playing the Wizard Gandalf in The Lord of the Rings movies."

"My, my, my. Have you ever thought of being a tour guide if your day job doesn't work out?"

Conrad continued with, "So here we are at the Pitt Building. Up these stairs and right this way. This housed the printing and publishing offices for Cambridge University Press for a hundred years in the 19th and early 20th centuries."

Trailing Conrad as he entered the building and started up the stairs, Libby asked, "Isn't this the same Press that published Sir Isaac Newton's theories on gravity, and Sir Charles Darwin's theory of evolution?"

"Right you are, but you're missing the point. They also publish my bestselling books today, *Essential Psychopharmacology* and *The Prescriber's Guide.* That's why I know this building."

"Well pardon me, 'Lord Conrad,'" Libby said with a mocking, deep curtsy.

"I'll ignore that. I've been here many times. They've moved the press offices, but still use it as a conference center."

Bounding up the middle stairs with Libby in tow, Conrad arrived at the receptionist and said, "We have a rather urgent situation that requires we interrupt Professor Chamberlain. Can you please fetch him?"

"He won't be happy," the receptionist snarled. "He's in an official meeting of the Press Syndicate."

"Please," Conrad pleaded. "It really cannot wait."

In a flash, out popped an elderly man who was surprisingly spry but seemed to be a bit irritated, with a folder of papers in one hand and an odd cane in the other. He wore an ancient university robe, looking ever the part of a university don straight out of central casting for a 19th century English professor. More than a bit rumpled, necktie askew, hair disheveled, robe unbuttoned, the good professor could have been mistaken for any number of academics who prowled the streets of Cambridge or sat in the buildings they had just passed over the past several centuries since the founding of the University of Cambridge more than 800 years ago.

"Professor Chamberlain! It's Gus Conrad."

"Goodness gracious. Gus Conrad," the professor said, lightening up from his somewhat huffy look that he had leaving the Darwin Room where he was interrupted from his meeting. "It's been a long time. And who's your beautiful girlfriend?"

"Well, actually Dr. Conrad is my boss. I'm Libby Warburton, Adam's mother."

The professor asked the receptionist, "Is the Newton Room available for a quick minute?"

"Yes, Professor Chamberlain. Make yourselves comfortable in there."

All three entered the Newton Room across from the Darwin Room, and sat down on chairs in the empty conference room—a modern rendition of neo-classical design.

"Libby, I'm so sorry about your Adam. Victoria texted me about his death, but only after I'd already walked over here from my office. It must be horrible for you. Victoria texted that Adam's mother and my former student Gus Conrad would be meeting me here before I got aboard my train for a fact-finding trip to the Imperial War Museum."

"We don't have much time before we have to get on our way," Conrad said.

"Your trip to the Imperial War Museum today is more important than ever," Libby added.

"What is it, young lady?"

"It's tragic of course. My Adam is dead." Libby's eyes teared-up all over again.

"Of course, young lady, of course. This is a horrible situation."

"But that tragedy is compounded now because Dr. Conrad is being blamed for it, which is ridiculous. I know the man and he couldn't have done it. We need your help to find the real murderer before the authorities catch up with us here."

"Then why are you in the U.K.? Wasn't he killed in the U.S.?"

"Didn't Victoria tell you that she found evidence in U.S. Army Intelligence files that the Patrons are active again under the Americans?"

"Yes, and they are evidently killing U.S. soldiers because the authorities think they're cowards. You think they killed Adam?"

"Yes. Not only did Adam have PTSD, he also had that damned Medallion of his great-great-grandfather, Papa Nigel."

"Yes, Victoria told me. So you think Adam's possession of that mysterious old Medallion threatened the army with exposure of their current Patrons and led to his death?"

"Yes, and that's why we need your help to find his Papa Nigel's records and use them to lead us to records of current operations of the Patrons."

"Prodigious and shocking, all this," the professor remarked.

"We're going to the Bethlem Royal Hospital right now to see if we can find out what happened to Adam's great-great-grandfather, bearer of that damned Medallion 59. You probably know he died there under suspicious circumstances during the Great War. His death was listed officially as a suicide, but Victoria found his name on the list of victims of the Patrons, so it probably was murder. He got *shell shock* himself and threatened to expose the Patrons back then."

"That could explain the absence of his war records in the usual places in our archives. This also helps me to know where to look when I get back to the dusty records room at the museum in about an hour."

"Victoria said she's gonna do some investigating near Cambridge," Conrad interjected. "Let's all decide to rendezvous tonight back at the Three Horseshoes Pub in Cambridge to share whatever we've found out today."

"What a nasty set of developments," Professor Chamberlain said, stroking his chin with his fingers and getting upset. "Dastardly cads are responsible for these diabolical deeds, no doubt. It would appear we have a double-murder mystery thrust upon us to solve. Let's hope it doesn't take another hundred years to do it."

Chapter 82

MAUDSLEY HOSPITAL, LONDON, AUTUMN OF 1917:

Lieutenant Warburton, haggard and tortured by his thoughts, was now tormented into thinking that death was may be his only option. He decided he might have one last act of heroism and courage left in him as he walked to the receiving area of the hospital where the Royal Post was collected for outgoing deliveries. With a sigh, he dropped his second letter in as many weeks into the iconic red post box, reading its addressee in his own handwriting as the message of truth about executing cowards with *shell shock* slid down the slot.

> To: The Right Honorable MP Snowdon,
> C/O: The House of Commons
> London

Chapter 83

ON THE ROAD TO BEDLAM:

"This trip to the Bethlem Royal Hospital in Kent should be relatively straightforward if we don't hit traffic. An hour, hour and a half tops. We go down the M11 to the M25 and around London on the Orbital across the QE Bridge to the Bethlem Royal Hospital on Monks Orchard Road in Beckenham, South of London," said Libby as she wheeled out of the car park of Clare College and into a petrol station down the road. "Let's fill Sally up with petrol right here."

"Wow, gas is really cheap."

"What? Are you crazy?"

"See it's only 1.32 a gallon. Back home it is over four dollars."

"1.32 pounds Sterling. And that's per liter, not per gallon," Libby informed.

"Omigod. That's over eight bucks a gallon. I stand corrected."

With Sally's belly full of fuel, off they shot, down the M11. "So, maybe you can do a better job finishing explaining how *shell shock* changed from one war to another than you can negotiating the price of British petrol," Libby quipped.

"Okay, Okay. I deserved that. Last time I think we were talking about the term 'gross stress reaction' used by psychiatrists right after World War II."

"Whatever happened to that diagnosis?

"They scrapped it."

"What?"

"Yep. In the 1960s, America was in the midst of the failure of its military intervention in Vietnam and there was considerable political pressure on psychiatry from the military to sweep psychological injuries due to the war under the carpet so as not to further inflame public opinion."

Libby veered suddenly to the right, passing a car at high speed. "Sorry about that, still getting adjusted to Sally is all. Please continue."

"Anyway, during the Vietnam War, military psychiatrists honestly thought they had beaten the problem of psychiatric reactions to warfare because at that time, there was the lowest incidence of psychological casualties of any war in the prior century."

"They really believed that psychological reactions to combat had vanished?"

Conrad shook his head yes. "I was actually taught that during my training in psychiatry. It was the common delusion among the military and their internal psychiatric experts. Soldiers often showed problems not in combat nor in Vietnam, but months and months later after getting home. The obvious explanation to any antiwar psychiatrist worth her salt was that these symptoms were not caused by fighting in the jungles of Vietnam but by returning to the destructive sociopolitical environment of the U.S."

"Seems rather silly now, doesn't it?"

"Yes, but at the time, what could be better than getting rid of all psychological problems of Vietnam combat soldiers? Experts at the time pointed to psychoanalytic theories that were incompatible with the notion that traumatic experiences in adulthood could be responsible for long term psychological disturbances."

"Amazing," Libby interjected in disbelief. "Sounds like the baloney we hear at Fort Hood today."

"Yep. Just like the British military scrapping the diagnosis of *shell shock* during World War I, the American military and psychiatric establishments during the Vietnam War ditched the idea that there could be psychological reactions to warfare."

Libby listened intently as she whipped around traffic passing on the right like a pro in a car made for climbing mountains, not taking the curves at Monaco.

"Watch out, Mario, you're gonna get picked up for speeding."

"You should talk, Mr. Aston Martin."

"I know we're racing against time, since it's clear we could be apprehended any minute. I at least want to be arrested in one piece and not for speeding," Conrad said, faking a brace for a crash with his hands shielding his face.

"If you're calling me racecar driver Mario Andretti, then I should tell you Sally and I can outrun any cop, so put your hands down and stop whimpering. We'll be at the M25 in less than twenty-five minutes now. So what happened to psychiatry after Vietnam? "

"At first, American psychiatry was saying that experiences in war could no longer cause psychiatric disturbances. Instead, soldiers who suffered breakdowns were predisposed to do so by their childhood experiences. It was their own fault."

"Yep. I've heard that one before."

"Psychiatry had suddenly cured all psychological war wounds by blaming them on pre-existing psychiatric problems or an evil society. Psychiatric records for Vietnam vets were full of details on the supposed childhood traumas of these soldiers but thin on details of their combat experiences, which at that time, amazingly enough, were considered irrelevant."

"Blame it on the soldier so the military has to take no responsibility for psychological wounds of warfare, seems to me," Libby said.

"But if you can believe it, everything changed again around 1980."

"If you weren't an expert on this topic, I'm not sure I'd believe what you're telling me this morning," said Libby.

"Antiwar psychiatrists had already mobilized as had veterans organizations, to insist that psychiatrists recognize a 'post-Vietnam syndrome.' Psychiatric illness due to war was back! And they coined it P---T---S---D."

Conrad looked nervously at his watch, wondering if his face was plastered all over British television news yet. "I'm gonna call Victoria in a bit to see if she's tracking the U.S. news over here and Interpol about our escape out of the U.S. We left California airspace a little over 12 hours ago, and it's still only about 3 A.M. on the East Coast there, so our stuff might not hit the news cycle in the U.S. for another three hours or so if we're lucky. It's already caught up with us here, at least in the papers."

"Relax, Gus. We're now on the M25. Only fifteen or twenty minutes and we'll be there."

"Should be able to get into Papa Nigel's medical record files well before lunchtime," Conrad said looking at his watch. "Anyway, so now psychological reactions to combat in Vietnam were normal reactions to an evil war."

"Not the fault of the military or of combat?" Libby asked very sarcastically.

"Either the fault of the flawed individual or of the evil in society."

Libby rubbed her eyes. "I'm getting a headache listening to the insensitivity and ignorance of both the army and psychiatrists. Hurry up because the hospital is straight ahead now. Where's that sun now? Seems even drearier than when we landed."

"Okay. Quickly then, psychiatry turned from supporting the military's point of view that there was no psychological reaction to war, to thumbing its nose at the military by saying that this conflict was uniquely associated with long term and widespread psychological injury to U.S. troops."

"However, it was still caused by pre-existing conditions or by an evil society, not by the military or by combat. So the army was still off the hook in terms of having responsibility to treat these soldiers or give them disability pensions," Libby said as she pulled up the entryway of the Bethlem Royal Hospital and looked for the visitors' car park

"Isn't it amazing that PTSD entered the psychiatric lexicon as a 'political concoction' and the result of political lobbying by antiwar psychiatrists, and not really due to careful research?"

As they passed by the entrance to the hospital, Conrad looked at the main building and said to himself, *what a place.*

Libby mused nervously and almost to herself, "I guess we'll find out now whether Papa Nigel's *shell shock* was a psychiatric problem or a 'political concoction' for him."

Chapter 84

MAUDSLEY HOSPITAL, LONDON, AUTUMN OF 1917:

Days turned to weeks and weeks into months at the Maudsley Hospital for Lieutenant Warburton. His drinking had become heavy as he found a reliable source of wine from one of the stewards whom he bribed for his supplies of liquid relief. He was increasingly irascible, and sat alone in his room brooding during the day, even skipping some meals. He was ashamed, felt guilty, and was convinced life was no longer worth living. He could not get the image of Jennings' face out of his mental vision. He was tormented by it and flashbacks of the firing squad intruded into his consciousness unrelentingly.

His old sidearm was hidden at the bottom of his locker, loaded. It was banned in the hospital, but he had smuggled it in anyway. He'd thought about ending it all for more than a year now and daily for the past several weeks. Problem was, during the whole time at Craiglockhart, he couldn't bring himself even to touch his handgun. He hadn't cleaned it fully since delivering the kill shot to Jennings. However, now more and more desperate, these past days sitting alone in his room at the Maudsley, he began to obsess constantly about that gun. Several days ago he finally got up the nerve to look at it, pulling it out from under all his belongings at the bottom of his footlocker where he had hidden it. He didn't spend long looking at it that first day, since Jennings' face appeared in its place, obscuring his view of it. The next day, however, he touched it again, precipitating a searing hot feeling in his trigger finger and right hand, as well as his face and neck. It was so bad it made him slam the cover shut on his footlocker and try to wash the feeling out of his hand. But as always, he was unsuccessful at doing that. Eventually, Lieutenant Warburton worked himself up to the point of being able to take his old gun out of the holster and toy with it in his lap, including today. *Might not even fire any more,* he thought. *I have killed before, so I am certain I could kill again.*

Chapter 85

BEDLAM HOSPITAL:

" *The infamous Bedlam Hospital,*" Conrad thought to himself as Libby hunted for parking in the visitors' car park. Looking up again at the entrance to the main building of a modern-looking Bethlem Royal Hospital, Conrad noted that it stood in stark contrast with its historical reputation as he recalled past visits here for academic meetings and research collaborations. Today, things were quite different—running for his life while trying to solve murders stretching back more than a century.

The main hospital building had a sweeping driveway coming up to the entrance, large circular flower gardens across from the driveway, and a nearby car park. Several additional buildings were neatly arranged in a campus-like setting, with mature trees and grass lawns separating numerous Tudor brick buildings with bright white windows, none more than two stories high.

"Feels very peaceful," Libby responded as she scanned the surroundings. She pulled into a parking place in the visitors car park, yanked on the parking brake, and stepped out of old Sally as Conrad was already on his feet, scanning the beautiful grounds.

"Looks like a university, not a madhouse," Conrad said, admiring the grounds. "This setting is quite relaxed and suburban. Hard to believe it's part of London."

"Yes, beautiful Bromley, a borough of London," Libby responded.

"Even on a bleak day like today, seems like a pastoral setting," Conrad mused aloud.

"Lots of green parkland all around. I must say, I'm getting quite a different impression from what I was expecting when you told me it had a notorious reputation."

"Let's see what we can find inside."

Conrad strode ahead of Libby, held open the massive door to the main building for her, then walked up to reception. A young woman with punk-hair was consumed by texting on her smartphone, ignored Conrad, but apparently was the one on duty.

"Good morning. I'm Dr. Augustus Conrad from Stanford University in America, and I'm wondering if I might see some records of one of your psychiatric patients from the Great War."

"Great war? I didn't know any war was great," the receptionist responded absently without looking up from her smartphone, clicking faster with her thumbs than with the gum in her mouth.

"Sorry, I mean World War I."

"Well then, why didn't you just say so?" she said still looking at her smartphone's screen. "In that case, you want the museum in the building over there," she said pointing with a rudely painted fingernail that had some esoteric Gothic rune on it, still looking down at the screen on her phone. "Got an appointment?"

"No, but if there's any way we could see those archives we'd be most appreciative." A television mounted on the wall of the waiting area tuned to BBC 1 was playing in the background but with the mute on. Conrad winced as he saw his picture pop-up on the screen with the newsreader talking silently about the murder in Palo Alto. Fortunately, no one seemed to be watching the screen and the receptionist was now looking at Conrad and not at the television. He pulled his baseball cap a bit lower over his head.

"I'm doing a research project and would like to see some hospital records for a patient hospitalized at the Maudsley in 1917."

"Well, we do have the old Maudsley records here, as well as those from some other places. But you'll have to see Dr. Bessely. He just returned from his conference in Cambridge. Let me give him a ring. Have a seat over there," she said, pointing with another rude fingernail to the waiting area, "and I'll let you know what he says when he calls back."

As Conrad and Libby took seats in the waiting area, Conrad said, "Interesting how this place doesn't creep me out. It could pass for any other modern psychiatric facility."

"You're beginning to really creep me out with all these references to the notoriety and bleak history of this place. What's so ill-famed about the Bedlam Hospital?"

"That's a long story. Originally a Catholic priory called 'Bethlehem' or 'Bethlem,' it first housed monks. The Church converted it to a hospital for psychiatric patients in 1259. Now called the Bethlem Royal Hospital, it's arguably the oldest continuously operating psychiatric hospital in the world."

"Wow. This place must be even older than the University of Cambridge."

"Actually, it's not. The University of Cambridge was founded in 1209," Conrad remarked.

"The 13th century must have been a rockin' time. Did I just say that? The 13th century? Hard to believe. This building certainly seems a lot newer than that."

"Oh, for sure. The Bethlem Royal Hospital has been built and re-built many times and in many locations over the centuries. In fact, it once was situated on the very site of the current Imperial War Museum, where Professor Chamberlain is working today."

"Interesting. A lot older than buildings in Palo Alto."

"You think?" Conrad remarked as he popped another jawbreaker candy in his mouth.

"Perhaps the most blatant emblem of the reputation of this place is the very word 'bedlam,' a Cockney mispronunciation of 'Bethlem.' That word—bedlam—was actually coined by visitors to this place centuries ago, and came into the English language then as a description of the conditions at this hospital at the time. Of course 'bedlam' now means 'uproar and confusion.' During past centuries, the Bedlam Hospital became representative of the worst excesses of asylums—full-up chaos and confusion. Finally came the so-called 'lunacy reforms' where they tried to improve conditions for psychiatric patients with passage of the Lunatics Act in the 1800s."

"Lunatics? Sounds more than old-fashioned. Sounds pejorative."

"Yes, I'm afraid so." Conrad looked nervously at the BBC 1 news playing silently on the wall, now on to another local story. He began to feel a bit over-stimulated, so took a deep breath, trying to relax and not trigger another flashback.

"Mental illness has been stigmatized since time immemorial," Conrad continued, lecturing to calm his nerves. "Terms originally with objective medical meanings eventually came into the English language as put-downs and verbal slurs."

"Sort of like *shell shock* in World War I and PTSD today."

"Exactly. I wonder what's holding up Dr. Bessely?" Conrad said as he slowly moved his neck back and forth to look at the receptionist who was again hard at work texting and ignoring visitors.

Conrad looked nervously at his watch, and then caught the eye of the receptionist on the phone, hopefully with Dr. Bessely. "This hospital reminds me the British have been leaders in using, then degrading psychiatric nomenclature for centuries. For example, their Lunacy Acts of 1890 referred to lunatics, which became 'Person of Unsound Mind' in the Mental Treatment Act in the 1930s, and then 'mental illness' under the Mental Health Act in the 1960s. Americans used these same terms. Did you know in 2012, our Congress enacted and our president signed legislation that removed the word "lunatic" from all federal laws?"

Just then, a short, balding man with a ruddy complexion, bookish glasses on top of his head, and his shirttail half-untucked, came up to them with a fast stride, hand outstretched. "Dr. Conrad? Dr. Augustus Conrad? I'm Simon Bessely, consultant psychiatrist here and curator of the museum for the Bethlem Royal Hospital. So great to see you here. Although we've never had the pleasure of meeting, I've read all your books. Especially love your book *Essential Psychopharmacology*. I use it in my teaching over at the Institute of Psychiatry. Wish you'd told us you were visiting so we could've prepared for you," he said pumping Conrad's hand vigorously.

"Hello, Dr. Bessely, glad to meet you, too. Or should I say, Sir Simon? Congratulations on your knighthood."

Dr. Bessely blushed. "It's an honor, but a bit much and completely undeserved."

"You're too modest, Sir Simon. I'm sorry we've missed the chance to meet in person until now, but I've also read your books, especially your highly acclaimed works on *shell shock* and military psychiatry." Turning to Libby, Conrad continued, "I'd like you to meet a nurse who works with me, Libby Warburton."

"Glad to meet, you, too, Miss Warburton."

"The pleasure is all mine, Sir Simon," Libby said with the slightest hint of a curtsy as she looked down and shook his hand. "Call me Libby."

"So, Libby, what brings you here?"

"I apologize for the lack of advanced notice," Conrad interjected. "My trip only came up at the last minute. We're here to do some research at Cambridge, and at the Imperial War Museum. If it wouldn't be too much trouble, we'd like to see your museum, and if not inconvenient, would also like to take a look at the hospital records of her great-grandfather, a British Army officer who was hospitalized at the Maudsley in 1917."

"A great-grandfather from the Great War, huh? Well, you can certainly see the museum."

And with a bit of a lurch, Dr. Bessely turned on his heel and motioned them to follow at a rapid pace. "You know, we have documents dating back to the 16th century. We have medical records of patients hospitalized back to the mid-1700s, hand written and preserved. You can't really appreciate how much psychiatry has changed unless you look at how diagnosis and treatment were recorded over the centuries since then."

"Fascinating, Dr. Bessely," Conrad replied at a half-jog, following an enthusiastic Dr. Bessely out the main building and over a walkway with Libby trailing behind.

THE THREE OF THEM soon arrived at the entrance to another beautiful brick building nearby. Dr. Bessely held the door open for them and Libby asked as she walked through the door, "I suppose that means you'll have hospital records for patients from the Great War in here as well?"

Not answering, Dr. Bessely continued in his state of reverie as he entered the building behind them. "Our museum just ahead specializes in the work of artists who have suffered from mental health problems, especially former Bethlem patients such as William Kurelek, Richard Dadd and Louis Wain. Ah, here we are," he said as they arrived at the entrance to the museum inside the brick building. He fumbled with a ring of keys, finally found one that fit and swung the museum door open. "See those beauties?"

"Incredible. What are they?" asked Libby.

"Our pride and joy. Two marble statues from the gates of the 17th century Bethlem Hospital by Caius Gabriel Cibber, known as *Raving* on the left and *Melancholy Madness* on the right."

"A bit spooky," Libby replied as she stepped back a bit.

"I'll bet quite a bit of suffering passed through those gates back in the day," said Conrad.

Anxious to find her Papa Nigel's records, Libby asked again, "What about records from the Great War?"

Conrad looked at his watch nervously while Libby silently wondered if the authorities had detected their car yet. *We could be arrested any moment,* Libby thought. *Let's get this show on the road. Gus looks ready to freak out,* she noted as Conrad shot yet another piece of candy into his mouth.

"As you know, we opened the Great War section of our archives a few years back but, curiously, you two are the first ones to ever ask to see any of these records," Dr. Bessely said looking at Libby with suspicion. "Your request seems a bit unusual to me. The Bethlem is a bit out of the way and many don't know we have any Great War records here. Couldn't I interest you in something else?"

Libby thought, *maybe it's time to turn on the charm.* "Dr. Bessely, Sir Simon, it would mean so much to me just to see if there are any records of my great-grandfather. I'm British by birth but live in the States now. I've often wondered about him, especially now on the hundredth anniversary of the Great War. He was an officer you know. Just a quick peek? I'd be forever grateful."

"You should've notified me well in advance so I could've checked with the proper authorities. Also, it may take a while to determine if we even have his records here. Most of them were sent to the War Department."

"Yes, I know and please pardon my bad manners popping in on you all unannounced. Don't you think a Knight and Commander of the Order of the British Empire is proper authority in this case?"

Dr. Bessely, blushed, seemed to hesitate, and then considered that Libby's suggestion was accurate, and suddenly changed his mind. "Fine, you have a point there. Right this way."

Libby looked at Conrad and silently raising her hands and shoulders in a *whaddaya think about that?* move behind Sir Simon's back, got Conrad to smile back.

"Aha. We arrive at our record room," Dr. Bessely exclaimed proudly as he led them to yet another door inside the museum. Floundering again for the right key, he finally opened the door to the immense record room, flipped on the overhead lights, which blinked on with a welcoming buzz, as they entered a dank, dusty set of library stacks filled floor to ceiling with old medical records. "Inhale," requested Dr. Bessely. "Don't you just love the smell of old books and papers?" Hesitating for a moment with his eyes closed, breathing in deeply and clearly enjoying the moment, he continued. "We have a veritable treasure trove here from the Great War."

Libby thought he seemed to have switched from being a bit suspicious they were there to looking like a proud papa. "First, let's look up your great-grandfather in the database and see if we even have his files on hand." Bessely went over to an empty computer terminal, flipped a switch and booted it up. "Now, what's his name and date of birth?"

"Nigel Leslie Warburton, date of birth, 23rd March 1890," Libby replied.

With quick motions on the keyboard, he tapped in the information, waited a moment and the screen highlighted a name in a long list of patients from 1917. "Well, what do you know? There he is big as day. Hospitalized at Craiglockhart, Scotland, from the 17th April, 1916 to the 14th of August, 1917. Then he was transferred to the Maudsley on the 15th of August, 1917 until his discharge on the 3rd of October, 1917."

"He wasn't discharged, he died there," Libby said.

Dr. Bessely seemed stunned by this revelation. "Oh, my, my, my. Then his records might not be here. Or maybe it would not be appropriate for you to see them if they are."

"We recognize that you must be discreet about access to anything that might be sensitive. But if you think about it, how sensitive would his records be if they are still on file here and nobody has looked at them in a hundred years and these are open archives?" Libby reasoned.

"You make a good point, young lady. Against my better judgment, let's take a look. If we have them, according to this, they should be in Section 17, shelf K." Dr. Bessely spun to his left and with several quick strides, turned to one of the shelves, pulled his reading glasses down from the top of his head and placed them on the tip of his nose, and lovingly pulled a dusty file of old papers off the shelf and carried it like a newborn baby past several empty carrels and laid the papers carefully on an open table. The whole room was deserted and chilly as the three of them were the only ones present.

"These papers are a century old," he said, looking at them like a proud father showing off his child. "So you must be very careful with them. I will ask you both to put on a pair of white gloves in the boxes on the table before you touch anything. May I also ask why you are so interested in your great-grandfather's records and at this time?"

"My son was an army soldier who was just murdered in the United States. I think there may be some connection between his death and the death of his great-great-grandfather," said Libby as the memory of the horror hit her in the gut like a championship fighter landing a body blow to his opponent.

Dr. Bessely suddenly became visibly upset. "Then I believe I should take these files back. They are only for scholarly purposes, not murder investigations. As chief archivist and museum director, I cannot allow anything other than scholarly work to be done here, and cannot allow any use of these materials that could bring dishonor to our hospital. We're working so hard these days to improve the image of mental illness and especially of the Bethlem Royal."

"Sorry if I upset you," Libby said. Backtracking quickly, she added, "Mostly, I'm just trying to seek 'closure' for myself. You know how we Americans need our 'closure.'"

Dr. Bessely thought the comment somewhat odd, given Libby's English accent. Nevertheless, he continued to listen for the moment.

Libby added, "Dr. Conrad here is the scholar and a champion of those with mental illness, as you know. He plans to use the opportunity to see these files in order to add material to his lectures that de-stigmatize the field," she said as Conrad nodded in agreement.

"You Americans and your 'closure,'" Dr. Bessely said disapprovingly. "Well, all right, I guess," he said, looking at them now more mistrustful than ever. "I'm sure you know these records are especially sensitive because they come from the *shell shock* era and until a few years ago were considered classified as military secrets."

"We understand and will be respectful and appropriate. We'll only be a few minutes as we plan to look at the Great War archives at the Imperial War Museum right after we're finished here."

"Yes, I certainly expect you'll be careful with those papers," Dr. Bessely said, clearly not at ease. "I shall leave you to it for a while and then I'll return after I do a few things I must complete this morning." With that, he spun again on his heels and wheeled out of the room.

"A bit quirky don't you think?" posed Libby.

"He's very leery of our visit. We need to look through these and get outta here as soon as we can. Assuming he's not gonna lock us in here until the authorities come to arrest us."

"Whatever. Let's get started," said Libby as she tried on a pair of white gloves. A bit big for her, she slid them as far as she could over her fingers, sat down in front of the records, and opened it delicately and gasped at what she saw.

Chapter 86

BEDLAM HOSPITAL, LONDON:

"Hello, Commandant?" said Dr. Bessely in a nervous whisper, cupping his hand around his mouth and his cell phone.

"Yes."

"Did I interrupt you? I know you may still be in conference at Madingley Hall. I was given this number to call in case of problems."

"No, you didn't interrupt me. We broke early for lunch."

"Of course. I shall get straight to the point. I have a couple of suspicious visitors here at the Bethlem Royal's museum looking into the archives for the records of a World War I lieutenant they say was hospitalized at the Maudsley and died there. I gave them the records to view, but now I'm having second thoughts and wonder if that was such a good idea. This is the first time anyone has ever asked to look at psychiatric records from the Great War since they became public, so I thought I'd better notify you."

"Yes, your call is appropriate, and thanks. Who's the soldier they are investigating?"

"Some Lieutenant Warburton, supposedly the great-grandfather of one of the visitors."

The Commandant bolted forward in the chair.

"Like I said, they seem suspicious to me," Dr. Bessely continued, "because they're looking into an old death they think might be linked to the recent death of the lady's son."

The Commandant shot onto both feet, thrusting the chair onto the floor behind, standing abruptly, in a full state of alarm. "You should have never allowed them access to those records."

"Yes, yes, indeed yes. So sorry, so sorry."

"Anything else?"

"Some silly thing about 'closure,' whatever that is," Dr. Bessely continued. "I was just wondering if her son was one of your guys, since she said he was a soldier in your army.

The Commandant seethed with anger as Dr. Bessely pressed on.

"I could see from the archives the great-grandfather was one of our guys, plain as day, right there to be seen in our open archives if you know what to look for. But I didn't let them know that."

"You say visitors? How many?"

"Two, a man and a woman. I know the man by reputation because he's a famous psychiatrist in my field, a Dr. Conrad from Stanford."

The Commandant physically winced although no one was there to see it. *Conrad's slipped out of California and is now in the UK. Bastard's probably closing in on our secret activities,* the Commandant thought frantically.

"And the woman," Dr. Bessely continued. "I forgot her name now, but she's looking at records from 1917, and says are from her great-grandfather."

"Not Libby Warburton by any chance?" the Commandant asked, seething.

"Yes, yes, that's it. How'd you know?"

"Just my instincts."

"Shall I keep them here, or let them go when they're done? They said they're off to the Imperial War Museum to see more records from the Great War after they're done here."

Startled, the Commandant thought for a moment in silence and finally said with a smile, "No, let them go. This is perfect. Absolutely perfect."

Chapter 87

L ibby brushed her gloved fingertips carefully over her great-grandfa-ther's name on the front of the folder. Although it was faded and fragmented by time, it was indeed his name.

"This is really his," she said out loud as tears welled-up in her eyes.

Conrad looked over Libby's shoulder, standing behind her seat as she opened the folder gingerly. "Looks like the first part of this folder is from Craiglockhart," he said.

Both read the first page silently:

> *This 26 year old white male officer from the British Expeditionary Force, France, presents for evaluation and treatment of neurasthenia. ...*

"'Neurasthenia.' That's the term they were using by 1916 for *shell shock* in officers while the very same condition in lower ranks was called 'hysteria,'" Conrad said.

"The handwriting is so neat, almost like a work of art, cursive, in ink probably written with a quill, and actually, beautiful," said Libby.

"Completely unlike a doctor's handwriting today, that's for sure."

As Libby carefully turned the pages, each cracked a bit, exhibiting yellowing, brittleness and dryness. "It's like I can almost feel him in here."

Then after a pause, she read aloud:

> *... claims to have nightmares after shooting a soldier*
> *in the head for cowardice.*

"Omigod. Then it *is* true. Papa Nigel did kill one of his own soldiers. How horrible. Papa Nigel was obviously part of the British Army executing their own men as cowards, the very same scandal Professor Chamberlain discovered once the World War I archives were opened. How shameful," Libby said aloud, embarrassed and disheartened.

"Hang on a minute. He was probably only following orders."

"They said that at Nuremberg, too."

"Let's not jump to conclusions before we finish looking at these records carefully."

"This is further proof Papa Nigel was a Patron of Perseus. I'm gonna take a picture of this page with the camera on my iPhone."

Conrad reached over Libby's shoulder with his own gloved hands and carefully began turning page after page, scanning the file as he went. "Look here," he said as he read aloud:

> *... Re-experiencing the traumatic event day and night ...*
> *... States he shot a soldier at close range when the execution*
> *squad he was leading failed to land a kill shot ...*
> *... Relating well to fellow patients. Made friends*
> *with Sassoon and Owen.*

"Siegfied Sassoon and Wilfred Owen?" Libby asked. "They're famous British poets from the early 20th century who were also hospitalized at Craiglockhart. Did you ever see that movie Regeneration or read the novel it was made from? I think written by Barker, Pat Barker?"

"Maybe a long time ago. Wasn't it really a political statement about the evils of war?"

"Yes. Sassoon was sent to Craiglockhart because he was a conscientious objector—wouldn't go back into combat. Had become a war hero, but then soured on the war and began writing anti-war poetry. Since he was famous and well-connected, the British Army decided to call him crazy and send him to a psychiatric hospital rather than execute him as a coward, like they obviously did to others."

"Quite an example of the class system at work in early 20th century Britain. Here's some notes signed by Dr. W.R.H. Rivers, the famous psychiatrist at Craiglockhart."

"And a real-life character in both the novel and the movie," Libby said as she turned over page after page.

> *... Not sleeping. Nightmares.*
> *... Drinking heavily to suppress re-living the execution over and over.*
> *... thinks he is the one who should have died.*
> *... Pessimistic and thoughts of death.*

"They may have diagnosed your great-grandfather as having 'neurasthenia,' but there are clear signs of what we would call today survivor's guilt, flashbacks, hyper-arousal and nightmares," Conrad said softly.

"Those are the very diagnostic criteria for PTSD today," Libby said emphatically. "I wanta take pictures of some of these records as well," as she began snapping away.

Libby looked up at Conrad as he leaned over her shoulder again to view the documents as she was taking pictures. Their faces now inches apart, Libby noticed Conrad was contemplating her lips. *Is he going to kiss me?* she asked herself. But Conrad hesitated. Libby looked deeply into his eyes, telling him silently, *go ahead.*

Conrad returned her intense gaze for a long moment, but after what seemed an eternity of awkwardness, he leaned back, returning to the task at hand. Continuing their conversation as though nothing had just passed between them, Conrad said, "Yep. Your Papa Nigel had PTSD for sure, suffered for what he did and felt very bad about it. He didn't make any progress after months at Craiglockhart, so he was transferred to the Maudsley Hospital, which must be these documents in the back half of the folder."

Libby just sighed and shook her head at Conrad in silence. Then, turning the page, she noted the exquisite cursive handwriting continued on different paper, heavier stock and in better condition with each page having the heading printed at the top:

Maudsley Neurological Clearing Hospital.
No. 4 London General Hospital Subsidiary

"Wow, look at this," Libby said.

> *... Spewing nonsense.*
> *... Goes on and on about the Patrons of Perseus and Medal-*
> *lion number 59.*
> *... Says he sees the face of the man he executed on everyone's*
> *face.*
> *... Seems tormented. Says he feels the hot blood of his victim*
> *on his shooting hand, and the pungent smell of burning*
> *brains in his nostrils. Clearly delusional.*

"Wow. Papa Nigel was really upset," said Libby sadly. She clicked a few more pictures. "You suppose he was losing touch with reality?"

"Not really. Those sensory perceptions are probably real things he really felt at the time then they became emblazoned like a branding iron indelibly into his memory. Just like what we see in PTSD combat soldiers today as well."

Libby noted Conrad suddenly seemed far away and in pain. "You all right?"

After a long pause, in which Conrad appeared to be collecting himself, he finally responded, "Oh, nothing, nothing at all. I was just thinking about something else."

"I could swear you were having some sort of flashback yourself."

"No, no, just tired," Conrad lied. "Sorry, we must press on."

Towards the end of the sheaf of loose papers in the folder Libby read:

> *... Ranting and raving, and causing trouble by contacting his*
> *MP. Claims the army is lying by denying it is executing its own*
> *soldiers with shell shock.*
> *... Had a visit from a high ranking officer from the war office,*
> *and clearly has become much more upset and out of control*
> *since that visit.*

Then the entries into his records end on 2nd April 1917.

"What day did he die?" Conrad asked.

"3rd April 1917."

"And look at this."

"Seems like something's been removed from his file."

A single sheet of heavy paper made up the last page in Lieutenant Warburton's file. Written on it was:

Death records removed for official enquiry.
- British Intelligence Service
- War Office of Special Investigations

"Damn," Conrad exclaimed. "That means America has those records now and have classified them as top-secret."

Chapter 88

LONDON:

The Commandant picked up a secure phone and dialed. Hearing a grunt for a greeting, the Commandant asked, "869? This is 912. Wanted to see if you're still freelancing."

"Commandant? What a surprise. Of course. What's the assignment?"

"Just broke for lunch at the Madingley Hall meeting. I'm now reviewing current targets with our operatives on site. Why aren't you attending the meeting at Madingley this year?"

"Mostly retired now."

"I need a sharpshooter. Current expertise of our operatives includes explosives, hand-to-hand, close range actions. No sharpshooters in town at this time. You game?"

"Must admit, sounds tempting. Things sure got more entertaining the past couple of years once you took over."

"We're serious now."

"Infiltrating and disrupting civilian meetings was never as much fun as assassination."

"Enough of the small talk. Yes or no?"

"If the assignment doesn't require me to rely too much on my bum knee, I'm in. Otherwise, I stay retired from all that, as I've told you."

"This just requires sharpshooting. Still qualified as a sniper?"

"Of course."

"Still located in central London?"

"I blend into the crowds quite well here and feel at ease in London."

"Just as I thought. You're perfectly positioned. However, that only helps me if you can drop everything immediately and make your way over to the Imperial War Museum."

"Going to pay me to enhance my cultural education at a museum? Sweet deal."

"I need you to take out two civilians who're going to be there within the hour."

"You sure? The Imperial War Museum is closed now for renovations. Not going to open again until the one-hundred year anniversary of the start of World War I."

"They have a contact inside the museum who works on the files there and he's going to let them in. You can sneak in if you disguise yourself as a construction worker."

"Do you want clean kill shots from a distance, or do you want them wounded and then tortured for a while before death?"

"Now, 869, let's not get carried away. This is strictly business. No fun allowed."

"Just checking. It's not the way you usually have me handle these things. So, who are the targets?"

"Two Americans, a man and a woman."

"That should be easy. There'll be no visitors or staff to worry about and there should also be lots of construction people about, and no metal detectors active. Will make it easy to slip in and out."

"I'll send you photos of the targets to your secure phone, and they should be there within an hour, probably going to the archives section, so you can set up there."

"Usual price?"

"Double."

Chapter 89

EN ROUTE TO THE IMPERIAL WAR MUSEUM, LONDON:

Conrad exhaled deeply as Libby gunned Sally back onto the M25. "Google maps says eleven miles to the Imperial War Museum, estimated time is twenty-nine minutes," he said.

"We'll be there in twenty. You think Sir Simon'll be upset with our leaving and not saying good-bye?"

"I'm just glad we got out of that place before we were recognized as fugitives and arrested there. Gotta keep moving."

"By the way, you became a bit unzipped in there, almost like you were experiencing a flashback or something."

"Just over-reacting to everything that's going on."

"Seemed to me like it was a lot more than that. You looked like you were about to come unglued when talking about Papa Nigel's PTSD branding sensations into his memory."

Conrad involuntarily winced as she said it. "See what I mean? You okay now?"

"I'll tell you about it sometime later. Right now we have some murderers to catch before they catch us."

"Okay, I'll hold you to that. For now, why don't you touch base with Victoria?"

As she asked, Conrad was pulling his tote bag from the backseat of the Range Rover, hearing that rattling sound again as he moved it. "Want an energy bar? Looks like we're gonna miss lunch."

"Sure," said Libby as she took it from him and unwrapped it with one hand while steering with the other.

Conrad started rifling through his bag, the old tote he picked up at his Lake Arrowhead home, to see what was making that jangling sound and deep in a side pocket, he pulled out a bottle of pills. All of a sudden, he felt flushed. The blood seemed to drain out of his head as he read—Oxy-Contin. Prescription was dated twelve years ago. He thought to himself, *I thought I got rid of all these long ago,* and put them away quickly and without a word.

Conrad dialed Victoria on his burner and put her on speaker phone. "Hi, Victoria, this is Dr. Conrad and Libby calling."

"Glad you called. Lots to report."

"Same here. Libby and I just finished up at the Bedlam Hospital. We found Papa Nigel's psychiatric records and confirmed he participated in executing British soldiers for cowardice, and he apparently got *shell shock* from doing it. Records also confirm he called himself a Patron of Perseus and had Medallion 59."

"That's further confirmation the Patrons of Perseus were members of a secret execution squad of the British Army during the Great War. Also confirmed that each member at the time got one of those Medallions, each uniquely numbered," said Victoria.

"Well, Papa Nigel apparently tried to resign from the group. He was in touch with Parliament about their activities because he felt it was wrong their actions were being denied in the press at the time," interjected Libby, speaking loudly so Victoria could pick up her voice. After a beat, Libby seemed to ask herself aloud, "You suppose that's why Papa Nigel died? Maybe the Patrons wanted to silence him?"

"Could be," answered Victoria.

"Anything new on Interpol or the news about us?" Conrad asked nervously.

"It's all over the BBC and the papers. Sorry, guys. They know you left California, flew here from Tijuana and landed at Stansted. American authorities have asked British police to arrest you."

Conrad slumped in his seat. "That means they'll be using all those surveillance cameras to look for us. Don't have much time left," he said as he pulled his baseball cap down further. "London's the worst place in the world to hide with all its cameras."

"You've got no choice but to go for it," Victoria encouraged. "Gramps called me and has a treasure trove for you too important to miss. I would think you still have a couple of hours before MI5 and London Metro surveillance connects the dots."

"We'll be there in about fifteen minutes," said Libby, bearing down on Sally's accelerator.

"Okay," Victoria continued. "No need to call him. I'll relay his message for you now. Gramps said for you to go around back of the museum where there's a sign for 'deliveries,' and park there. After the Elephant and Castle roundabout ..."

"Elephant and Castle?" asked Conrad.

"Quiet, I'll explain later," Libby interrupted. "Sorry, Victoria, what do you do after the Elephant and Castle roundabout?"

"Yeah," Victoria continued, "at the Elephant and Castle roundabout, exit on St. Georges Road, turn onto Lambeth Road and then pick up Gramps at the entrance to the museum off Lambeth. He'll get you 'round back with a permit and take you to see what he's discovered. I'll call him now to tell him you're only a few minutes out."

"Thanks. What's the update from your end?" asked Conrad.

"Just following up a hunch ... but I think I may have found the link between Papa Nigel's death and Adam's."

Conrad looked at Libby as both sets of eyes grew wide.

"What?"

"Not on the phone. Let's just say it has to do with an American psychiatrist I discovered buried in the American Cemetery next to Madingley Hall."

"Whoa!"

"I'll have to give up hacking into U.S. Army Intelligence records and go Neanderthal now."

"What?"

"You know, look at hard copy. I'll show you what I've found once you get here. Pick up Gramps and text me when you're done at the museum and on the way here."

"Where shall we meet?"

"Three Horseshoes Pub again," and with that, Victoria clicked off.

"Elephant and Castle?" Conrad asked Libby. "You sure have some weird street names in England. When I was at Cambridge, I was always flummoxed by many of the street names in-and-about the city. You know, like Queen Edith's Way, Worts' Causeway, or even Pakenham Close."

"I heard tell the name 'Elephant and Castle' came from a coach house that used to be on the site of the current roundabout. Took its name from a blacksmith and cutler who had previously occupied the shop in the 1700s. Seems the shop owner had a coat of arms for cutlers on his door."

"Very interesting. So what's the connection to an elephant and a castle?" Conrad asked flatly.

"The coat of arms for cutlers features an elephant with a castle on its back, possibly meant to be a howdah—an elephant's saddle—rather than an actual castle on the elephant's back. Cutlers used this elephant and castle as their guild symbol because they used elephant ivory in handles of the knives they made."

"I wouldda never dreamed that would be the answer to the history of a roundabout in London." After a pause, Conrad felt better of reminding Libby they were the next victims listed on the Patrons' hit list.

Chapter 90

MADINGLEY HALL, CAMBRIDGE:

"We've been hacked," Rossi shouted, then exploded into the conference room at Madingley Hall, where Richards was meeting with Major Benson, head of army psychiatry at Fort Hood.

"Hold on Rossi, who's been hacked? Your personal computer?"

"No, Richards'. Army Intelligence computers. They've been hacked."

"Now that's not so good. Any damage done? Any files altered or deleted?" Richards asked.

"That's the thing. According to my staff back at the Pentagon, it doesn't look like any files have been deleted or altered," Rossi answered, calming down a bit. "Seems like it might've just been one of those college hackers doing it for fun rather than a real spy. But the bad thing is most of the time was spent looking at the old Patrons' files, which are still classified by the British and World War I."

"That's ancient history. We were thinking of making them public now anyway. The Brits already have made similar files open access ten years ago."

"And see what that got them. A godforsaken 'shot at dawn' scandal," Rossi fired back, spewing spittle all over.

"Yeah, by our favorite reporter at *The Washington Post*. Any idea who's doing this?" Richards asked.

"Not really. But if I had to guess, if not a nuisance joyrider through our files, it would be that good for nothing fire-eater from *The Post* looking for another headline and another meaningless award."

"Jennifer Roberts?" Now Richards was getting upset. "I've already had my run-ins with her. She's trouble. But she's no computer hacker. Maybe somebody's working for her, or is leaking to her what they find."

"Now it's time for you to relax," Rossi said. "Remember, we're flying back to D.C., first thing in the morning."

"Advice noted. In the meantime, I guess this computer hacker can't really do any damage. All the files that are sensitive are here in Cambridge in underground storage. Hard copies, not digital. Nobody knows these records are here. And they're not accessible to reporters, or hackers, or even freedom of information requests from the Congress," Richards responded.

"Good points. Plausible deniability and all that stuff, I know. In reality, the files here don't even exist," Rossi said with a wicked laugh. "The only lead we have on the hacker is he or she is using multiple ISP addresses and pinging themselves all over the world. Interesting, however, is that one tracing leads to here in Cambridge over at the university. You suppose anybody there, say like in that old man's group who heads the World War I open files, could be involved?"

"Ah, yes. The old-man Professor Chamberlain. Wouldn't be him but maybe somebody sophisticated with computers in his group. Why don't you have your team check that out? In the meantime, we both need to relax. We're on our way home tomorrow. Meanwhile, there's nothing in the digital records online we can't live with making public. So what's to worry about?" Richards asked rhetorically.

Chapter 91

LONDON:

Sure enough, Professor Chamberlain was waiting for Libby and Conrad outside at the museum entrance, leaning on his shooting stick, scarf flailing in the wind, which had picked up a bit with the sky still very bleak now at mid-day. "A bit hyperborean out there," he said rubbing his hands together to warm them as he rumbled into Sally's backseat behind Libby.

"Hyperborean? You mean cold?" asked Conrad.

"Of course. Snappy. Siberian. A two-dog-night. Didn't you learn any English when you were at Cambridge, young man?" Professor Chamberlain asked with a crooked smile on his craggy face bearing a cold red nose.

"Thanks for arranging for us to look at the files you found. I can't wait. I hope this wasn't too much trouble for you," Libby said to him in the backseat.

"Ah, they don't call me 'the sleuth of the archives' for nothing, young lady. This is what I live for, and today I hit a gusher," he added, continuing to rub his hands together, but this time in delight. "You'll see," he said as he directed them to drive around the back and showed his security pass to the guard patrolling the area. As Sally slinked past the museum policeman, he continued to look at them suspiciously and for a bit too long for comfort.

"Do you suppose the guard has identified us?" asked Conrad. "I hate being on the run and looking over my shoulder every moment."

"No, no, no," disagreed Professor Chamberlain. "He's just gawking at your beautiful girlfriend, I should think. Or wondering what an old fool like me is doing with such a lovely chauffeur on this fine day."

Libby blushed as Conrad made and then dropped eye contact with her.

"Still, a bit unnerving for me," Conrad admitted. "If the authorities identify us while we're still at the museum, we're as good as captured."

"Not to worry, so many more interesting things just ahead to think about than that," scolded Professor Chamberlain gently.

As they got out of the car and approached a rear entrance door, it appeared solid if worn and rusted in places and yet essentially impenetrable. Professor Chamberlain punched in a code on a corroding keypad next to the entrance and a green light quickly went on with a beep, and despite the size of the mammoth steel door, the excited professor pushed it open with practiced ease.

"Ah, there it is. Open. Follow me." And with a brisk pace that surprised Libby, Professor Chamberlain took them quickly through a huge maze of corridors, from enormous heating ducts occupying most of the passageways as they squeezed along aside, to massive plumbing pipes overhead, they walked briskly past room after room full of shelves overflowing with various artifacts, identifying tags dangling everywhere. "The items in all these rooms are all part of The Great War Archives. They rotate into the viewing areas over time. We need to go in the records room where I've been successfully wildcatting this morning. Still a bit of a distance from here. Shall we press on?"

"Sure. I guess that a shooting stick is solely a decoration," said Libby with a smile.

"Just for my old bones on occasion, especially when walking in the countryside. In here, I'm a young man once again." As they reached a large exhibit area, he stopped and said with delight, "Ah, we have arrived at our first stop. I want to show this to you before we get to the really valuable gems of information I just found this morning."

"Okay, but let's not take too long because we still have lots to discover before the police catch up to us," Conrad said, fussing again while looking at his watch. "Interpol has now put out a bulletin on Libby and me asking for us to be apprehended."

"Don't you know how to relax and enjoy the moment, young man?"

"No, he doesn't," answered Libby for Conrad, shooting him a sideways glance and popping another jawbreaker into the eagerly awaiting palm of his hand.

"Not to worry," responded Professor Chamberlain. "We shall only be a moment."

Then, ushering them into the middle of a huge exhibit area, maybe the size of an American football field or a British soccer pitch, Professor Chamberlain suddenly stopped and looked up and pointed with his shooting stick at the windows ringing the room some forty feet or more above. "See that? There's a Cockney pickpocket in the upper gallery. I can see he's having a fine day fleecing the low-price crowd."

Suddenly pivoting and pointing his shooting stick at a lower set of windows. "And there. See that fine lady, fanning herself and enjoying the entertainment?"

Libby and Conrad looked at each other quizzically. Nobody was there.

"And now, quickly, to your right, dear doctor." Professor Chamberlain was now pointing his shooting stick at a huge olive drab Sherman Tank from World War II standing next to Libby. His impish smile and quick movements of a man half his age were the signs of sheer rapture. "Mind the beggar, right there."

Libby and Conrad were spellbound with a sense of awe mixed with more than a bit of confusion.

"And behind you, fine Lady Warburton." Whirling to the other side, Professor Chamberlain, now poised himself in the *en garde* position, as though a fencing master pointing his foil at a gentleman's opponent. His sorry old shooting stick actually was pointing at a set of Thunderbird missiles mounted on a World War II launching pad that extended in the air over twenty-feet high. "Wary of the madman."

Libby and Conrad were beginning to wonder who was the madman. Libby finally stated tentatively, "Professor Chamberlain, you're clearly in your element here."

Suddenly, Professor Chamberlain dropped his shooting stick to his side and said with a twinkle in his eye, "Had you going there for a moment, didn't I?"

"Well, you were clearly having a joyous few winks on the stage, Professor Chamberlain," Libby added, clearly relieved the professor had returned to himself. "One could even say it looked like you were having a bit of pure reverie."

"Yes, but I think we were both worried that, how do you Brits say it, you had 'lost the plot,'" added Conrad.

"Nonsense man. Can't you feel it? You're standing in the center of the oldest psychiatric hospital in the world."

"Not that again," Libby said rolling her eyes. "I thought we just left that place."

"Hasn't your expert psychiatrist boyfriend told you the full story yet? Tsk, tsk, tsk. Augustus, I thought I taught you better than that years ago at Cambridge."

Libby blushed, but no one seemed to notice. With a pause and a bow, Professor Chamberlain continued. "Lady and gentleman, you are standing now in the central section of the Bethlem Hospital. The wealthy alderman and sheriff of London, Simon Fitz-Mary, founded the Priory of St. Mary Bethlehem in 1259, on the site which is now part of the Liverpool Street station, over there," Professor Chamberlain said while pointing to the left once again with his shooting stick. Placing the stick to his side again, he leaned on it like a cane with one hand as he reshaped his moustache with the other, and then continued.

Conrad and Libby looked at each other, but said nothing.

"In the 14th century, the priory began to specialize in care of the insane. In 1547, Henry VIII granted the hospital to the City of London, which eventually moved it to a new building in the Moorfields in 1676. The story I just told you actually took place at the Moorfields location. Until 1770, a series of heads of the Bethlem Hospital made themselves rich by charging admission to the public to see the psychiatric patients for entertainment purposes. Evidently, fine ladies on the lower gallery at high prices, and cockney pickpockets on the upper gallery for a tuppence, were equally fascinated by the beggars, debtors, madmen, prostitutes and lunatics in chains on the floor. Sunday afternoon entertainment before television and football—either the English or the American version—consisted of coming to watch the bizarre antics of the inmates of this hospital. Some of course called it bedlam, which they could safely observe from galleries as a social occasion. "

"That's disgusting and dehumanizing," said Libby with a scowl on her face.

"Yes, and it eventually led to the more humane lunatic acts of the 19th century. This viewing of patients as entertainment was banned in 1770, and the hospital eventually moved to where we are standing in 1815 until 1930, when it moved to Beckenham where you just visited."

Suddenly, Professor Chamberlain seemed back in his element, pointing his shooting stick straight ahead. "See peeking out over there? You just missed her. It was Mary Nicholson, who tried to assassinate George III in 1786, and then was admitted here." Twirling left, he pointed again to another military artifact. "And there is Jonathan Martin, committed in 1829, after setting fire to Yorkminster; and of course," aiming the shooting stick like a shotgun to his right, "there you can find the renowned architect A.W.N. Pugin, who designed the Houses of Parliament and St. George's Roman Catholic Cathedral opposite the museum today."

Now Libby was laughing. "You really make history come alive Professor Chamberlain. Do you give all your students lectures like this?"

Conrad laughed to himself, feeling a touch of jealousy at the theatrics of the professor making his teaching more memorable than any Conrad had mustered himself.

"Of course, but let's test that out and see what the young chap with you from America remembers from his time in Cambridge. You, young bloke, tell me about Tom Rakewell and William Hogarth."

"Me? You mean me?" Conrad asked fumbling for words and feeling more than a bit embarrassed. Stroking his chin with his forefinger and thumb for a moment, Conrad finally said, "Well, I remember Hogarth was the famous 18th century English artist who created canvases and eventually engravings of several scenes from the life of Thomas Rakewell."

"Well done, old boy. You must've had a masterful teacher at Cambridge," Professor Chamberlain said with a wink at Libby. "Yes, those elegant sketches are considered by some to be the world's first ever storyboard. In eight scenes, Hogarth depicts over time the decline and fall of this 'rake' from spendthrift son of a rich merchant who wastes all his money on luxurious living, gambling and prostitution in London, to Bedlam inmate finally confined in chains. Remember the last one in the series, young man?"

"Any psychiatrist worth her salt certainly knows that one," said Conrad with a grin. "Finally considered insane and violent, the 'rake' is shown as an inmate of Bedlam, with only his fancy wife Sarah Young, in her fine clothes with high society fan in her hand, there to comfort him. Shown as well is the rake being simultaneously entertained by a man posing as King George, and various grotesque, disturbed and suffering co-habitants of Bedlam all about. An emblem of the worst excesses of abusive mental health treatment in its full glory."

"Excellent, excellent. Lecture finished," and off he marched out of the great room with a limp. Shouting over his shoulder as he exited, Professor Chamberlain said, "Now it's to the musty papers and the incredible truths I have uncovered. That will be my true gift to you today."

Chapter 92

IMPERIAL WAR MUSEUM, LONDON:

Medallion holder 869 sporting a hard hat and carrying a set of fake architectural plans rolled up in one hand and a black ballistic nylon drag bag in the other, passed unnoticed through a construction entrance into the Imperial War Museum. Cement mixers, stacks of cement bags, scaffolding, a silent skip loader, and a dozen men were strewn about the large hall as 869 entered the museum and made his way through the maze of organized chaos typical of an industrial construction site. Having memorized the floor plan of the museum, 869 continued past the large exhibit hall, all the way to the archives room, and slipped inside. The lights were on, and papers and files opened on several large tables next to each other. *Someone has already been here and that someone is sure to return soon,* the sniper said to himself. He then spied a stack of boxes at the far end of the room piled high. *Perfect. This is going to be one of the easiest hits ever,* he thought to himself as he began to assemble his Ruger M77/22 with integral Tac-Ops suppressor. After mounting the Leupold Mark 4 PR 1.5-4x20mm scope with the SPR reticle, he checked the ten round rotary box magazine. He favored its .22 caliber long rifle round for close-work indoors—despite its small caliber, it had devastating killing power. He found bigger rounds were messy at times and he needed to get in-and-out ASAP after the hits. Readying himself for action, he said to himself with practiced precision, *rifle—check; silencer—double check; scope—triple check. Ready for assassination.* His internal chuckle said it all.

Chapter 93

IMPERIAL WAR MUSEUM, LONDON:

With great delight, Professor Chamberlain led Libby and Conrad into the large room that housed archival records and papers from the Great War.

"This looks more like the main reading room of the Stanford library with a ceiling that reaches to the stars, than a musty old storage room in the back of a museum," said Conrad.

"What a room," Libby added. "Sort of like Cambridge University in a way. You feel a part of history just by walking into this place."

"And this is only the Great War documents archive," replied Professor Chamberlain proudly. "There's a similar room for World War II and yet another room for our later conflicts. Too many wars, I should say."

"How many documents must be in here?" asked Libby. "There are shelves from floor-to-ceiling all around this massive room. You clearly need a ladder to get to the upper shelves," she said pointing to one of the ladders on wheels next to a nearby shelf.

"Millions of documents, hundreds of millions of pages," replied Professor Chamberlain.

"How many people work in here?" asked Conrad.

"We have a dozen large tables each with a dozen chairs, so easily over a hundred could work here at the same time, although we rarely have anything approaching that number," answered the professor. "Although closed temporarily due to renovations, when in full swing, we tend to have only a few visitors or scholars working at a given time, because research often requires lots of space. Most scholars work by laying out hundreds of documents at a time, first finding them, then organizing them into related groups on different tables, and only then moving from location to location in order to actually read and analyze each lot of interconnected documents."

"Looks like some scholar is working that way right now," Conrad said as he looked over about a half-dozen large tables piled high with stack after stack of folders.

"Yes, indeed and that scholar would be me," replied Professor Chamberlain, bowing to them theatrically.

"Genius at work, I guess," said Libby to the professor with a smile.

"We shall see. But, now I have a real treat for you. More of a feast, actually. Libby, in front of you are the answers to your questions about your great-grandfather."

"Fantastic. Let's eat," said Libby with excitement.

"You are the guest of honor, young lady. Have a seat right here so we can get started," Professor Chamberlain said, pointing at a seat in front of the first stack of folders at the nearest table. "Augustus, you stand behind her and look over her shoulder as I point things out for you two."

Libby and Conrad moved obediently where directed. "Now, the curtain goes up and the show begins. Look first at these," Professor Chamberlain said, clearly enjoying his performance as a theatrical presentation of information to them.

"Once you told me to search for the military records of a Lieutenant Nigel Warburton, I hit a gusher," he said, moving his hands quickly in a full arc as far as he could reach upward and then gracefully back down as though tracing the pathway of exploding oil spouting straight up and then down. "I had already come across his name several years ago as the leader of the execution squad for the well-known case of Private Simon Jennings. As you will recall, Private Jennings became the 'poster boy' for the worst abuses of the British military in the Great War—executing *shell shock* victims as cowards. His case was particularly well-documented in our files, including the complete transcript of his court-martial."

"Yes, we read about him in the exposé by the investigative reporter who worked with you on this project, Jennifer Roberts of *The Washington Post*," Libby responded. "I had no idea Papa Nigel led his firing squad. It's so shocking and shameful."

"We're in touch with Ms. Roberts right now, hoping she can help us solve Adam's murder and get me off the hook," Conrad said. Looking again at his watch, he continued, "I sure hope this information of yours is not a detour from that specific problem, since time is of the essence as I'm already plastered all over Interpol."

"Patience, Augustus, patience. Libby, can't you teach this man to savor his experiences rather than quaff it all down without fully experiencing the libation of the moment?"

"I'm working on that Professor Chamberlain, but Gus is a difficult case."

"Indeed he is."

"So, what happened to my great-grandfather?"

"Yes, yes, yes. Hold on, you're about to find out." Taking out his shooting stick once again and sweeping it in a 360 degree arc, scanning the entire horizon of the room in a complete circle, Professor Chamberlain said, "All documents have now been scanned into a digital database, including every piece of paper in this room."

Libby was clearly impressed by the enormity of the task, and saw Conrad also nodding without saying a word as they caught each other's gaze.

Pivoting with the flair that was clearly his style once he got going, Professor Chamberlain now lurched to the left and pointed his shooting stick at a section of shelves. "For example, there you will find all remaining military communiqués, written correspondence and memos among all civilian leadership and army personnel prosecuting the Great War from the British side."

Sweeping his shooting stick in a full circle again around the entire circumference of the room, Professor Chamberlain continued, "But nowhere in this room will you find the military records of the millions of soldiers who fought in the Great War, since those were not sealed by His Majesty's Government. They have always been considered somewhat open files of the War Department, available to appropriate parties such as military personnel and civilian government officials. In many cases, the families also had access to these files, especially at the times of the deaths of any of the soldiers in that horrible conflict."

Without warning, Professor Chamberlain now lurched again to the right with his trusty shooting stick pointing to shelves close-by, aiming shotgun-style again. "But over there we have the military records and related files for each of the 306 documented cases in which the British Army officially executed *shell shock* victims as cowards. For example, we have the exact transcript from Private Jennings' court-martial in there. These are the same cases that have been publically recognized with the 'shot at dawn' memorial. As you know, a Parliamentary pardon was authorized for each of these cases after the government was so thoroughly disgraced by this scandal."

"So, those are all the cases you uncovered. Very impressive," said Libby in awe.

Now pitching to the right next to them, and swinging his shooting stick slightly farther to the right, Professor Chamberlain continued, "And there sit several hundred additional suspected cases of *shell shock* executions, with as yet incomplete information but remaining under active investigation. Each was court-martialed and executed, but ostensibly for desertion, criminal acts or insubordination. These cases are obviously of intense interest to their surviving relatives."

"Well done, but may I ask, please, what does all this have to do with my great-grandfather?" queried Libby, herself now becoming a bit impatient.

"Yes, we're enjoying your comprehensive orientation to the work here, but," looking nervously yet again at his watch, "it's already mid-afternoon now and time is of the essence if we're to use this information to find out who killed Adam and what the link might be to Papa Nigel's Medallion."

"Ah, I shall point that out straight away," said the professor with a wink at Libby. With a rapid twirl, he suddenly did an about-face and was now turned away from them with his stick. "Over there are the records of 147 officers held in secret for seventy-five years. In front of you is a list of each of them. The folder is entitled 'Patrons of Perseus' and on top is a list of all of them one through 147. Look down at number 59, would you please."

There it was. Libby gasped as she read aloud, "Lieutenant Nigel Warburton." She pulled out her cell phone camera and snapped a picture of the list.

"And organized in the several stacks of records on the table in front of you are the military records of those 147 on the list of the Patrons of Perseus. We found almost all of them except the last one on the list. Each was clearly involved in executing cowards during the Great War."

"Can I see Papa Nigel's personal file?"

"In due time, young lady, in due time."

"Professor Chamberlain, please be sensitive to our situation. We'll be caught at any moment, please professor," Conrad pleaded.

Chapter 94

MAUDSLEY HOSPITAL, SOUTH LONDON, AUTUMN OF 1917:

The following day Lieutenant Warburton didn't show up for any meals, and missed his appointment with his doctor, staying shut-up in his room all day. Finally, two of his fellow patients knocked on his door.

"Lieutenant Warburton, come join us for dinner," one shouted through the closed door.

"Yeah, we need some companionship," added the second officer.

There was no answer.

The door was locked, but concerned about his long absence, they forced it open and were aghast with what they saw. Lieutenant Warburton was lying on the floor in a pool of spent blood. Next to his body was his sidearm, which had obviously been discharged against the roof of his mouth. An empty glass sat next to a bottle of Glenlivet on its side on the small table next to him. A note was in place under the empty glass.

"What the fuck! He killed himself," exclaimed the first officer.

"Not at all," said the second officer as he inspected the scene and proclaimed, "The bastards got him."

Chapter 95

IMPERIAL WAR MUSEUM, LONDON:

Number 869 was positioning himself at the far end of the room, about a hundred feet away from where *the three of them* were viewing records. Perched atop of a stack of pallets and behind a tall stack of boxes, 869's sniper rifle, balanced on a bi-pod, was now set up with an ideal sighting of his two targets below. However, the professor kept moving about frenetically in front of his targets and 869 was awaiting his opportunity for two clean kill shots ... one ... two!

Chapter 96

MADINGLEY HALL, CAMBRIDGE:

In the waning late-afternoon light, Victoria drove her Mini to the car park of the American Cemetery, pulled on the parking brake and stepped outside. She walked quickly up to the entrance, feeling cold wet air with a foreboding chill, and noticed the wind had picked up significantly. She pulled her hoodie over her head and looked up to see an overcast sky with dark clouds threatening from above. Stepping inside the main entrance to the American Cemetery, she saw immediately to her left there was a visitors' building with a bronze plaque in front, a huge flagpole opposite a long narrow reflecting pool, and to the right, a massive marble wall with thousands of engraved names emblazoned all over it. Popping inside the Memorial building at the end of the wall, Victoria noted it was separated into a museum and a devotional chapel, neither of which seemed to be heated and both of which were deserted. Looking outside, she saw crosses in the thousands across the manicured grass. These markers exploded over the thirty-acre site, arranged in precise geometric rows in gentle curving arcs across the well-kept grounds, with the occasional Star of David disturbing an otherwise perfect symmetry of crosses. Just beyond lay Madingley Hall, about half a mile ahead. Walking outside the Memorial building, past the enormous sea of crosses, she came to Cambridge Road and decided to follow it to Madingley Hall as it slipped beneath the A428 highway above, arriving at the main gate of the cemetery and its grounds after only ten minutes of brisk walking.

Victoria crossed the street to the property where Madingley Hall sat up the road and past the porter's lodge just beyond the main gate on the left. Next to the porter's lodge was a church, St. Mary Magdalene, that was obviously still in use but was small, dark and in an appalling state of disrepair. Victoria had researched this entire area three miles from Cambridge city center, and recalled this church dated from the 12th century. Inside the main gate and to the right, about a dozen sheep were grazing lazily in a fenced grass paddock several acres in size. The paddock was surrounded by mature trees all along its border and followed the entry road up to Madingley Hall itself. Walking along the road, after only a few hundred yards, Victoria came to the front lawn on the right, a beautifully landscaped area called the Walled Garden straight ahead and a large empty car park to its left. The Tudor-period brick and mortar hall itself was situated just to the right and somewhat beyond the Walled Garden. Two cars were parked directly in front of it—a small, late model Mercedes at the sign "Reserved for the Director" and an old banger, shooting brake that was next to the Mercedes.

Victoria thought her view of Madingley Hall from the entry road was indeed quite grand as she was walking up towards the main building. Even in the gloom of the late-afternoon mist that burned her cheeks as she jogged slowly up the road to the entrance porch, Madingley Hall was most impressive. Looking up, she saw a clunch carving above the door with a restoration of Tudor royal arms depicting a greyhound and a dragon, a Tudor rose and the initials KH, indicating none other than King Henry the VIII. Other carvings under huge bay windows included one with the initials PE and the arms of Edward, Prince of Wales, son of Queen Victoria and later King Edward VI, who once lived here when he attended the University of Cambridge down the road. Beautiful brown and white brickwork restored the exterior throughout and there were two turrets, one immediately to the left of the front porch, which Victoria noticed, as she entered the porch and pulled her hoodie down to better look around.

An invisible voice from the reception area just inside the porch and to the left caused Victoria to startle, "May I help you?"

Victoria walked tentatively up to reception and saw an elderly gentleman with bad teeth and in desperate need of having his hair brushed. A flannel shirt, denim work pants and well-worn boots served to fill-out his failed attempt at sartorial excellence. "Hi, I'm Victoria, a student at Cambridge, and was just looking around a bit."

"Not a problem. I'm Derrick, the porter. Gets kinda quiet and lonely out here. Too far off campus for the important people, but we make do."

Victoria already knew Madingley Hall was largely used by the university as a sop to the general public to counter claims of elitism by letting the old ladies of Cambridge hold their basket weaving, flower arranging and Pilates classes here as a community service. Evidently, they didn't have too many of such meetings.

"Can you show me around?" Victoria asked.

"Delighted, my child. No one seems interested in the old place anymore. Just let me get the keys."

Victoria watched as Derrick went over to a board mounted on the wall and plucked a ring of keys off a hook. He then took long strides past her and stopped outside a set of double doors just opposite reception and put a key in the lock and swung the doors open.

"This is the dining hall, built in 1540. The ceiling is its most striking feature, installed by Colonel Harding in the 20th century using plasterwork from Jacobean molds."

Victoria could see three long rows of tables for seating more than sixty, plus a head table for another twenty, in the traditional English boarding school style. On one wall was a renovated fireplace with the date 1589 clearly showing and an over-mantel displaying a marble bust of Queen Elizabeth I—The Virgin Queen. "What's that?" she asked pointing to some columns to the left of the entrance to the Dining Hall.

"Oh, that's Stair Hall, which leads up to the Board Room, the Hickson Room and the Long Gallery and down to the old tunnel."

"Tunnel?"

"Well, young lady, there's lots of tunnels in Cambridge."

"Whatever for?"

"Different purposes. Built over the centuries. Some tunnels today go under major streets in Cambridge for pedestrians. During World War II, one tunnel under Corpus Christi College, Cambridge, was rumored to have been a place to hide if Hitler had successfully invaded England. Now they're mostly used as wine cellars."

"What about the one here? Can I see it?'

"Don't see why not. In almost fifty years working as Porter of Madingley Hall, I've only been down there a couple of times, and not for many years. No reason to go there, really."

"You've been here a long time."

"Yes, the university purchased the estate in 1948, after a string of families over the centuries all nearly went bankrupt with the upkeep. I started working here in the 1960s and am retiring next year. This way," Derrick said as he made his way across the Dining Hall to Stair Hall and went down the stairs.

"Sure you don't want to go up? It's more interesting up there. Probably just cold and damp down there. It leads over to the American Cemetery and Memorial across the highway."

"No, I prefer an adventure. Why an American Military Cemetery here, anyway?"

"It's the American World War II military cemetery in Britain. Almost 4,000 American servicemen and women are buried there. Mostly crew members of British based U.S. aircraft."

Leading the way, Derrick soon came to a heavy metal door, found a key on the ring and turned it, opening the way to the tunnel. Switching on some lights, he said, "I'll lead the way, but not too far."

Victoria felt a strong chill go up her spine as she entered the dark, dank passageway—a heavy mustiness seemed to suck the oxygen out of the tunnel.

Derrick broke the silence as they took several paces down the corridor, and said, "The only ones down here anymore are those soldiers a few times a year. They're the ones meeting at Madingley now. Down here are all the records of the thousands of Americans buried across the way, plus all those missing in action listed at the Memorial."

"Would that include those of an American, Colonel Alexander Miller, buried there?"

"Why yes, I suppose. Funny you should ask. I knew Colonel Miller before his death. It was he who's the one that got the deal with the university to store records of the Americans buried in the cemetery here after the war. The university was grateful for the financial support from the U.S. Army to help with the upkeep and restorations. The university also needed funds to convert the stables to residences, and make Madingley Hall into a small conference center. Now, let's get out of here. I'm cold."

Victoria could see down the hall a ways that various rooms came off the corridor, presumably record rooms. "Are those the record rooms?" she asked before turning around.

"Far as I know."

After ascending the Stair Hall back into the Dining Hall, Derrick said, "There's lot more to see upstairs. Follow me." Taking the stairs up another floor, he poked his head into one room, saying, "This is the Saloon." He continued to move across the way, motioned down the hall and said, "And over there's the King's Room—a small conference room."

"What's that door," Victoria asked, pointing to a solid oak door on the far end of the King's Room.

"Oh, that's the entry to the turret stairway."

"Not the one Prince Edward used to sneak his girlfriends in and out is it?"

"Legend has it, that's the very one. I see you're acquainted with the lore, some call it a myth, that when Queen Victoria leased Madingley Hall for her son, Edward, Prince of Wales in the mid-19th century, so he'd have some place proper to live as a Cambridge student, he was a bit of a playboy."

"Some dormitory," she said as her eyes-wide-open scanned the hall.

"Yes, gardens, stables, horses, servants, all for one man, but he was the Crown Prince and eventually became King Edward the VII. During his mother's reign, he was betrothed to a German princess, but, according to legend, had plenty of girlfriends he got in and out, fooling his palace handlers at the time."

"Let's see the stairway."

"Haven't been down these turret steps forever. You know, it's from the mid-1500s, part of the original building. Let's see now," Derrick said as he fumbled for another key. "There we go." He opened an oak door barely five-feet tall.

"They were short back then, I guess," Victoria said, almost needing to duck as she entered the turret staircase winding tightly around and around the inside of the same turret she saw on the left of the entrance hall when she first came into the building.

"Yes, indeed. Mind your step, these 450-year-old stairs are narrow and dangerous."

The two of them descended from the King's Room, round and round. Suddenly, Derrick stopped at another door, opened it and said, "Now we are back at reception."

"Yes, but these stairs continue to go down. Where to?"

"I think there used to be a door to the outside. That's supposedly how the mistresses got in and out."

"Can we see?"

"Well, all right." Turning around, Derrick led the way downward to another oak door, tried the same key and pushed hard, opening the door onto the front lawn, onto the grounds, and next to the main entrance. "There you go. That's how it was done. Don't think I've ever been out this way before."

"Thanks so much, Derrick. I've got to be going. Maybe I'll come back to see the rest of the building and the grounds on a nicer day."

And with that Victoria thought, *Alexander Miller's records are surely down there. Medallion holder 147. And I bet so are the records of the modern Patrons. I've got to get in there and copy those records. But how?*

Chapter 97

IN THE TUNNEL UNDER MADINGLEY HALL, CAMBRIDGE:

The Commandant sat at the head of the conference table in the storage room off the tunnel connecting Madingley Hall and the American Cemetery for the second time on the same day. "Sorry to trouble you all again today, but recent developments require us to add some additional tasks to our ongoing activities." The same dozen or so expressionless faces as before were seated again all around the small conference table in the records room off the corridor of the tunnel. "888, in addition to the two new names added to the target list earlier today, we have some new problematic developments."

"Yes, Commandant. Do you want us to add more names?" 888 replied with paradoxical deference in his burly voice.

"Unfortunately, we have enemies who're hacking into U.S. Army Intelligence files."

A stir and mumbling erupted in the room. "Omigod." "Terrible." "Who is it?" All exclamations coming at once from various members seated at the table.

"Gentlemen, gentlemen. Listen up. Seems like a skilled computer hacker, working with an investigative reporter, have compromised U.S. Army security, and we've now designated them both as targets for espionage."

"What records did they breach?" 888 asked.

"Ours. The Patrons. But only those online," the Commandant replied.

"Then maybe we aren't so bad off," said one of the other operatives.

"They sound dangerous to me. What's the order?" asked 888 in a concerned voice.

"Execution, by any means necessary and as soon as possible," the Commandant barked. "One of them is in America and the other is in the U.K. We're in touch with operatives in the U.S., so you in this room can focus on the enemy from the U.K."

"Who are they?"

"We have put the following two names on the list. Jennifer Roberts, from *The Washington Post*, in Washington, D.C."

"And who else?"

"Victoria Chamberlain from Cambridge."

Chapter 98

"**I** shall get straight to the point," the ever energetic Professor Chamberlain said.

That would be novel, Libby thought to herself.

"With all due respect, Professor Chamberlain, we have an emergency here," Conrad pleaded.

Ignoring Conrad, and this time lurching to his left, Professor Chamberlain continued, "Finally, over there on that table lay the military records of those individuals under current investigation who are either known or suspected to be executed, assassinated or murdered by the 147 documented Patrons of Perseus during the Great War. None had a legitimate court-martial. Now, on which pile do you think your great-grandfather's records exist? Over here?" he asked, pointing to the folders of those killed by the Patrons of Perseus, "or over there?" he asked, now spinning to his right, pointing to the folders of the killers, the Patrons of Perseus themselves.

A long pause ensued during which Libby looked back and forth between the two piles of records, clearly too befuddled to answer, as Conrad checked his watch once again.

"Aha! Your great-grandfather's folder is over here," Professor Chamberlain shouted triumphantly, but now exhibiting anger for the first time as he pointed his shooting stick almost violently at the stack of folders of men executed by the Patrons.

"Your Papa Nigel, as you call him, or Medallion Number 59, as the Patrons of Perseus called him, was visited by Medallion Number 1 at the Maudsley Hospital. That is significant because at the time, Medallion Number 1 was also the leader of this secret, unethical and illegal society. The leader was also known as the Commandant of Perseus, whereas the regular members were all known as Patrons of Perseus."

"For real?" Libby gasped.

"Not only that. Three days after Number 59 was visited by Number 1, Medallion Number 59 was dead."

Libby began to cry.

"And, disgustingly, we see your great-grandfather's name come up on the kill list of Number 84 over there," Professor Chamberlain said, now swinging his stick back to the pile of the Patrons of Perseus. "It seems Number 84 specialized in making murders look like suicides at the time. He was a diabolical cad. Other Patrons in that pile specialized in making the murders they committed look like somebody else murdered their targets. This was their tactic for sometimes simultaneously framing an enemy while eliminating someone they thought was a coward."

Stunned, Libby slowly said, "So Papa Nigel was killed by his own secret organization."

"Yes. He was threatening to expose the Patrons of Perseus and their activities with letters to his MP at the very time British military leadership was under fire but lying publicly by falsely reassuring the Parliament there was no instance or policy where any British soldier was executed for cowardice if he had *shell shock.*"

Libby was silent, tears rolling down her cheek. Conrad stood behind her and placed his hands gently on her shoulders.

"Papa Nigel was killed by his own organization and his death was made to look like a suicide," Libby said softly.

"I'm afraid so, young lady," Professor Chamberlain agreed in a soft tone with a tear in the corner of one eye.

"But he was actually a hero, Libby," Conrad said gently.

Suddenly it dawned on Libby. "That's it. That's what's also happened to Adam. The modern Patrons killed my only son to protect their secret and framed you for it because they think you're an enemy of the army."

"That's probably true," agreed Conrad enthusiastically. "But that theory will appear crazy, unless we get solid proof for Jennifer Roberts. Professor Chamberlain, the Patrons began as a purely British organization, and that was more than a hundred years ago. Have you found proof this organization continues to exist?"

"Not from Britain," he answered with a wry smile.

"So you mean from America?" asked Libby with a quizzical look.

"Yes. And now the *coup de grâce*," Professor Chamberlain said, thrusting his stick fencing-style at the documents for the Patrons of Perseus. "The link to Adam comes from Number 147 on that list of Patrons. In fact, it's the very last one on the list we have from the Great War era. Also, it's the name of a young American doctor, soon to become a psychiatrist, Dr. Alexander Miller."

"Alexander Miller? Is he buried in the American Cemetery at Cambridge?" Libby asked.

"And that is where we go next," Professor Chamberlain said, spinning behind Conrad as Conrad remained standing behind Libby who was still sitting at the table.

Thwat! Thwat! The sounds came from behind.

Both Professor Chamberlain and Conrad shouted out in terrorizing pain simultaneously and hit the floor.

Libby screamed and ducked under the closest table.

Professor Chamberlain, blood roiling out of his mouth, clenched his bullet-pierced chest with one hand and punched an alarm under the table where he lay with his other hand and said as he collapsed, "The answer to Adam is at Madingley Hall. Go get 'em, Libby. Go get 'em."

Chapter 99

IMPERIAL WAR MUSEUM, LONDON:

"Gus, you're hit," whispered Libby.
"Yeah, it's my right side, upper thigh. A through-and-through. You okay?"

"Shaken but not shot."

"Let's get the hell outta here," Conrad said wincing and grabbing his thigh.

"You're bleeding."

"Not too bad. Let's worry about that later."

"What about Professor Chamberlain?"

Checking for a pulse as copious blood continued to rush out of the professor's chest, Conrad replied, "He's gone."

A moment of silence as the two scanned the area, looking for the assassin, then, "We need to stay low and get out of here. The killer could be anywhere," Conrad whispered.

They crawled on all fours out of the Great War documents room, into the dark corridor, as Conrad dragged his leg behind him.

Once in the outer corridor, the searing pain of the wound settled all around Conrad and he couldn't see anything in his field of vision.

"We've got to get outta here before we're goners, too," Libby said.

Libby helped Conrad scramble to his feet, and while Conrad punched his entry wound with his right hand to stem the bleeding, more blood trickled down the back of his leg. Libby took his left arm and led him as quickly as they could go, Conrad dragging his right leg down the corridor and out the massive external door and into Sally without encountering the gunman.

Once in the Range Rover, Libby revved it, and crashed through the parking barrier, past a stunned security guard. In a blink she was on Lambeth, straight to the A13 and on her way to Cambridge. As she drove, Conrad reached for his tote bag in the back to grab an undershirt. He quickly tore it into rudimentary bandages and made part of it into a tourniquet as well.

"Looks like it missed bone, as well as the femoral artery, thank God. It's above the knee, but right through my quad and out the back. Pain is frickin' unbearable. Hand me that water bottle. I'll wash it out a bit."

"Here," Libby said as she handed him a half empty water bottle. "Hold on for now, I'm calling Victoria." Steering with one hand, punching the phone with her other, she yelled, "Victoria, Victoria. Call the police. We've been ambushed at the Imperial War Museum."

"What?"

"Just call 999."

"You mean 911," Conrad gasped.

"No 999. This is the U.K.," Libby retorted.

"Oh, right," Conrad remarked.

Then, into the phone, "I am afraid your grandfather may have been mortally wounded. We had to leave him behind as we made our escape. So, hurry, hurry. Dr. Conrad's shot, but I'm okay. Call me back as soon as you can." She ended the call and continued to drive frantically.

Conrad, now barely conscious, heard the familiar rattle coming from his tote bag as he tore his undershirt into bandages. "It's not bleeding badly, but I can't take this pain."

Libby, now at full speed on the M11, ignored Conrad for the moment and mumbled to herself, trying to get her bearings. *About sixty miles to Madingley. Looked that up earlier. About seventy-five minutes with traffic, but with any luck, I could make it in an hour.* "Gus, we're gonna have to stop and get that looked at."

"No chance," he fired back in a wincing voice. "We need to get to Madingley first. I'm sure that security guard back at the museum has already given the cops Sally's registration plate. Hard to miss."

"GALSAL."

"We'll be arrested soon if we can't get to Cambridge ahead of them. I can't take this pain, though."

Suddenly, Conrad realized there was a solution at hand. He fished the noisy bottle of pills out of his tote bag, opened it up and tapped two OxyContin into the palm of his hand. The normally snow white pills were now dirty brown with age. *Wow, that's weird. I'm already feeling pain relief just handling these pills and not even swallowing them*, he thought to himself. Clearly tempted by the excruciating pain in his right thigh, Conrad thought again, *it was such a struggle getting clean from these damned prescription opiates twelve years ago, was it worth risking a relapse?* Just then, Libby hit another bump, jolting him, and Conrad shouted out in pain, getting the answer to his question. He leaned back in ecstasy as the old pills dissolved on his tongue, and he felt like he ascended above his own body in a blue haze as the pain dissipated. *Still potent after all these years,* he thought, and drifted off again as Libby sped up the road to Cambridge.

Chapter 100

LONDON:

Quickly, 869 dialed the number, knowing he was in trouble. "912, this is 869. Bad news. Hit Conrad but not a kill. Warburton not hit. Collateral damage to some old man who stepped in front of my shots."

"You idiot. Did you follow them?"

"Negative. Alarm set off and priority was on me escaping without capture. Cops everywhere, but at least I eluded them."

"So has success eluded you?"

"Do you want me to finish the job once they resurface?"

"869, you're not only immutably retired now, but permanently de-activated. We shall never need your services again."

"But—"

The Commandant hung up, knowing any job needed doing well often had to be done by oneself. And then the Commandant whispered aloud, *"I'll terminate them myself."*

Chapter 101

As Jennifer pulled into the parking lot for Au Pied de Cochon, she noticed a tired old building with a fancy name. Doing a bit of research on the place before departing for lunch, she learned "the foot of the pig" had been here for several decades as a neighborhood restaurant that was a place to eat rather than dine. Word was the restaurant would soon be replaced by a more modern but generic "Five Guys" that promised to have far less character. Rumor had it that heavyweight boxing champion Mike Tyson evidently had gotten into a brawl here once. The restaurant also had a notorious reputation from the Cold War Era. Legend also had it that in 1985, a high-ranking Soviet defector slipped away from his CIA escort during a meal here, seeking refuge back in the Soviet Embassy around the corner and about a mile away.

Walking inside, Jennifer scanned the premises and saw an unpretentious eatery that had probably not changed in decades. Informal, with a polished bar top and tables sporting artificial marble tops, it was trying to be a French brasserie. Slowly she became aware of the pungent smell of smoke, cheap wine and life under a freeway without soap coming from behind her. Startled by the sudden movement, she turned to accost a man with matted hair, a wild beard, and pale blue eyes that looked ten years younger than his worn face.

"Jennifer Roberts?" a kind voice implored.

Taking a step back, Jennifer responded, "Yes, are you Jordan Davis?"

The man nodded yes, his furrowed brow seeming to bear the weight of the whole world upon two furry moustaches mounted above tired eyes sporting strangely delicate lashes. Tattered tennis shoes poked out of the bottom of baggy cargo pants two sizes too large for his gaunt body. On top he wore a torn and unbuttoned trench coat over at least two mouse-eaten sweaters, a shirt or two and a colored t-shirt or two, forming layers of clothing on his chest. *Probably all the clothes he possesses,* Jennifer thought to herself.

"Let's sit down and get you something to eat," she said.

"Good enough. I'm starved."

Jennifer noted the man looked malnourished and seemed to be carrying the burdens of a difficult life without complaint on fragile shoulders. He moved deliberately yet gracefully, sliding into his seat across from her at the table where the waitress escorted them as she placed menus on the table and then departed. When the waitress returned, Jennifer ordered a salad and Jordan asked for a steak and mashed potatoes with plenty of gravy.

"So, Jordan, thanks for meeting with me. What can you tell me about your sister?"

Jordan got straight to it. "We grew up in a dysfunctional home. Ellen is five years younger than me. I tried to look out for her, and tried to be the man of the house after our dad flew the coop when I was about ten."

Jordan stroked his matted beard as he spoke with long, elegant fingers ending in hard bitten nails, all arising from a dirty hand, with rough, cracked skin on the palm and heavily scarred knuckles.

As the waitress put down glasses of water, Jordan stopped speaking. When she left, he continued, "Mom was complete and utter chaos. In and out of cuckoo wards, drunk tanks and jails until she finally took an overdose and killed herself. It was bedlam living with her."

Jennifer's thoughts quickly turned to Conrad and Libby at the real Bedlam Hospital, and then pivoted her attention back to Jordan.

"Ellen was fifteen and I was twenty when Mom died. Ellen then flew the coop too and shacked up with some old bugger, and I joined the army."

"Sounds like a difficult childhood for both of you. How'd you and Ellen get along?"

"At first, pretty well. I was her only support system and tried to be there for her. I went to juvie many times to help get her released."

"Juvenile hall?"

"Yep, prison for underage criminals, which Ellen was. Shoplifting, truancy, eloped from her group home, and once tried to torch her group home. Actually did set a cat on fire once."

"Was she violent or just disturbed?"

"Life wasn't easy for her and she was really on her own once mom died. Later I heard that Dad had molested her while she was growing up, but who knows? She tried to off herself more than once as a teenager, and they put her in the looney bin at least twice for that. She took drugs all the time, and went bonkers once. They called it a psychotic break, and thought it might have been bipolar, just like my mom. I didn't get my bipolar until I was getting kicked out of the army on a psychiatric discharge about five years ago."

"How'd she get straightened out?"

"I'm not sure she ever really did, although after she married that guy and got her abortion, he helped her get her GED and start college."

Jennifer thought, *Jordan's confirming just what Ellen's ex told me.* "Yes, I know, I've spoken with her ex-husband."

"Nice guy but a sucker for her manipulating ways. He was like putty in her hands. Anyway, after that she got a ROTC scholarship and then joined the army, and they put her through medical school as well. A full-ride all the way."

"Well, I'd say she really turned herself around after such a tough start to her life. What makes you say she maybe never really straightened herself out?"

Just then the food arrived, and Jordan wolfed half of his down before Jennifer even picked up her fork. She let him finish before she resumed questions.

"So, what do you know about Ellen in more recent years?"

"Ellen and I really didn't have much contact once she was in med school and training. I was also in the army, but stationed all over the place, including three deployments to Iraq. Ellen went to Iraq, too. She was deployed after my last tour there, so we never overlapped. I tried to contact her for help about six months ago after she got that big shot position over at the Pentagon, but she treats me now like I'm radioactive."

"Do you know why?"

Just then the waitress came by. "Did you even taste it?" the waitress asked Jordan with a smile. "How about dessert?"

"Sure. Apple pie and ice cream."

"How about you, ma'am?" the waitress asked Jennifer.

"No thanks. I'm still working on this salad. You could bring me a cup of coffee, though."

"Comin' right up."

Jennifer resumed, "So Jordan, why did Ellen start ignoring you?"

"Well, I certainly didn't make her proud since I was given a psychiatric discharge from the army after my third deployment. I've had bad PTSD ever since my second deployment, plus all of a sudden I got a wild manic episode once I got home from my third deployment and started drinking and getting into fights. The army discharged me with bipolar as a pre-existing condition, and said I didn't have PTSD. I think they did that just so they can say my bipolar is my own fault, and then they don't have to give me any disability payments or medical care from the VA. So, I've been homeless the last five years. Ellen's ashamed of me and worried I'll spill the beans about her family full of loonies and her own psycho past."

"You've certainly had your own challenges. I'm so sorry to hear about your struggles. With your sister in such a prominent position in psychiatry, I would think she could get the VA to reconsider your case and get you some help."

"Ha," Jordan said between huge bites of apple pie á la mode.

"What Ellen really doesn't want is for anyone in the army to know about her past. She thinks it'll interfere with her all-important career if the head of army psychiatry is seen to be a psychopath, a murderer and someone who comes from a family full of mental illness including having her own mental illnesses."

"*Murderer?*" Jennifer stopped chewing and dropped her hands to the table, almost losing the silverware she was holding. "Did I hear you say *murder?*"

"Yeah, forgot to mention."

"Forgot to mention? You're just gonna slip that in here?"

"Let me explain. Ellen got into a fight with another kid at the group home where she was living as a teenager. She was tried as a juvenile but pleaded self-defense and was acquitted."

"Well, maybe that was the correct verdict."

Jordan looked up at Jennifer like she was a brick short of a full load.

"I don't think so. She's actually dangerous. Don't you get it? Nobody seems to get it. When I asked her about killing her roommate, she admitted she did it on purpose. And when I asked her why, you know what she said?"

Jennifer gulped and then offered, "What?"

"She said she did it just to see what it felt like to kill someone."

"Oh, my god. I see what you mean that she's dangerous."

"She also told me she would kill me if I ever told anybody, so for God's sake, don't tell her I gave you this information."

"Of course, not. Your secret is safe with me. I can see why Ellen might think this information in the hands of army superiors, who aren't sympathetic to psychiatric illness, might ruin her career."

"So now you understand. Do you think Ellen is the type of person who should be a doctor, let alone a psychiatrist, particularly one in charge of all psychiatry in the army?"

"You know, that's the same question her ex-husband asked me."

Jennifer paid the bill and slipped some pastries at the checkout counter into a bag for Jordan and they departed.

Chapter 102

"Jennifer?" Victoria asked breathlessly over the phone.

"Yes, what's wrong Victoria?"

"Everything. I'm back at the Three Horseshoes waiting for Libby and Dr. Conrad to arrive. My grandfather's been murdered and Dr. Conrad's been shot."

"Omigod. Can't be."

"Everything's falling apart. We could all be dead by the end of the day."

"Let's just pause for a moment and regroup. It's bad but we're not all going to die. First of all, take a deep breath."

Victoria complied audibly, as a moment of silence passed.

Jennifer continued. "You gonna be okay to deal with this?"

"But we are all gonna die. Already two deaths, one right after the other. Adam, then Gramps. It's so unfair."

"Slow down. You're not making sense. Your grandfather was an incredible friend to me. I'm completely undone by this myself. Let me think. Who'd want to shoot a harmless Cambridge professor?" Jennifer had all she could do to not lose it on the phone.

"They were looking at files at the Imperial War Museum and got shot by a sniper there."

"Sniper? That's serious business. Sounds like a special ops hit."

"I think they were actually aiming for Dr. Conrad. He was only hit in the leg but refuses to go to the hospital. He's on his way here. Should arrive in a few minutes."

Jennifer's fast-lane thinking was spinning out of control, providing no answers to the crisis that was unfolding.

"It's all falling apart," Victoria repeated. "We still don't have the files you need to prove what's going on."

"Victoria, this has become far too serious for you to keep playing this game. You need to get Dr. Conrad to the hospital and let the authorities take it from there."

"It's the authorities we're investigating, Jennifer. Listen to this. I snooped around Madingley Hall today when Dr. Conrad and Libby were in London. There are military conferences being held there. Between the American and the British Armies."

"You're clearly taking far too much risk with your snooping, Victoria."

Paying Jennifer no mind, Victoria continued. "And there's a secret underground passage connecting Madingley Hall with the American Cemetery and Memorial. I snuck in there today and found out where they probably keep the files you need to prove ongoing operations of the Patrons of Perseus. I didn't have the chance at the time to lift any files or make any copies."

"Victoria, you listen to me. You can't fight one army let alone two. You must stop this immediately and get help."

"No. We've already decided we're going back this evening now that the conference has ended. We'll break in after everyone is out of the underground storage room and asleep in the dormitory area at Madingley."

"Victoria, don't do it. I beg you, this is far too dangerous. Let me follow-up on some things I've already initiated and get some serious help for you. I've already launched action here at a very high level, and you just need to give me a little bit of time to get you that assistance."

"Jennifer, listen to me. You don't understand. We're out of time. Things are moving far too fast to wait for that help. We have to expose this assassination unit and shut it down tonight."

"Why tonight?"

"I don't know how to tell you this, so I'm just gonna blurt it out. Dr. Conrad and Libby are no longer the last names on the list of victims of the Patrons."

"Then who are?"

Victoria gulped. "You and me. Neither one of us may have much more than a couple of hours to get this done."

Chapter 103

EN ROUTE TO CAMBRIDGE:

Jolted forward by another bump, Conrad awakened once again in his passenger seat alongside Libby, who was still preoccupied with the road as she hurtled faithful Sally at top speed towards Cambridge.

"Sorry about that. We just made the turn-off for Madingley," Libby said without looking at Conrad and missing the grimace on his face, as her eyes looked intensively at the road ahead. "We're gonna meet Victoria at the Three Horseshoes again and figure out our plan of attack for Madingley Hall. How're you doing?"

Trying to relieve the discomfort in his leg, Conrad shifted his weight, but to no avail, flinching with the new onset of pain he caused himself by repositioning his leg in his car seat. "Fine, until that last bump."

Then, looking down at his wounded thigh, he was knocked back in time to the pain he felt in his car right after his accident with his wife and newborn baby. *Oh, no.* Seeing the blood all over his thigh triggered it. Like so many times over the past decade, Conrad suddenly heard the screech of tires, explosion of glass, grating of metal, and smell of flaming rubber. *Here we go again,* he thought as the flashback gripped him for the millionth time, tearing apart the contents of his body while terror scorched his guts. Waiting for it to pass, it ended like it always did with deafening silence and the devastating sense of loss of both his wife and daughter as though it had just happened. Willing himself back to the present, he quickly shut himself down emotionally, feeling numb.

I need to get my wits about myself, he thought and felt better as he detached from the reality of the moment.

"Gus, you okay? I thought you left us for a moment."

"No more bleeding, but it's throbbing like a bugger and driving me out of my frickin' mind right now."

"Did you have another one of those flashbacks? Sure we don't need to take you to a hospital?"

"No, I have another plan," Conrad said, as he fished out the pill bottle from the tote bag on his lap and chomped down four more Oxys.

"What are you taking?" Libby asked out of the corner of her eye.

"Just some mint candy," he lied. "I need a bit of energy. Want one?"

Libby shook her head no.

That glorious, familiar blue haze, thought Conrad, as the bitter taste of four more Oxys exploded in his mouth. *All is well with the world. Peace and tranquility.*

"What did you say," Conrad asked aloud as he willed himself out of his trance.

"I didn't say anything, but here we are," Libby responded, as the crunch of gravel in the Three Horseshoes car park greeted them once again. She brought Sally to a full stop and quickly dismounted from the driver's seat. Moving nimbly around to the passenger door, she helped Conrad get out.

"Let's not make a spectacle of this, or we're going to be noticed," said Conrad, wincing silently as he got to his feet.

"Here. Just put your arm over my shoulder and lean on me," Libby said, as she positioned herself with the well-practiced maneuvers of a skilled nurse. The warmth of Libby's body brushing against his wounded thigh—which managed to cover most of the bloodstain on his pant—momentarily removed the coldness penetrating in his right limb, and also provided a bit of warmth between his limbs as well.

"Slow as we go," continued Libby, her eyes and her posture encouraging careful forward movement as a single unit working together.

"There's Victoria," Conrad grunted between clenched teeth as they floated over the threshold of the pub entrance. "Let's go sit down and try and not get noticed."

A few paces later, Conrad slumped into his seat, face contorted and body recoiling as his weight transferred off his feet. *Not too much pain once*

I stop moving, Conrad thought, then noticing the artificial calm of his mind competing successfully with his underlying instincts that he was under a greater threat than just pain from a bullet wound.

"You okay, doc?" asked Victoria.

"I'm fine," Conrad replied, reassuring no one. "Let's get on with our plans. What did you learn and what's next?"

"I have so much bad news, I don't know where to start." Victoria paused, tears welling up again in her eyes, voice breaking. "Gramps is gone."

Conrad and Libby looked at each other nodding with realization that their worst fears about Professor Chamberlain had been realized.

Sitting silently, both Libby and Conrad were unable to find the words to respond.

"Just as you guys feared. Found dead of his gunshot wound," Victoria continued, "and the police are all over the case down at the Imperial War Museum."

"We're so sorry, Victoria," Libby finally said as her kind eyes met Victoria's before turning downward, and touched both of Victoria's hands on the table with both of hers with tenderness.

As Conrad looked on, it seemed to him that the two women had just formed a strong bond now that both of them had lost loved ones in this unfolding tragedy. The three of them just sat there for a long moment, no one seeming to know what to say.

Victoria finally broke the silence again. "Secondly, the other bad news. While I was waiting for you guys to arrive, I hacked back into the U.S. Army Intelligence files to check out the list of victims of the Patrons to see if it's changed."

"Well?" Libby asked when Victoria said nothing for a beat.

"It has."

"Victoria, what's going on?"

After another beat, Victoria finally said, "Both Jennifer Roberts and I have been added to the list.

Libby gasped.

Conrad, shaken out of his stupor and only following all this superficially due to his pain and opiates, was suddenly alert and attentive. "Incredible. Now we're all being targeted. Can this get any worse?"

Nobody said anything, too stunned to process all these events. Finally, Victoria interrupted the lull in the discussion. "And if all that's not bad enough, Interpol is on to you two guys in a big way and has identified your cell phone, Libby, and knows you're driving Sally."

"How would they know that, Victoria?" Libby asked.

"They're Interpol, that's how. So, you can't use Sally anymore. Once we're done tonight, I'll ditch her in central Cambridge, so the car doesn't lead the authorities to Madingley any quicker than your cell phone may already have."

"This is not good," Conrad responded, combing his hands again and again through his hair. He then held his head in his hands on arms propped on elbows sitting atop the pub table with his eyes closed. "This is not good at all," he repeated. *How did they trace our cell phone? I only used a burner,* Conrad thought to himself.

"There's some good news," Victoria offered.

"Let's hear it," Libby replied. "We certainly could use some of that."

"I traced the history of the last known Patron of Perseus from World War I, Alexander Miller. I think his story's going to blow this case wide open."

Conrad opened his eyes now, watching Victoria as the new information unfolded.

"Alexander Miller was an American, a young doctor actually, sent by the Yanks as an observer embedded in our British Army during the Great War. He was already a doctor at age twenty in 1916, joined the U.S. Army, and was sent to Britain as a medical observer in 1917, after the Americans joined the war."

"How could he be a doctor that young?" Libby asked.

Now fully awake again, Conrad sat up and entered *lecturing professor mode.* "That was before the modern era of medical education. A medical degree was typically awarded before World War I after only two years of study. Regulation of the medical profession by state governments was minimal or nonexistent then, so American doctors varied enormously in their scientific understanding of human physiology and the word 'quack' flourished, and rightfully so."

"Well, this quack Miller developed a special interest in psychiatry," Victoria continued, "and became so involved in the treatment of *shell shock* in the British Expeditionary Force during the last two years of World War I, that the British made him a member of the Patrons of Perseus at the end of the conflict, the last known member from that war, and the only American."

"I know that name. I have a picture of the list with his name on it from the museum right here on the camera in my cell phone." Libby said as she punched it up.

"Is that still on?" Victoria asked with obvious alarm.

"That's how the cops have traced us," Conrad said in a panic. "Omigod, omigod, it's all over."

Libby closed her eyes and buried her head in her hands, obviously realizing the huge mistake she had made. "Guys, I'm devastated. What a stupid thing to do. There, it's off now, and the battery's out as well."

"Don't worry. There's no way to undo this one, so we must just move on," Conrad said, trying to be reassuring but not doing too well as his obvious panic betrayed his true feelings. "Seems burner phones can no longer be trusted."

Victoria, mature beyond her years, continued. "Let's get practical, not emotional. The authorities now know we're at the Three Horseshoes, but they're not gonna know we're on our way to Madingley Hall."

Trying to cheer Libby up, Conrad said, "We still probably have a little while before they figure that out."

Victoria took one hand from each of them and said, "Look at me. It's imperative we use our last remaining minutes to scan records on file at Madingley Hall. We need proof tonight for Jennifer Roberts or else no one is gonna believe us and the killing of soldiers is gonna continue."

"Okay," Libby said softly. "What's the plan?"

Chapter 104

No sooner had Jennifer returned to her desk following her lunch meeting with Jordan Davis, than Bert yelled, "Hey, Roberts. Your friend, Colonel Richards on line one."

Jennifer picked up the line. "Colonel Richards? This is Jennifer Roberts. Thanks for calling back. I have a few questions about your reaction to the report of your Fort Hood soldier Sergeant Adam Warburton's death at Stanford."

"As the official press contact for the Pentagon on this matter, I can only tell you it's still under investigation," Richards responded in a matter-of-fact tone. "What I can tell you, however, is the young man's psychiatrist, Dr. Augustus Conrad, is wanted for questioning about the case, but the doctor seems to have disappeared."

"Is the army aware of anybody else who may have had a reason to want this soldier dead? Or possibly whether this could have been a suicide?"

"As I said, the matter is still under investigation."

"Are you aware that this soldier was in possession of a World War I Medallion from the Patrons of Perseus once owned by his great-great-grandfather, a British Army officer at the time?"

A prolonged silence came from the other end of the line. Finally, Colonel Richards responded, "As far as we know, there's no truth to that and it hardly seems relevant to the current investigation."

"Oh, I think it might be very relevant. Sources tell me the Patrons of Perseus might still be in existence under U.S. Army control. Any truth to that, Colonel Richards?"

"You have a very vivid imagination, Ms. Roberts. Perhaps you have too much 'Patrons of Perseus' on your one-track mind ever since you reported on them in the British Great War Archives, thus discrediting the British Army for your Pulitzer. I think you need to find a new story."

"Speaking of a new story, sources tell me you have a very curious background for the head of army psychiatry, including a brother who's an Iraq War veteran with PTSD but can't get help from the VA. Then there's a mother with bipolar issues who committed suicide and it appears you have some interesting psychiatric history of your own when you were an adolescent."

"Ms. Roberts. It's clear you're a muckraker, intent on discrediting the army and its loyal leaders, including myself. Your sources are incorrect and slanderous, and I suggest you not pursue this line of questioning if you ever want access to official Pentagon and army sources for your future stories. Assuming of course, you ever want to write stories that are true. This interview is over," she said in a biting adversarial tone.

Chapter 105

THREE HORSESHOES PUB, CAMBRIDGE:

"Okay, here's the plan," Victoria said as she picked up her computer bag sitting on the floor by her chair, and pulled out a laptop and a portable document scanner.

"Look at this little baby. A portable hand-scanner with Wi-Fi capabilities. Latest version, just released."

Victoria also fished a USB flash drive out of a pocket on the outside of the bag, and said, "Another tool of the trade. This is how we get the proof we need to blow this secret sky high without keeping it on a laptop that's difficult to move around when one's in a hurry."

"Good thinking," Libby remarked.

Conrad, now fully alert, followed with, "What the hell?"

"We break into army files in the tunnel tonight. I know how to get in. First we go and find the files of Alexander Miller. If we can do that, I think it'll lead us to the files for the activities of the current Patrons."

"This sounds quite unlikely, Victoria. And dangerous."

"Nothing's more dangerous than letting the Patrons continue to kill soldiers, including Gramps who's already died because of them. He'd want me to finish this the right way. Everybody on board? This is the time to opt out if you're not up for it."

"I'm in," said Libby.

"So'm I," Conrad added.

"Here's what I suggest. Libby, you're still ambulatory, so once we get into the tunnel, you stand lookout at the top of the tunnel to warn us if anyone comes to discover us." Reaching into her computer bag, she pulled out a black object and handed it to Libby, "Here's a torch for you."

"Torch?" Conrad asked with surprise. "We gonna burn the place down?"

"Dr. Conrad, don't you remember, in England, 'torch' means flashlight?" Victoria retorted.

"Oh, yeah, of course. Not really hitting on all cylinders tonight."

"And here's a torch, rather flashlight, for you, too, Dr. Conrad. I'm gonna need you to hold it while I look through the files and then scan the documents."

Libby interjected, "Before we even get to how you think we're gonna break into army records, what makes you think the files of this Dr. Alexander Miller are going to lead us to the Patrons?"

"It's the only thing that makes sense. He's the link between World War I British Patrons and modern day American Patrons."

"How so?" asked Libby. "I do see the link between the two organizations. Both groups are obviously assassins and both groups focus on soldiers with *shell shock*. But how does Alexander Miller make that link?"

Victoria continued. "I researched this guy and found out he came home to the U.S. after World War I and the army sent him for training in psychiatry. He continued a career in the army for thirty years and was one of their only psychiatrists between the two World Wars. Later, he became a leader of army psychiatry during World War II. He's the one who got the U.S. Army to collaborate with Madingley Hall when they built their Military Cemetery across the way. And I learned that the University of Cambridge liked it because the U.S. Federal Government paid them to store the records of all those buried in the cemetery. Miller developed Madingley Hall into a site for ongoing collaboration between British and American military psychiatry, which continues today."

"I can see how it would make sense to have this joint operation sited at Madingley," said Conrad. "That way, the British could deny the existence of the Patrons and claim they were disbanded, because all their records after the Great War were classified by the Americans, and they could deny the existence of the Patrons because they were able to keep their key records out of official Army Intelligence files and instead on file here outside of the U.S., and with a trusty ally in the U.K. Brilliant."

As Victoria shoved her scanner and computer into her bag, Libby shook her head and said, "I think the better description is 'diabolical.'"

Chapter 106

Conrad limped out of the Three Horseshoes Pub as Victoria reached down and picked up a long fat branch the wind had blown out of an oak tree. "Here. Use this as a walking stick."

"Thanks. That'll be handy."

"I'm gonna drop you guys off at the entrance to Madingley Hall. I'll park, then we'll go into the Dining Hall for one of their public lectures. Tonight's speaker is the Head of Computational Science at Microsoft. His title is 'If Donald Rumsfeld were a scientist.' Supposedly a play on words for 'known unknowns,'" Victoria said.

"Where's Donald Rumsfeld when we need him?" Conrad asked. "It's not the known unknowns I'm worried about. It's the unknown unknowns that could get us tonight."

Libby slipped Conrad a mint. "Cool it, Gus. You need all your wits tonight."

"So this is the plan," Victoria continued. "I already registered each of us for the course tonight. Since you guys are plastered all over the media, you need to be sure you don't attract any attention. Wear your ball cap low around your eyes, Dr. Conrad. Here, I've got one for you too, Libby. Also, all three of us will enter the Hall separately so no one thinks we're together. Let some people get between us."

"Then what?" Libby asked.

"Sit in the back row. But not together. Just before the lecture starts, I'll get up and then you follow a few minutes later, Dr. Conrad, and Libby, you follow at a distance. Come through the doors inside the Dining Hall on the left, and I'll lead us to Stair Hall. We'll all take the steps down to the tunnel."

"Isn't it locked?"

"Leave that to me," Victoria said.

Soon they were all standing separately inside the Dining Hall sipping white wine and trying not to be noticed when Victoria slipped out the back. She came up to the reception area, and found the lights on but no one there. Evidently Derrick and his staff were busy getting things organized for the night. Looking over her shoulder quickly, Victoria darted to the back of the reception area, pulled a ring of keys off the hook, and nonchalantly reentered the Dining Hall as if nothing had happened.

"Where were you just now?" Libby asked as Victoria passed by as though she didn't know her.

"All systems go," Victoria whispered without looking back at Libby. "Ready? Wait, then follow me, slowly, looking only straight ahead to arouse no suspicion. Put your wine glasses down first. Then we'll disappear behind those wooden columns and nobody'll notice."

And with that Victoria slipped around the wooden Ionic columns at the side of the room in the back, and started down the stairs. Conrad followed, leaning on his make-shift cane with Libby bringing up the rear.

Confronting a large metal door at the entrance to the tunnel, Conrad no sooner said, "Now what?" than Victoria pushed it open. "How'd you do that?"

"Follow me." Victoria turned her torch on, and said, "Libby, here's one of the torches. Stay here. If that door opens again, run as quickly as you can to alert us. We're gonna be down there a ways in their storage room for a good while because there're several documents to find and scan. Dr. Conrad, let's go."

Conrad felt the pain returning to his leg in great surges, as he moved but he tried to ignore it and keep quiet. Finally, after about a hundred yards, he asked Victoria, "Can we stop and rest a moment?" Conrad's tote bag was hanging on a strap around his neck. He took off his ball cap and found a handful of joy pills and when Victoria wasn't looking, swallowed them dry in the dark, then said, "I'm ready now."

About another hundred yards or so of limping on his stick, and a large record room with glass windows appeared just off the corridor. "Let's see if I can get in," Victoria said, fumbling for the keys and trying one after the other.

"Where'd you get those?" Conrad questioned.

"Not from hacking a computer, that's for sure," she said just as the door suddenly yielded to one of the keys. Once inside, Victoria swept her light across the room. "This looks like something out of the 1960s. Can you believe it? Typewriters. Carbon paper. Filing cabinets. No computers. No printers. We're going to have to do this by hand. Good thing I have a Neanderthal with me."

Conrad heard Victoria but was silent.

"That was supposed to be a joke," Victoria insisted.

"Oh, yeah. Sorry, just tired."

"So, let's find Alex Miller's records. Looks like this bank of filing cabinets across the back is for all those buried in the cemetery." Opening a drawer and rifling through Victoria said, "These appear to be all in good military order, alphabetical, and the letter 'M' is here." Victoria opened a filing cabinet drawer halfway across the archives. "No, not here, I'll try the next drawer. Ah, here are the Millers, several of them, and of course Alexander Miller at the front of the Millers. Thick file," she said as she pulled it out with two hands. "Let's take it over to the table and examine it. Can you hold that flashlight, or torch, for me so I can see well enough to scan?"

Just then, they both heard a loud "bang" and they dropped to the floor, hoping against hope to escape detection.

Chapter 107

Still lying in a state of complete panic on the floor of the conference room—torch off. Both Conrad and Victoria barely daring to breathe— nothing actually occurred for several minutes. "Damn," Victoria finally said aloud. "That was just the conference room door slamming shut. I didn't close it when we came in and the draft down the tunnel sucked it shut with a slam. False alarm. Sorry."

Trying to replace his heart down in his chest where it belonged rather than in his throat where it was just jammed right then, Conrad breathed a deep sigh of relief.

Back at work at the conference table, Victoria said, "Can you believe it? I can even hack into the university's private Wi-Fi signal down here. Madingley Hall is a remote site for Cambridge's Intranet. Okay, ready-to-go, let's see what we want to scan."

Paging through the files while Conrad held the light, Victoria looked through Colonel Alexander Miller's military records, documents showing his service in both World Wars, and then receiving security clearance as a member of Army Intelligence. "Look at this," Conrad said, pointing to one document. "Dr. Miller had both the U.S. Navy's top psychiatrist Rear Admiral Francis Braceland, and the U.S. Army's top psychiatrist Brigadier General William Menninger visit here during the Second World War. Both of these men went on to become major figures in

American psychiatry after the war."

"That doesn't help us. Read on," Victoria said, obviously trying to encourage Conrad to stay on task.

Conrad then replied, "Says here Miller retired after thirty years in the army in 1947, and relocated to the U.K., to work out of Madingley Hall as a civilian contractor until his death in 1972, when he was buried next door. He was able to engineer deaths of cowards and many others he thought threatened army cohesion and the warrior spirit, well into the Vietnam War."

"A real piece of work. Still, not all of what we need."

"Now here's what we really want. He was the second Commandant of the Patrons of Perseus until his death."

"Great," Victoria exclaimed. "That's the proof we need that the Americans took over the Patrons after the Great War and continued their activities at least until 1972. Give me those documents and I'll scan them in. Keep looking."

"And here's the list of new Patrons from the 1930s until his death in 1972. Miller was number 147 and this list goes up to number 350. So, I think this indicates about 200 new Patrons were added to the organization over forty years. And aha," Conrad said eagerly, all indications of pain draining from his leg, "this here seems to be the list of their victims up to 1972. Interesting, Libby's Papa Nigel was number 59 on the list of Patrons and also number 650 on the list of victims from the Great War."

"Probably 306 of these victims are the same ones Jennifer Roberts and Gramps uncovered in their 'shot at dawn' project. Give me that one, too, and keep digging," Victoria said, working feverishly feeding documents through the scanner as they spoke. "Now we need documents proving the activities of the modern day Patrons. That's the information most critical for us and for Jennifer Roberts."

"But those records will probably not be in the bank of file cabinets across the back wall," she said as she pointed, "because these are archives only for those buried across the way. Let's see if there's a more recent set of files for activities of the Patrons after 1972, in one of these other cabinets," Victoria suggested.

Conrad began scanning his flashlight across the other side of the room and came upon a large modern looking exhibit case for vertical files that was quite different from the old, rusty four-drawer file cabinets they had already searched. With the flashlight Conrad could see this filing cabinet had glass windows, and at the top displayed the label *Psychiatry*. "I'll bet this is what we're looking for. After all, the Patrons transitioned from leadership by British combat officers to an American military psychiatrist, and they existed largely to target psychiatric patients." Looking more carefully, Conrad could see the cabinet was actually a very large four drawer file cabinet for vertical files organized neatly in a locked glass cabinet.

"But it's locked," Victoria said, trying to open the glass door.

"Give me that chair." And with that Conrad smashed the glass and started to look through the files now liberated. "I think this is exactly what we want, Victoria," Conrad said, as he quickly took out file after file. "These are Iraq and Afghanistan soldiers, all suicides. About a hundred of them."

"And this seems to be a master-file," Victoria said as she took out a file from another drawer. "In fact, I've seen this document before in the Army Intelligence files I hacked online. It's the list of all army suicides for the past year with an asterisk next to about half of these names, and with another asterisk at the bottom next to the word 'Madingley.'"

"So your original hunch was correct. The files here are only the ones with asterisks on your master-list. No wonder there's an epidemic of suicides in the army," said Conrad.

"And look here. There's a gap between 1972, and two years ago when the names began to be entered again. And all the names for the past two years have the same number next to them. Number 912. Obviously one of the most recently appointed Patrons."

"Suppose 912 is responsible for all the recent deaths?"

"Looks like the Patrons stopped assassinations after 1972, when Miller died, and restarted them again only two years ago. You think 912 might be the new Commandant?"

"Looking quickly at a couple of these files, I'm seeing they all contain psychiatric records and discussions about PTSD. Start scanning as many of these as you can," said Conrad, feeding Victoria one document after another as the frustratingly slow scanner took its time sending valuable proof to the flash drive on her laptop.

After finishing that batch, both Conrad and Victoria plunged again into the broken file cabinet. "Omigod," Conrad said excitedly. "I've just hit the jackpot. Here's the official set of orders for these hits. And look at this one. It's the order here to kill Adam and frame me for murder."

Just then, Libby appeared at the door and frantically tapped on the window.

"Oh, she's locked out after the door slammed shut," Conrad said.

Victoria noticed that lights were now illuminating the previously dark corridor. "This is not good," she said as she opened the door and Libby rushed in breathlessly.

"They're on the way," Libby blurted out. "I heard two people opening the door, saying something about missing keys from reception, so I ran ahead of them as they entered and then they turned on the lights. They'll be here in just a few moments. What should we do?"

"I'm gonna keep scanning," Victoria said with determination. "We need these documents as well for Jennifer. I'll keep going until I'm stopped."

Abruptly, the lights in the conference room went on and the first man in an army uniform said, "What the hell are you doing here?"

The other one was a man with burly biceps and a paunch, and had the handgun from his holster already drawn. "They're obviously stealing records. Hand me that flash drive, bitch."

Victoria continued scanning, ignoring him for the moment.

All of a sudden, Conrad said, "Colonel Richards," as he recognized who the one was in uniform.

"Well, well, well, Dr. Conrad," Colonel Richards said. "I see you've been a busy little beaver here compromising Army Intelligence operations. Consider yourself under arrest."

"You can't arrest us," Conrad rebutted.

"Well, let's just call it being detained. Think you can convince my colleague here otherwise?" Richards pointed her head to the burly man with huge biceps, and pistol from his holster drawn and pointing at him. "And who do we have here? If it isn't little Libby Warburton?"

Libby appeared crestfallen and defeated, and could only mumble at first, then a raging anger forced her to say, "You're the ones responsible for Adam's murder. You're atrocious human beings," Libby screamed. "You're murderers."

"Stop your scanning, young lady," Richards shouted at Victoria. "And who do we have here?"

"Victoria Chamberlain," Victoria said defiantly.

"Oh, yes, our little computer hacker. Well, you're all being detained for violating the espionage act. 888, put the FlexiCuffs on all of 'em?"

While he took them off his belt from behind his back, Victoria slowly removed the flash drive containing all the files she had scanned.

"So, Ms. Warburton, you can hand over your son's Medallion," Richards demanded. "And you can give my oversized friend here the thumb drive, Ms. Chamberlain."

"That's mine," Victoria retorted.

"I said hand it over."

"Is this what you're looking for?" asked Libby, flashing the Medallion at Richards defiantly.

Victoria and Libby then looked at each other and understood without a word what they must do next to save their skins. Victoria nodded and they simultaneously threw across the room the precious items their captors so desperately wanted. "Run!" Victoria shouted.

The flash drive flew into the back of the room and the burly operative dove after it. The heavy gold Medallion appeared to hit the glass file cabinet in the opposite direction, landing with a loud crash, and Richards went after it.

While their captors momentarily took the bait and went after their treasures, all three bolted in the opposite direction out the conference room door, with Conrad moving the slowest, but managing to squeeze out enough adrenaline to counteract his pain as he shifted into survival mode.

After retrieving the precious treasures in the dim light, Richards yelled, "After them," as she and her operative bounded behind the trio of interlopers only steps behind.

The burly special operative yelled, "Shall I shoot or do you want them alive?"

"No. Finish the job. You'll get credit for three hits if you do."

The three trespassers made their way almost to the door leading back into Madingley Hall when shots rang out, with deafening effect and echoed from the restricted environment of the tunnel.

"Anybody hit?" Libby asked.

"No."

"Not here," added Conrad. "Don't need another gunshot wound at this point."

Libby shoved Conrad through the door first just as 888 was upon them, but Victoria managed to slam the door in his face, gaining them a few precious seconds and shouted, "This way."

Victoria found the key to the turret stairway and motioned for them to follow. Last to enter the secret stairway, Victoria pulled the turret stairway door shut just as Richards and 888 blew into the reception area behind them. She said sotto voce, "Go down, not up."

Clambering as silently as possible down the stairs behind Libby and Conrad in the dark, Victoria could hear behind her Richards saying outside the turret staircase, "Where the hell did they go? They couldn't have just evaporated."

Smiling to herself, Victoria thought, *I'm sure this is the best use of the turret stairs since Edward was a prince.*

Reaching the bottom of the turret stairs first and now confronted with another oak door. Libby said frantically, "It's locked. What do we do?"

"Not to worry," said Victoria, as she unlocked the door, shoved it open and let all three of them, with Conrad slowing down, escape from Madingley Hall into the darkness outside.

Chapter 108

MAUDSLEY HOSPITAL, SOUTH LONDON, AUTUMN OF 1917:

A rmy investigators wrapped up the case quickly. It was not clear when the gun went off as no one admitted to hearing it.

The first patient-officer to find Lieutenant Warburton's body speculated, "Must have happened some time since dinner last night."

"Yeah, probably," the second patient-officer responded. "Maybe no one reported a gunshot because the men scream so much at night. Also there're large distances between rooms."

"I wish I could say that I'm surprised, but given old Warburton's psychiatric condition and his admitted thoughts of suicide, this outcome was not unexpected, just tragic."

"I think the evidence will show Lieutenant Warburton must have had a final drink of Scotch whisky, left a suicide note and then pulled the damn trigger. I heard the inspector say examination of the gun showed blown-back bits of that man he executed almost a year ago still inside the gun barrel, with layers of saliva, presumably Lieutenant Warburton's, caked on the outside."

"Just one problem. Lieutenant Warburton was scheduled to have family visit tomorrow. Why would he do this now?"

"If they don't find an answer soon, that question could haunt his family for the next hundred years."

Chapter 109

MADINGLEY HALL, CAMBRIDGE:

Victoria was already opening the door of her Mini parked in front when Conrad realized he was again in excruciating pain from his frantic run through the tunnel. Unable to continue running, he slowed down to catch his breath as Libby raced towards the car.

"Hurry, Gus," Libby pleaded.

Conrad noticed as Libby seemed to turn white in front of him and screamed, "No, no, no." All of a sudden he felt a jolt of electricity explode through his body, immediately collapsing him to his knees and then someone shouted,

"We got him."

It was the last thing Conrad heard before everything went dark.

SATURDAY

Chapter 110

AIRBORNE TO WASHINGTON/DULLES AIRPORT:

Up early to get to Heathrow and now en route back home to Washington, D.C., Dulles International Airport, Rossi and Richards had barely said a word to each other all morning.

"I missed you last night. Where were you? I could've used some of that incredible 'relaxation' you can provide. Seems like you're just sulking today."

"Go screw yourself, Andy. I'm tired and grumpy. Just leave me alone." With that, Richards noticed the seatbelt light go off, so she plumped up her pillow and placed her business-class seat flat and got ready to take a nap.

"Before you get all comfy, I'm afraid I have a bone to pick with you."

"I said, go screw yourself."

"Seems you're getting a bit uppity at these Madingley meetings, and I'm not really on top of what all your Special Forces requests are for. You're also having these various side meetings in which I'm not included, like those you had yesterday and last night in the tunnel. Case you've forgotten, *I'm* the head of Army Intelligence and you gotta keep me fully informed. I'm beginning to feel you're not doing that."

"We'll talk about it when we get home."

"You bet we will. Maybe a good old-fashioned review of all your Special Forces requests over the past year is a good way to start."

"You can be a real pain, Andy."

"Unless you want to be blindsided by all of this in front of General Morelli on Monday, I suggest you stop by my apartment Sunday to go over these matters together."

"Like I said Andy, you're a real pain in the ass."

"I'll take that as a 'yes.'"

Chapter 111

WALTER REED HOSPITAL, BETHESDA, MARYLAND:

Conrad was trying to open his eyes, but extreme grogginess made his lids feel like they weighed a ton each as he was unsuccessfully emerging from a deep sleep. Giving up, he settled back and stopped trying to open his eyes, but abruptly became aware of a pounding headache and dull, burning pain in his right leg. Now awake, he could finally open his eyes fully. As he tried to focus on his surroundings, Conrad saw only blurred images of a few people who were standing around him, but he couldn't recognize a single face yet.

"Look, Gus is waking up."

Conrad recognized the voice as Libby's.

"Gus, you awake? It's Libby here. Victoria and I are both waiting for you to wake up."

Conrad mumbled something and closed his eyes again, but his ears were open. "I think he said he has a headache," Libby said to the nurse who was just now alongside Conrad's bed. That was all Conrad needed to awaken fully, and he jolted upright, now realizing that he was lying in a bed. Looking around, he saw Libby and Victoria, and thought it looked like he was in a hospital room as the dimmer switch in his brain slowly lit it up to its usual blazing intensity. He then noted that somebody was raising his bed into the sitting position.

"Where am I?"

"You're in Walter Reed," Libby answered.

"What'm I doing here? And how'd I get here?"

"Slow down, Mario, now *you're* going over the speed limit again. Let me explain."

A smile came to Conrad's face as he recalled teasing Libby about driving like Mario Andretti in London just the other day. "Okay, okay. Bring me up to date."

"Gus, you're in Walter Reed because Senator Benham had the CIA take all of us into protective custody outside of Madingley Hall last night, and fly us back to Washington, D.C."

"How'd that happen? The last thing I remember is walking out of the turret staircase at Madingley Hall while being chased by Richards and her goon."

"The CIA Tasered you and then knocked you out with a drug, while they whisked Victoria and me away before those guys ever caught up to us."

"How'd the CIA get involved?

"Your friend Senator Benham arranged all this, thanks to being tipped off by Jennifer Richards. She got the CIA in England involved."

"If they were saving me, then why Taser me and knock me out? And why only me and not you and Victoria?"

Now Victoria spoke. "I guess that was easier since you were the wounded one."

"And you always ask too many questions," Libby added.

"Guilty as charged."

"That reminds me," Libby continued. "Since we turned over the files of the Patrons including the order for U.S. Special Ops to murder Adam and frame you, the murder charges against you are in the process of being dropped."

"Great news. Now, only being detained for espionage?"

"Senator Benham is working on having those dropped, too, which should happen before Monday."

"What day is it today?"

"It's Saturday afternoon," Victoria answered. "We flew out of the London on a CIA transport leaving just after midnight there last night."

"You obviously were unconscious," Libby said, "but we arrived here at the hospital in the middle of the night local time, when you were admitted."

Conrad shifted uncomfortably in the bed, suddenly craving pain medication. "Wait a minute. How did you show them that order from the Patrons? I saw Victoria throw the flash drive away from the door so we could escape. Everything we risked going to England was lost before we even got outside of Madingley Hall."

Victoria smiled and said, "Dr. Conrad, can you look outside your window and tell me what you see?"

"What? You answer my question with a question? Well, I see green grass, and a cloudy day."

"Yes, clouds. That's where all the proof went. All the documents from Madingley Hall are up there."

"What? In the clouds."

"No, Einstein. *The cloud.* The Internet. Turns out I had a weak Wi-Fi signal in the tunnel and was able to simultaneously send the documents to the cloud as I scanned them onto the flash drive."

"Fantastic."

"So, I had sent Jennifer Roberts everything she needed to complete her story on the Patrons, and I did that last night from Madingley Hall."

"Well done," Conrad smiled.

"As a matter of fact," Libby added, "Jennifer Roberts' racing right now to complete her story by the deadline so it can appear in tomorrow's Sunday *Washington Post.*"

"Too bad we lost the Medallion."

Just then, Libby pulled it out of her purse and brandished it with a smile.

"How'd you get that?" Conrad was confused. "I saw you throw it when Victoria threw the flash drive."

"I showed Richards the Medallion, but unhooked it from the heavy chain and threw only the chain, and kept the Medallion safe and sound. The darkness in the corner of the room where I tossed it meant she couldn't have known what I did until someone tried to retrieve it."

"Brilliant! Unbelievable. Like an NBA basketball head fake. So when can I get out of here?"

"Not so fast, Mario. We're all in protective custody," Libby said with a smile.

"What?"

"That's why there're MPs guarding your door. Remember, the senator made sure of it," Libby said, motioning to two muscular MPs standing with arms crossed on either side of Conrad's hospital door.

"There are two more of those guards outside your room as well," Victoria elaborated.

The nurse was bustling about, adjusting Conrad's IV and making notes on the chart hanging at the foot of his bed.

Libby continued, "You should also know that the FBI Legat in London, with the help of MI5, raided the files at Madingley Hall and turned them over to the FBI, Washington. So, we're here until it's all resolved."

"Yeah. Libby and I are staying in a really cool room used by the Secret Service when they stay here to guard the president," Victoria said.

Libby continued. "Richards and Rossi are flying home today. The FBI has them under surveillance and have initiated an investigation of them as well."

"When can I get out of this hospital bed?"

"You're still on intravenous antibiotics, following cleaning and dressing of your gunshot wound last night."

Just then, a young military doctor walked in with two more military nurses accompanying him. "Dr. Conrad, may we come in?"

"Of course. You my doctor?"

"Yes, Major Flanagan here. Just want to check that wound," he said as he peered through the reading glasses precariously positioned at the end of his slender nose. He gently pulled back the dressing and then pushed it back into place. "Coming along fine. Probably be a couple of weeks till it's back to normal. In the meantime, you need another day or two of IV antibiotics. And if there's no fever or obvious infection that's spread, we can discharge you on oral antibiotics."

"Anything for pain?"

The doctor looked over at Libby, who took a pill bottle out of Conrad's tote bag that was on the chair beside his bed and shook it, making that rattling sound.

"Like these?" she asked.

Conrad felt caught and looked down.

"Yes, like those."

"Libby, why don't you tell him what we know?" said the young military doctor with a smile.

"Gus, you shouldn't be surprised we found these in your bag. I already figured out yesterday that you'd been taking them all day. Because you were formerly addicted to pain pills, I can understand why you deceived me because you were also deceiving yourself. And in more than one way."

"What do you mean by that?"

"You know these pills are expired."

"Yeah, so what?"

"We're having them analyzed by the lab, but the preliminary report already shows the pills in your tote bag are over twelve years old and they contain essentially no active ingredient any more. It's all been oxidized with age. Didn't you see how these normally snow white pills are now all brown?"

"Yea," Conrad said sheepishly, "but that can't be right. I felt a real kick from them."

The doctor interjected, "Did you feel that kick before or after you took the pills?"

"As a matter of fact, it was well *before* I swallowed them. I had less of a kick and more of a calm *after* I took them."

"Since you're the psychiatrist and psycho-pharmacologist—an expert in drugs, I'm surprised you were so readily fooled, Dr. Conrad."

"Goes to show you that a man who treats himself has a fool for a patient."

"Excellent point. You must know that narcotics give you a kick the first few times you take them. But once you're addicted, your brain releases the pleasure neurotransmitter dopamine not when you take the drug, but when you anticipate taking the drug, before the pill even gets into your brain."

"Yeah. I felt a high just hearing the rattle of the pills, seeing them in my hand and tasting the bitterness in my mouth before swallowing."

"Just as predicted for someone who's addicted."

"I should've known that," Conrad said, feeling ashamed as he thought to himself ... *and it doesn't help that I have a bit of PTSD. That's strongly linked to addictive behavior.*

"So, let's not fully re-establish your addiction to pain pills, Dr. Conrad. Here's the bad news. No opiate pain relievers for you. Only non-narcotic analgesics."

"Uggh."

"You'll survive, Gus," Libby interjected. "Here, take one of these," she demanded, handing Gus a mint. "These aren't too addicting for him, are they doctor?"

"Not in low amounts," the doctor replied as they all laughed.

No sooner had the doctor and nurses exited than a brassy, good-looking and impeccably groomed woman dressed to the nines with an air of both class and authority entered, escorted by two men in black suits who looked like FBI agents.

Conrad recognized the senator immediately. "Barbara, whatever brings you here?"

Chapter 112

YORKSHIRE, ENGLAND, SPRING OF 1958:

Gertie Jennings was by the bedside of her sixty-two-year-old mother Sarah as the doctor took the stethoscope from around his neck, folded it and put it back into his black doctor's bag. Her mother's failing health meant life was coming to an end, and the family's general practitioner was asked to stop by and make a final evaluation of Sarah.

"It's bad, isn't it?" Sarah asked.

"You've had a long and rich life, Sarah, and it's all up to the Lord now. Are you comfortable?"

"Yes, my breathing's fine."

Turning to Gertie, the doctor added, "Okay, you let me know if there's anything else I can do for you or your mother."

As soon as the doctor departed, Sarah said, "Gertie, I suppose I shan't wait any longer. I've burdened my soul with a 'secret' and have told nobody, but it would be unfair not to let you know something important about your father before I die."

"Daddy?" Gertie asked. "We never talk about him. Something from the Great War?"

"Yes. You know he died in France during the war in 1916, but I never told you the whole story. It's so awful. So embarrassing. I've told no one for some forty years. When I got the official notification from the War Office back in 1916, I stuffed it down my blouse so no one would see it."

"What did it say, Mama? What?"

"I guess there's no easy way of saying this. They notified me your daddy was sentenced to death for cowardice and shot at dawn. That's why we got no war pension."

Gertie was thunderstruck. It took a while for the revelation to sink in. After a moment, she asked, "You mean killed by his own men? Shot like a traitor? Surely daddy would have done nothing to deserve that."

"I'm certain it was a horrible mistake. Your daddy was treated for his nerves—*shell shock*—during the war, first in France, and then he was shipped home for a few months of treatment at Netley, where he wrote me letters about his condition and we visited him once. You were too little to remember."

"I remember you telling me about that."

"Your daddy got better and was sent back to the trenches in France but apparently relapsed. Instead of giving him more treatment, they shot him like an animal. I'm so angry and so ashamed." Sarah began to sob uncontrollably.

Gertie, stunned with this news tried to comfort her mother. "Mama, did you look into this at the time to get to the truth?"

"Yes, but it was futile. The newspapers then all said that the army never shot anyone with *shell shock*. The Parliament denied it as well."

What Gertie suddenly realized was that the burden of this secret had now passed from her mother to herself. What Gertie could not know at the time was that she would hold this horrible knowledge silently for another thirty some years herself.

Chapter 113

It was always cold sleeping on the hard cement of the parking garage, but it wasn't anything Jordan Davis hadn't endured on many homeless nights spent upon park benches under newspaper blankets or lying on sidewalks in a sleeping bag. This time, Jordan had a reason for choosing where he slept. He was waiting for his sister Ellen to return to her car.

If there was one thing he knew how to do, it was how to wait. Seemed Jordan had spent most of his life waiting, since he had nothing better to do. *You can see a whole lot just by observing,* Jordan reflected, laughing to himself as he recalled this was a "Yogi Berra saying." Jordan was a New York Yankee fan and enjoyed the sayings coined by the Yankee baseball star and folk philosopher Yogi Berra.

Jordan realized that some would consider what he was doing as stalking his sister. But he looked at it more as monitoring than stalking. That was how he discovered Ellen's routine. Since moving into her office at the Pentagon, her pattern now was to drive from her home to this parking facility and then to take the subway to the Pentagon from here. After work, she reversed the pattern to get home. However, last night she never showed. *Maybe out of town,* he thought. *Might as well wait until she eventually gets here. Nothing better to do.* So he spent the night sleeping on concrete.

It was Saturday, and few cars remained on the weekend in the parking structure, and no people were visible. The parking garage was used mostly by commuters who left their cars here for a commute to the Pentagon on the train. It was dark, even during the daytime, like a poorly lit cave of several stories. Gloom inside the parking garage was exaggerated by the lack of sun outside in the mid-morning in Washington, D.C.

Jordan monitored things from behind a pillar near Ellen's black Toyota Camry. *A doctor and a military officer should be able to afford something more upmarket than that,* Jordan thought. He chuckled to himself as he thought more. *You can take the girl out of the trailer-trash of her past, but you can't take the trailer-trash entirely out of the girl.*

However, Ellen was now acting too uppity to help him get veterans benefits or medical care now, but he had a way of always turning up when he needed something and could keep her from avoiding him entirely. *Monitoring,* thought Jordan. *Not stalking.*

Jordan heard the click-clack-click-clack of expensive high heels on cement and the sudden "oink" and "thud" of her car unlocking from the remote key in her hand. As she reached for the handle of the car, he stepped out from behind the pillar as her back was towards him, and put his gloved hand over her mouth, stifling any attempt of her to yell, grabbing her around the waist with his other arm, and then sandwiching her between his body and her modest car.

Chapter 114

YORKSHIRE, ENGLAND, 1992:

It was one of those ugly, dank Yorkshire Monday mornings in 1992, thirty some years after her mother Sarah Jennings' death. Gertie Harris, daughter of Private Simon Jennings of the 1ˢᵗ Yorkshire Regiment that fought valiantly on the Western Front in France during the Great War, sat down with her cuppa tea to read *The Times* of London. Now in her late-seventies, Gertie had been born during the Great War, a conflict in which her father, whom she only knew as a baby, had died in shame. Gertie froze completely as she read the article on the front page. The British Parliament had just announced it was going to begin opening its secret government archives of the Great War to the public after decades of secrecy.

She read:

> *The Great War Archives are to be opened to the public in tranches, with the earliest records of the war to become public first. Noted historian Professor Trevor Chamberlain, of the University of Cambridge, has been appointed to supervise the publication and distribution of the archives. To accommodate his task, the first wave of documents will be moving to the history department of Clare College at Cambridge University from their dusty boxes currently in storage for the past seventy-five years at the Imperial War Museum in London.*

Immediately, the thought occurred to her, *I wonder if daddy's records are in there? Maybe they could finally prove he had shell shock and was wrongly executed. I'm going to contact this professor fellow and see if he won't help me.*

A FEW WEEKS LATER, Gertie returned from her errands in town, including collecting her post. She was in a hurry to open an official-looking letter from the University of Cambridge. She read:

> *Dear Mrs. Harris:*
>
> *I received your letter inquiring about your father, Private Simon Jennings of the 1st Yorkshire Regiment that fought valiantly on the Western Front in France during the Great War. I am pleased to confirm I have been able to locate his documents in the public record, including his military orders, his hospitalizations in Le Havre and in the D Block at the Royal Victoria Hospital in Netley, his court-martial and his ultimate execution by firing squad. My colleagues and I believe his case exemplifies one of the greatest miscarriages of justice by the British Army in the Great War. I fully support your overture for a Parliamentary Pardon, and I will do everything in my power to help you attain this for your father. I believe working with the press so the public can put political pressure on the current Parliament may be the most effective way to proceed, as the current position of the Parliament is, as you know, unfavorable.*
>
> *My deep and sincere condolences for you and your family regarding your father, and I stand ready to assist you in any way possible.*
>
> *Yours very truly.*
>
> *Professor Trevor Chamberlain*
> *Mellon Professor of History*
> *Master of Clare College*
> *University of Cambridge*

Gertie put the letter down as tears welled up in her eyes. *Papa, can we now remove the unjust shame?* she asked herself. Knowing she was almost eighty-years-old meant there was not much time left to clear the name of Private Simon Jennings—her dear Papa.

Chapter 115

WALTER REED HOSPITAL, BETHESDA, MARYLAND:

Senator Benham smiled as she looked over at Conrad in his hospital bed at Walter Reed National Military Medical Center. "Well, Gus, how're you holding up?" she asked as she came over to Conrad and they exchanged air kisses on both cheeks.

"As good as can be expected," Conrad responded while he looked first at his IV and then at the wound on his right thigh. "Thanks, by the way, for saving my ass."

"And a wonderful little tush it is, if I remember correctly."

Conrad smiled and everyone around him blushed and looked down with smiles.

"So, are you gonna be up to testifying at my hearing in Senate chambers by Monday afternoon?"

"I think so. What should I expect, and what should I prepare for?"

"By then the proverbial shit will have hit the fan from the publication of *The Washington Post* story on Sunday and the appearances of Jennifer Roberts and me on the Sunday morning news shows."

"What exactly is gonna be in *The Post*?"

"I've seen a draft of the article, the first part of a series. Jennifer did get all the materials you guys scanned at Madingley Hall and put together an amazing exposé. For the first part tomorrow, she'll report how the Patrons were taken over by Colonel Alexander Miller at the end of World

War I and then ran the Patrons until his death in 1972, continuing to mercilessly assassinate American soldiers for cowardice. The article goes on to show that as a psychiatrist, Miller arrogated to himself the ability to distinguish mental illness from cowardice and dealt out death as punishment for hundreds more cases after World War I, and Americans to boot."

"Anything else?"

"After Miller's death, Jennifer found that the Patrons functioned as an advocacy group for over forty years to work against cowardice and preserve the warrior culture of the army, but no longer as an assassination unit of the army. Then recently, the assassinations started up again, apparently under the regime of a new Commandant. Looks like someone new recently appointed themselves as the one to decide who has a mental illness and who is a coward needing to be killed, and reactivated the assassination squads."

"Just like Dr. Miller did decades ago. This whole thing is so disgusting. Evidently nothing learned from history and the scandal from World War I and shooting *shell shock* victims. And to think that psychiatrists of all people have been in the middle of this over the past century."

"One more thing. Jennifer has proof that the Patrons killed Adam to keep the reactivation of their organization as a hit squad secret, and for fun, they framed you. Must be because you're so charming, Gus."

"What?"

"Think about all the tact and diplomacy you showed in communicating to the army their deficiencies in mental health care at Fort Hood," Senator Benham remarked sarcastically while rolling her eyes. "Not to mention your testimony for the defense and against army prosecutors in Sergeant Bales' case."

"Oh, *that* tact and diplomacy of mine. Now I know what you're talking about," Gus smiled. "Sorry, a little hazy from the meds."

"Yeah, right," Senator Benham said derisively. "So, answer me. Are you ready for your testimony?"

"If they let me outa here, I'm ready and rarin' to go."

"You should be able to read the article in *The Post* tomorrow and that'll also help you prepare. If you're up to it, you should watch the morning news shows on Sunday. Jennifer and I leaked notice of her article for the Sunday *Post* and she'll send it to them ahead of publication so they can prepare for our big media blitz tomorrow that'll air just after the paper hits the stands. In addition to what's being reported in the first article of the series on Sunday, we intend to release a bombshell that won't appear until later in the written series."

"Wow. And what's the bombshell?"

"Wouldn't be one if I told you now, would it? You'll learn on Sunday if you listen to the programs."

"You doing a full court press of all five morning shows?"

"You mean am I pulling a Ginsburg? Then the answer is yes."

"What's a Ginsburg?" asked Libby.

"Ah, that means doing NBC, CBS, ABC, Fox and CNN—the big five—on a single Sunday morning," Senator Benham responded. "First and most famously done by Monica Lewinsky's family lawyer when he defended her during the Clinton scandal. His name was William Ginsburg. He was even lampooned on Saturday Night Live by John Goodman, if you remember."

"Yes, but don't we call it pulling a 'Rice' now?" Conrad teased.

"Don't go there, Conrad, remember, I'm a Democrat."

"Sorry, but can someone here please translate for me," asked Libby.

Conrad answered quickly, "A 'Rice' is doing all five shows and lying about something like Benghazi."

"That's up for debate," Senator Benham shot back.

"Anyway, that's Sunday. What about Monday?"

"On Monday morning, I'm gonna grill Army Vice Chief Morelli on mental health care for soldiers and veterans. He's scheduled to appear before the Senate Armed Services Committee first thing in the morning. I expect more than C-Span'll be there to greet him from the media. Then, we'll have your testimony on Monday afternoon."

"What's the line of questioning gonna be for me?"

"I'll ask you to relate your experiences working with military psychiatry, active duty soldiers and veterans and give you a chance to tell the media what you think needs to be done to bolster national security, fix army psychiatry and get our armed forces ready for defending America in the 21st century."

"That all?"

"It's your chance for another fifteen minutes of fame and a national bully pulpit, and we all know how much you're gonna like that."

Conrad did indeed like the sound of that. "I'll be ready. That is, if you're ever going to let me out of custody."

"I can certainly let you out of custody for the murder and for espionage soon, but not out of protective custody."

"Protection from whom?"

"Well, there are a few troubling things you should know," Senator Benham said as she sat down next to Conrad's bed and touched the top of his hand with the palm of hers. "First of all, you're still on the hit list of the Patrons. We've not been able yet to rescind the order from the current Commandant to Special Ops. Our intel people are working on that. Secondly, Libby, Victoria and Jennifer Roberts are also still on the hit list. Libby and Victoria are being protected with you here. This hospital is set up for VIPs needing security, including the president himself, so it's a good place for all three of you to stay until everything's been resolved. Jennifer Roberts has a security detail assigned to her around the clock to keep her safe."

"Quite an operation, Barb. I can't thank you enough."

"Until we can neutralize the kill order, you're all gonna need continued protection."

Silence everywhere. Conrad swallowed hard and then said, "I guess that means we better take very good care of our security guards here, and make sure they have all the coffee they want so they are plenty alert and happy. Starbucks, gentlemen?" he asked, looking to the door.

Chapter 116

A young Jennifer Roberts, fresh out of Northwestern's Medill School of Journalism and now a cub reporter for *The Washington Post* put her feet up and took a well-deserved sip of wine now that she was back in the relative quiet of her Washington, D.C., apartment with her newspaper and her cat. Jennifer again picked up that morning's edition of Sunday's *Washington Post*. It was the winter of 1993 and Jennifer reread the headline for her story co-written with her colleague from the British newspaper *The Guardian*, which was the result of months of investigative reporting. The headline shouted:

British Archives Uncover World War I
Executions for *Shell Shock*

Cooling her heels after appearing on the Sunday morning network news shows, phones were ringing off the hook and E-mails were coming in over the digital transom at an exponential rate. Jennifer realized she had uncovered a vast and deadly scandal. Finally able to breathe a sigh of relief after having published the first of her pending stories, the full significance of the story she and her British colleague had uncovered was beginning to hit her. She'd worked several months without a break with her secret contact, Professor Trevor Chamberlain of the University of Cambridge. She was both abhorred by what she had learned and grateful for the help of the professor, who agreed to work with her on uncovering the story for the public good after he discovered the heinous practice of the British Army soon after the British Parliament opened its World War I archives seventy-five years after the end of the Great War.

WEEKS LATER, JENNIFER WAS WALKING through the lobby of *The Washington Post* and picked up a copy of that day's British paper, *The Guardian*. She couldn't believe what she read. Dateline: 23rd March, 1993.

Prime Minister Denies Pardons for World War I *Shell Shock* Executions

Jennifer had worked so hard to expose the practice of the British Expeditionary Force executing hundreds of *shell shock* sufferers as cowards, she was sure the only just thing to do at this point was for the British government to make amends for this travesty of justice, but the official bureaucracy was stone-walling. She read:

> ... *Today Prime Minister John Major has refused pardons for any of the executed soldiers citing the paucity of documentary evidence, the fact almost all relevant witnesses were long deceased and his Government's opposition in principle to passing official reinterpretations of the actions of soldiers in a war which had taken place previously.*

Seething, Jennifer said to herself, *we must start a major public campaign to clear these men's names.* Meanwhile, however, the official British response to her story from 10 Downing Street was to deny these men had *shell shock*, but were instead cowards and deserters and were dealt with appropriately in the heat and fury of warfare in France. A hue-and-cry for pardons and reparations was being made by relatives of those executed for *shell shock*, but the official response from the British Parliament was this was a regretful necessity of warfare and no action should be taken at this point. No longer able to deny the deaths, the official response was to make these men cowards. And nobody likes a coward.

Chapter 117

WALTER REED HOSPITAL, BETHESDA, MARYLAND:

Libby was reading *Oprah* in a chair in the corner of Conrad's hospital room at Walter Reed and Victoria was texting on her smartphone while Conrad rested with his eyes closed.

Suddenly, in marched a man with a syringe, in a nurse's uniform. "This is for you, sir," he said to Conrad as the two hulking military police stepped aside, then watched—assuming a parade rest position, feet apart, arms crossed, backs against the wall and looking disinterested.

"Wait a minute," Libby said looking up. "I'm a nurse and Dr. Conrad here just got his antibiotics. What's that?" she asked coming up to the nurse and trying to look closely at the syringe in his hand.

With that, the nurse pushed her violently onto her backside, turned, grabbed a handgun out of the holster of one of the MPs before he could react, and fired it at Conrad while being tackled by the other MP, so missed his target. Soon the intruder was on the floor, face down, with FlexiCuffs in place behind his back. The room quickly filled with police, and at the middle of all the activity, Conrad sat in his bed, stunned, ears ringing, nostrils stinging with gunshot powder, but unhurt as the shot went into the wall over his head.

Libby picked up the syringe. "Potassium chloride. He was gonna kill you."

"He almost did."

"That was way too close," Victoria said. "I wonder if you and I were next, Libby. This is really tearing me apart. When's it gonna be over?"

"It's clear none of the hits on us have been cancelled yet," Libby said looking even more shaken than Conrad.

Chapter 118

WASHINGTON, D.C, 1995:

A s Jennifer walked into the offices of *The Washington Post* with a sense of pride painted on her face, she was met by the editor, the owner and all the senior staff right next to her desk. "Congratulations," said Ben Bradlee, Executive Editor. "Let's hear it for Jennifer," he yelled to all in the immense newsroom. A resounding cheer went up all around, embarrassing Jennifer, who wished she could have just passed through a wormhole and into an alternate universe. However, she knew this was heady stuff. It was 1995, and Bradlee was an icon in journalism, having overseen Woodward and Bernstein's work exposing the Watergate scandal. He didn't just drop by for any reason at all.

"Come along to the conference room for a champagne toast," he said. "It's not every day *The Washington Post* wins another Pulitzer Prize."

Jennifer knew the winner of the Prize was the reporter and not the paper, but this was no time to point that out to an icon. Suddenly, a deep sense of injustice and dissatisfaction swept over her as she now felt very guilty with all the praise, knowing hundreds of innocent assassinations still awaited pardons.

Chapter 119

Jennifer Roberts picked up both *The Guardian* and *The Times* of London in the lobby of *The Washington Post* and after reading the headline of *The Guardian*, felt a wave of satisfaction race through her body.

Shot at Dawn Memorial Honors Those
Executed for *Shell Shock*

> *Private Jennings and his comrades had finally received the recognition they deserved, Jennifer thought. But it took long enough. It's already 2001,* she said to herself.
> *... a new monument was dedicated today at the National Memorial Arboretum near Alrewas, Staffordshire, honoring the 306 British soldiers executed during World War One for desertion and cowardice, many of whom were probably suffering from shell shock due to their experiences in war.*

However, Jennifer soon cringed as she saw the corresponding headline in *The Times*.

Monument Recognizes Deserters and Mutineers
Executed during WWI

> *... 306 men documented to be executed by the British Army in the Great War included 266 shot for desertion, 18 for cowardice, seven for quitting their posts and two for casting away their arms.*

Nothing about *shell shock* or any injustice to the men, only the implication the monument was an injustice to those who did not get *shell shock*.

Continuing to read the various headlines, Jennifer said to herself, *progress of a sort, I guess, but this wrong will never be righted until these men are pardoned.*

Jennifer knew that since the last time there had been an official refusal of a pardon, the public had pushed for a memorial instead, and despite a change of government in the meantime, the new Prime Minister Tony Blair seemed in no mood for taking on the controversy and pardoning these men. Pushing as hard as she could as a foreign journalist and thus without much clout, she knew from her British colleagues that the armed forces minister in Britain considered the possibility of pardons under the royal prerogative, but concluded few if any individual cases would meet the requirements. They determined the law, as it stood at the time, was followed. Instead of a pardon, all officials were willing to do at the time of the change in government was to release a statement that was unacceptable to relatives of the victims including Gertie:

> *Those executed were as much victims of war as the soldiers and airmen who were killed in action. ...*

Jennifer realized with sadness nine years had passed since the British government had opened its archives—eight since her original exposé. Things were working out well for herself professionally, however, since she wrote her Pulitzer Prize winning series "Shot at Dawn" seven years ago, and received her Pulitzer a year later. Many additional years had now passed, and the only result was a controversial memorial. No pardons. Gertie was now eighty-seven years old and in failing health. Time was running out.

Chapter 120

Pressed up against her car by her assailant, Colonel Richards executed a well-practiced defensive move, twisting the assailant's arm and planting a kick strategically in his groin. As she withdrew her foot, she gained her composure and laughed at the dark figure grasping his groin. "You!" Richards laughed, snarling in contempt. "Don't you realize what I could've done to you? You'd be smart to leave me alone."

"Do you have to practice being condescending or does it just come naturally to you, Ellen?"

"Grow up, Jordan."

"I need some money. I just got out of the hospital again and I'm hungry and homeless."

"Tell me something I don't know. You're a loser with a psychiatric discharge from the army, so don't ask me to cry for you."

"All my money's gone. I spent it on my meds. You need to help me. Please? You won't let me stay with you anymore, so the least you can do is help me get off the street and get a hot meal."

"I learned my lesson about you years ago. You're never gonna get better or stop trying to leech off me. You're to stay out of my space and you'd better get the hell outa my life if you want to have any more life of your own."

"Then help me get into the VA. If I stay away from you, it still doesn't change who I am or our mutual secret. You have to help me." An impish smile spread over Jonathan's face. "Or do you want me showing up when your bosses are around, or spread our little secret on the Internet or to your staff? Doctor-Colonel-Psychiatrist-Extraordinaire—poof, all up-in-smoke," he said as he clasped his hands together and then raised them as if there was a cloud of smoke.

"You son-of-a-bitch, Jordan." Ellen took out several twenty-dollar bills from her wallet and threw them on the hard concrete floor of the parking garage away from her car. "You better know what you're doing. That's the last you're gonna get. Don't get cute with me, because I refuse to let you blackmail me. You'll not get away with this again. Believe me, don't try it again."

"Yeah, yeah, yeah."

"Listen carefully. This is the last time I ever want to see you. If you decide to make trouble and try to tell anyone or even see me again, I promise it will be the last time you'll see anyone else for that matter. The army has ways of making people disappear. Don't make me use them on you."

"I was just messin' you about. I'd never do anything to really harm you. It's just that I'm desperate and could really use your help knocking down that VA bureaucracy for me. Once I'm in, I'll be gone from your life forever."

"Alright, let's make amends," Ellen said with a depraved smile.

Ellen's sudden shift in affect from murderous to sickly sweet made Jordan quite suspicious. "Okay," Jordan said tentatively.

"Then come over to my apartment for dinner tomorrow night and we'll discuss your future."

"I can always use a dinner." Just then a creepy feeling came over Jordan, not knowing what really to expect tomorrow night for dinner.

Chapter 121

WASHINGTON, D.C.:

Stunned, yet excited by all the documents she received last night by Internet from Madingley Hall, Jennifer Roberts had gotten right to work. By mid-morning the next day, Saturday, Jennifer was back in her office at *The Washington Post*. "Bert, thanks for coming in on a Saturday. I think I'll make deadline for Sunday's paper. Make sure you tell them I want this *above the fold.*"

"Yes, ma'am, the editor already knows."

"So we have copies of many actual documents, and now numerous sources who confirm having seen the documents or who confirm knowledge of the army's operation of the Patrons. There's way too much for one article. Like I said, this thing is gonna have to run for a week. Like a serial thriller, except this time it's real."

"Yep." The phone at main reception in the newsroom rang and Bert went over to answer it. He listened for a moment, then said loudly, "Jennifer, Senator Benham on line two."

Jennifer picked up. "Hold for the senator." In a few moments, she heard, "Hello, Jennifer? This is Senator Benham."

"Hello, hello. And what a day it has been, senator."

"Here, too. How're you holding up?"

"Fine. Working like crazy. And thanks for all the information. I'll obviously keep it highly confidential that you've been one of my sources.

However, some may very well suspect you if we appear on the news shows together."

"I don't really care what they think."

"You got us scheduled for the full Ginsburg?"

"You betcha. I'll have a limo waiting to take us from one studio to the next. It's gonna be a helluva day tomorrow."

"I'm just finishing my story now, so I better get a bit of rest tonight if I can, since I didn't really sleep last night."

"Do whatever you need to do in order to be ready to go tomorrow. We really need your insights. When the time is right, we'll drop our bombshell. Let me do it, okay?"

"It's all yours."

"As you know, this has become a matter of national security, and a scandal that's gone on for far too long. A hundred years, if you include the British. By the way, how's that security detail going for you?"

"I'm sure the agents are just bored, since all I've done since they came to my apartment last night is work at home and then come into the office at *The Post*. They're just sitting around and drinking coffee and getting bored."

"Ah, the glamour of a news reporter. But bored is good. We don't need any excitement for your security detail. We still have no indication your threat has been neutralized nor that the hit on you has been cancelled. We're feverishly working to find the operatives hired by the current Commandant as we speak and countermand their orders."

"Thanks so much, senator."

"The least we could do. Meanwhile, you and I are gonna blow this scandal sky-high tomorrow."

"I agree. Hold on to your seat."

"Might be just what we need to get the army to reform its psychiatry programs, so might be a blessing in disguise."

"I'm counting on it."

SECOND SUNDAY

Chapter 122

WASHINGTON, D.C.:

The ever energetic Jennifer Roberts was getting ready in the green room of *Meet the Press* with a quick check of her makeup and hair. She was preparing to go in front of a national news audience in a few minutes for the first time since she did interviews for her "Shot at Dawn" exposé that won her the Pulitzer Prize several years ago.

Senator Benham suddenly burst into the green room with her security detail in tow. *Amazing woman. Always looks like a million bucks,* Jennifer thought. *Maybe that's because a million bucks is just pocket change to her, yet she, unlike most people of wealth, is concerned about more than herself. She's always been a great force for the military.* "Good morning, senator."

"Sorry, I had to take the call. Are you ready to go?" the senator asked.

"Ready as I'll ever be."

An audio technician came into the green room bearing two microphones. "Ladies, come right this way onto the set and get mic'd up."

While moving to the set, Senator Benham continued, "I reread your article in *The Post* this morning in the limo on the way over here. There's a second Pulitzer in this for you, I'm certain."

"Thanks, but what I really want to see is the Patrons shut down once and for all."

"That's step *one*. If this becomes a big enough scandal, it could even transform the way a bureaucracy as large and cumbersome as the U.S. Army treats psychological war wounds."

"At least they should forever stop killing soldiers with PTSD."

"We can only hope, and give it our best shot today, pardon the pun," Senator Benham replied, and then sat down at the round-table. As the technician attached her microphone to her silk blouse, he brushed the fulsomeness of her firm breasts, causing her to look up with an expression that said *you were a little too close, buddy.*

Just then, retired Major General George Harmeyer entered the studio, his aide-de-camp toting a large briefcase, and shook the senator's hand and then Jennifer's. "Good morning, General Harmeyer," the senator said. Two air kisses, and she added, "Don't mess my makeup. Thanks. Let me introduce you to Jennifer Roberts from *The Washington Post.*"

"Good morning, Ms. Roberts," the general said with a wink.

"I'm gonna pretend I didn't see that," the senator said.

Now Jennifer watched as retired Major General Jonathan Booker, former Surgeon General of the U.S. Army, came in and sat down without saying hello or giving anyone eye contact.

"Good morning, General Booker," Jennifer offered.

"Morning," he replied without looking at her.

"And a jolly good morning to you, too, General Booker," the senator said sarcastically.

The host of *Meet the Press* entered off camera and said, "Good morning all. Everybody ready?" Then, with the host looking into the camera, which panned across the members of the panel, Jennifer tried to relax as he introduced all of them on air and then began. "A shocking story released today in *The Washington Post* exposes the practice of the U.S. Army killing its own soldiers for cowardice because they have PTSD. Here's the headline of today's article by Pulitzer Prize-winning investigative reporter Jennifer Roberts and an excerpt from her article:

Secret Army Unit Assassinates PTSD Soldiers for Cowardice

... U.S. Army intelligence documents released to the Post have uncovered the continuation of a century's old practice of executing soldiers with psychiatric conditions.

The host turned to Jennifer and asked, "So, Miss Roberts, what did you learn from your reporting?"

Jennifer took a big breath and began. "Sources inside the army and documents uncovered from Army Intelligence files show the U.S. Army is killing its own soldiers they deem as cowards, making the deaths look like suicides and occasionally, murders."

Everyone at the table gasped even though they had all read it earlier in *The Post*.

The host regained his composure and followed-up with a question, "Stunning if true. Seems too fantastic to believe. Why do you think the U.S. Army would do that, senator?" the host asked as he turned toward Senator Benham.

"It's a misplaced sense of the warrior myth in the army culture that equates heroism with devotion to the army, manliness and fearlessness. Those who don't measure up to this ideal are often ostracized and isolated at a minimum and executed at the extreme. Armies have been doing this for centuries and it has to stop."

"Jennifer. How did you get those documents?"

"As you know, that's confidential, but I have multiple sources and copies of the actual documents."

"Sounds like another Edward Snowden may be operating here somewhere in the background. General Harmeyer, what do you think?"

The portly general drew himself up straight in his seat and said, "It's high time for the army to pivot away from an old-fashioned view of the ideal soldier, to that of the modern warrior, who is diverse in gender, sexual orientation, and who may suffer not only a blast wound in combat, but a psychological one."

"May I interject here?" General Booker asked as he interrupted. "With all due respect to all of you around this table, everyone in combat experiences post-traumatic stress, but with resilience training, and rest after combat, there are few true cases of long-term combat related problems. PTSD is an over-utilized term for those who brought their problems into the military with them and are going to bankrupt this nation with their expectations of a lifetime pension as a reward for their pre-existing psychiatric difficulties."

Senator Benham retorted. "That's an outdated and over-tired response, General Booker. Although I'm sure there are cases of abusing the system for personal gain, mental health experts tell me the much larger problem is the inability of the army to reconcile the notion of heroism with the fact even heroes can become psychologically traumatized by warfare."

"May I add something here?" General Harmeyer asked. "I agree with the senator and think we must recognize the army needs to understand you can't prevent psychological problems by simply screening them out of the military at the time of recruitment, or by resilience training after recruitment. That's proven to be a flawed strategy because it assumes normal people don't get traumatized by war, and they can be trained to keep psychological trauma from happening after experiencing combat."

"Thanks, General Harmeyer," Senator Benham said inserting herself quickly before anyone else could respond. "It's beginning to look like psychological trauma is a normal reaction of many individuals to the realities of combat, just like bleeding is a normal reaction to a gunshot wound. The army shouldn't shun the soldier with a psychological injury any more than they would ever think of failing to save the soldier with a blast injury."

The host turned to Jennifer. "I'd like to ask you Ms. Roberts if this isn't more or less a modern equivalent of the 'Shot at Dawn' scandal you previously uncovered several years ago, documenting that the British Army killed hundreds of its own soldiers because they had *shell shock* a century ago?"

"Indeed. It's amazing how little has changed in a century," Jennifer responded. "In World War I psychological reactions were called *shell shock* and the major armies in that conflict—the British, the Germans, the Italians, and the French—executed soldiers with this condition by firing squad, sadly mistaking *shell shock* for cowardice and desertion. Today, we call it PTSD and we're either allowing these soldiers to deteriorate without treatment, commit suicide by neglecting them, or dumping the survivors into an incapable VA system. At worst, we've now uncovered we're even executing present-day soldiers by a secret assassination squad, making it look like suicide and contributing to the epidemic of apparent suicides by active duty soldiers today."

"That's a very serious charge," the host challenged immediately. "I assume you have unimpeachable sources before you decided to make such an allegation."

"We have copies of actual army documents as irrefutable evidence, including copies of official orders to carry out recent actions of the Patrons of Perseus, the name of the army assassination unit."

"Do you have any idea who's being killed and why they were selected for death?"

"Just as in World War I, it's relatively random. A few hundred have been killed as of today, and we're investigating how they were chosen. It appears one of the army command went rogue and reactivated the assassination squads of the old Patrons of Perseus from World War I about two years ago."

Senator Benham now pressed a comment. "The plans were to eliminate high profile and embarrassing cases that could compromise the army's ability to recruit or to maintain the warrior myth, I should think."

Trying once again, a clearly frustrated General Booker inserted with exasperation, "What nobody is recognizing here is your story, Ms. Roberts, represents yet another compromise of national security. We've got to stop these leaks from intelligence files. No one seems to be talking about that."

"Yes, I agree with that," Senator Benham shot back. "We do have to prevent these outrageous leaks. But so long as Army Intelligence abuses its power by illegally and immorally assassinating its own soldiers with psychiatric problems, it's likely leaks will continue. I think we should prioritize changing army policy and the warrior culture regarding the shame and stigma of psychological war wounds. If we work hard to identify these conditions, and treat them openly and without shame or injury to a soldier's career, there'll be nothing to hide."

"Senator Benham, how far up the line-of-command in the Pentagon does this modern 'shot at dawn' scandal extend? To the White House?"

"We have no evidence that anyone in the White House has any notion of these activities," the senator replied.

Jennifer interjected, "Our sources and documents indicate that the modern organization of the Patrons of Perseus is being run by a select group of former special operation soldiers led by a self-appointed leader called the Commandant."

"Who's that?" the host asked.

Jennifer answered. "We've eliminated the Chief and Vice Chief of the Army as suspects. Our sources and documents point to another army officer working in the Pentagon."

"We're still working to confirm the identity of the Commandant and have the lead suspect under surveillance," Senator Benham added.

"Since there's evidence of orders that are still active and continuing assassinations, we must proceed with extreme caution until the Patrons are shut down."

"I think the public has a right to know the identity of this Commandant. Can you name him?" the host asked, pushing Senator Benham for an answer.

"This is preposterous," shouted General Booker. "You'd better be careful before you go around maligning our brave officers serving this country."

"I agree we must be careful, General Booker. In fact, given the sensitivity of the situation, I can disclose we've also ruled out the head of Army Intelligence. He seems to have been duped by the real Commandant," Senator Benham added.

The host continued to press his case. "Senator, for the sake of any innocent soldiers who may still be active targets of the Patrons, I believe you have a duty to disclose his name. And also to disclose your sources so we can evaluate whether to believe these horrendous claims," the host fired back.

"In this country, you're innocent until proven guilty. We're continuing to investigate and the prime suspect remains at large until we can get enough evidence for an arrest warrant. As you can imagine, there're also jurisdictional issues yet to be worked out among the army, the FBI and Justice. You don't just arrest a high-ranking army officer, especially one who works in the Pentagon, without having all your ducks in a row."

"Then let me ask it this way, senator. Who's your prime suspect and who's under surveillance?"

Jennifer looked at Senator Benham and during the tense pause, she gave her the slightest nod. *Here's the bombshell,* Jennifer thought. *We're gonna expose the Commandant now and see if it leads to our chief suspect panicking and making a big mistake.*

"I can answer that question," Senator Benham responded. "Our prime suspect is Lieutenant Colonel Ellen Richards, head of army psychiatry."

"A psychiatrist? Running an assassination squad?" the host asked incredulously as those on the panel sat bolt upright, everyone obviously astounded at the revelation. Even many of the technicians working the show were stupefied and shocked.

"A regrettable possibility, according to our investigation," the senator replied. "You'd think psychiatrists would be the natural advocates for soldiers with PTSD, but over the past century, army psychiatrists have instead been complicit with commanders of the armies throughout the world to identify and shame those with psychological reactions to warfare as cowards."

Jennifer chimed in here. "In fact, the previous Commandant was also a U.S. Army psychiatrist who headed the Patrons from the end of World War I until the end of the Viet Nam War. Senior psychiatrists in the army have for too long arrogated to themselves the right to determine who is mentally ill and who is a coward, and if a coward, what the punishment should be, including death."

"Amazing doesn't cover the bombshell you just dropped," the host exclaimed. "Who'd a thunk it? A psychiatrist and a woman leading a modern army assassination unit while manipulating her boss and the Vice Chief of the Army. One smart piece of work."

"Dangerous and diabolical, I'd say," Senator Benham continued. "She's now under very tight surveillance, but still at-large."

"Wow. I'd like to continue this conversation for sure, but I'm afraid we're out of time," the host said, butting in. "It's been a truly stunning hour and I might add, shocking. That said, remember, if it's Sunday, it's *Meet the Press*."

As soon as the host signed off, Jennifer and Senator Benham quickly removed their microphones and dashed to their limo to go to the next network studio.

JENNIFER SLIPPED HER SHOES off in the backseat of the limo after their fifth interview in a row, as Senator Benham slid-in next to her.

"Quite a day," Senator Benham finally said out loud.

"That's for sure."

"We just completed a real whirlwind."

"Yep. The full Ginsburg," Jennifer noted.

"Hopefully we've spooked Colonel Richards into turning herself in to authorities before she does anything desperate or foolish so we can put this whole miserable chapter of 'shot at dawn' to rest."

"The sooner, the better on that. I'm still an active target. I'd like to get these guys off overtime," Jennifer said motioning to the two men in her security detail facing her in the middle seat of the limo.

"Good point. Hopefully, we've nailed shut the operations of the modern Patrons."

"Maybe they'll begin to rethink the definition of the ideal warrior, and recognize the contemporary warrior is much more likely to experience a psychological war wound in modern military service than a physical wound, or even death."

"We'll hammer that at the hearing tomorrow."

"Good luck with those hearings. I'll be watching. From our discussion today on *Face the Nation*, it appears this is not a partisan issue, and Representative Stephens from the House Armed Services Committee showed you have the political support from the other side of the aisle."

"Agreed. This is like the recent VA hospital scandal a few years ago. Far too important for partisan bickering. We need to work together to transform how we treat soldiers with PTSD not only when they're on active duty, but also when they become veterans."

"The well-being and long term viability of our active duty military depend upon it."

"Not to mention, so does our national security."

Chapter 123

Trying to collect herself, Colonel Ellen Richards was beginning to realize just how horrible the last few days had been for her and that her demise was near. A close call at Madingley Hall with Conrad, and now with the FBI having raided her secret files regarding the operations of the modern Patrons of Perseus and having turned them over to the Department of Justice, she knew that meant she had probably been under surveillance for some time now and her operations would soon be exposed.

Feeling glad to be able to get home to plan her next course of action, Richards was also feeling the burden of all the accumulated grudges in her life. Booting up her computer, she opened her favorite file: "Manifesto." Her masterpiece was easily the best way she could express her grievances to the world, much like the way the famous Unibomber Ted Kaczynski did. Her "Manifesto" would leave behind vindication for what she had done in her life and what she was about to do. A long time in the planning now, Richards knew it was time for her final act to begin and wanted to recheck the "Manifesto" so it was perfect before she posted it online for all to see. Then everyone would understand the injustices she had experienced from the beginning of her life, and the destruction mental illness in the world had caused in her life. Reading to herself, she scanned the 150 page document for the thousandth and final time since drafting it over the past year.

> *... alcoholic father abused me sexually and then abandoned*
> *me at age seven.*
> *... crazy mother abandoned me twice, first at age ten when*
> *she developed bipolar disorder, and then at age fifteen*
> *when she killed herself.*
> *... unjust psychiatric hospitalizations for me as a teen,*
> *punishing me for normal problems of growing up.*
> *... selfish husband abandoned me age nineteen when he*
> *learned about my past.*
> *... brother with the same bipolar illness as my mother,*
> *shamefully inadequate in his coping with combat experi-*
> *ence, a threat to my career.*
> *... high-ranking soldiers throughout the army squandering*
> *national security resources on unjustified pensions paying*
> *soldiers for their own inadequacies and laziness.*
> *... army is now abandoning me after loyal service to*
> *preserve the warrior hero.*

Richards was suddenly interrupted by her cell phone. Looking at it, she said to herself, *ha, Rossi. That's timely.*

"Hello, Andy."

"Hi, Ellen, just confirming you're coming over this afternoon?" Rossi asked with the expectation of hearing a "yes."

"I'm just waking up and getting organized. I'll be over in about an hour."

One more thing I have to do before instigating the plan this afternoon, Richards thought to herself. With that, she took her iPad and snapped a selfie. Then she turned on the video and began to speak into it.

> *This is Colonel Ellen Richards of the U.S. Army, head of*
> *psychiatry and loyal army officer. I'm leaving this video*
> *behind to explain what's about to happen later today and*
> *why. Despite dedicating my career to psychiatry, mental*
> *illness has ruined my life. I've been victimized by my father's*
> *alcoholism and pedophilia and by my mother's craziness and*
> *suicide. Both abandoned me. I've been victimized as well by*
> *my brother's shameful psychiatric collapse in response to*

combat. Imagine that, of all things for the head of army psychiatrist to endure, it was not enough to have a family full of mental illness to torment me and complicate my life, but my own brother denigrates my service to the army by his own inability to serve honorably in the same army where I'm trying to help save the last vestiges of the noble warrior spirit. How ironic.

Despite all these obstacles, I'm proud to say I've persevered, and have risen to the top of my field. I've bravely reactivated and commanded the Patrons of Perseus to keep our army pure and to eliminate threats. And for this, I'm about to be ostracized, punished or worse. After everyone else has abandoned me, finally, the army is about to do the same.

I'll wreak my vengeance upon those who'll deny my important acts of service to the army. The army head of intelligence has to go. He'll never fully support the activities of protecting the army with the Patrons the way it is needed. He wants his second star too badly.

Also, my brother will have to go. He's the scourge of the army and represents all I detest in weakness and inability to serve his country, choosing instead self-pity and the easy way out.

Finally, I'll need to leave as well, but I'll do so in a blazing burst of glory. Not by suicide. Anyone can do that. Even my useless mother found this was the one thing she could do successfully. No, and not "suicide by cop," as many have done this before. Instead, I'll show you that mine will be a demise by a never before witnessed means: "suicide by army." This will be my legacy. It'll lead you to read my "Manifesto" and then you'll all understand. I will not have lived and died in vain.

With that, Ellen posted the video on YouTube, and E-mailed her "Manifesto" to a long list of recipients, and then set her final plan into motion.

Chapter 124

WASHINGTON, D.C.:

A determined Ellen Richards arrived at General Rossi's apartment, looked up at the gray sky threatening rain, with a chilly breeze this Sunday afternoon, and knocked.

Answering the door, Rossi said, "Come right in. Anything to drink?"

"I'll have a diet Coke," she answered as she unbuttoned her stylish coat.

"Nothing stronger?"

"No. I still have a bit of a headache. Probably desynchronosis. You know, jet lag."

"Sure it's not from this?" He asked, pointing at today's Sunday edition of *The Washington Post*. "Have you read it?"

"Yeah, see how much the press hates the army?"

"We'd better discuss it. I need to know what's going on. The Sunday morning talk shows and now the Internet are abuzz about you. Some ridiculous idea that you're the new Commandant of the Patrons of Perseus and you've re-activated assassination squads to kill our cowards. Crazy, I know. Can you imagine the bullshit the press can manufacture? Anyway, the proverbial shit is gonna hit the fan tomorrow when we get to the Pentagon, so we need a plan."

"That's assuming we go to the Pentagon tomorrow," Richards said, deadly serious.

"Very funny. You look completely zoned out. You need to pull yourself together."

"I'm plenty together. In fact, I'm better than together. I'm *resolved*. This whole thing will be over before you know it."

"This thing is barely getting started, and it's far from over. And by the way, you look like a robot—not all together."

Ellen just scowled back.

"Whatever," Rossi continued. "What about those allegations in the paper? Did we really kill a couple hundred soldiers since you became head of psychiatry? I don't recall signing off on any murders, only on operations to infiltrate outside organizations and disrupt them."

"Of course you do."

"And what about this framing of Conrad? You mean we killed the soldier from Fort Hood and framed Conrad for it? Not that I mind that much, but you should've told me."

"Then you should read and understand my *requisitions* more carefully before signing them," she said laughingly.

"Well, sometimes I'm otherwise occupied at the time, in case you don't remember."

"Oh, I remember. I purposely seduced you and let you think you were forcing yourself on me just to get you to sign them without reading them."

"Woo hoo. Now you're hurting my feelings. You mean it was not because of true love and my magnetic personality and obvious sexual prowess?"

Richards made no response and just looked back at him blankly.

"We have to shut down the Patrons. And somebody has to take the fall. I think we can set up for Morelli to take it. He's such a clueless buffoon. A pretty face with no substance. Everybody knows that, so he's the perfect fall guy. What do you think? The rest of us can act all innocent and such, just following orders, and so on," he said seriously.

"Do you think that'll do it?"

"I'm counting on it. No way I want this incident to sink my career."

"So, we play dumb and when army investigators come in or the FBI grills us, we tell them it was all Morelli."

"Right," Rossi said.

"And what about protecting the nobility of the warrior?"

"That's gone. The world's changing, Ellen. We're probably gonna have to give more resources to psychiatry, but if there's a big uproar started after publication of *The Washington Post* article today, we can count on Congress just increasing the budget rather than stealing it from the army command or other programs at the Pentagon. We still win." A smile grew on Rossi's tanned face.

"I'm glad you're so optimistic and think it'll be that simple."

"I do. Anyway, come over here, I need to relax," he said as he motioned to her.

"I know what that means. Let me go into the bathroom first and change."

"Okay," and with that Rossi took his clothes off and climbed under the covers in his bed that would have been the envy of Caligula himself.

Richards came out in a moment, similarly unclothed, carrying a small makeup-bag she placed at the head of the bed as she slinked under the covers next to Rossi. Soon she was on top, thrusting again and again, with Rossi groaning, about to climax. Reaching forward, not losing a beat, she withdrew a subcompact Glock 26 handgun, and with Rossi completely unaware, shot him right between the eyes. As Rossi's member faded, Richards felt a warm bolt of electricity surge from her groin and she flushed in pure reverie. *Now that was the best orgasm I have ever had,* she exclaimed to herself. *So, on to the next task.*

Chapter 125

Trying to relax now that he was out of bed and off IVs, Conrad began to pace up and down his hospital room. Libby sat nearby thumbing through a copy of *Cooking Light*. Victoria stood in the corner, speaking quietly to some mates back in the U.K. and two very alert MPs stood inside the hospital door.

"Settle down, Gus. You need to rest and get ready for your big day testifying in front of the Senate tomorrow afternoon. Have a mint."

"Thanks. You know, these work better for my pain than ibuprofen."

"Soon this will be all over. By the way, I've been wanting to ask you about those flashbacks I have seen you experience more than once. Or at least that's what they look like from the outside. Is that what I think they are?"

"Yes, I have to admit, I do have flashbacks due to a horrible auto accident I experienced more than ten years ago. Caused my back injury that led to my opiate addiction of which you are now well aware."

"So, you have a bit of PTSD yourself?"

"I guess so. Only triggered by certain sounds, smells or the sight of horrible amounts of blood."

"Most people with back injuries after a car accident don't have PTSD. Why do you suppose you developed it?"

"Long story."

"I'm not going anywhere right now."

"Well, I don't really like to speak about it."

"I'm just trying to understand and be supportive."

"I know. It's just hard to discuss. I can start by saying that I was married at the time and my wife had just given birth to a baby girl."

At that moment, the nurse entered the room saying, "We need to clean that wound out and change the dressing for you one more time before you leave for your testimony tomorrow, Dr. Conrad. Since you can't have any opiates and this is going to be painful, let me just give you this sedative to knock you out for an hour or so while we work on this."

And with that, Conrad got a shot, dozed off and his nurse went to work on his gunshot wound.

Meanwhile, Libby sat there aching to learn more about Conrad's flashbacks.

Chapter 126

Richards calmly entered her own home after driving the few miles back from Rossi's. It was a modest, semi-detached house she rented on the army base at Fort McNair, near the Pentagon. Aware she was now under very tight surveillance but not yet arrested meant the case against her had not yet advanced sufficiently for that. It also meant she still had enough time to implement the final phase of her maniacal plan.

Richards cleaned-up and started dinner in anticipation of seeing her brother in a few minutes. The surveillance agents—probably FBI—wouldn't think anything was suspicious when her brother came, and it was likely Rossi's body wouldn't have been discovered yet. Richards guessed with the high profile nature of her crimes, that not only FBI surveillance but also an Army Ranger unit and other law enforcement agencies would be outside—sooner rather than later, inasmuch as her house was officially part of Fort McNair Army Base. Rehearsing her plan again in her head, she said to herself, *all is going according to plan. My brother just needs to get here soon.*

As the steak was broiling and the mash potatoes were being whipped, she heard the doorbell. "Come in. It's unlocked," Richards yelled.

Her brother, looking tired and forlorn, and more than a bit apprehensive, entered.

"Hello, Jordan. You want something to drink?"

"I'm on the wagon. Just a Coke, please."

"Here you go. Have a seat. I'll just finish up here and we can eat in just a second. Hungry?"

"You know I am."

"Of course, of course. We'll fix that soon. Steak and mashed potatoes with gravy. Your favorite. And guess what's for dessert?"

"Not apple pie and ice cream?"

"The same."

Jordan relaxed noticeably. "So, to what do I owe this treatment? I thought you wanted me out of your life."

"Well, let's just say it's complicated. We'll discuss it when we sit down."

Looking at the sculptures placed throughout the living room, Jordan said, "Ellen, your weird collection creeps me out every time I see it. It's sick."

"What, my animal collection?"

"Some collection. They all look angry. They're all killing something."

"Good observation. And so they are. You see, I collect predators. I admire all predators."

"Some hobby."

"See the eagle with talons tearing apart the fish?"

"Yuck."

"I'm starting to collect predatory insects next. Wish I could find something tearing the wings off a fly. That's one of my favorite images."

"That's twisted."

"How about the one with the pride of lionesses ripping apart the zebra?" she questioned.

"I like zebras."

"Everybody has to eat."

"Let's stop talking about predators killing something in order to eat," Jordan requested.

"Okay, then let's sit down and eat ourselves."

Jordan dug into his steak, and asked, "So, you gonna help me get my VA benefits and medical care?"

"Of course not."

"Then why did you have me come over?"

"To tell you that you represent all that's wrong about mental illness in the army."

"What do you mean? That's cruel. It's not my fault."

"Oh, but it is Jordan. Anybody with your family history should have never gone into combat."

"Well, you have the same family history and you joined the army."

"That's different. Nobody in the army has to know about my past or my family's history of mental illness. Because of you, everyone will know."

"Well, it's managed to remain a secret from them so far. Unless I tell them, which I won't if you help me get the benefits I've earned, how would they ever know?"

"Because we're both going out in a blaze of glory." Just then, Ellen took the Glock out of her purse and fired a shot into the wall.

"Why did you do that?" Jordan asked as he rocked back in his chair.

"Because the army is now waiting outside and that'll bring them to my door."

Jordan had noticed several soldiers nearby when he walked up to his sister's front door but thought nothing of it. After all, it was an army base. But now he understood why.

Just then, a bullhorn shouted at her door, "Colonel Richards. We know you're in there. Come out with your hands up."

"Well, Jordan," Richards said calmly, now pointing the gun at him. "Show time. How does it feel to be a hostage? Let's wait until they call my cell."

As predicted, in just a moment, her cell rang. "This is Major Leroy Jackson, Army Special Forces. We know you've killed General Rossi and you're in there with your brother. We heard a gunshot. Is he okay?"

"Talk to him yourself." Richards handed over the phone to Jordan.

"Yeah, I'm okay but my sister has gone nuts."

"That's enough, give it back." Now speaking into the phone with one hand and the other pointing a gun, Richards said, "So, why don't you come in here and get me?"

"Colonel Richards, we don't wanna do that. Why don't we end this peacefully? Let your brother come out first. Then throw your gun out and come out with your hands up. That way nobody'll get hurt."

"You've obviously watched too many cop shows, Major Jackson. You don't seem to understand. You're not running this show, I am." And with that she put the Glock up to her brother's head, wrapped her free arm around him holding the back of his body tightly to the front of hers so his body could act as a shield for her, and said calmly to Jordan, "Now, walk with me slowly out the front door."

"No."

"I said walk or I'll pull the trigger right now. It's your only chance of getting out of this alive."

"Okay, okay, relax. I'm moving."

As they exited the townhouse, Richards could see six army soldiers from Special Forces in full-tactical gear and with their automatic-assault rifles trained on her from all directions. *Looks like an old-fashioned firing squad,* she said to herself calmly. Richards could also see more than one news van pulling up and getting set.

"Colonel Richards, that's good. Now put the gun down and let your brother walk toward us and nobody will get hurt."

"I have something to say to you in the news media back there first," she shouted.

"All right, but make it quick. I'm the only one who's going to speak with you, but we can all listen."

Their cameras were all now rolling from a safe distance.

"To all of you out there, be aware ... the army has lost its way. I've done my best to purge the service of mental illness, but have confronted many obstacles. My mission is not done. I'm going to kill my brother in front of you all, as an example of the problem I have with veterans asking for care they don't deserve and wanting payment for problems of their own making."

A shockwave of emotions hit those within earshot of her words.

"Don't do it," Major Jackson pleaded. "There's no need to end things this way. Let your brother go, and put your gun down. We can discuss your mission then."

"No! The time is now. I'm done. Read my 'Manifesto.' Watch my video. All will be clear."

Pausing for a beat, relishing being the center of attention, and with calmness and resolve, Richards continued. "Now watch this. Good-bye Jordan." With that she pulled the trigger. As Jordan dropped lifeless, she pointed her gun at the riflemen but did not fire. Suddenly, several dozen killer rounds of hollow-point ammo riddled her body before she could hit the ground.

SECOND MONDAY

Chapter 127

Senator Benham took note that her Senate hearing chamber was ablaze with whispering members of Congress, witnesses, and journalists thick as thieves. Senate aides took their seats in the elevated area behind the senators, who were simultaneously positioning themselves behind their nameplates and microphones towering over the witnesses below and in front of the cameras—hoping to get as much Face Time as possible. *A perfect place for political theater,* she thought. The gallery was much more crowded with observers and news media today than normal. On the floor, there was standing room only for staff, VIPs, and additional media. Several of the highest ranking leadership in the U.S. Army sat at witness tables preparing for a highly public grilling. Senator Benham, much accustomed to holding hearings in this expansive room, knew today would be much higher profile than the routine fact-finding meetings that often occurred with the Senate in this room—she was whetting her appetite for what was about to transpire.

An entire gaggle of army generals sat side-by-side in front of her elevated perch, with four-star General Peter Morelli in the middle. More junior rank officers, legal counsel and various aides sat three-deep in full-dress uniforms behind the generals, at the ready to supply documents or to whisper verbal input to the witnesses on the hot seat who faced their Senate inquisitors. *All just another act in great American political theatre,* the senator thought again, and was ready now for the curtain to go up as she emerged into the Senate chamber energetic, fully composed and exuding power and authority as she sat down in the chairperson's seat to play ring-master in the middle of her three ring circus. A buzz was all about. Suddenly, Senator Benham brought her gavel down and spoke into her live microphone, "Order. Let's come to order now." Rap rap rap. "Order, please," and the crowd came to an anticipatory hush. "Will the witnesses please identify themselves for the record?"

"General Peter Morelli here and two of my staff, General Anthony Beckman, Army Surgeon General and General Charles Jones, Commanding General at Fort Hood. My boss, General Casey, is with the president and joint chiefs this morning and as you may have heard, my head of intelligence, General Andreas Rossi, has met with an unfortunate demise yesterday and won't be joining us."

"Thank you, General Morelli," Senator Benham replied. "Yes, I'm aware of the tragic incident and will be asking more about it in due course. For now, I'd like to ask you to respond to allegations in the press that the U.S. Army has maintained a secret assassination squad to kill its own soldiers deemed cowards."

The crowd in the room audibly inhaled almost in unison with that statement by the senator.

"I saw the reports and am totally unaware of that activity. We're in the process of confirming or refuting that allegation, and I've asked for an immediate investigation."

"I remind you, you're under oath. Is it not your responsibility to know what's going on in your office?"

"Yes, of course. But as this is alleged to be part of Army Intelligence operations, the details would not be appropriate to release here in open session."

"Do you know anything about the Patrons of Perseus?"

"That is a national security issue, and I cannot speak to that in open session."

"Don't you feel if the U.S. Army is killing its own soldiers, this should be declassified?"

"Perhaps, but that's not up to me."

"Ugh, Lindsey, can you help me here?"

"I'll try. Good morning, General Morelli. Lindsey Mann, senior senator from South Carolina here. I've read the official classified security briefings for our committee and of course the news coverage, but I want to get on the record your responses to several specific questions. Firstly, did you authorize a special assassination unit of the U.S. Army to kill your own soldiers when they were deemed to be a national security threat because of developing PTSD?"

Heads throughout the room pivoted toward the general.

"I respectfully decline to answer on the basis of national security concerns."

"And is this special assassination unit a continuation of the World War I unit known as the Patrons of Perseus?"

"I respectfully decline to answer on the basis of national security concerns."

"And have the Patrons of Perseus been led by U.S. Army chief of psychiatry Lieutenant Colonel Ellen Richards, with authorization from U.S. Army head of intelligence Brigadier General Andreas Rossi?"

"Same answer, senator."

"And did the current U.S. Commander of the Patrons of Perseus kill an American soldier with direct ties to the World War I Patrons of Perseus that began in the U.K., then frame an American psychiatrist for his murder, and finally, target for death this psychiatrist, the soldier's mother, those assisting them finding the truth about these operations, and indeed the reporter who uncovered this story?"

"I respectfully decline to answer on the basis of national security concerns."

"Madam, chairman, I yield the floor again to you."

Cameras were heard clicking like machine gun fire. Whispers echoed in the large room.

"Well, very, very interesting General Morelli. In open hearings, I guess you can try to get away with hiding behind the veil of national security, but we'll have a closed-door session tomorrow, and I instruct you to provide answers to those questions. I don't want to hear you've started an investigation, hoping this issue will go away by the time the investigation is done. We call that 'kicking the can down the road' around here and I'll have none of it. To proceed today, I insist on answers to the following line of questions or will be prepared to hold you in contempt, ask for a special prosecutor, and have you indicted. Are we clear on this, General Morelli?"

Morelli remained stoic, and said, "Yes, senator."

Senator Benham had a wry smile on her face. *Didn't call me ma'am. Guess the old bugger can learn a new trick,* she said to herself.

"No games, now General Morelli. I want answers or, I repeat, I'll hold you in contempt. Firstly, I realize the army has tried to tackle the behavioral health issues of its soldiers during the recent and ongoing conflicts in Iraq and Afghanistan, as well as over its long history largely by trying to train their way out of mental illness and preserve the classical warrior culture. Do you still think that's the way to go now and what are your plans for the future?"

"I must admit recent events have shaken the army, from tragic Fort Hood shootings, to suicide shootings at other army bases such as Fort Lee and others, to horrific mass murders in Afghanistan by a lone gunman. And that doesn't even include the terrible spike in active duty suicides. Yes, I'm upset. And I think we have to acknowledge what we're doing isn't working."

"Well, thank you for your candor, General Morelli. Do you think you can fix it or do we need to get a new Vice Chief of the Army who is up to the task? And if you think you can do it, what are you plans for moving forward?"

"It's clear we need to make an assessment of the allegations now surfacing in the press, and investigate the activities of the U.S. Army in the U.K., as well as the leadership and priorities of U.S. Army psychiatry."

"That's all very well and good, General Morelli, but that sounds like vague platitudes. First, deny knowledge of the problem, then promise an investigation, then refuse to answer questions during the investigation, and then when the problem blows over and we all go on to other things, you hold no one accountable. That's the apparent operational plan of the current administration. But you cannot get away with that. I want an action plan. Now, what is it?"

"I can give you my personal commitment we'll begin to reform the army's culture of the warrior hero, and the army's priorities of identifying and treating mental illness among our soldiers, particularly those serving in combat."

"How are you going to do that when your priorities are on resilience training rather than on identification and treatment of psychiatric disorders?"

"I have to admit, our resilience training, while strengthening the will of good soldiers, has not prevented the onset of PTSD or the increase in suicides."

"It now appears at least some of your suicides may have been mur-

ders, but even accounting for that, you have a definite spike in army suicides and now more than twenty percent of current Iraq and Afghanistan war veterans have PTSD, many combined with mild traumatic
brain injuries, substance abuse, depression and suicide attempts and
completions. You seem to have a long-standing policy of looking the
other way, and then dumping these soldiers into the VA. In case you
haven't been following the news recently, we have an overburdened VA
medical and disability system, and it cannot deal with the pending
onslaught of unmet need that'll occur when we begin discharging
hundreds of thousands of soldiers in need of mental health care into the
VA from the army. What's the army going to do to help manage this problem
rather than just cause it and then dump it onto another agency to solve?"

"I agree this problem is far too enormous for us to continue to give
it low priority in the active duty environment, and I'm forming a special
commission to give us recommendations on how to reduce these problems, and manage them in the army before these soldiers are discharged."

"Another commission? We've seen that administrative ploy and it
amounts to nothing as shown by the current state of affairs for army
mental health. Damn it, why have a new commission when the answer is
already in front of you? My understanding is civilian mental health experts have already given you recommendations for doing more than just
enhanced mental health screenings during recruitment to keep out the
vulnerable and then resilience training after recruitment to strengthen
the weak. According to proposals presently on your desk, you've already
been advised you need much more robust mental health diagnosis and
treatment resources within the military for each-and-every soldier."

"Well, that takes money."

"You need to request funds for those programs and a high priority
for that funding. If you do so, I will see to it that you get those funds,"
Benham said looking over at Senator Lindsey Mann who nodded silently
in agreement.

"Of course, we have budget problems, but you have to request funds
for specific new programs or you're never going to get them off the ground
or hire the additional mental health staff you're going to need. In reality,
your history has been to make mental health care a low priority that always
gets pushed down in favor of weapon systems, more salaries for more
officers, and in terms of medical care, more resources for blast injuries,
always cutting mental health priorities during budget negotiations. This

must stop. Your priorities must change."

"I very much agree, Senator Benham."

"I want to see your next budget with a plan for a major increase in army psychiatrists, psychologists, nurse practitioners and nurses. I want to see a robust training budget for your current mental health professionals. I want to see more culture change to show the classical warrior myth of the ideal soldier is outdated and frankly, dangerous."

"Yes, ma ... I mean, yes, senator."

Cameras began clicking and lights flashing in the direction of Senator Benham.

"And General, if I don't see changes pronto, I'll do everything in my power to see you are removed as Vice Chief of the Army." Staring down at Morelli, she finished with, "And don't test me."

General Morelli sat mute, as if he'd been a young school boy scolded by his teacher.

Within a nano-second reporters charged for the doors to make their newspapers' deadlines.

Chapter 128

Pacing up and down in a private waiting area with a television monitor off the side of Senate chambers, Conrad was working off nervous energy and even excitement while listening to the proceedings and occasionally turning to watch them. Awaiting his turn in the Senate chamber to be questioned, Conrad said out loud, "I've never done anything like this before." Libby and Jennifer Roberts were waiting in the room with him.

Libby just smiled reassuringly and said, "You're a natural for any audience. Just kick in to 'professor mode' and you'll nail it. And if that's not good enough, here is a whole roll of mints. In fact, I suggest you take one now."

Conrad smiled. "I guess you're right. Thanks," he said, looking into her kind eyes and allowing himself to feel an undeniable attraction to her. Then he popped a mint into his mouth and was immediately back to obsessing about his upcoming testimony. "Jennifer, you've seen lots of these hearings over the years. Any suggestions for me?"

"I've seen them, but thankfully have never had to testify. My suggestion is to be yourself. Show sincerity. Don't be evasive. You have the knowledge and information, just speak from your heart and not just your brain."

"Yes, that's a particular problem for you, Gus. You need to let people see your heart. I'm pretty sure there's one in there somewhere," Libby said, putting an index finger on his breast over his heart and pushing it while shooting a beaming smile up at him and within inches of his face.

"Thanks, ladies," Conrad said, awkwardly backing up from Libby and beginning to pace again.

"Jennifer, I'm looking forward to working with you closely on your follow-up stories. You're a real hero here. I guess I should say heroine?"

"Thanks, Dr. Conrad. I'll also need you to fact check some of my future stories and I'd like to quote you if you're willing."

"We'll see about the quotes," Conrad said.

There was a moment of silence, then "And Libby," Conrad finally asked, addressing Libby. "Where're you going after all of this? No real reason any more for you to stay in Texas."

Jennifer interjected with a suggestion. "How about staying here in Washington, D.C., to work with Senator Benham? I'll also help any way I can. With that new commission Senator Benham will announce this afternoon, and with you and Conrad serving on it, there'll be plenty for you to do here."

"Yes, Libby," Conrad added. "Both you and I and several other experts from the civilian, military and VA worlds are going to be appointed to help develop proposals and implement projects to transform army psychiatry. We especially need to train many more nurse practitioners who can diagnose and prescribe. That's right up your alley. I'm sure the senator could use someone local who she can trust to keep the commission on track."

"I don't know. I haven't decided yet. I need some time," Libby said.

"Understandable. Libby, no matter what you do, you need to know I cannot thank you enough. You risked not only your own freedom for aiding me when I was a fugitive, but eventually you risked your own life to get to the bottom of this. After the hearing is over tonight, I think I owe you a dinner."

"I think you owe me a lot more than a dinner. How 'bout a job?"

IMMEDIATELY CONRAD felt small and foolish with his offer of a simple dinner, and realized that his invitation diminished the role Libby had played in this whole affair—and as he was slowly beginning to admit to himself, what she had come to mean to him on a deeper level as well. "You know, that sounds like a great idea. I'll be asking the government for resources to recruit and train a large number of mental health professionals for the army. That includes civilian contractors, since many mental health professionals don't necessarily want to join the army. With your help, my emphasis will be on training nurse practitioners all across the various army bases in this country. We see them as the backbone of a new psychiatric service for the army so it can get its medical and psychiatric priorities right for the 21st century. I would really like to have you help me lead that venture."

"Gus, you don't get it. I was thinking about a nursing position in Palo Alto."

Chapter 129

LONDON, 2007:

Now ninety-two-years-old, Gertie heard the news. Ninety years after her father's death; fifty years after she learned how he died; and more than fifteen years after the opening of the British Great War Archives, it finally came now in 2007. Private Simon Jennings had been pardoned, along with 305 of his comrades. It wasn't an overturning of any conviction or sentence, and there was no surviving relative or anyone else who was to be given any compensation. It was simply that each of the executed soldiers was, by a modern-type of legal fiction, said to be pardoned in retrospect for the offense for which he was executed.

However, after her long battle, Gertie was grateful and satisfied. Perhaps without fully realizing her choice of words for a father with *shell shock*, she said to herself, *"I prayed it would happen in my lifetime, but I never thought it would. It's come as a shock today. We were determined, for my mother's sake, because she always said Papa was no coward. She said he was a very brave soldier who fought for his country and died for his country."*

Later, Gertie was upset to read mixed reactions to the pardons. The famous military historian Correlli Barnett told *The Daily Telegraph*:

> *These were decisions taken in the heat of a war when the commanders' primary duties were to keep the Army together and to keep it fighting. They were therefore*

*decisions taken from a different moral perspective. For the
people of this generation to come along and second-guess
decisions taken then is wrong. They were done in a
particular historical setting and in a particular moral and
social climate. It's pointless to give these pardons. What's
the use of a posthumous pardon?*

Other news coverage was more favorable, arguing:

*... so few of those sentenced to death had actually been
executed that to be shot at dawn was a form of random
chance rather than the application of legal principles,
especially since there is evidence in several individual cases
of the miscarriage of justice. Current understanding of shell
shock as a psychological war wound related to modern cases
of PTSD dictates that the families of the deceased should
not have to live with shame.*

Without any knowledge of what was going on in the modern military, the fact the controversy was at least under discussion, gave Gertie hope that by the standard of knowledge in the present-day, that no wrong had been committed, either by soldiers with *shell shock* in her father's era nor by today's soldiers with PTSD.

Chapter 130

WASHINGTON, D.C.:

Following the public humiliation of their chief, General Peter Morelli, General Anthony Beckman and General Charles Jones returned from the Senate hearing and sat down with their chiefs of staff at the Pentagon for a debriefing. "That senator bitch is so arrogant," General Jones seethed.

"Just wait until that asshole Conrad starts to testify this afternoon. He's hell bent on ruining the army, our culture, and our budget," General Beckman added.

"Neither Conrad nor that Senator Benham broad have ever even been in combat. They don't understand that unless there is a warrior mentality in the army, men won't fight."

"Or women."

"Yeah, that too. We can at least try to turn them into men."

With that, all erupted in laughter and the tension in the room came down a notch.

"Idiot politicians and doctors don't understand when it comes right down to it, a warrior doesn't fight for his country or even for his own life," General Jones continued. "A warrior fights for the guy next to him. Take that away and you have no fight in an army, and nobody to command and you'll never win a battle."

"So what're we gonna do?"

"I have half-a-mind to pop that fucking psychiatrist before he testifies this afternoon," General Jones spouted.

"What? That'd be too dangerous to pull off, although I don't think the idea is a bad one if we could get away with it."

"I just hate what Conrad is doing to my soldiers' morale at Fort Hood. Don't understand why he has such a hard-on against the army, especially Fort Hood."

"He has far too much influence with that senator and that reporter."

"And with civilian psychiatry."

"Got any ideas how to neutralize him going forward?"

"Not going to be easy. He's rich and doesn't have family."

Chapter 131

"Order, order," Senator Benham said as she repeatedly pounded her gavel after lunch. "The Senate Armed Services Committee is back in session. Hope everyone enjoyed their lunch. Let's get on with it."

Dr. Augustus Conrad was seated nervously at the witness table all by himself, popping one hard candy after another. Libby sat behind him as his silent cheerleader. Conrad looked back at her just before he began, feeling grateful for such a solid friend, someone he could really lean on.

Members of the press were at the ready, anxious to report on any issues that might sell papers.

"Please give your name for the record," Senator Benham instructed.

"Dr. Augustus Conrad, Professor of Psychiatry at Stanford University in Palo Alto, California."

"Thank you, Dr. Conrad. I understand you have consulted for the military in the area of mental health over the course of your career?"

"Yes, I've taught courses at many facilities, including Fort Hood, Walter Reed, Tripler, Camp Pendleton, and others. I conduct a regular course for psychiatrists and mental health professionals at the Naval Medical Center in San Diego, also called Balboa."

"What are your credentials?"

"I've written forty-two books in my field, including the top two bestselling textbooks. In addition, I've published over 500 scholarly papers in the medical literature. I'm also a full professor at Stanford and the editor-in-chief of a major medical journal. Recently the University of Cambridge in Great Britain has recognized my work with an Honorary Fellowship."

"Thank you again, Dr. Conrad. And I understand you wrote a report for the army, which you published in a medical journal and it got you into a bit of hot water with the army. Can you summarize your findings?"

"Certainly. I visited Fort Hood on several occasions, interviewing numerous soldiers in their Warrior Transition Unit, and instructed over a hundred mental health professionals and several hundred soldiers in command—the cadre—at Fort Hood who were assigned to the WTU."

"Isn't the Warrior Transition Unit the one set up after the Walter Reed medical fiasco a few years back in order to prevent runarounds and bureaucratic delays for wounded soldiers in the army?"

"Yes, but it doesn't work in psychiatry."

"Mental health professionals and command soldiers alike felt there was not a rapid access to appointments for patients with psychiatric difficulties. Is that true, doctor?"

"Yes, that's true."

"And what did you find out about the quality of psychiatric care these soldiers received?"

"We found the troops themselves had justifiably low levels of confidence in army mental health care. They felt there was a potentially dangerous lack of availability of psychiatric records, excessive use of pain killers, and too many psychiatric drugs being prescribed by several doctors per soldier without being aware of each other's prescriptions. And they were right."

"While there, did you learn anything about the army culture for soldiers with psychological wounds?" Senator Benham asked.

"Yes. Soldiers in command thought PTSD was not a real medical illness caused by military service and most soldiers with PTSD were either exaggerating or faking it."

"Really? All very sobering, Dr. Conrad."

"Senator Benham," the man sitting directly on her right interrupted.

"The chair recognizes the distinguished Ranking Member of the Armed Services Committee from Oklahoma."

"Will you yield the floor so I can ask one question?

"Certainly, Senator Inhofe. But just one question. I have a lot of ground I need to cover this afternoon."

"I thank the distinguished senator from California. Now, Dr. Conrad, I want to make something perfectly clear and get it on the record here. Are your criticisms of the army because you think war is wrong, and we should not have entered the wars in Iraq and Afghanistan?"

"No, not at all. My findings and proposed solutions are not intended to be political in the least. I'm a scientist. And I'm highly supportive of the army's mission, but want to make sure it pays attention to a long neglected area—mental health—that's beginning to become a threat to military readiness, especially in being prepared to defend our country moving forward."

"Thank you, Dr. Conrad. I yield the floor again to the distinguished senator from California."

Senator Benham continued without missing a beat. "Dr. Conrad, any solution to this dilemma of deficiencies in mental health care in the army other than just throwing money at the problem and hoping it goes away?"

Just then, Conrad noted Libby took a look at her phone then bolted for the door at the back of the room. He paused for a moment, distracted, wondering where Libby was going. He then pressed on. "As a matter of fact, I think the solution is entirely within the reach of the army."

"Please continue with details. Please, doctor."

Conrad turned around and stole a look at the door to the Senate chambers hoping to see Libby, but she was gone. He reluctantly continued. "My sincere wish is to wake up the army and assist them in preparing to fight 21st century wars. Whether the army likes it or not, it needs strong programs to deal with psychiatric problems in their soldiers, other than simply trying to manage this by screening out recruits with psychiatric problems before they enter the service, or by giving new recruits resilience training to prevent psychiatric disorders. Those expensive programs aimed at resilience training are in my opinion complete misallocations of the army's resources, ineffective and hugely wasteful, with no evidence they prevent psychiatric illness. Instead, army resources should go towards more and better trained staff with a significant boost in civilian contractors."

"Why are you focusing on the army? Is this not an issue for the entire military?"

"Likely it is to a certain extent, but the problem is far less in the other branches of the military. I've had the opportunity to work with numerous U.S. Navy psychiatrists embedded with army troops in Iraq due to the lack of sufficient numbers of army psychiatrists, and able to compare the psychiatric care given to sailors and Marines on the one hand and soldiers in the army on the other. To a person, they've told me of their abhorrence to the low standards of mental health care and poisonous attitudes to mental illness in the army, as compared, for example, to the navy, who, of course, takes care of Marines as well as sailors."

"So, you suggest we focus on the army?"

"In a word, yes. At least to begin with. The army also has the problem of being a much larger organization, of having to take lower quality recruits, and of being under pressure to fight wars using large numbers of troops."

"Just how big a problem are psychiatric war wounds for the army?"

"There are ten times more psychological war wounds than there are battle casualties to the body. But ninety percent of the army's medical resources go into treating battle casualties to the body. There are also a hundred times more psychological war wounds than there are combat deaths. We estimate that there are over a half million soldiers with PTSD in the army today."

"Half a million? Sounds like a misalignment of medical resources and priorities."

"Exactly. And big problems for the VA are coming as soon as these active duty soldiers are discharged and become vets."

"That's another story we don't want to get into here today. Specifically, what do you suggest we do?"

"Actually, the army already knows what to do. Remember, the army is where trauma care was invented, where medics in the battlefield were pioneered, and where army medical innovations including Medevac, helicopters, ambulances and triage for trauma victims were invented and then imported into the civilian world. Army trauma care has become 'the gold standard' not only for the military, but for civilian medicine throughout the world. What we need are similar innovations in army medicine applied to psychiatry."

All in the Senate chamber sat momentarily mute.

"Any specific ideas?"

"Yes. You could consider the army, with all its soldiers, has in some ways the best PTSD laboratory in the world to find large numbers of cases, develop and test new treatments and also reduce bad outcomes such as substance abuse and suicide. In fact, I have two specific ideas I have proposed for the army to evaluate in order to prevent PTSD."

"Go ahead briefly, if you can."

"Yes, Senator Benham. My first idea is to take a page out of the chapter written recently by the NFL and American football."

All eyes were riveted on Conrad, with everyone in the gallery wanting to know what was up his sleeve. Continuing, Conrad said, "The idea is to promptly identify soldiers who are highly aroused, emotionally upset or experiencing significant insomnia following a combat mission, a fire fight or after having observed a horrible traumatic event."

Conrad noticed that he had the entire Senate gallery listening intently. "After finding these soldiers, then sit them on the bench."

"On the bench? What do you mean?"

"Remove them from the front lines to cool off and recover, just as we do now if someone has a concussion during a football game. We used to send football players with concussions right back into the game, only to have them get another concussion before the first one healed. We now know this leads to bad outcomes. My suggestion to prevent PTSD is to rotate in fresh troops to take the place of those who are hyper-aroused by combat and experiencing overactive startle responses and bad insomnia. Allow them to recover away from the front lines after a brief respite. Although this would potentially require more troops in the short run, it could prevent bad outcomes overall for our warriors. I suggest we compare soldiers who are allowed to recover before re-entering combat to soldiers who pursue combat continuously despite high levels of hyperarousal and emotional upset. My prediction is that allowing a cooling off period will prevent development of long lasting PTSD."

"Certainly an interesting idea. What's your other suggestion?"

"I think we can take advantage of the fact that women will soon be entering every combat role now open to men in order to see if embedding women with small combat squads could make a difference in reducing PTSD." As soon as he said that, Conrad noted that you could now hear a pin drop inside the Senate chamber.

"Dr. Conrad, we usually hear that embedding women will be dangerous to the military's espirit de corps, will lead to sexual abuse, and that women will not hold their own with heavy rucksacks and lifting. How could the presence of women in combat prove beneficial in reducing PTSD?"

"My idea is to test the frequency of PTSD in combat units with men only, to those with both men and women. I believe one potential dividend of having women in combat units would be to soften the hyper-masculine warrior ideal thereby allowing all soldiers to become aware of their emotional reactions to what is happening to themselves rather than suppressing those emotions. The theory is that having an outlet for emotions in combat—something traditionally done better by women than by men—would lead to less PTSD in everyone. Just an idea."

Lots of murmuring and talking in an excited wave swept across the Senate chamber. As it died down, Senator Benham said, "Very clever, Dr. Conrad. Never heard anybody suggest there might be an actual advantage of having women in combat, but this is clearly creative and worth pursuing, if not at least progressive and open minded."

"I guess the point is, the army has the potential to test various ideas like this and to determine if we can find ways to reduce or even prevent PTSD," Conrad continued. "The army only has to make it a priority. There are many mental health professionals poised to help. All the military needs to do is to ask. If we all work together, we should be able to significantly reduce psychiatric casualties, eliminate a great deal of suffering while not overburdening our already overflowing VA medical system. We can do it. I know it. We can do it."

With that, applause erupted in the Senate chamber and a crescendo of cheers dominated the moment as the gallery leaped to their feet. Cameras fired off shots as reporters darted for the doors. Nobody heard Senator Benham state "adjourned" with a single rap of her gavel.

Conrad stood, took a deep breath and reflected on the incredible journey he had been on. Turning around to see if Libby had returned yet and to congratulate her with a strong impulse to give her a hug, he was instead confronted with a frantic Jennifer Roberts. Her face appeared ashen white.

"Jennifer. What's wrong? Where's Libby? I can't see her. Where'd she go?" Conrad demanded.

"That's the problem, Dr. Conrad," Jennifer responded.

"What do you mean? She was just here."

"She's gone."

Acknowledgments

This book would not have been possible without the dedication of my editor, Marko Perko. My muse, my champion, and the inventor of the "Marko Mocha." He inspired me to take a detour from my academic writings and embark on a journey to write fiction. Jennifer, Victoria, Annette and especially Cindy all read drafts of the book and provided constructive input during its formative stages and also gave encouragement when I needed it. All four of these voracious consumers of commercial fiction provided invaluable input to this debut novelist, helping to shape the final version. For facts and information about the history of post-traumatic stress disorder from *shell shock* to the present, I wish to thank my many colleagues across the fields of psychiatry, psychology and neuroscience who provided input over the years. For perspectives on military psychiatry, I thank the hard-working mental health professionals at the Naval Medical Center in San Diego.

Glossary

astasia abasia – the inability to walk or stand despite good motor strength and voluntary coordination; can be bizarre and not suggestive of an actual neurological illness

barmy – eccentric, foolish, mildly crazy, cracked

balneotherapy – the treatment of diseases, injuries or other physical ailments with baths and bathing, especially in natural mineral waters

Bedlam; Bedlam Hospital; Bethlem Royal Hospital – bedlam is a scene or state of chaos, wild uproar, confusion, an insane asylum or madhouse; Bedlam Hospital is slang for the Bethlem Royal Hospital in London

blighty, blighty wound – a wound or furlough permitting a soldier to be sent back to England from the front

blokes – man, fellow, guy

bollocks – rubbish, nonsense, an exclamation of annoyance or disbelief; to muddle or botch

BOLO – an acronym for "be on the lookout" used for the picture of a person being sought by law enforcement

bugger; bugger you, bugger up – a fellow or lad, usually a despicable or contemptible person; vulgar, to sodomize; slang meaning damn; bugger off is to depart; bugger up is to ruin, spoil, botch

Cambridge American Cemetery and Memorial – a cemetery and chapel outside of the village of Madingley near Cambridge in England opened in 1956 and commemorates American servicemen who died in World War II

casualty station – also known as casualty clearing station, a military medical facility behind the front lines used to treat wounded soldiers

CID Army criminal investigation command – criminal investigation department; detective division of the army police

Craiglockhart; Slateford Military Hospital at Craiglockhart, Scotland – Craiglockhart and Slateford are villages in Scotland outside of Edinburgh; site of a military psychiatric hospital for officers with *shell shock* during World War I

D Block, Netley Hospital – psychiatric unit of the Royal Victoria Hospital in Netley, near Southampton, England, for British 'other ranks' with *shell shock*

daft – senseless, stupid, foolish, insane, crazy

dishabille – dressed in a careless, disheveled or disorderly style; undress; naked

dodgy – risky, hazardous, chancy, dangerous, tricky

dressing station – a military post that gives first aid to the wounded located near a combat area

DSM – the Diagnostic and Statistical Manual of the American Psychiatric Association; a list of the criteria for mental disorders; also known as the 'psychiatrists' bible.'

'E' Ring of the Pentagon – the outer ring of the Pentagon, generally occupied by senior officials

faradization – to stimulate or treat muscles or nerves with induced alternating current

fobbed off – to cheat someone, to put off by deception or trickery

Fritz – slang, sometimes offensive, for a German soldier

frog – slang, extremely disparaging and offensive, a contemptuous term used for a French person

Hun – old slang, disparaging and offensive, a contemptuous term used to refer to a German, especially a German soldier

hydrotherapy – curative use of water to treat physical disability or injury, often by immersing in water

hysteria – psychoneurotic condition; conversion disorder in which physical symptoms such as paralysis or blindness are without apparent physical cause and instead appear to result from psychological conflict

Imperial War Museum, London – a British national museum founded to record the war effort and sacrifice of Britain and its empire during the first World War, now expanded to include later conflicts

Jerries – slang for a German or German soldier

Le Havre – a seaport in northern France on the English channel at the mouth of the Seine River

Legat – the US FBI's (Federal Bureau of Investigation) international program, or legal attaché who liaise with the principal law enforcement in a foreign country

lost the plot – to stop acting rationally

lunatic – an insane person or person of unsound mind

Madingley Hall – a stately home in the village of Madingley outside of Cambridge, England, built by Sir John Hynde in 1543, rented by Queen Victoria in 1860 for her son Edward, the future King Edward VII to live in while he was an undergraduate at Cambridge University; now a conference center of Cambridge University

malingering – to pretend to have an illness, especially to shirk one's duty

Maudsley Hospital; Sir Henry Maudsley – a hospital in South London, opened in 1915 as a military hospital and then a psychiatric hospital since 1923; merged with the Bedlam/Bethlem Royal Hospital in 1948; Sir Henry Maudsley, a pioneering British psychiatrist

Medusa – in Greek mythology, the monster with the face of a hideous woman with live venomous snakes for hair; an emblem of evil or rage

mental – daft, out of one's mind, crazy

milksop – a weak or ineffectual person; feeble, wimp

minenwerfers or minnies – mine launcher, German name for a class of short range mortars, nick-named "minnies" by Allied forces

motley – diverse, varied, disparate, incongruous, jumble, hodge-podge

MP – member of parliament (British)

Netley Hospital – a large military hospital in Netley, near Southampton, England used extensively during World War I for treatment of *shell shock* in 'other rank' soldiers; D block (Victoria House) and E block (Albert House) formed the psychiatric hospital

neurasthenia – weakness of the nerves; fatigue, anxiety, exhaustion of the nervous system

off the rails – losing track of reality

other ranks – in the British armed forces, all those who do not hold a commissioned rank (those who are not officers)

Perseus – in Greek mythology, hero, God of heroism, son of Zeus, the hero who beheaded the evil Medusa

plot, lost the plot – to stop acting rationally

poltroon – a wretched or contemptible coward

pneumatotherapy – use of compressed or rarified air in treating disease

PTSD – post-traumatic stress disorder; a mental condition triggered by a terrifying event with symptoms such as flashbacks, nightmares, severe anxiety and recurrent uncontrollable thoughts about the event; in the military, often associated with mild traumatic brain injury as well; related to *shell shock* and battle fatigue of past wars

rails, gone off the rails; off the rails – losing track of reality

RAMC – Royal Army Medical Corps

Royal Victoria hospital for war neuroses at Netley, Hampshire, England – see *D Block Netley* and *Netley Hospital*

scrimshanking – to avoid one's obligations or share of work; to shirk work

shirker – a person who evades work, responsibility, or duty

sister – a term for a senior female nurse in Britain; a remnant of the historical religious nature of nurses

Slateford Military Hospital at Craiglockhart, Scotland – Slateford is a suburb of Edinburgh, Scotland, near Craiglockhart Castle; a World War I military hospital for officers with *shell shock* built here; famous patients include the war poets Siegfried Sassoon and Wilfred Owen; and famous psychiatrist Dr. W.H.R. Rivers

Somme, battle of, river – a river in northern France flowing into the English Channel; battle of the Somme took place between July 1 and November 18, 1916 on both sides of the River Somme; more than one million men killed or wounded in perhaps the bloodiest battle in human history

stationary hospital – a base hospital in France, part of the casualty evacuation chain, farther back from the front line than the casualty clearing stations, generally located near the coast and close to a railway line and a port

TBI, traumatic brain injury; mild TBI or mTBI – a brain injury resulting from a violent blow or jolt to the head; mild TBI excludes injuries where damage is done from objects actually penetrating the skull; may cause only temporary dysfunction of brain cells, or more serious injuries can result in long term complications; symptoms may overlap with PTSD or be confused with PTSD

trench foot – a medical condition caused by cold, wet and unsanitary conditions; feet become numb, red, and infected with a decaying odor

twitch, on the twitch – to move in a jerky, spasmodic way; a sudden involuntary or spasmodic muscle movement

Veronal – the brand name for barbitone, a barbiturate tranquilizer

Victoria Cross – the highest military decoration awarded for valor in the face of the enemy to members of the armed forces of British Commonwealth countries, introduced by Queen Victoria

Warrior Transition Brigade; Warrior Transition Unit. WTB, WTU – US Army established WTUs at major military treatment facilities during the Iraq and Afghanistan conflicts, aiming to give personalized support to wounded soldiers; established in the wake of medical scandals at Walter Reed Medical Center; attempt to build unit cohesion, teamwork and help transition of the soldier back to the army or to civilian status; in practice, highly bureaucratic and relatively ineffective for psychiatric conditions

Western Front – the fortified trench network stretching from the North Sea to the Swiss frontier with France during World War I, where Allied forces, especially British, fought German forces, and remained essentially unchanged for most of the war

FURTHER READING

Relevant Publications by Stephen M. Stahl, M.D., PhD.

1. Stahl SM and Grady MM, Stahl's Illustrated: Anxiety, Stress and PTSD, Cambridge University Press, New York, 2010
2. Stahl SM, Stahl's Essential Psychopharmacology, Anxiety Disorders and Anxiolytics, Chapter 9, pp 388 – 419, Cambridge University Press, Cambridge, 2013
3. Stahl SM and Moore BS (Eds), Anxiety Disorders: A Guide for Integrating Psychopharmacology and Psychothcrapy, Routledge, Taylor and Francis, New York, 2013
4. Stahl SM, Crisis in Army Psychopharmacology and Mental Health Care at Fort Hood, CNS Spectrums 14: 677-81 (2009)

Publications on World War I and on *Shell Shock* from the World War I Era

1. Barker, Pat, Regeneration, Penguin Books, London, 1992
2. Sassoon, Siegfried, Memoirs of a Fox-Hunting Man, Penguin Books, New York, 1928
3. Sassoon, Siegfried, Memoirs of an Infantry Officer, Penguin Books, New York, 1930
4. Jones E and Wessely S, *Shell Shock* to PTSD: Military Psychiatry from 1900 to the Gulf War, Psychology Press, Taylor and Francis Group, Hove, UK, 2005
5. Binneveld H, From Shellshock to Combat Stress: A comprehensive history of military psychiatry, Amsterdam University Press, Amsterdam, 1997
6. Micale MS and Lerner P (Eds), Traumatic Pasts: History, psychiatry and trauma in the modern age 1870-1930, Cambridge University Press, Cambridge, 2001
7. Lerner P, Hysterical Men: War, Psychiatry and the Politics of Trauma in German, 1890-1930, Cornell University Press, Ithaca, 2003
8. Shephard B, A War of Nerves: Soldiers and Psychiatrist in the 20th Century, Harvard University Press, Cambridge MA 2000
9. Barham Peter, Forgotten Lunatics of the Great War, Yale University Press, New Haven, 2004
10. Reid, Fiona, Broken Men: *Shell Shock*, Treatment and Recovery in Britain 1914-1930, Continuum Press, London, 2010
11. Wessely S, The life and death of Private Harry Farr, Journal of the Royal Society of Medicine, 99:440-3 (2006)

Contemporary Publications on PTSD (Post-Traumatic Stress Disorder)

1. Young A, The harmony of illusions: Inventing Post-traumatic stress disorder, Princeton University Press, Princeton, 1995
2. Diagnostic and Statistical Manual of the American Psychiatric Association, 5th edition, American Psychiatric Press Inc, Washington DC, 2013

3. Hoge CW, Once a Warrior, always a warrior: navigating the transition from combat to home including combat stress, PTSD and mTBI, GPP Life, Globe Pequot Press, Guilford, CT, 2010

4. Freeman SM, Moore BA, Freeman A (Eds), Living and Surviving in Harm's Way: A psychological treatment handbook for pre and post deployment of military personnel, Routledge, Taylor and Francis, New York, 2009

5. Jones E, Fear NT, Wessely, S, *Shell shock* and mild traumatic brain injury: a historical review, American Journal of Psychiatry, 164: 1641-5 (2007)

6. Hoge CW, Auchterlonie JL, Milliken CS, Mental health problems, use of mental health services and attrition from military service after returning from deployment to Iraq or Afghanistan, JAMA 295: 1023-32 (2006)

7. Hoge CW, Castro CA, Messer SC, McGurk D, Cotting DI, Koffman, RL, Combat duty in Iraq and Afghanistan, mental health problems and barriers to care, New Engl J Med 351:13-22 (2004)

8. Milliken CS, Auchterlonie JL, Hoge CW, Longitudinal assessment of mental health problems among active and reserve component soldiers returning from the Iraq War, JAMA 298: 2141-8 (2007)

9. Figley CR and Nash WP (Eds), Combat Stress Injury: Theory, Research, and Management, Routledge, Taylor and Francis, New York, 2007

10. Moore BA, Penk WE (Eds), Treating PTSD in Military Personnel: A clinical handbook, Guilford Press, New York, 2011

11. Southwick SM, Charney DS, Resilience: The Science of Mastering Life's Greatest Challenges and Ten Key Ways to weather and bounce back from stress and trauma, Cambridge University Press, New York, 2012

12. Shay J, Achilles in Vietnam: Combat Trauma and the Undoing of Character, Scribner, New York, 1994

13. Shay J, Odysseus in America: Combat Trauma and the Trials of Homecoming, Scribner, New York, 2002

Publications on British Sites and Hospitals, London and Cambridge

1. Arnold C, Bedlam: London and Its Mad, Pocketbooks, Simon and Shuster, London, 2008

2. Chambers P, Bedlam: London's Hospital for the Mad, Ian Allen Publishing, Surrey UK, 2009

3. Madingley Hall Guide: Institute of Continuing Education, University of Cambridge, Cambridge University Press, Cambridge, 2008

4. Boyd S, The Story of Cambridge, Cambridge University Press, Cambridge 2005

5. Gray R and Stubbings D, Cambridge Street Names: Their Origins and Associations, Cambridge University Press, Cambridge, 2000

Colophon:
This book was designed using Garamond Premier Pro, developed by type designer Robert Slimbach in 1988. The typeface is based upon the type created by the French metal type punch craftsman, Claude Garamond, and his contemporary, Robert Granjon, who designed the italics face in the 16th Century. Together, these faces harmonize to combine an unprecedented degree of balance, elegance, and readability.